Praise for the novel

"Jessica R. Patch has penned a beautifully written, gritty psychological thriller that will stay with readers long after the story is finished. *A Cry in the Dark* is highly recommended."
—Nancy Mehl, author of the Quantico Files series

"Jessica R. Patch has done it again! *A Cry in the Dark* grabbed me on the first page and kept me reading until 2 a.m. to finish it."
—Patricia Bradley, author of the Memphis Cold Case novels

"With twisted psychology and relatable characters, readers will feel like they discovered the *Criminal Minds* version of a fiction book. I definitely recommend reading this book after dark for the full effect, and be sure to lock your doors before you go to sleep."
—Jaime Jo Wright, author of *The Souls of Lost Lake*, on *A Cry in the Dark*

"With twists and turns, secrets and salvation, *A Cry in the Dark* is a keep-you-up-at-night ride that proves Jessica R. Patch is at the top of her game."
—Jodie Bailey, *USA TODAY* bestselling author of *Deadly Cargo*

"Gritty and terrifying, *Her Darkest Secret* pulled me into a pulse-spiking story and I will never be able to look at nursery rhymes the same way again. Ms. Patch masterfully weaves a chilling plot with authentic characters and a villain that won't let readers sleep until they find out what happens next."
—Natalie Walters, Carol Award finalist and author of *Living Lies* and the Harbored Secrets series

"*Her Darkest Secret*…is a taut psychological thriller with deeply relatable characters. Patch's brilliantly created plot will keep readers turning pages until they reach the shocking conclusion."
—Nancy Mehl, author of the Quantico Files series

"*Her Darkest Secret* keeps you on edge until the very end! Patch knows how to masterfully weave a suspenseful tale. This is one book you won't want to miss."
—Christy Barritt, *USA TODAY* bestselling author

A

CRY

IN THE

DARK

JESSICA R. PATCH

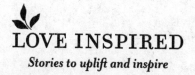

LOVE INSPIRED

Stories to uplift and inspire

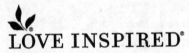

LOVE INSPIRED®

Stories to uplift and inspire

Recycling programs for this product may not exist in your area.

ISBN-13: 978-1-335-66257-6

A Cry in the Dark

Love Inspired
22 Adelaide St. West, 41st Floor
Toronto, Ontario M5H 4E3, Canada
www.LoveInspired.com

Printed in U.S.A.

To my precious, beautiful friend Emily Shuff.
You walk in truth, live in light and shine both wherever you go.
Can't wait to see how your ministry to young women
impacts generations to come. Go make disciples.
Find those who cry in the dark and help lead them into marvelous light.

A

CRY

IN THE

DARK

Prologue

Fifteen months ago, Adam had promised to let her go.

If that was even his real name.

With smoky blue-green eyes, a strong jaw with a cleft, and a confident air, he'd radiated wealth, power and hope—to give her a better life.

Now, Reeva huddled at the head of the squeaky bed with a thin, stained mattress, bloody legs drawn up to her chest and her body exhausted and sore.

She'd done what he'd asked—no, demanded.

Finally.

Submitted. Obeyed.

Because he'd promised fifteen months ago he'd let her go if she did.

Glancing down at her belly, all loose skin and flabby, she vowed she'd find a way out, again, if he'd lied. But he'd released Chrissy only two months ago. And Debbie a month before that.

Eve remained though. She'd been here the longest.

High-pitched squalls drew Reeva's attention to the side of the bed, but she refused to go near it. Didn't want to see it. Smell it. She covered her head with the lumpy pink pillow, drowning out the sounds and the scent of the baby basement. Cold. Dank. Moldy. Even in summer, Reeva had never been warm enough.

Twice she'd almost made it out of the house.

Twice Adam had caught her and made her pay. Her broken arm hadn't healed properly—the one with the brand he'd given her that first night, after he'd offered to take her for ice cream. After that lie, he'd bound her hands behind her back and blindfolded her. She had no way to know where she was or how far from Memphis he'd taken her—if they'd even traveled out of Bluff City.

He'd done unspeakable things to her. The branding the very least painful. She'd accepted the searing burn, inhaled the singed flesh through tears. But she'd refused to cry after that first night, and she'd refused to accept the comfort of the other girls in partitioned rooms. False comfort.

"It'll be okay. Do what he says."

"He won't hurt you if you do what he says."

"It'll get easier. You'll get used to it."

Reeva didn't want to get used to it. Didn't want to obey. But after six months and the failed escape attempts, she'd realized she had no hope. No light. No salvation.

She could only trust that when she produced, he'd let her go.

The door to the basement screeched open, pops of light from upstairs blinding her. Down here in the darkness, there were no windows. No sunlight. No dawn of a new day.

Feathered footsteps brushed along the wooden stairs.

Eve.

Eve had access to the whole house. Reeva wasn't allowed

upstairs. Neither were Ann or Polly. Ann had finally produced, but she hadn't been able to leave yet. Adam had to be sure the child was well and healthy—or Ann would have to produce again.

"Reeva," Eve whispered and set a tray of soup, crackers and tea on the edge of her bed. "You need to feed her, Reeva. She has to be healthy before you go." Reeva turned her head, exhausted and weak.

"You know he's never going to let you leave, Eve. You're his favorite."

Eve, only a year or two older than Reeva, sighed. "I don't mind. He's good to me. If you wouldn't fight him, he'd be good to you too."

Nothing was good about Adam.

Reeva turned to Eve. "He's done something to your brain. You're not thinking clearly. You have a home. A family. A life outside the baby basement." If she could get out into sunshine and away from here, she'd see that.

Eve ignored her pleas to come to her senses. "What will you name her?" Eve asked.

Reeva wiped her runny nose and turned her face to the cool concrete wall again. "I don't want her," she whispered, fear and guilt mingled with panic. How would she care for this baby? Why should she? She hadn't even looked at her once since she'd birthed her only an hour ago with the help of Eve.

Eve huffed and carefully lifted the swaddled babe in her arms, but she continued to bleat. Reeva covered her ears to avoid the urge to take the baby. Deep within, a sense of duty to the child swelled. Told her she was a part of her. She needed to be protected and loved and...fed.

"You are a pretty little girl, aren't you?" Eve stroked her cheek. "I hope my baby is as lovely as yours." Eve had been here longest—at least since Reeva had arrived—and yet she hadn't produced. Why would Adam care so much about a girl who couldn't produce quickly? "Ann's little boy is precious. They leave tomorrow. Adam told me."

Freedom. But was there freedom after this? Would he come for the children at some point? Come back and take her for more babies?

Footsteps clunked on the wooden stairs.

Adam.

"What is going on down here?" he asked as the baby continued to wail. His voice was quiet and tender; she'd never heard him raise it. But there was no need. The evil that pulsed in his eyes kept them under control. Kept them quiet.

"Reeva was about to feed Baby Girl. She's strong. Over seven pounds." Eve beamed as if she had been the one who'd endured hours of labor and pain with nothing to dull it. She forced the crying infant into Reeva's arms, but she felt nothing until she finally looked upon her face.

It was a beautiful face. Heart-shaped lips and a button nose.

Another wave of maternal instinct crashed over her. Stronger. Greater.

But no matter what she tried, the baby fussed and screeched—as if she knew she'd been imprisoned too. Felt the hopelessness and pain. The shame.

Reeva ran her hands along her thick dark cap of hair, and a glimpse of promise rushed through her. Tears sprang to her eyes but not of desperation and helplessness.

Tears of new life. New hope. This was the one good thing from the nightmare she'd been living. Baby was hers. Needed her. Depended on her. She would keep her safe. Feed her and make sure she was healthy so they could flee this place. Go somewhere far away.

"Hush now," she cooed and snuggled the baby to her breast. But she wouldn't eat, wouldn't stop wailing. Until her face turned purplish blue. What was she doing wrong? Why didn't her daughter feel secure in her arms? "There there, little one. Mama is here. I won't let him hurt you. It'll be okay now."

Except it wasn't. Frustration and despair sank her heart as she felt powerless and helpless to even comfort her own daughter.

Adam cocked his head and frowned. "Let me have her."

Reeva hesitated. She didn't want her baby to be stained by his touch.

"Reeva," he demanded softly. "Give me my daughter. My lovely, lovely little girl."

Swallowing fear, she reluctantly handed the bundle to Adam. "Don't—don't hurt her."

He received her gently—he'd never been gentle with Reeva. "Why would I ever hurt my own daughter?" He stroked Baby's cheek with his index finger. "Oh there, little girl, Daddy's here. Daddy's girl. You are a beauty indeed." His proud-papa face disgusted her. "She has my eyes and chin. Maybe even my nose." He kissed Baby's brow. "You're your father's daughter, aren't you? My very first baby girl. That makes you extra special."

The baby quieted. Opened wide eyes with dark lashes and stared into her father's eyes, her purplish skin now fading to a rosy, healthy glow as the crying subsided.

Even cooed.

And Reeva knew in that moment, she'd birthed a monster.

Chapter One

Memphis, Tennessee
Monday, October 16
8:00 a.m.

Ever the dutiful daughter, Violet Rainwater climbed the cracked steps of the sagging apartment complex, wishing someone would put her out of her misery.

Inside, the putrid scent whacked her upside the head—like the smell of assisted-living centers where residents were far from assisted. She entered the elevator and punched the button for the second floor. As she stepped out, fluorescent lights spasmed overhead and drew out a dying hum signaling a ballast was about to go kaput.

An apartment door on the left opened, and an ancient woman with crags deeper than the Grand Canyon glared, a cigarette hanging from her lips. A floral housedress hung off her bag of bones.

"Morning," Violet said, ignoring the burn in her eyes from the smoke as she strode past the woman.

"Yeah, what's so great about it?" She snarled and snatched her newspaper off a welcome mat with a sunflower.

Violet paused, turned and studied her. Nothing flowery about her. A woman hardened by life. By disappointment. Failures. Same face Violet would peer into three doors down.

"You're breathing, aren't you?" she asked. Why was she even engaging with the woman?

"Barely." She huffed and pointed to Violet's face. "I remember when I was young and pretty."

Violet had heard that one before. But surface-lookers didn't stick around long enough to go past skin-deep, or they'd see what she saw when gazing long enough in the mirror. None of it would be defined as pretty.

Pushing thirty-five, she'd experienced more than any person should in a lifetime, and that was before becoming a forensic psychologist and an FBI agent with the Strange Crimes Unit. It was only natural.

Strange crimes were in her DNA.

"We're all worm food eventually," she quipped and carried on down the hall for her Monday morning ritual. She'd been enduring it for the past two years, since she'd transferred into the SCU from the Violent Crimes unit out of Jackson, Mississippi. The Mondays they were out of town on a case were a reprieve. She'd rather be hunting killers with the SCU than doing this.

The SCU South Division covered the Southern states, and there were more bizarre crimes—many with strange religious undertones—than one might imagine, which kept their specialized task force traveling often. Only three months had passed since they'd finally closed the Nursery Rhyme Killer case—a local Memphis cold case—and they hadn't traveled since. Didn't mean there wasn't work to do like review open cases and process mountains of abominable paperwork.

Violet shuddered remembering that hot July night the Nursery Rhyme Killer had gotten the jump on her. Her colleague Fiona Kelly had been staying at her home, cramping her style, and she'd assumed the noise had been her. Otherwise, she wouldn't have been ambushed.

As he'd trained a gun on her, staring her down, he'd seen the same thing Violet had quickly recognized.

Glaring, undeniable and shocking familial traits. She'd understood the possibility of having half-siblings out there from wild rants or incoherent patches of information muttered while her mom fitfully slept, but this had confirmed it along with a brief conversation about their moms and the circumstances surrounding their births.

He'd shown her mercy and let her live.

She hadn't returned the favor.

Violet reached apartment twelve at the end of the hall; her chest constricted and the ball in her gut tightened. Why did she do this to herself? Why did she keep coming back knowing it would never change?

Grandmother had made it crystal clear that she only tolerated Violet, and most days Mom wouldn't even speak to or look at her. She rapped on the golden knocker hidden underneath the rag wreath with a welcome sign hanging in the middle.

Violet had never been welcomed here. Not in the apartment or in the lives behind the door.

But they kept letting her in, knowing she'd have money to give them like she did each and every month. Penance for being born and a strain on their lives. She swallowed hard and touched the hollow of her neck as her skin flushed hot. This feeling never changed either.

She could psychoanalyze it all day long and give herself a clinical pep talk along with a rational plan of action, but the heart could care less about psychology and a glossary of terms. Even her own therapist concurred with her mind's counsel. But her heart said something else, and it led her up this gnarly path almost every single start to the week.

Grandmother opened the door, her hair recently set and her nails painted light pink. Neither Grandmother nor Mom made it past five feet. Violet towered over them at five foot nine. Got her height from dear old Dad too.

"Hello, Violet," she said, her voice identical to the late Olympia Dukakis.

"Grandmother." She entered the too warm, cramped apartment and set the Gibson's old-fashioned donuts on the counter. Mom's favorite. Plucking a white envelope from her purse, she laid the money on top of the breakfast box.

Mom sat by the window in her recliner. She was petite and frail, and her dark brown hair hung in a loose braid down her back and needed a shampoo. Mom had never taken care of herself. Had gone weeks without bathing and days in the same old sweatpants and T-shirt.

Growing up, Violet hadn't understood what depression meant and all that it entailed. Part of her motivation for pursuing a psychology degree was to understand her mom. And to figure out what might be wrong with herself.

"Hello, Mom," Violet said softly and sat on the burnt orange sofa across from her. "You having a good week?" Violet cocked her head and studied her. Nails gnawed to the quick. Pale cheeks sunken like craters and dark half-moons under her silver eyes. Sleep had eluded her for some time. Violet remembered the screams emanating from Mom's room and Grandmother's calm and steadying voice helping her chase the nightmares away.

A nightmare named Adam who had abducted Mom at only fifteen and held her in a place she'd called the baby basement. Then he'd set her free. But Mom reminded her for years after Violet hit puberty that she not only looked like the monster who had created her, but she acted like him in some ways too.

She wasn't sure if Mom was repulsed by her or feared her. Maybe both.

Either way, Adam releasing her hadn't actually freed her. Mom finally responded to her voice.

"It's Monday, Violet. Not much of a week yet." She kept her gaze focused outside at the traffic leaving exhaust in its wake.

"I mean since last Monday. I brought you old-fashioneds from Gibson's. You could stand to eat, Mom."

Mom whipped her head around and glinted. "Don't tell me what to do. No one tells me what to do. And stop calling me Mom. I hate that." She snatched a pack of Marlboro Lights off the side table and lit one up, inhaling deeply. Smoke plumed and curled around her face as Violet bit back a cough.

"Right," she whispered.

Grandmother eased into the recliner next to Mom's. Sandwiched between the plush chairs was a small table with Southern cuisine magazines in a tall stack, an ashtray full of butts and ashes, and a half-empty cup of coffee. "Saw the news about a nasty killer the SCU caught in Oregon."

Four divisions of the Strange Crimes Unit covered the country, working with local law enforcement and other agencies, and had authority to take a case over, unlike some of the other federal agencies. Her special agent in charge had to pull rank on only two cases. He'd rather work with the locals and not ruffle their feathers, and most often the local agencies welcomed their expertise.

"You help with that?" Grandmother asked.

"No. Not my division, and they didn't ask for assistance."

She rubbed her clammy palms on her thighs. "You need anything? I brought you some money, but if you need anything…"

"We do all right. Always have." She arched an eyebrow. "When you weren't making trouble, of course."

Violet's insides burned. She couldn't deny that truth. The fires she'd started around the neighborhood, the items she'd been caught—on purpose—stealing. The morbid fascination with death that consistently sent Grandmother into an episode and her mom on a tangent about being her father's daughter.

She supposed she was her father's daughter.

Which is why she'd been fixated on finding him. Entering law enforcement had given her access she wouldn't have otherwise had. She'd searched for years, coming up empty until the Nursery Rhyme Killer. Even with Fiona's help these past few months, they had zip.

But she would not rest until she faced him to see the truth. Was she like her father? Could she end up like him?

That one incident. That one girl.

But she'd had it coming.

"Of course." She stood and straightened her blazer.

"I'll see you next Monday unless I'm traveling." She waited a beat. No one had anything to say to her. She dipped her chin. "Grandmother. Reeva."

Mom didn't wave or say goodbye. She never did.

Out in the hallway, she picked up her pace to escape when a blond, curly-haired kid bounded out of the elevator, her mother already calling for her to slow down.

She ran right into Violet, the child's sticky hand leaving residue on her pant leg.

Lovely.

"Hewoo," she said, and her sparkling blue eyes peered into Violet's. Innocence. Goodness.

"Hello," Violet said, uncomfortable and irritated at the

stain on her pants. But it had no comparison to the stain in-side her soul.

"You're pretty."

The preschooler wrapped her arms around Violet's leg like a leech.

"Mommy says I'm pretty too."

Must be nice, and it was true. The kid was cute. The mom, with an exasperated expression, threw her hands in the air. "Charlee!" Her smile was apologetic. "Sorry, she never meets a stranger."

Violet awkwardly lifted her leg, the kid attached, and mo-tioned for the mother to peel her off. "Might want to teach her stranger danger. Or she's going to end up in parts in some-one's freezer."

The woman gaped and her face blanched. She scrambled to untether her daughter's tiny arms from Violet's leg. "Come on, honey." She gripped her hand and turned back to Violet. "Why would you say something like that?"

"Why not?" She stepped into the elevator and shrugged. "It's possible." Violet might have done the woman a favor, waking her up from a fairytale. There was entirely too much of a false sense of security in the world. No one thought any-thing bad could happen to them.

Until it did.

The doors closed and her phone rang.

Asa Kodiak. Special agent in charge of their SCU division and one of the very few people Violet would consider a friend besides Fiona. She answered. "What?"

"And a good Monday morning to you too," he said through his grit-and-gravel voice.

The elevator opened, and she hurried outside, escaping into the fresh October air. Third week in the month and it was only now starting to feel like fall in Memphis. "I don't have time for pleasantries." She frowned at her sticky pants. "I've had enough of that for one morning."

Asa grunted. "We have a case. We leave in an hour and a half."

And that was why she and her entire team kept bags packed. Quick exits. "Where?"

"East Kentucky. A place called Night Hollow. Branches out from a little town called Crow's Creek." He sighed. "Three bodies found around midnight by some people partying in a cave. All female. The latest victim is pretty fresh. Not sure how long she's been deceased. I want to get there quickly and try to preserve the integrity of the scene. Who knows how contaminated it might be by now. Bodies been removed by the coroner already. Couldn't leave them for animals and weather to eat away any possible remaining evidence."

"Why us?" Where was the strange and bizarre that rang the SCU bell?

"The victims' eyes have been removed and their eyelids sutured shut."

"So?" It was grotesque but would still fall under Violent Crimes.

"And a series of numbers have been carved across the forehead of the most recent body. Some nicks on the skulls of the other two suggest they'd also had the same forehead carvings, or similar ones."

Ah. Now it was getting strange. "They have any idea what the numbers mean?"

"Not a clue. It gets worse, but I'll brief everyone when we meet."

"We flying or driving?"

"Both. Flying first. Meet at the airport and pack for two weeks. Not sure how long we'll be there. Louisville agents will be there waiting on us to pass the baton. Cami is setting up our room arrangements."

"Who's handling the crime scene processing? Locals or the ERT?" she asked.

"Evidence Response Team."

Their people. Good.

"Everything is going to the Quantico lab."

"Kentucky State Police didn't want in?"

"They've passed the buck to the FBI. I'll fill you in more on that when we have the team together," Asa said. "Media is already swarming. Dubbed him the Blind Eye Killer."

"Lovely. See you in an hour."

The back door leading into the kitchen stuck, and he put some grit into it. He'd have to fix it. The fact Mama hadn't already ridden him about it must be a fluke. Nag. Nag. Nag. All the time. Every day.

"Sonny! That you?" Mama called in her high-pitched squawk. The tone like vermin scratched along his spine.

"Yeah," he returned then muttered, "but I hate being called that, and you know it, you hag." He entered the tiny kitchen, the linoleum fading and peeling back at the edge of the dingy cabinets.

He plopped a plastic bag with two foam containers of food from the Meat and Three Veg on the table. Mama's house slippers swished against the old hardwood as she shuffled toward the kitchen. "What'd you get?" she asked.

"Beans, greens and cornbread." He removed a box and placed it at her seat at the head of the four-chair table. But it had only been him and Mama sitting at it for more than twenty years.

After situating their food, he poured two sweet teas. She grunted and wrapped her bony fingers around the glass. Her hair had been pulled back in a severe bun at the nape of her neck. She'd never worn it any other way.

Once he'd seen it spilling down her back. When he'd been spying on her and Mr. Franks next door. His daughter had been pretty. And Sonny had wondered what her hair would look like spilling down her back.

Sonny sat across from Mama, and she held out her hand. He instinctively clasped it, and she blessed the food.

"Amen," he muttered and splashed hot sauce on his greens. Bitter like Mama. They ate in silence, the TV as background noise from the living room.

"What's troubling you, Sonny?" Mama asked, holding her fork in midair as if the Good Lord Himself had whispered Sonny's sins into her ear. "What have you done that needs repentance?"

"Nothing, Mama." Sonny's insides jittered and his pulse pounded. He couldn't meet her eyes.

She got to her feet.

His stomach knotted, but underneath the fear and humiliation of a grown man about to be inspected, rage simmered. Mama slowly rounded the table, circling him and sniffing, then her glint pierced his soul.

"I smell her on you. The hint of perfume lingers on your shirt." With every syllable, spittle from her disgust dotted his lips and nose. "You've given in to temptation." She poked him in the chest, her sharp nail pressing through the cotton fabric, stabbing him.

Invisible ants crawled under his skin and his bones rumbled as he pictured picking up the vase of silk lilies on the table, bashing in her skull and watching her bleed out like a pig on the faded floor. A thrill zinged through his middle until the slap across his cheek snapped him into the present with a venomous sting.

"How many times have I told you? How many times is it going to take to teach you the lesson of morality? You rotten boy. You shall be judged."

"Don't," he whispered. He knew what came next, after his sins were found out. After she pronounced him guilty. "I haven't been bad, Mama." But he had. He'd been very bad.

It wasn't his fault. He couldn't help himself. Couldn't stop himself.

Until it was over.

Then the shame and the overwhelming guilt flooded his system and the rumbling started. The rumble in his bones and the ants crawling under his skin.

It was their fault. Like sirens singing him to shore and ensnaring him.

"Get in the bedroom. Right this minute."

No. No, he hated this. He slammed his fist on the kitchen table, the glasses sloshing tea and the vase teetering. "You don't tell me what to do anymore! You can't make me."

She stepped into his personal space, her dark eyes boring into his, and he cowered.

Like he always had. Like he always did.

"You. Will. Take. Your. Punishment. Or you'll burn in the pit for eternity. Do you want to burn for eternity, Sonny?"

Tears burned his eyes and wet his cheeks. "No, Mama. Don't let me burn," he pleaded as paralyzing fear overcame him, but he forced one foot in front of the other until he reached Mama's bedroom.

He knew the drill. Been here many times before.

It was time to face the collage of crosses on the wall, reminding him of his sins. Slowly, he unbuttoned his shirt.

"That's a good boy," Mama cooed. Her cool hand ran down his bare, scarred back, her nails raising gooseflesh on his skin. "This is for your own good."

"Yes, Ma'am," he mumbled.

He braced himself as the dresser drawer squeaked open.

"Say it," she demanded.

He balled his fists. "Forgive me for I have sinned," he whispered. "'Lust not after her beauty in thine heart; neither let her take thee with her eyelids.'"

And the first lash of forty to come lit his skin up like raging fire.

"Again! Say it."

Chapter Two

Monday, October 16
3:20 p.m.

Violet slumped against the window in the back seat of the black Suburban the team had rented at the regional airport. On the drive to Slate County, they'd stopped for greasy fast food, and she'd choked down a grilled chicken sandwich with a wilted piece of romaine and too much mayo.

Asa drove and his ex-wife, Fiona—who he was now dating again—sat shotgun. Weird to date a former spouse, but it was working for them. Asa had been less grouchy and Fiona wasn't quite as hardcore. Softness had smoothed her edges since they'd caught the Nursery Rhyme Killer. Fiona had closure to her past. Something Violet craved like water to a parched throat in August heat. Closure and answers.

Next to her, the team's religious-behavioral analyst played on his phone, groaning when he lost. Tiberius Granger grated Violet's nerves about eight hours a day, but he was one of the smartest men she'd ever met, which he downplayed by behaving like an overgrown child with a smart mouth and no filter. At least he smelled nice.

"You'd think I'd be a pro at this game by now. I've only been playing since I was twenty." Frustration and disgust laced his tone.

"That's sad." Violet curled her lip.

"It helps me think."

"That's sadder."

Ty waved her off and went back to his game.

Sprawled out behind them was Owen Barkley—their criminal pattern theory expert; he hummed along to music with heavy bass thumping through his AirPods. Owen was a paradox. A gentlemanly rake who she was fairly certain had a secret romance going with their computer analyst, Selah Jones. She'd remained at the Memphis field office with their admin assistant, Cami. They were short an agent, but Asa couldn't seem to find the right person to fit the SCU bill.

"How much longer?" Ty asked. "I'm about to pop. One too many Monsters."

Violet swallowed hard to relieve the pressure in her ears as they wove up the east Kentucky mountains flanking the narrow highway. A blue cloudless sky met the October foliage dressed in gold, crimson, rust and orange. And somewhere nestled deep within the glittering colors, three women had died in a gruesome, cruel fashion.

Nothing pretty or glittering about that.

"Crow's Creek is twelve minutes away according to GPS, but the holler where the crime scene is located is further in the hills," Asa said. "Hold it."

"You sound like my mom."

Violet stared out the window, ignoring the banter.

"What do you think, Violet?" Ty asked.

She scrunched her nose. "I think you shouldn't drink so many energy drinks. You definitely don't need them."

"About the case. I don't care what you think about my thirst-quenching habits." He winked and handed her an iPad with the preliminary report and photos the Louisville FBI had sent them. She scanned the photographs but refrained from wincing.

The most recent victim was crumpled in a heap near a pile of rocks, her eyeless sockets exposed, sutures hanging from her eyelids. She must have ripped them out. Her mouth gaped in horror. Her long dark hair was matted and in disarray. Bruising from several rough blows to her face revealed she'd been beaten prior to death, and the marks around her neck indicated strangulation by bare hands; finger impressions had formed a ring along the sides of her neck. She couldn't be sure what kind of marks were hidden beneath her filthy rumpled clothing. They didn't have a coroner's report yet. Violet could only speculate based on the crime photos. What she did know was Atta Atwater had been twenty-four. Born and raised in the hollow—or holler, whatever.

The other two victims had been in the cave longer than Atta, and due to time, wild animals and the damp environment, they hadn't been able to identify them yet. But two women had been reported missing in the past three months. If the missing women were the victims in the cave, they had a three-month timeline to work out from.

"I can't say until I see their bodies, study the crime scene and hear the official cause of death. Right now, it's simply tragic." Violet handed Ty back the iPad.

Fiona shifted in the passenger seat, her hair a tad longer than her usual short cut. After catching the Nursery Rhyme Killer, Fiona had talked Violet into unlocking her guest room and letting her inside.

I know what's behind here. I had a room like this once too. Never let anyone in. It was all about me and Rhyme. It nearly destroyed me. It did destroy my marriage. Let me help you, Violet. Let me in.

And Violet had. Fiona was the first person to see the work she'd done behind-the-scenes to track Adam. Violet didn't cultivate relationships. She had her reasons. But their working in tandem and talking about topics personal to Violet had developed something akin to friendship. Unfortunately, it hadn't brought anything new with Adam.

Fiona's right eye drooped, a little lazy but not too noticeable unless she was tired. And already they were all tired. Traveling often took it out of them.

"Cami texted," Fiona said. "The closest hotel is in Pikeville, but that's a little over an hour away from Crow's Creek, so she found a place in town. We can be on site easier and not have to make a drive late at night when we're spent. Below our lodging budget too. Bureau will love our frugality." She nudged Asa's arm.

"I did the research, and Crow's Creek is less than three thousand people," Owen said. "What kind of accommodations are we talking?"

"An old boarding house?" Fiona's tone sounded more questioning than confident and didn't reassure Violet that their lodging was going to be on the up and up.

"I got bad vibes, Fi Fi McGee," Ty said.

"I hate it when you call me that."

"I know," he said as brotherly love laced with playfulness radiated in his light blue eyes. Their team was tight-knit, but Violet chose to hover on the outer edges. Until she knew for sure she wasn't like her father in all the ways she suspected she was, everyone was safer at a distance.

She was safer.

Fiona glanced at Ty. "You think those numbers carry a religious connotation?"

He shrugged. "Can't say yet."

Typically, the crimes that landed in their laps had religious or ritualistic undertones, though they weren't always easy to detect at first in some cases, and if Violent Crimes had a full plate, regardless of if there were odd religious undertones, they'd take a case off their hands.

"If we could figure out the meaning behind the carved numbers, it might give us a leaping head start," Fiona said.

Ty huffed. "Fiona, I don't like working under pressure."

She threw him an are-you-kidding-me expression. "All we do is work under pressure."

He splayed his hands. "Now you know why I repeatedly say I hate my job."

It won him an eye roll.

They turned off on KY 15. North Fork Kentucky River rolled to their left, and to the right, ridges of limestone, shale and sandstone rocks painted an earthy landscape; above the crags, the Appalachian Mountains rose to the sun and the increasing altitude clogged Violet's ears. She swallowed, forcing them to pop and adjust.

"Shouldn't be too far up."

Little roads branched out with signs revealing several hollows, which were nothing more than unincorporated communities of people. Violet had done a little digging, and the only hollow she found interesting was Loretta Lynn and Crystal Gayle's old homeplace in Butcher Hollow. Once home to miners and their families until the mines closed. Many moved out, but there were those who remained. Living off the land. Doing life their way.

She wondered how the folk in the hollow would take to outsiders coming in and disrupting that way of life. Asa said in the briefing earlier that an anonymous call came in to the State Police at two in the morning from a bar in Crow's Creek called the Black Feather. The man informed them that bodies had been found, but they better come out because the local law enforcement wasn't going to properly investigate. Not sure if that was true or not. But locals probably weren't going to roll out a welcome mat for any other agency, including the SCU.

They continued to wind up and around, Violet's stomach turning at the curves. She should have taken a Dramamine. A small green sign reading Night Hollow signaled them to the mouth of the hollow. It hungrily opened, swallowing them up, its tongue a narrow dirt road carpeted with colorful leaves, potholes and puddles from an earlier rain.

Ty perked up, his golden-brown hair in disarray and his eyes vexatious as he pocketed his phone.

Asa shot him a sharp glare through the rearview. "Don't even start it." But his warning fell on deaf ears as Ty was already picking an air banjo and humming the music to the movie *Deliverance*. A movie Violet was only familiar with because she was a secret film buff.

Fiona pivoted in her seat and turned her nose up. "Really?"

But at first glance, Ty wasn't that far off base. The atmosphere seemed to morph. Inkier. Ominous. Something malevolent hovered, and Violet shifted in her seat, the vehicle heavy with silence as they entered the great yawn. Would this place swallow them whole? It had devoured three women already.

The road wound sharply, providing only one car width of room. Unpaved driveways led to small double-wides, trailers and cabins with sagging roofs. Nothing about this place gave off welcoming vibes, so she hoped they wouldn't need to turn around in one of those driveways or pull over to let another vehicle pass.

A black lab and a dirt-crusted mutt moseyed along the tall strands of grass edging the road, their tongues lolling. Violet cracked her window, the SUV too stifling. The rush of water wending the path of the road slicked over stones and sloshed along the creek bank.

As they continued their ascent, the lush woods thickened like a fortress and the air outside cooled as they plunged deeper into the belly of the hollow. Violet massaged the area behind her earlobe and stretched her mouth to relieve the pressure in her ears once more.

Outside a rusty aluminum trailer on their right, a rail-thin woman hung clothes on a droopy line, her hair blowing in the breeze as three little girls with the same blond locks ran and screeched barefoot through the overgrown lawn, rustling up the free-range chickens. Their clucks echoed, and they paused as the team veered past.

Asa growled and slapped the steering wheel. "There went the GPS."

"You know what happens to those who get lost in the backwoods?" Ty started in on the air banjo again.

"Knock it off." Owen's tone was sharp and somber as he sat ramrod, his eyes warily surveying their environment. Men with guns stood on porches, stony-eyed. Children gathered behind them, their little heads poking out from between their legs to get a look at the newcomers.

With local police coming through since midnight last night then State Police and feds, it had been a circus up here. Owen removed his AirPods and kept a hand on his holster. His dark eyes were trained on the man who stood at the foot of his gravel drive, his beard touching his belt and his gun in an aimed position. "I do *not* like this place. And I got a feeling none of these good ole boys are gonna like me."

Fiona turned in her seat again, adjusting her seat belt. "We all need to tread lightly. I suspect nobody is happy about any of us being here. But I hear you, O. And we got ya."

Violet shivered as goose bumps broke out on her arms, and the hair at the nape of her neck stood on end. It wasn't the demographic that rubbed her wrong but the awareness of an eerie presence. Unsettling. Rancorous. As if darkness had staked its claim, ready to fight to keep its hollow under its cold bony thumb. The kind of merciless evil that didn't play by any rules. Or fight fair.

Violet closed her eyes. They'd fought this kind of monster before.

But something felt...personal. Like the place was eyeing her alone as its tasty morsel. The mouse that the cat toyed with before sinking its teeth into.

"Leave it to Violet to nap through a freak show like this. Ice in your veins, woman. Ice." Ty snorted.

Let him think what he wanted. Ice did run in her veins. But the cold she felt at this moment had nothing to do with DNA.

"Where are we?" Asa paused on the road. "Talk about being out in the middle of B...nowhere."

"We out at Aunt Gussie's, no doubt," Owen quipped. "Where exactly is the crime scene?"

"A cave back in the hollow. There's supposed to be a road that leads us to it, but I haven't seen anything except driveways." He eased on the gas and continued the climb until up ahead a flash of yellow caught their eyes.

Crime-scene tape had cordoned off a small dusty road, and a Slate County patrol car with two deputies stood post, keeping out anyone who wasn't law enforcement. Asa rolled down his window and flashed his creds while introducing himself and the SCU team. The deputy handed him the logbook to sign them in, then he parted the tape to allow them through.

They inched up the bumpy road, being jostled like dice in a clammy palm. The road—if it could loosely be called that—opened up into hilly terrain, lacking grass. A UTV's dream. The cave was enormous, a rock formation that climbed and stretched beyond the trees. Boulders had formed a porch of sorts covering the dark opening, wide enough to fit a couple of trucks. Cans and cigarette butts littered the surroundings.

Looked like a perfect party place. Why hide bodies inside unless the killer wanted them to be found?

Asa parked behind Louisville's federal vehicle, and they clambered out, stretched their legs. Violet straightened her charcoal gray blazer and smoothed her matching slacks. Her knee popped and she winced. Owen opened the hatch and passed out their FBI windbreakers. Maybe it'd cut out the wind seeping through her thin blazer and silk shirt underneath. She donned it and checked her watch.

"Almost four o'clock."

"Yeah. I really don't wanna be out here after dark." Fiona shivered. No. No she wouldn't.

Asa discreetly squeezed her hand and winked. "You stick real close to me."

"Enough of the flirting already," Ty whined and slid into his windbreaker. "Get married again and get a room, would ya?"

They'd be losing light in forty minutes. "Or we could get to work."

A lanky, bowlegged man approached, his badge noting him as the sheriff. Removing his hat, he spoke from underneath a Tom Selleck mustache, but that was as far as the similarities ran. His comb-over tuft blew like a lone strand in the wind and his beady dark eyes homed in on her, squinted as if he was trying to place her familiarity. "Whichuns of you is gonna be in charge?"

"I'm the special agent in charge. Asa Kodiak." He held out his strong arm, and the sheriff hesitated then shook his hand.

"Sheriff Jackie Wayne Modine." Pleasantries and introductions were made, but they rode an undercurrent of mistrust on both sides. Nope, no welcome mat. "I'll tell you like I told the others who're still here and the State Police before 'em. We can handle this case."

Before the sheriff could further voice his opinion, the two federal agents out of Louisville exited the cave, and the blond muscular one waved at Asa. "Hey hey," he called. "Good to see you and glad to pass this one off." They approached and he hugged Fiona. "You look amazing. I knew I should have beat Asa to the punch in the Academy. You and I could've been a sweet, sweet thing."

Fiona blushed at his brazen teasing, and Asa rolled his eyes and introduced the old friend and cad as Agent Kip Pulaski. The dark-haired man with the runner's build who'd been standing quietly and observing was Agent Bill Thompson.

The sheriff's cell phone rang. "Pardon me. Not that it matters," he mumbled and traipsed out of earshot.

"He's a real piece of work. Not happy that we're here at all and pretty ticked about the anonymous call to the State Police," Agent Pulaski said. "We've been trying to track who that caller might be."

Violet suspected it would be easier to find a needle in a haystack.

"Rain came in a few nights ago. It's muddy back there," Pulaski said. "If y'all have rubber boots, use 'em. Coroner took the bodies around eight this morning. What little trace evidence we found, we held for you to see, but it's ready to go to Quantico."

"You already reinterview the first ones on the scene, the people who found the bodies?" Asa asked.

Agent Pulaski nodded. "Figured you'd want to do it all yourself though. Third time's a charm, right? We still have ERT combing. The cave is deep, and we're pretty sure the vics were alive in here for a period of time. Not sure how long."

"How do you know that?" Violet asked.

"Scratch marks on the cave walls."

"What else do you know?" Asa asked.

"This is the primary location. But they were tortured else-where first. Too much equipment to bring in and too dark for what he did to their eyes—removing them then suturing the lids. Hoping they weren't awake for that. Our most recent victim ripped out the sutures and went into a frenzy based on the wild muddy shoe prints and sludge caked to her boots. But he killed her here."

For all that was good. "I want to see inside."

"Bears in there?" Ty asked, scratching his head. "I'll take my chances with a serial killer. Not so much a bear."

"I guess we'll find out," Owen said. "I'm not underesti-mating either one."

They headed for the mouth of the cave.

"Who identified the most recent victim?" Asa asked.

"Homicide detective for the sheriff's office Criminal Investi-gations Division. A Regis Owsley. When the partiers found the bodies, they called 911. He came out with a couple of deputies. She's a local," Agent Pulaski said. "Atta Atwater. Sheriff says she cleans houses for a living. No family except for a brother."

Local deputies provided them with helmets with attached lights, and they set off for the cave. "We have floodlights set up inside too. Help collect evidence," Agent Pulaski said.

Inside, a glow from farther in the cave gave them a small amount of illumination. The air was chilly, and the smell of decay and copper thumped Violet's gag reflex.

Water trickled down the rock and flowed into small crags, leaving pools of water.

As they continued deeper into the belly of the cave, the walls narrowed to single file; their boots sloshed and kicked up water. "I wouldn't think most partiers would come back this far." Too cramped. It was possible the killer thought he had hidden them well after all. But some inebriated young adults had gotten brave and explored. Violet had to shift to face the wall and move sideways. "Not a claustrophobic's paradise," she muttered as they all pivoted and groaned.

"Watch your step," Agent Pulaski said. The opaque rock was slick and slimy. Finally the passage widened, and they stepped up into a cavern. "This is where we found the most recent vic. In that crevice. The other two were about ten feet back."

Violet studied the rock walls and squatted, shining her light near an evidence marker noting scratches in the mud-caked wall. Upon closer inspection, she noticed the other piece of evidence—a human fingernail embedded in a small crack of the rock, proving the marks were human, not animal.

Violet let her mind drift until she was the Blind Eye Killer. "He wanted her confined, afraid and clawing for a way out. The crevice may have given her false hope that it was a tunnel leading to freedom. Or the killer placed her here after killing her. Hide her better."

Why would the killer remove their eyes, suture the lids closed then leave them here only to come back and kill them later? It was risky. She closed her eyes, inhaled. What would she have done?

"I don't want them to see. See their way out? See me? Their final moment?" Not sure. "I want them blind and afraid. Panicked. I want to watch that. See them come to if they'd been put under, which I tend to think they would be. It would heighten my delight when they realized they couldn't see. Weren't in the place they were before. Couldn't open their eyes. Then it would dawn that their eyes had been sutured. They'd touch them, panic. Go into a frenzy." She looked at the rest of the team. "He wouldn't want to miss that."

"Go on," Asa said.

She closed her eyes again. "I'm here. Tucked in a quiet

corner where I can have my fill. I have light. I can see them. But they won't be able to detect light because their eyes aren't simply closed."

She walked back toward the narrow opening. Far enough he would be out of reach but have the best view.

"I watch them claw through the pain and hysteria as they rip the sutures from tender, sore eyelids, and it's a thrill. But not as big a joy as when they finally have them out and they still...can't...see. It's possible the meds that put them under or knocked them out have them groggy enough to not even know they only have empty sockets."

"That's sick!" Ty shuddered.

"Keep going, Vi," Asa said and hushed Tiberius. "Stay in that place."

A place she hated but that came easily. A dark place—like a cave in her own mind.

She closed her eyes again, then repeated her initial thoughts. "He wanted them to know that the pain was for nothing. It changed nothing. They were still blind. Alone. Afraid. Without rescue." She opened her eyes. "That's why he didn't kill them at the secondary location. But here. He wanted the ambiance of the cavern to mimic their literal darkness. Wanted them to grope along the walls, hunting for false freedom. They'd call out, cry out. But it would be utterly useless."

Fiona rubbed her chin. "He enjoyed that. Watching them have hope they could get out, survive. He needs control and power, every single second down to their death belongs to him. As if they owe it to him. He's probably a man who has little control in the real world, where he can't entertain his fantasies."

He took their lives and left them to rot in this outer darkness. As if they were nothing more than garbage for the wild animals.

Asa turned to Ty. "And the numbers? Anything in this cave give insight into them?"

Tiberius adjusted the helmet on his head and surveyed the conditions. "The numbers themselves don't, but I'd like to see them—see how they're etched and discover the type of instrument he used. It may be significant. Offhand, Violet said something that rings a bell religiously. 'Grope in darkness.' There's a verse in the Holy Bible. In Isaiah, I believe, about the corrupt being blind and groping in spiritual darkness. And there's one in the book of Job about making them grope in darkness and there is no light. Also, in the book of Genesis there's the angels striking the men at Lot's door blind because they wanted him to send out his visitors—who were angels—for the men of the town to sexually abuse."

Violet pinched the bridge of her nose. "Anything else? In any other religion?"

"Yeah, plenty," Ty said. "And if we were in New Orleans or closer to the Mexican border or even in the desert, I'd name them, but we're in the Bible Belt for Christians. Most likely if a religion has been twisted by a killer, in this region, it's going to be Christianity at the foundation. Could have some jacked up mixes but unlikely. I'd prefer to start with the cornerstone then work outward."

"So this could be a metaphor of some kind," Fiona noted.

"Possibly. I need to know more about the victims to help me discern if religious undertones are involved."

Violet stood. "And I need the victimology to work a more solid profile." Technically, they could call out a behavioral analyst from Quantico to join their task force, but most team members of the SCU division had at least one agent who had gone through training at the FBI to build profiles. The South Division had one: Fiona. She'd never worked in the BAU, but she had been trained. Violet had done work in forensic psychology—and there was her inner self who easily thought ominous thoughts—and preferred victimology over profiles, but she could do either.

Asa rubbed the back of his neck. "Owen, see if you can't find us some sort of geographical pattern to pinpoint where the killer may live or work in relation to the cave. I want to know where they underwent the torture. And why this cave."

"The location of the eye removal probably isn't too far from the cave due to the risk and the fact this place is isolated," Owen said as he moved toward the opening of the cave. "I'm gonna survey the woods. If I'm not back in twenty minutes, send out a search party," he jested.

"If you get lost, you're the worst geographical profiler ever to navigate the earth," Ty said.

Owen waved him off and exited the cave.

"I want to see where the other bodies were located," Asa said.

"We'll need a command post too," Fiona added.

After they finished examining the cave, they reentered the dusky evening, and Violet smacked into someone. "Sorry."

"Hello, Violet."

"John? What are you doing here?"

John Orlando wasn't surprised to see Agent Violet Rainwater on the scene. The case was bizarre, and Violet's job was all up in the whackadoo. John had seen some crazy things as a detective with the Louisville PD before moving three years ago to Memphis and working in the Missing Persons Unit. Occasionally he was faced with gruesome scenes, but not like when he worked homicide. Now he helped families get closure. Like he'd been helped when his late wife went missing.

"I got a call from a friend at the Louisville field office. Said a few women had been found in a cave and it related to a case

I'm close to." John wasn't one to flash around his wife's tragic death. The sympathy card wasn't his game. Pity eyes and weak pats on the back fell flat each and every time.

Callie wouldn't have liked that either. She'd been independent, tough as nails and in love with her agency. Been with the DEA almost twelve years before she died. That last year of marriage had been their toughest. Stella had been only three months old and Callie wanted back in. Back undercover. Indefinitely.

Scads of bad memories surfaced since he'd been here on the scene.

"Oh." She paused. "Well anything you can tell us will help. How long has your vic been missing? Do you think it's one of the women in the cave?" Violet brushed a long dark strand of hair that blew in front of her face. His gut squeezed like it always did when he encountered Violet. The last time was three months ago when a case he was working connected with hers. The first time was a year ago when she came to him about looking into a few missing persons from over thirty years ago. Never explained why. And he never asked. He understood the need to keep things private, but they'd had several conversations about missing persons, one of them over a lunch he'd wished had gone longer.

John avoided eye contact by scratching his left temple with his right hand. This wouldn't stay hidden. He should have known this. "She's not missing anymore."

"John." Asa greeted him with a hearty handshake. "How've you been and what brings you to this scene? To Kentucky?"

His chest squeezed and heat ballooned across his brow and ears. He motioned them to a more private area to keep their conversation confidential. "Uh...my wife, Callie, was DEA. Went undercover in Slate, Letcher and Harlan counties almost four years ago. Meth ring. Big money. Big circulation.

She went missing six months into the assignment." He'd never forget that phone call.

John, it's Greg. Callie's missing.

"Another agent, Greg Bigsby, was undercover with her. And he's still under. Some sting operations take years—you know this." He was hemming and hawing. "Two weeks after she went missing, the DEA found her in an old abandoned mine on the outskirts of Crow's Creek. She'd been…" Even now it was too difficult to talk about. "She'd been beaten up, strangled. And her eyes had been sewn shut. Postmortem." *Thank You, Lord.* From the scuttlebutt, these newest victims had been sewn up prior to death and had been missing their eyes. At least Callie hadn't suffered that.

"I'm sorry," Asa said. The others gave condolences.

Except for Violet.

"What exactly are you here to do?" she asked.

That he didn't mind sharing. "Initially I came to help determine if whoever killed these women killed Callie, but I'd like to help in the investigation if possible. I have some time saved up I could use."

Fiona and Asa exchanged knowing glances. A fine line separated revenge from justice. Asa pawed his face. "I—"

John held up his hand. "I'm not here on a vendetta. I've made peace with Callie's death. Forged a new life. But one more hand on deck can't hurt, can it? I have inside contacts here," he said in a whisper. "Greg is still trying to compile evidence to put a guy they call Whiskey away. I think he's behind Callie's murder, and he might be behind your victims' deaths too. I'm not here as a vigilante."

Asa's jaw twitched, but then his eyes acquiesced. "I'm down an agent in my unit. Fiona filled the other spot. Budget cuts. You're right. I could use a helping hand, especially if the locals won't take kindly to us."

They wouldn't.

"What about your daughter?" Violet asked.

John was torn. After Callie died, he'd needed help raising Stella, so he'd moved to Memphis, where his sister lived and could give him a hand. Stella saw her cousins as siblings and would love being there while he was here, but he had grown used to being home with her every night. "If my sister tells me she's having a rough time, I'll leave. But for now, I'm in."

Asa shook his hand again. "My team, my rules, Orlando."

John caught Violet's mouth twitch. Asa Kodiak was known for being large and in charge, but fair and excellent at his job. John had no problems submitting to authority. Asa was showing him courtesy. And John believed it was divine.

"Welcome to the team then," Violet said.

Violet herself was top-notch. Reminded him somewhat of Callie. Never showed an ounce of fear. Like Callie had been, Violet might be attracted to danger too.

John was certainly attracted to her.

But attraction was where it would stay. For the very reason he'd lost Callie—dangerous job. And he had a sneaky feeling Violet was married to it.

"I see a game of rock-paper-scissors in the near future as to who gets stuck working with us as a liaison." Ty chuckled.

"Just because that's how you and Owen divvy up responsibility doesn't mean it's how everyone does." Fiona gave him a stern expression.

"Doesn't mean they don't either." Ty checked his watch. "It's been twenty minutes. Let's vote. Who thinks Owen's dead?"

John raised his eyebrows. For a man on an elite team, Ty didn't seem to be too serious about it.

Owen emerged from the tree line holding up his arm and pointing to his watch. "Twenty-one minutes, bruh. I see no SAR."

"Figured you were dead, making a search and rescue point-less, *bruh*." Ty shrugged, but John sensed the deep loyalty and brotherhood between the two men. Violet had quietly slipped away. Was John the only one who'd noticed? It was hard to not notice when her presence wasn't around.

As if he had no choice, he moved from the conversation and found her near the cave entrance. "Whatcha doin'?"

Violet slowly pivoted in his direction, her face devoid of expression. He'd never actually seen her teeth revealed in a smile, and he felt a pang in his chest. What would keep one from a big genuine grin? Even on occasion?

"Wondering what significance this cave holds. Why this one? I know it's Owen's job to figure out why the killer chooses his locations, which can help us find him, but..." She touched the limestone with her gloved hand and ran her finger down the side. "Did he play here as a child? Experi-ence a traumatic event inside? Or was it simply convenient?"

John understood. "I'll leave you to let the cave talk."

Her eyebrows briefly raised. "Why do you say it like that?"

"When I worked homicide, I often went in alone. The crime scene talks if we're listening. Kinda like a lingering voice that wants to speak up, speak out from that dark place. Reminds me of Abel's blood crying out for justice and reach-ing God's ears. Places...people talk."

She cocked her head, and a small *hmm* escaped her lips. He turned to leave when she stopped him.

"You can stay. Maybe it'll talk to you too."

Somehow he knew her invitation wasn't airy. Not one she often offered.

To stay.

"Thank you."

Remaining quiet, he tiptoed through the trees, the grass reaching his waist in a few spots. Rock and loose boulders cluttered the area as he climbed and stumbled his way around the side of the cave, looking for other entrances and for... something.

He turned and surveyed his surroundings. Wait a minute. What was that? He watched his step through the high grass until he met a tree line and a worn footpath carved through the middle of the forest. "Violet!"

She appeared from the high grass, her windbreaker buttoned and debris dotting her dress pants. "You find something?"

He pointed to the trail. "Someone—or multiple some-ones—travel this enough to keep it bare. Wanna see where it leads?"

"I absolutely do." Violet's eyes lit up, a little on the bluer side, and she met up with him at the tree line. She retrieved her cell phone as they entered the heavily wooded area, and her thumbs worked the keyboard. "The last thing I need is Ty asking for votes on if I'm dead or not," she muttered then growled. No cell service.

"He's..." What was the best word choice? "Comical."

"He's hiding his big fat brain behind it." She ducked at a low branch.

"That your professional diagnosis?"

"Maybe." A hint of mischief tugged at her lips. "It's prob-ably some deep-seated issue, but I told myself I wouldn't di-agnose my colleagues unless they asked. Though sometimes, it's difficult not to shrink them."

The path wound uphill and curved into a yard. An old sunken-in cabin with a decaying porch came into view. In the trees beyond were remnants of a kid's play world or an intri-cate deer stand. Rickety rungs climbed an old tree and led to a shelter, maybe a tree house. A rope bridge connected from that tree and ran about a hundred feet to another small, un-covered platform. John glanced from the contraption to the ground. Had to be around fifty feet or so. Maybe less. John would never let Stella go up there to play.

The overgrown yard was littered with rusty toys and dozens of beer cans. A faded and torn sofa rested on the saggy porch, some of the boards rotted away.

"Secondary crime scene?"

"Perhaps." Violet moved to the wobbly wooden porch steps and switched on her cell phone flashlight. The sun was quickly fading. Most of the windows had been broken or cracked. The house radiated ominous vibes. Wonder what it would say to Violet?

"Be careful. Boards look weak."

She tested the planks, then moved forward a slow step at a time. "It's sturdier than it appears."

Yeah, well, John outweighed her by a hundred pounds if he had to guess. Keeping fit came with the job, and he needed to be healthy, but after Callie's death he spent extra time at the gym. His stress reliever. A time to work out his feelings. Wrestle with the pain and the anger.

Deal with the guilt over the circumstances that arose before Callie went undercover. John still blamed himself in some ways and allowed that last heated argument to torture him.

They could have worked through the turmoil surrounding their marriage. Turned back to their faith earlier. But it had taken the tragedy to bring John to his senses and back to the God he once loved and served.

Why did it have to always be tragedy?

"John, you okay?" Violet stood at the open door, studying him.

"Yeah. Yeah." He shook out of the past and grinned. "You're not standing there profiling me, are you?"

"Do you want me to?" One sculpted eyebrow rose.

"Not particularly." He stepped through the door ahead of her.

"What happened to ladies first?" she asked, but he noted her easy tone.

"Safety over chivalry."

She followed him inside. "That also seems chivalrous."

Since she appeared to be talking to herself he ignored her.

The stale air mixed with urine and the stench of decay. Old furniture had been toppled, and the stuffing was protruding from an armchair. Looked like animals had made nests. No sink. No light switches. Not uncommon in the hills and hollers of Kentucky. Many had no electricity or running water. John had been born and raised in Hazard, so he knew a thing or two about Appalachian living.

The cabin was less than a thousand square feet if he had to guess. One living area that opened into a cramped kitchen minus a sink or electrical outlets. No kitchen table. Only two rickety chairs hinting there once had been. John searched for any evidence suggesting the victims had been brutalized here. Wooden walls and floors carpeted in dust, debris and wood shavings.

"Hey, look at this." John motioned toward the ribbons of wood. "Isn't this odd?"

"Wood in a log cabin with a bunch of other junk? No."

Frowning, he examined them closer. "These are from whittling. Who is going to come into this dilapidated place and sit down and whittle?"

Violet flipped her hair from her face and stared at the droppings as if she were bored to tears. "The killer? Whittle while you work," she quipped.

Before he had a chance to laugh, her eyes grew wide and she clamped a hand over her mouth. "Shoot me now, I've been around Tiberius too long."

He did laugh then and pulled out his phone to get a few photos of the shavings, then he moved into the narrow hall-

way. A bedroom at each end. A closet in between. No bathroom. The smaller room housed a full-size bed, old blue
tattered curtains. No sheets. Only a dingy, soiled mattress.

Violet entered. "It's like they fled the cabin. Or vanished.
In a poverty-stricken environment, why would one leave behind all their meager belongings?"

"I don't know," John murmured and spotted an old pencil box on the dresser. "Do you happen to have an extra pair
of gloves?"

She dug into her pocket and handed him a set. He rum-
maged through the items in the box. A pocket knife, a few
quarters, a child's white Bible and a suede coin purse. He
opened it and inside was a faded photo of a girl, maybe seven
or eight. Blond pigtails. Pretty. He used his cell phone camera
and took a photo of the picture and the coin purse.

"You think this means something?"

Violet placed her finger in the cleft of her chin. "My gut
says everything here means something."

John's gut echoed Violet's. Something sinister hung in the
air, like a taunt to come further inside. To step into the past
and see the nightmare with a firsthand view.

But like words spoken that couldn't be taken back, what
they might see couldn't be unseen.

And some things should never be looked upon.

As they exited the cabin, Violet paused and turned her head
toward the woods.

"What is it?"

"You feel that? The sense of being watched?"

He didn't.

But maybe it was because he wasn't the one being watched.

Chapter Three

Rage kindled in his blood like flames that couldn't be quenched. They had no right to be here. To handle his things. He'd seen the law drive up earlier, carry out the bodies.

Atta had always fascinated him. The way her body curved and her hips swayed as she walked. Dark long hair that slipped over her shoulders like satin and big eyes with long lashes like elm switches. Skin smooth like the stones from the crick running through the holler.

He balled his fist, his nails digging into his palm as the two intruders finally left. Then he got a good look at the woman agent in her FBI windbreaker. She was celestial. Same long hair as Atta. Anger subsiding, he studied her as his blood heated and his abdomen tightened.

She was careful in stepping off the porch, and the lawman held her elbow to aid her balance. As if he was some great protector. He grunted.

He knew men like that. Tough and cocky. Believing a

pretty woman might show him affection if he behaved in a gentlemanly way.

Never worked.

Didn't matter how kindly he was or how many doors he held open or even how many gifts he gave them. They didn't want him. Never said yes.

Only no.

He was sick to death of hearing no.

How many times had he rescued a damsel in distress at the Swallow? Been the knight in shining armor, protecting them from a tragedy waiting to happen at the hands of a drunken letch. And yet, they'd rather be in the arms of those men than his. He would have treated them like queens. Been gentle and given them their heart's desires.

But no. No. No. No. The words echoed in his ears until he plugged them with his fingers to drown out the word he hated most.

The word he heard most.

Wasn't fair.

Wasn't right.

Wasn't going to ever happen again.

The pretty agent paused like a doe caught in the crosshairs. Alert. At attention but frozen. Cocking her head, her gaze pierced through the woods, cutting right to him, right through him. She didn't cower. Didn't run. Didn't retreat. But smiled. Didn't she? Her eyes fixed on him the way sunlight glittered on the lake—a bright spot in the shadows.

He wanted her.

Something about her was familiar.

He watched her begin moving again, his mind running away with his fantasies.

Maybe the pretty agent wouldn't say no.

Maybe he'd take what he wanted even if she did. But he'd

have to be careful, a step ahead. After all, she wasn't alone. But she didn't know the holler like he did.

And the holler had ways of presenting prime opportunities for a man with patience.

Rubbing her aching and tired back, Ruby slammed the door of her ancient clunker that needed a new muffler and clambered up the cabin's steps, opening the screen door with a screech and hollering, "Mother, it's me." She smelled the remnants of fried chicken and her mouth watered.

Mother rounded the corner in her pink housedress, her aqua eyes young for a woman of eighty-three. Thick gray hair hung to her waist in a braid. "Child, hush. Lula is taking a nap. I know it's late, but she was tuckered out after dinner. You hungry? I saved you a plate." She moved with precision to the oven and removed a warm plate of fried chicken, mashed potatoes with country gravy, cornbread and butter beans.

"That looks amazing." Ruby sat at the table and wasted no time digging in. "Clark Powell was on a bender today. Do you know how hard it is to do your job with a sloppy drunk?" Ruby shuddered thinking of his bourbon breath and sweat-stained shirt. The man hadn't bathed in days. His house had been a nightmare. Food-crusted plates and empty beer cans had littered his kitchen. She sopped up the butter-bean juice with her cornbread. "I heard a special federal agency was called in to investigate Atta's death, and the anonymous call from the Black Feather said that local law enforcement wasn't gonna do nothing about the murders, so that's why the State Police cut and run and here they are. Saw Regis earlier."

Mother sat across from her with a glass of water. "He say anything else?"

"Just that the two other bodies were most likely Tillie and Darla." Her eyes burned at the thought of losing now three friends. "They're fixin' to bring in Tillie's sister from Bowling Green, and I guess Amy to see if they can identify the… remains. If anyone would know if it's Darla, it'll be her roommate. They practically shared a closet." She pushed away her plate at the thought of friends rotting in a cave to the point they were unidentifiable by their faces. "Who would do this?"

"I don't know, but until we do, you watch your back." Mother's worried brow concerned her. Ruby rarely saw Mother fret. She always said the Good Lord didn't need worriers. He needed warriors. Taking care of the needs of others was warrior work, and that was what she did; and those who loved her followed her example.

"Well." She gulped her sweet tea. "We'll figure it out. I can't stay hidden in my house. I have to work." Work to eat. Pay bills. Take care of Lula. "Oh, Regis also mentioned the feds would be setting up shop at the sheriff's office, but no one wants to work with them." No surprise there. The holler had its own way of dealing with folks and seeing to justice. "Anyway, since he's the original detective on the scene, the short stick fell to him. He said he wasn't too upset and he'd keep tabs."

Mother tapped her long oval nails on the nicked wooden table. "He has good reason."

Ruby paused midbite. She supposed they all had good reason. Her stomach roiled, and Lula's cries startled her.

"I'll get her. You finish up now." Mother scurried from the room, and in a few beats brought in Lula, her dark hair damp on her forehead. Mother kissed her cheek. "Such a sweet baby. Look who's here."

"Mama!"

Ruby's heart swelled, and her anxiety and worry faded away—at least for a moment. This life she had always wanted to escape dimmed in the presence of her three-year-old's chubby face. She had Ruby's dark hair and chin dimple, but her daddy's dark eyes. She took her baby from Mother and hugged her tight.

Lula made everything better. She was the only good thing Ruby had ever done. And she worried about Lula's future in the holler.

"What did you do today while Mama worked?"

"I played with Festus."

Ruby chuckled. That old black lab belonged to the holler. Folks took turns feeding the poor thing. He ate better than most kids. "Well, good. Let's go home."

Mother raised an eyebrow. "Keep your doors locked."

She shuddered. For a few days after Tillie had disappeared, she thought maybe she'd run off. Thought maybe Darla had gone to meet her, but deep down, the truth screamed they hadn't left of their own accord. Wouldn't.

Couldn't.

"Yes ma'am." She kissed Mother's cheek. "Say bye-bye."

Lula kissed Mother's cheek. "Bye-bye."

"Thanks for keeping her. Love you."

"Love you too, hon. Be careful." She saw them to the car, and they said their goodbyes twice more, then Ruby drove up into the holler, where her small double-wide was nestled along the trees with the crick running behind it.

Once inside, she kicked off her shoes and groaned at her own kitchen. It had nothing on Clark Powell's kitchen, but even so. After all her cleaning, the last thing she wanted to do was her own chores, but Mother said godliness was next to cleanliness. 'Course Ruby had no idea if that was true. She didn't read the Good Book as often as she ought to, but she did attend church and prayed daily.

"Mama, can I go play?"

"Yeah, baby. For a minute. It'll be too dark before long. Don't get too close to the crick, now, okay?"

"Yes, ma'am." Lula bolted out the back door and into the backyard, where Ruby had made her a sandbox. She watched from the kitchen window. Innocent, sweet Lula.

She went to work on the stack of dishes in the sink, peeping through the window to keep an eye on her. Once the last dish was in the drainer, she yawned and stretched her back. Padding to her room, she pulled the day's cash from her purse, and with nerves humming skimmed a hundred-dollar bill from the top and shoved it under her mattress then put the rest in an envelope and sealed it.

"Mama!" Lula hollered, and Ruby jumped as if she'd been caught with her hand in the till. Heart racing, she pasted a smile on her face.

"Baby, don't be scaring me like that." She noticed Lula had something. "What's that?"

"Him left it for me! Isn't she sweet?" Lula handed Ruby the rag doll. Made of white cloth and button eyes. Hand-stitched red lips. Black hair made from yarn. She wore a silky floral dress. Ruby rubbed the material. Was that made of... A lump formed in her throat.

"Who is 'him,' baby?" she asked and turned the doll over, examining the other side.

"Him. I call him *Him*. Him leaves me stuff by the crick sometimes."

Ruby's blood chilled, and her hand touched the hollow in her throat. "Do you talk to Him?"

Lula shook her head. "No. But I seent Him. He waved to me from the trees. I can keep her, can't I?"

Ruby rushed through the house and opened the back door, scanning the woods. She couldn't see Him, but gooseflesh broke out on her skin and her pulse sounded like cotton swooshing in her ears.

She felt unseen eyes gazing in her direction, watching. Lurking. Prowling. Planning.

She swallowed hard, trying to shove down the feeling she'd experienced three separate times in the past two weeks. Eyes prying.

Inching backward into the house, she closed and locked the door. Lula sat at the kitchen table with a ponytail holder and juice box.

Lula would have no idea when the mystery man had left her the items. No point asking. Except… "Baby, remember the day Mommy couldn't find her silkies and asked if you'd taken them?" Lula loved anything satiny or silky soft. Slips. Undergarments. She had no boundaries.

"Yes, ma'am."

"Did he leave you stuff that day?"

"Yes, ma'am. Mama, I didn't take your silkies."

"No…no, I know you didn't," she murmured. "Can I see what he left for you?"

Nodding, Lula scrambled into her little bedroom and returned with a tube of watermelon lip gloss, a silver compact and a half-eaten bag of Skittles.

Ruby's head buzzed and the room shifted.

Atta wore watermelon lip gloss, and she always had a family-size bag of Skittles in her car, even in summer. Those two things might be coincidences, but the compact was not.

Ruby had given Atta the compact as a birthday present last year.

Adrenaline raced through her veins, and she clutched the doll tighter. "You can never take any more trinkets from Him. Do you understand?" The need to escape, to flee, overwhelmed her. Mother. Mother would know what to do.

"But why?"

"Because *Him* is a bad man." Whoever Him was, he had taken things from Atta. Maybe even her life. Why was Him giving her daughter gifts?

And why had Him fashioned the doll's dress out of Ruby's undergarments?

John hated the coroner's office. From when he worked homicide to when he had to fly here and identify Callie. Same sterile, cold air. Stainless steel slabs and tools. He'd never been comfortable in these places.

He stood sandwiched between Violet and Asa. Fiona stood at the head of the table, and Ty and Owen had gone with the deputies to begin the command post set up. It surprised John that Asa allowed those two off the leash. The coroner stood near Fiona, a thick shock of prematurely white hair glaring under the fluorescent lighting. On two other tables, the other victims lay covered in thin white sheets. They hadn't been officially identified yet, but hopefully between family and a roommate, they'd have identifications within twenty-four to forty-eight hours. Really, it would come down to dental records to be sure the two victims were Tillie LeBeau and Darla Boone.

The coroner's assistant, Dr. D.J. Lanslow, looked more basketball player than doctor. "Cause of death is cerebral hypoxia."

She'd been manually strangled after being beaten. Her face, breasts and genitals had been severely battered and bruised as if he'd concentrated on those regions most.

"What can you tell us about the eye removal? Was it a hack job? Professional?" Violet asked.

Were they looking at someone with a medical background of some kind?

Atta's sockets gave her an alien look, and John's stomach churned. Lividity had set in, and her back, arms and thighs were dark purple. Gases had already begun to bloat her abdomen, and the scene was simply too ugly to stare at.

"They were taken cleanly, yes," Dr. Crocker said. "There's evidence a clamp was used, concluding it's possible someone has a medical degree or medical knowledge. Or someone who watched a million surgeries on YouTube and maybe practiced it on others—animals first. She ripped out her sutures, and therefore the eyelids are in shambles, so I can't speak to technique or form."

D.J. pointed to Atta's neck. "You can see the contusions and abrasions and the round bruises matching tips of fingers on the sides of her neck." His voice strained, and he cleared his throat then continued, "But the thumb pad prints in the recesses of her carotid reveal he was facing her when he strangled her. Possibly straddling her as she lay on her back. We know she died on her back because of the lividity. Not to mention the bruising to her trachea, proving he faced her when she was killed, and the hyoid bone has been fractured. He used a lot of force."

Angry force if the additional blows to her body meant anything. She would have suffered those perimortem too. And suffer she did.

John studied her neck wounds, noticed fingernail indentions.

"I found bleeding into the neck muscles. He used more force than necessary." Dr. Lanslow averted his gaze, and his nostrils flared then he cleared his throat.

"Did you know the victim?" Violet had picked up on the same emotion John had. Distress. Doctors were not squeamish, but something was giving him a struggle.

"No," he stated. "I didn't."

"You live in town or up in the hollow?" Violet did that intimidating glare he'd seen her do before, and Asa and Fiona exchanged a knowing glance.

"In town."

"All your life?"

"No. I moved here to work with Dr. Crocker."

"You ever go up in the hollow?"

"Maybe once or twice."

"Did you know Atta?"

"Yes." He shook his head. "I mean no. No. I did not know her." He rubbed his earlobe and broke eye contact with Violet. "I've seen her in passing. In town. I don't—didn't know her. Personally."

John wondered if Violet would pursue it or let it drop.

Violet kept her focus on him then abruptly backed off. "Fair enough." She gave Fiona an almost invisible nod.

Fiona stepped between Violet and Dr. Lanslow. "We need a time of death, and have you found the same cause of death with the other two victims?"

"Cause of death is the same. Fractures the same. Naturally, with the decomp I can't find any marks. Can't be sure their lids were sutured, but I'd guess that if my job was a guessing game. Their eyes had also been removed. One wasn't on her back, but I believe an animal, maybe a coyote, sniffed her out, moved her. I gave any trace evidence to your Evidence Response Team for analysis."

They'd need a manufacturer of the sutures. Maybe they could link the sutures with a hospital or vet clinic. Medical experience didn't necessarily mean human.

"Time of death is tricky," Dr. Lanslow said. "They were exposed to elements, but the temperature in the cave slowed decomposition. I'd have to say time of death was likely forty-eight to seventy-two hours ago for your most recent victim."

Either Friday night or early on Saturday. Definitely over the weekend. "We need to retrace Atta's steps. See where she went the week leading up to the weekend. Maybe we can find the last person to see her alive. Do we know where she worked or if she had family?" John didn't mean to jump in, but he'd been a homicide detective and now worked missing persons. This was what he did.

The SAC didn't seem to mind. Asa only agreed. "According to the sheriff, Atta cleaned houses in town and the surrounding counties."

"Family? Residence?" John asked.

"A brother. A chaplain up in the holler."

"Ty will want to know that her brother's religious," Violet said.

Asa agreed. "We need to get some dinner, stop in and pick up Owen and Ty then settle in at our lodging. Tomorrow, we can start fresh at the command post." He turned to the coroner. "Toxicology and rape kit?"

"We did a tox screen. Most anesthesia wears off and leaves the system, but Agent Pulaski with the Louisville FBI sent blood samples to Quantico. We did find a spermicide. I can't say definitively that she was sexually assaulted, but I can say she had intercourse prior to death."

Dr. Lanslow shifted from one foot to the other, but his face remained stoic.

Asa's lips twisted, and he puffed his frustration through his nose. "Okay, thank you for your help."

"I'll have my official report to you in a couple of days."

On their way out, Violet frowned. "I think Dr. D.J. Lanslow is hiding something. And I definitely believe he knew Atta Atwater."

"You think everyone is hiding something," Fiona said.

"Everyone is." She huffed and they climbed inside the SUV.

John buckled up. "We need to find out who she dated or if she was a fling kind of girl. Where she hung out. With whom."

Asa glanced in the rearview.

"Sorry."

"Don't be. All theories, suggestions and thoughts are welcome."

Totally cool dude. No narcissism or rivalry. No wonder young agents badly wanted on this team. "While we might be looking for someone with a medical background, we can't rule out other occupations or hobbies that would require sewing, stitching or removing body parts." He winced just saying it.

Violet draped her FBI windbreaker over her lap and shifted to face John. "Taxidermist comes to mind. Even a skilled hunter—which might make everyone up here a suspect. Or it could be someone who started out young cutting up cats and squirrels and who knows what else. We can't say for sure."

"Hopefully the tox screen will help us out. What other drugs would put someone under deep enough to remove their eyes without them waking from the pain?" Asa asked.

"No one said he gave her anything," Violet said. "We assume because we don't want to imagine him binding them head, body, torso, hands and feet. That's deplorable and diabolical. But it is still a possibility. Women poke out attackers' eyes all the time. Doesn't kill them."

John swallowed down the nauseating saliva forming in his mouth. "Callie's eyes were sutured postmortem, and her eyeballs weren't taken. No sign of sexual assault that they could determine."

"She was taken four years ago." Violet nibbled on her thumbnail. "Placed in a coal mine. Sounds like he was forming his signature with your wife, and now he's perfected it. Also, it's possible we have more victims in other locations.

Let's get Owen on caves and mines in the area. We can't comb them all, but we might be able to narrow down other crime scenes. If he is using tools—whether or not they were under or conscious—he's not doing it in the cave."

They needed to discover where.

"Maybe the ERT will link something from the cabin you and John found earlier to the victims or the scene," Asa said as he pulled into the tiny lot at the sheriff's office. "Ready to meet the team who doesn't want us here? And probably even more so since having to deal with Tiberius for the past forty minutes."

Fiona snickered.

"Someone does want us here, though," Violet said. "A man who wants to remain anonymous. Who believes that the local law won't do anything about these murders. Could be someone inside the blue line. Or media. Or someone who knows something."

They could ask about who might have been in the Black Feather bar that night around the time the call came in, but that didn't mean the locals were going to be forthcoming.

"We'll keep trying to find Mr. Anonymous, but I'm not expecting answers," Asa said, and they exited the SUV. Entering the small station, heads turned, all eyes on their team.

"How can we help you?" the woman at the reception desk asked.

"I got this, Bonnie." The CID detective from the scene earlier approached with his sports coat draped over his arm and car keys in hand. He was over six feet with a thick, salt-and-pepper military cut. His arms were beefy but his slight paunch said he also enjoyed beer. Crinkles creased around his dark eyes—so black they were almost blue. "Homicide Detective Regis Owsley." He introduced himself and shook hands with the team. "I'll be helpin' ya on the case."

"You were first on the scene?" Asa asked, but Regis's eyes were glued to Violet. Finally, he averted his gaze and answered Asa.

"I was. Quite a sight. Quite a sight." He pointed behind him. "I gotta be somewhere, but the room is all ready for ya. Your partners are in there. You need anything ask Bonnie here."

"I do have some questions for you," Asa said.

"And I'm happy to answer 'em. But I really do gotta be somewhere." He rushed out the door, and Asa frowned.

"Let's go see this room." As the team headed for the case room, John's phone rang.

Unknown caller.

Instead of following, he hung back and answered. "Detective John Orlando."

"If you think you're going to come up here and poke your nose into everything, I'll kill you with my bare hands."

Chapter Four

After grabbing a bite to eat at a meat-and-three diner that was literally called Meat and Three Veg—Violet only eating the veggies and wondering how much butter they had been cooked in—the team headed for their lodging accommodations. They were staying in an old boarding house that had been converted into a bed and breakfast, propped on the banks of the Kentucky River with the Cumberland Mountains encompassing it.

But it couldn't be described as quaint or cozy.

Looming and ominous, it boasted of deep-seated secrets and a past that would curl one's toes, from the cracked, peeling paint on the four porch pillars to the sagging dormers over the three windows across the second story. Soggy earth and a hint of brine from the river swirled with falling leaves, and the two glowing lights opposite the front double doors flickered.

"Are we being punked?" Ty retrieved his phone from his pocket. "I'm texting Cami right now."

Wasn't like they hadn't stayed in some odd places before.

"I'm willing to make the hour drive to a hotel in Pikeville. That's all I'm saying," Ty added. "Remember what happened at the last creepy home? *Fiona?*" He stressed her name and she frowned.

"Well, it needs work," she said cautiously. "But maybe the inside will be better."

Asa put his arm around her. "You didn't sell that, hon."

No. She hadn't. Fluttering called her attention to an old clothesline where a flock of crows perched, emanating raucous caws. Like something out of a Hitchcock film.

"Are we gonna stand here like teenagers afraid to go into the haunted house in a movie, or are we going to go in like dumb adults in a slasher film? Me? I prefer the juvenile approach." Ty glanced at his phone. "Cami says she didn't know it was creepy, but it provides beds, so get over it. I do not like that woman."

Fiona snickered, and Asa elbowed her ribs. Cami and Fiona had a salty past.

This was ridiculous. They were cowering like the Scooby-Doo gang, not top-notch federal agents who ate monsters for breakfast. "Enough already," she muttered and approached the house, climbing the concrete porch and ringing the doorbell.

John followed. "Beggars can't be choosers, huh?" The subtle scent of his aftershave tickled her nose. She never thought she'd be working a case with John Orlando—other than when she'd been working her mom's case. But here he was. He'd said he'd driven straight here once he got the call about the murders and hadn't thought anything else through. Seemed more level-headed than that, but it was concerning his dead wife. Hysteria got a pass. Ty said he'd bunk with Owen, and that opened up a room for John. The house was now at full occupancy.

Violet suspected they'd be here the whole two weeks, which was their longest possible stay in a location due to the budget and people needing a life. Sometimes it was only a couple of days or an over-the-phone consult. Violet didn't mind the traveling or the living out of a hotel for two weeks and guzzling gas-station coffee. What else did she have going on other than her hunt for Adam?

The front door opened.

Not much surprised Violet, especially after the Nursery Rhyme Killer and all that came with his identity, but to say she was taken aback at this moment was a gross understatement.

"Detective Owsley," Asa said.

Violet reined in her bewilderment. Why was the Criminal Investigations Division's lead investigator at their B and B? Was this why he had to rush out of the station? To be somewhere. Here. Did he know they'd be staying here? He recognized their shock and grinned. "Agents," he said in a gravelly voice, thanks to the nicotine.

"Do you own this place?" Talk about coincidence.

He laughed. Gritty but jovial. "Nah, Aunt Hossie does. But I played here all the time as a kid. Come in. Come in." He took her bags, and she glanced at John, who shrugged with his eyebrows, then she tossed another look to the team behind her. Ty's lips spread wide like the Cheshire cat.

"Hossie. Really?" he said through the side of his mouth and bypassed Violet into the foyer.

Inside, the house smelled like lemon and pine and many years gone by. It was clean, and the original hardwoods shined through the generations of wear and tear. "Do you live here now?" John asked.

"No. I got a little place up in the holler. Help out Aunt

Hossie once in a while and sneak a home-cooked meal a few times a week. Command post good enough for you?"

"Yeah," Violet said absently, surveying the interior. Rustic pine, soft blues and antique furniture. Fiona wasn't wrong. The inside was nicer than the outside.

"I'll show you to your rooms. Aunt Hossie's achin' with the gout. I sent her on to bed early. She sure did want to welcome ya, though." Regis traipsed up the steep wooden staircase, and John followed, leading the rest of the charge. Upstairs a hallway forked with two bedrooms on the left and three on the right, sandwiching a bathroom. "Any one you want."

Violet chose a room with mauve wallpaper and a Queen Anne bed with a pastel quilt. Not her style, and she winced at the collection of porcelain dolls sitting in a Victorian lady's chair with a faded velvety cushion. A bookshelf void of books was lined with more of them. Not all were porcelain, but each one looked well used. Great.

She'd picked the Chucky doll room.

Taking in her accommodations, she sighed. The wallpaper peeled in some of the corners, and the oval mirror hanging above the dresser was cloudy with black spots declaring its age. Regis wheeled in her bag and rolled it to the far corner of the room; his gaze was unsettling, same as at the SO earlier, and Violet cocked her head. "Anything you need?"

He cleared his throat. "Sorry, you…remind me of someone."

"Well, they say everyone has a twin." Violet might have dozens. Hundreds even. She had no idea how many young girls Adam had abducted over the years and fathered children with. Only a few names Mom had muttered when talking in her sleep.

Asa poked his head inside. "Seven a.m. Meet in the dining room. Breakfast and then go-time."

"Okay."

He let his gaze swing from her to Regis then back.

"Anything else?" she asked.

"Nope," he said and eyed Regis again, then patted the door-frame twice and disappeared.

Regis lingered, and she wanted to know why. "You want to ask me something. Ask it."

He scratched his head. "How long you been an agent?"

"Long enough to know how to catch a criminal like the Blind Eye Killer." Was he sexist or hunting for a reason to stay in her bedroom? Fat chance he was getting an invitation for the latter.

Leaning against the wall, he crossed one ankle over the other and folded his arms. "You think you'll catch him?"

"You don't?"

"Not if the holler don't want him found."

She stepped forward into his space, testing his reaction. He didn't shy away. Didn't mind her up close. Personal. "Why wouldn't they want justice for their community? I thought hollers were family even if they weren't related."

"I didn't say they didn't want justice served. I said they might not want *you* to find him. We got ways of doing things up here." He held up his hands in surrender. "Now, don't go gettin' me wrong. I'm a law dog. I'm here to help you, but you should know it's not gonna be none too easy, hear."

She heard him loud and clear. All the more reason they were to stay even though Sheriff Modine would love for them to leave.

"How did you know Atta?" She lived in the hollow, and he said he did too. No way they didn't know one another. Might as well get on with the victimology. Test Regis. See how much truth she'd get. Read his body language. Try to discover tells.

"I know everybody who lives in the holler."

That didn't tell her how he knew her personally though. "How well did you know Atta?"

"Well enough."

Evasive. "Do you think the killer's a local? I mean he'd have to be, right? Everyone knows who's comin' into the hollow."

"Holler. We say *holler* in these parts."

"Holler," she corrected herself. "It's one way in, and he probably didn't walk. Someone saw him or at the very least his vehicle. They'll know if an unfamiliar vehicle passed through." But would they tell her? "And who would actually be the ones to dish out that justice? Is there some kind of hierarchy?"

"You ask a lot of questions, law lady." He chuckled. "I 'magine he's familiar in some kind of way. His comin' in and out of the holler wouldn't raise suspicion. That cave isn't on any website or tourist brochure. Someone knew it. Knew how far back it went and that those girls could scream all day long and not a soul would hear. Yeah, I'm putting my money on a familiar face."

But not necessarily someone who lived in the holler. Possibly in town or in the county, or someone who used to live here and returned on occasion to visit. Violet wanted a list of the addresses for the homes Atta cleaned. Hopefully, she kept records and was on the up and up, not cash under the table, but Violet didn't have a good feeling about that.

"How sure are you that the other two bodies are Tillie LeBeau and Darla Boone?"

"Two months ago, Tillie LeBeau went missing, and one month ago Darla Boone up and disappeared. No reason to leave. No talk of it, and nothin' packed up and removed from their homes. I'd say I'm pretty certain." He backed into the hall. "Well, good night, agent. You sleep tight, now."

Violet closed the door behind him and rubbed her aching back and kicked off her shoes. The team had been sent everything related to the case as digital files, and she opened her laptop and collapsed on the bed.

Who was Atta Atwater? Why did this Blind Eye Killer choose her? What made her an easy target? Was it someone she cleaned for? Atta would have entered the homes of people she knew and of people she didn't. That was the risk anyone took when their occupation brought them inside homes.

They needed identification on the other two women immediately.

She closed her laptop and unzipped her suitcase, pulling out toiletries, pajama bottoms and a top in simple gray. She padded into the small private bathroom with ivory wallpaper dotted with rosebuds. Before she stepped into the shower, that same chilling foreboding prickled her skin like an unwanted touch.

Snagging the fluffy white towel, she covered herself and raked over the bathroom. No windows. The shades in the bedroom had been drawn, but something was here, lurking. The sense was palpable.

Scalp prickling and throat tightening, she reluctantly turned on the hot water then stepped behind the curtain. She did not like this house. She did not like this case.

Or maybe she'd seen one too many Hitchcock films. They hadn't actually seen Aunt Hossie. She might be facing the cellar wall, rotting in a chair.

Tuesday, October 17
8:45 a.m.

Rubbing the back of his neck, John listened in quietly as the SCU team discussed the case and created boards, tacking up photos of the victims, and Owen Barkley worked on a map, pushing blue pins into the location of the cave but also working on some software on his computer and mumbling about the coffee. Atta's home was in red, but he hadn't gotten much further.

After the call John had received yesterday, he was distracted. He'd recognized the voice instantly though he hadn't heard it in three years.

Greg Bigsby.

His wife's old DEA partner. After his threat, he set up a time to meet with John. Today at one o'clock. To talk him out of sticking around. It appeared their murder investigation might bleed into the case the DEA was building to take down a guy who went by the name Whiskey and ran a serious methamphetamine ring through the Appalachian hills, reaching all of the eastern Kentucky counties. Callie had been under a few months when she'd been murdered. Greg had been in much longer. Several years. Callie hadn't revealed much to John about the case other than she'd been going in as Greg's girl with hopes to become a Whiskey Girl.

Whiskey chose women to make drop swaps, and they were known as Whiskey Girls. According to Callie, women were less likely to skim the product or the cash and could be more easily corralled and managed than men. But not just any woman was hired. It took trust on Whiskey's part, and John hated what Callie might have had to do to prove loyalty and trust. She'd never cross lines, and Greg's stamp of approval would go far, but John knew she'd had to play a part, one he probably wouldn't have wanted to witness.

John not only hated the danger, especially when they'd only recently had Stella, but mostly he hated that Callie wasn't content being or doing anything else. He'd encouraged her to go back to work, but if she couldn't go back undercover, she didn't want to do it. She'd been a daredevil from the start. Their first date had been skydiving.

"John, you have an opinion? You're pretty quiet," Asa said,

standing in front of a whiteboard with a dry-erase marker in hand.

He pawed his face. "Sorry, just taking it all in."

Violet cocked her head, and he met her eyes. She didn't buy it, but she didn't call him on it.

"Fair enough," Asa said. "Violet, what have you found out since breakfast about Atta Atwater?"

Violet strode to the board. "Not much. We know from Sheriff Modine she cleaned houses and so did Tillie LeBeau and Darla Boone. ERT didn't find a laptop or any device except a phone. No digital record of the addresses or names for houses Atta cleaned. I'm waiting on a positive ID before looking into Tillie and Darla, but the housecleaning is a link."

"Cash business?" Asa asked.

"Selah found no records of taxes being paid in the past few years by any of the women. Which means most likely. Not surprising given where we are, and the fact tons of people work for cash off the books. Even servers don't input the exact tip dollar amount. That doesn't concern me. What's odd is Atta didn't have any social media accounts. What twenty-something woman doesn't have a social media presence of some kind? Selah's digging up any scrap she can find. I'd like to go through Atta's place, talk to her brother—in person. And once we have official identifications on the others do the same."

"Okay."

"Detective Owsley said the preacher man is out of town until Sunday. An annual week-long fishing trip. Alone." Violet frowned. "However, I did talk to him briefly on the phone early this morning. Reception was shoddy. He had no guesses to who might have killed his sister, but since she was gone, he was going to take the time in the woods to grieve alone. Seems weird, but people grieve in many ways."

"When was the last time he saw her?" Asa asked.

"Thursday morning when he paid a visit to Mother."

"Mother?" John asked.

"Imogene Boyd. Old lady in the holler. Everyone calls her Mother. He said Atta had stopped by to pick up a casserole for a girl named Betty Jane Dwyer. New mom. He was there to discuss the fall coat drive with Mother. Imogene. Whatever. Whoever. I'll want to talk to Betty Jane and Imogene Boyd."

"The cave is long, and the surrounding area is dense. I'd like to have another look," Fiona said. "Something might have been missed."

"Okay," Asa said. "Violet, you and John—if that's okay, John—work the victimology. Owen, keep doing what you're doing, and if you see a pattern, let us know. Once we get the IDs, we'll call you. Fiona and I will go over the cave again. See if we can get a few deputies to help. Even bring back the ERT for a second look. Ty, work on those numbers."

Ty saluted. "Six-two-zero-one-two-three-four-five-six. Bizarre, but I'm working on it. Be patient." Beside him, holy books from several religions were stacked, and a notebook with a few pencils and pens lay next to them. A laptop was open in front of him.

"Let's meet for lunch at one at the Meat and Three Veg. I saw it was meatloaf today." Asa grinned. "We'll rally and trade notes then go from there."

They broke and Violet sidled up to John. "You good working with me?"

"Why, are you bossy?" he teased and collected his phone and wallet from the table. He wasn't technically on duty, so he wore casual jeans and a cream-colored sweater with his Timberlands in case they ended up in the woods again. But Violet was dressed in a black pantsuit with a light green shirt underneath that made her eyes a smoky green color.

"I am, as a matter of fact," she said coolly, but he caught the amusement in her eyes. She wasn't easy to read, but maybe if he spent enough time with her, he'd catch on to her nuances. Not that he needed to be spending time with her—other than work of course.

"Well, good. I like bossy women."

A laugh escaped her nose. "Then I'm driving."

The sheriff's office had two unmarked units that they allowed the team to use while working the case. But John preferred his own car. Asa had told him to save the miles. Still. He didn't mind Violet driving it.

Directions in the holler were all about landmarks since there weren't road signs. They didn't go as far back as the cave but drove over a small bridge and a road that forked west of the crime scene. Passing a smattering of houses with kids playing and women on porches gawking, they finally wound into the mountains, where a cabin nestled into the pines.

The yard wasn't overgrown. The porch was clean, and two pots of mums flanked the front door. A welcome wreath hung on the screen door. Two rockers sat on opposite ends. According to the lead detective, Regis Owsley, Atta had lived alone. He guessed her brother would deal with the place now.

Violet grabbed the crime-scene kit from the back seat and unzipped it then handed John a pair of latex gloves and booties to cover his shoes. "We're about fifteen minutes from the cave. And no other houses are in view. If he wanted to watch her, study her patterns, he had the time and the space to do it. Or he may have already known everything he needed to—if she knew her killer."

John agreed then turned the knob. Door was unlocked. "Well, there goes me breaking and entering. I always liked that part when we had to search a house."

Violet raised her eyebrows and went inside.

The cabin was small but tidy and full of mismatched furniture. The living space and kitchen were all open and to the right was a hall with two bedrooms and a bathroom.

Violet moved into the kitchen. Opened the fridge. "She likes wine. Not much else in here to drink. Basics." She found a stack of mail on the counter and rifled through it. "Mostly junk."

John studied the living room, looked in baskets, bins and the entertainment cabinet. "This is the brother." He held up a picture of the two of them outside a little church by the creek. He was wearing a clerical collar. They had similar features. Atta had been pretty, with long dark hair, big blue eyes and apple cheeks. Tall and slender. Her smile and her teeth were crooked, but it added character to her face.

Violet gazed at the photo. "Keep it. If we canvass the town, we could use it. Brother's nice looking."

She amused him. "You think?"

"He's no Cary Grant, but yeah. In a conventional way."

He mused on the photo again. Didn't see it, but he was a guy so… "I'll check the primary bedroom."

"I'll take the other one."

John combed through Atta's room. Her nightstand held a few *Cosmopolitan* magazines and a gun. Her top drawers had lacy nightgowns and fuzzy handcuffs. "Definitely involved with at least one man," he called. The coroner said she'd had intercourse prior to her death, but he couldn't rule it a rape.

Violet entered the room. He held up the cuffs.

"Why are they always red or pink?" She frowned and held up a suede purse, the size of a small makeup bag. Atta's name had been sewn on it along with the phrase *I am dark but lovely.* "This is strange."

"That's Song of Solomon."

"Say again?" Her brow creased and she cocked her head.

"It's a verse from the book of Song of Solomon in the Bible. It's spoken by the beloved of King Solomon. Her brothers made her work in the fields, and her skin had been weathered by the sun. The book is poetry about marital love."

"She wasn't married. That we know of."

"No. And why have that sewn onto a suede pouch?"

"Could it have been a gift from her brother? He's the preacher man."

John wasn't sure. That would be a creepy gift from a brother.

Violet studied the purse and ran her fingers along the edge. "Sure is nice stitching." She held it up.

John inspected it further.

Like tiny little handcrafted sutures all the way around.

Positioned flush on his belly, he slithered until he could reach what he was after. The floor was filthy and littered with rodent droppings. He didn't mind them or the rodents who left them. He stretched out and found the cold metal latch then lifted it, and the flooring loosened. Inside the dark, earthen hole were his favorite things.

He ran his fingers over the silky materials and smiled then found a lacey item that had belonged to Atta. She had been so beautiful in blue, like her eyes. He snagged it and shoved it into his pocket. Tillie had looked best in green. He found the green swatch and let his memories shift back to when he'd first seen them on her. Like an emerald queen. Finding a sleek, see-through black piece, he chuckled. Bella Dawn. He'd used part of these as a little scarf on the cowboy doll he'd made for her son. The little boy played with it, saddling him on his plastic horse and making him ride across the grass behind their house. The multicolored material fit Ruby best because she was the most colorful. But he'd frightened her with the doll he left Lula. Ruby was far more observant.

He'd be more careful. Ruby had powerful people in her pocket—in her bed. That soured his mood, and as he sifted through his treasures, disappointment stabbed his chest, replacing anger.

He had nothing of Agent Rainwater's. Violet. He liked her first name, liked the way it made his tongue lick his upper lip. He repeated it softly, letting it fill him with excitement. No longer angry. And he wouldn't stay disappointed.

He had a plan.

It was risky, but the risk gave him a thrill that put his other escapades to shame.

And he loved it.

Chapter Five

Tuesday, October 17
1:05 p.m.

John entered a cracker box that had been planted on a gravel drive. Trucks, motorcycles and even sport-utility vehicles dotted the lot. In the right corner, a jukebox blared Hank Williams Jr.'s "A Country Boy Can Survive," and it mingled with the conversation, laughter, and clinking of glass bottles and glasses on the bar top. Place reminded him of the movie *Road House* with the late Patrick Swayze—before his character cleaned up the place.

He spotted Greg in a booth in the back corner next to the hallway leading to the restrooms. John raised his chin at the bartender and wove through the tables. Squeaking on the leather as he slid into the booth, he noticed Greg's appearance was harder, more chiseled than last he saw him. At Callie's funeral in Louisville.

When she'd been found, the DEA had sent undercover

agents in as family to retrieve her body and send her home for her funeral. Whiskey, the guy they were after, had never admitted to the murder, but he hadn't been too concerned according to Greg. That put him on John's list. If someone had come in and brutally murdered one of Whiskey's girls, why did he do nothing? No retaliation? Because he might be behind it himself.

Greg's hair had grown out to his shoulders in unkempt curls, and his beard was thick but short. Broad shoulders and biceps stretched his flannel shirt. He raised his eyebrow that had a slice through it from a work-related injury. Green eyes pierced John's, and his nostrils flared.

"What? Not happy to see me?" John asked.

Greg sipped his beer and leaned forward. "We're this close," he pinched his fingers together, "to bringing down Whiskey. It took me three years to gain his trust, two to get in the inner circle and now one more year in and I'm his right hand. You poking your nose around is going to put up his guard and de-rail my mission."

Was that all Greg cared about? Did justice for his partner not mean anything to him? "What about Callie? Whiskey could be involved in her death—"

"And if he is, I'll find out." If he hadn't found out by now, he might not ever. He set his beer down hard. "Then I'll make him pay. For the drug ring. For her murder. I need proof. I can get it. You can't. Stay away from him. Better if you go on home."

"I'm not going home. I'm working with the SCU on the case."

A server scooted up to the table with a pad in hand. "What can I get ya, honey?"

"Water. Thanks."

She raised her eyebrows and hurried away.

"If it leads us to Whiskey, it just does. The SCU isn't going to back off simply because the DEA is involved. I know the SAC. Never happen. He would work with you, but to back off a multiple homicide for meth—uh-uh. No go."

John hadn't heard from Greg since the funeral either. "I'm assuming you haven't gotten any new leads on Callie's death?"

For the first time since he'd sat down, Greg's pain showed. He dropped his head and shook it. "I wish I did. Whiskey might have dirty hands, and he might have had Callie killed, but now with this serial killing connecting to her... I don't think he's a serial killer. He's a rotten son of a goat, a dirty drug dealer and a murderer—though I need more proof—but not this kind of killing. It's possible one of his crew is capable of it."

"Name?"

"Nope. I don't need you questioning him on a tip that will then stoke Whiskey's paranoia with the question of who threw out the tip. He's got good reason to be like a spring wound tight. It's why he's never been caught. Extra precautions. If your investigation leads to this crew member, then fine. But don't expect holler folks to talk."

John rolled his eyes. "I know about mountain living, Greg. I was raised in Hazard. I'm sick of hearing no one will talk. Someone is going to at some point."

"Whiskey knows y'all are here. He's got eyes everywhere, which is why I chose a bar two counties over. Even now, I'm not completely sure I'm out of harm's way. Those eyes he's got everywhere are on each one of you too. You're too close to his operation."

"What about the local sheriff? Why isn't he doing anything about him?" Stupid question that John already knew the answer to.

Greg laughed. "Can't say Modine is being bribed, but he knows. Some in the SO are on the take, some afraid. People who cross this man, they disappear. You understand? Gone. Poof! Earl Levine went missing two weeks ago. He was here, then he wasn't. Days passed. They asked about him, but Whiskey said he wasn't coming back. Rumor had it that a couple months back, he'd been messing around with Tillie LeBeau. Got a little rough with her, and not long after that he and Atta had an altercation. Earl was here. Now he's gone. Now she's gone too. Her and probably Tillie. I've said more than I ought to."

"Not coming back from where?"

Greg shrugged. "Probably the grave."

The server brought John a glass of water and left without a word. He sipped it. "What do you know about the CID detective with the Slate County sheriff's office? Regis Owsley."

Greg gulped down the rest of his brew and slid the glass, foam running down the insides, to the edge of the table, signaling another. The better question was how deep in was Greg? They were forty-five minutes out of Crow's Creek. No reason to keep up the act, yet he was drinking at one in the afternoon on a Tuesday.

"I never seen Regis at the cabin."

John assumed *the cabin* was code for their meth lab or place of business. Probably was an old cabin somewhere in the holler. "But?"

"I've seen other deputies there. You can't trust everyone at the SO. I don't know if you can trust Regis or not. I haven't personally seen him friendly with Whiskey. But he's familiar with him. Everyone is."

"What about the sheriff? You say he knows about Whiskey. Has he ever been to the cabin?"

The server brought Greg another beer and winked then disappeared again. "Blind eye. Not a present one."

John's skin prickled at the term. These victims had been

blinded. Had they been turning blind eyes to something? To Whiskey's ring? Except that didn't fit for Callie. If she'd been killed by Whiskey, it was for not turning a blind eye.

That might be it. Maybe these women went to the law for help concerning Whiskey's crew abusing them, but Greg said not everyone could be trusted. They might have gone to someone they thought they could trust. Which meant their killer could be someone in law enforcement. That could be why the call came anonymously. Why the local law would do nothing. Were they protecting one of their own or going to mete out justice on their own terms?

"I don't think the sheriff's directly involved. Could be on the take, but I haven't been privy to all Whiskey's meetings yet."

"And that's what you want?"

"It's what I need."

John stirred the straw in his drink. "Any buzz about the murders? You don't want me pointed at Whiskey, point me somewhere else. You have to know something about Tillie LeBeau if one of the guys you are around daily beat up on her. What about Darla Boone—she's the other girl who went missing. She been around any of Whiskey's crew?"

Greg ran his tongue along the inside of his cheek. "I know she went missing, and I know the SO looked into it."

"Was Earl Levine questioned?"

"I don't know."

John found that hard to believe. He was only offering up information that wouldn't point to the meth ring. Which wasn't much at all. "He never said?"

"Not to me."

Liar.

"I guess we're done here. You're wasting my time."

"If I hear anything that will point you toward the dead

women, I'll call you. But if it could also lead to Whiskey... I can't. I've worked too hard. Lost...too much."

His life? His soul?

Callie? John's stomach knotted.

He stood. "Don't let this job turn you into one of them, Greg. Callie wouldn't have wanted that."

Greg circled the rim of his glass with his index finger. "No," he murmured, "she wouldn't. How's Stella? She must be how old now? She was just a baby at the funeral."

"Almost four. Growing. Sassy like her mom. Curious about everything." He hated being away from her. "See ya, man." Once he was out of the bar, he called his sister to check in and to FaceTime with his sassy, inquisitive kiddo. It lifted his spirits, and he remembered why he was here. To make the world a little safer for his own daughter and to get justice for her mother.

By three o'clock, he made it back to Slate County and Crow's Creek. He called Violet to find out where the team was and what she'd been doing the past two hours. He hated dipping out during their lunch and briefing, but he'd hoped this would be more important.

"Did you find anything useful from your undercover agent?" Violet asked.

"No. Well, not about Whiskey." He relayed the information about Earl Levine and Tillie LeBeau. "Could be him. Rejected. Got rough. Kills her, then Whiskey kills him. Got rough with Atta too."

"Tillie's sister came in an hour ago. Only family. Lives in Bowling Green. She couldn't identify the body, obviously, but they showed her some personal effects. She recognized her necklace. Gave it to her for Christmas last year. And we got dental records back for the second victim. It is Darla Boone. Waiting on dentals from Tillie to make it official."

Well, at least they knew.

"What do we know, if anything, about these women?"

Violet heaved a breath, and it filtered through the Bluetooth in the car. "Other than they all lived in the holler and cleaned houses, Tillie LeBeau was twenty-eight and hung out at the Black Feather."

Same bar the anonymous call to the State Police came from.

"Asa and Fiona are talking to Tillie's sister then going to interview employees and the manager. Darla Boone was twenty-five, also cleaned homes. And that's all we know right now. How far out are you?"

"Thirty minutes."

"When you get back, we'll visit Darla's and Tillie's homes. Talk to Darla's roommate, Amy."

"One other thing," John said. "About the department." He relayed what Greg had told him about some of them being involved and others turning a blind eye and John's possible theory about why the women ended up dead.

Violet's end of the line was silent for a few moments.

"Well," she said, "since we don't know which ones we can and can't trust, then we have to go in not trusting any of them. I think we might need to create a command post at the B and B. For things we don't want them to see. I'll talk to Asa."

"But Regis Owsley has access to the house. For all we know, he has keys to every room."

"True, and I don't like that place to begin with. It's like someone is watching our every move. Did you get any creepy vibes last night?" she asked.

"No. But to be honest, after a hot shower, I was out. We'll need to be careful with what we say at the SO and with what we put on the board, then at the B and B, we watch our backs."

"Yeah, because I got a sick feeling someone wants to stab them."

Darla Boone's trailer was probably decades old but was tidy inside and smelled like cigarettes and cinnamon. An ashtray with a handful of butts, a few coated in lipstick, sat on the glass-top coffee table.

Darla's roommate, Amy Miller, sat on a late-eighties model couch, tears forming a curtain over her big brown eyes. She was rail thin, but not unhealthy, and her hair hung loose around her shoulders.

Violet sat on the club chair next to the couch, and John stood leaning against the wall that led down a hallway to Darla's bedroom.

They needed to retrace all these women's steps, starting with Atta since she would be the most recent and more memorable, but since Amy had been Darla's roommate, she would know more about her disappearance. "Tell me about the last night you saw Darla."

"I told all this to Regis. Sorry, Detective Owsley, when he came. And I don't mean to sound insensitive, but I have somewhere to be in twenty minutes."

Somewhere to be. That was fast becoming a well-used phrase in Night Hollow. "Once we ask you some questions, you're free to go, though we'll probably stick around if that's okay with you."

"Yeah. Fine. Just turn the lock when y'all leave."

"About the last time you saw Darla..." Violet redirected.

"Five weeks ago this Friday night. We'd gone to the Black Feather for a few drinks and to listen to a live band outta Pikeville."

Again. Same bar the anonymous call came from.

"Darla loved music. And crocheting. She'd listen to old

vinyl while making hats or scarves or baby blankets. It was her thing."

"Did she meet anyone at the bar? Dance with anyone?"

"She danced with a couple of guys who'd come in from Pikeville to see the band. Strangers. But that was nothin'."

"Did she talk to or hang out with anyone local?" Violet asked.

Amy fidgeted and ran her hand down her thigh. "Probably. It's been weeks. I had a good buzz going and played pool for a while with some friends. I wasn't watchin' her like a hawk, you know?"

"Who left first?"

"I did. Around midnight. She said she'd catch a ride." She wiped her eyes. "I should've stayed. I should've stayed the night Atta died too."

"You saw Atta the night she died?"

Amy nodded. "She came in the Black Feather around one Saturday morning. She'd been in a fight. Didn't want to talk about it." She pointed to her eye. "Had one of those little bandages on her eyebrow. Guess someone had split it open. She went to the back, and I left. Told her to call if she needed me."

"You see her with anyone when you left the bar?"

She shook her head.

"Any idea who might have roughed her up? Or bandaged her eye?"

She slid her bottom lip between her teeth and flicked her nail, avoiding eye contact. "No," she murmured. Violet wasn't buying it.

"Back to Darla. Do you know who she was going to catch a ride with?"

"Didn't say. I mean locals were crawlin', and anybody would have given her a lift. No big."

Clearly it was. And the bar was possibly the last place Atta Atwater had been before she died. They'd run that trail next.

"What about Earl Levine?" John asked. "Was he in the bar?"

John had told her this guy was one of Whiskey's crew and had roughed up Tillie, and he had an altercation with Atta not long after. Could he be connected to Darla Boone as well?

Amy's eyes widened. "Yeah," she whispered. "How you know about Earl?"

"It's our job. We're good at it too." Violet held Amy's eye contact. This woman needed to know that Violet wasn't a pushover and wouldn't stop until she uncovered every truth. "Did Earl dance with Darla? Talk to her? Could he have been her ride?"

Amy inhaled deeply. "Maybe," she squeaked. "Darla knew Earl. He grew up in the holler a few years ahead of us. Dropped out at fifteen. He wasn't always…he used to be a decent person. But…"

But Whiskey.

"He drinks a good bit. When he's drunk, he can be unruly."

"Do you have any idea whose homes Darla cleaned? Any at all? She ever talk about anyone scaring her or acting odd?"

Amy's neck flushed red, and she fidgeted, looking at her jeans. "No. I don't know anything about that."

Lies.

Why? "Someone she cleaned houses for might be the killer. They might have killed Tillie and Atta too. She never once told you where she was going or whose houses she cleaned?"

Amy shook her head.

Violet tamped down her temper; she was getting nowhere, and the fact Amy was withholding information told her enough. She was either protecting someone, or she was afraid of someone. "We're gonna look around now, okay? Detective Owsley look around?"

"I don't know. Maybe."

"Nobody fingerprinted anything?"

"We thought she'd run off. No one suspected she was... had been..." She sniffed and covered her face.

"That's all for now, Miss Miller. You're free to go. We'll lock the door."

She nodded, and as they entered Darla's room, they heard the front door open and close.

Violet snapped on her gloves, and John took a few photos. "Who knows if this room's been disturbed since she went missing."

"Who knows if anyone stole incriminating evidence." Violet heaved a sigh and started in her nightstand drawers. Books, junk, flashlight, gum. Nothing of importance. "Find anything significant?"

John poked his head out of the tiny closest. "No." He felt around the inside, hunting for hidden spaces or boxes. "Unless the pink bunny counts?" He held up a raggedy childhood toy and shook it. "Kinda looks like one Stella carried around when she was two. We had to tote that thing all over creation. Child wouldn't nap without it."

Violet noted the joy in John's voice when he talked of his little girl. It was genuine and pure. Stella had no idea that someone loved her beyond words, so much it came through like a ray of light from his warm brown eyes. No one had ever spoken with joy or even a hint of happiness when discussing Violet. The emptiness turned her insides cold.

"She has no idea what she has in you, John. Or...maybe she does."

"You got kids?"

"Me?" Hardly. It wasn't that she didn't like children. They

were entertaining and cute enough, but the awkwardness she felt around them was a little much. "No. I'm not cut out for motherhood. And that's okay. I've never really thought much about them."

"Oh." His tone held a trace of disappointment, and he shook the bunny in his hands. "I can't imagine life without Stella. I admit I was kind of freaked when I found out Callie was pregnant. She was too. She never—"

His abrupt cutoff said enough. Callie hadn't wanted children either. Which explained why a new mom would go undercover for an undetermined amount of time in a dangerous environment. It could kill her, and it had.

Seemed selfish to Violet. But she rarely judged anyone. She had no room. She'd done some pretty horrible things.

Things she couldn't undo or take back, and the worst part was she didn't regret some of them. That's why she wanted to track down Adam. Her gut told her if she could look into his eyes—same as her eyes—she'd know. She'd know if she was anything like him at all.

"Anyway," John said. "You ever been married?" He tucked the bunny back in the closet and dug around in the shoes. "I used to hide things in my shoes as a teenager."

"Yeah? What kinds of things?"

"Cigarettes." He laughed. "I was quite the rebel. Gave my parents a real run for their money. I figured my dad smoked, so I should get to as well. I grew out of it."

"I never smoked." She'd always been conscious about her health. If she ever got sick…she'd have no one to care for her. But that was too depressing to share. "I never married either."

"I'm surprised."

"That I never smoked?" She liked teasing him. It was easy, and he always seemed to know when she was making a joke. Fiona still had to ask, and she spent every day with that woman.

He chuckled and stood, his knee cracking, but she didn't remark. "Never married."

Violet had occasionally dated, but it was a rare thing. Never lasted long. "I scare men."

Crossing the room to the desk, he arched an eyebrow. "Like key their car scare them or...?"

A laugh bubbled in her chest, but she had keyed a car once. Her grandmother's. "Maybe intimidate is the right word." She was aloof. Cut and dry. Direct. Threw men off for the most part.

"You don't intimidate me, Violet. And I will kick your behind if I catch you keying my car. I'm all for gender equality," he teased again. John Orlando would no more lay a finger on a woman than he would his own daughter. But he was amusing.

No, he wasn't afraid of her or intimidated, which irked her. Why wasn't John unnerved by her?

"You'd never catch me. Never find a print. Trust me."

"I believe you," he murmured and opened the dresser drawer. "Hey, Violet..."

She walked over and peered into the dresser.

John took a photo then removed a small suede purse identical to the one they found belonging to Atta Atwater.

I am dark but lovely.

"Well, that's interesting." She handed John a plastic bag, and he entered the evidence then logged the information. "I wonder where they're getting these and if Tillie had one." Maybe Amy would know. They'd have to ask later. "Maybe we'll find one at her residence."

"Maybe." He stared at it through the plastic. "Perfect stitching like the other one. Same material. It might be nothing, but I feel like it's something."

"Agreed." She called Ty, set the phone to speaker, and he answered on the fourth ring. She heard Owen in the background cackling. "What's he laughing at?"

"The ringtone I use for you," Ty said through a chuckle. "What's up?"

She didn't even want to know what he'd set his phone to ring to when she called. "We've found two leather purses from two vics. Both have Scripture—the same Scripture on them. *I am dark but lovely.* John told me it's from Song of Solomon about marital love. Give me something."

"First of all, you could make your requests more cordial."

"Doubtful."

"Fine," he said and sighed. "John's right. It's about Solomon and his bride and gives some good marital advice. But some believe it has more poetic symbolism and speaks about Jesus and His bride, which is the church. It's about spiritual intimacy. The *I am dark but lovely* statement can mean that though she is dark with sin, she is still lovely because Christ died to set her free from her sins, and now she's pure and clean and lovely. Forgiven."

Violet sucked on her bottom lip, thinking. "Then whoever gave them this purse knows or believes these women are sinners but still pretty or salvageable or forgiven? Would he think he's their bridegroom or something?"

"Well, this is the SCU. So maybe. But if he thinks they're any of those things you rattled off, why kill them?"

Good question. "Maybe they committed adultery against him in some weird way. Or maybe whoever made the purses isn't the killer. Maybe the killer didn't care that they were dark very much, but that they were lovely." She glanced at a photo of Darla Boone and Amy. Darla was a looker. Even prettier than Atta.

"I don't know, but I'll be thinking because it's strange to make that your life verse. Or maybe not. Who knows."

"Any progress with the numbers on the forehead?"

"Not enough. But I'll see if I can find anything that might link to the book of Song of Solomon. The only number I am sure of right now is six. Because that's when we're meeting for dinner, and I'm starved. I was actually about to call you. Little place called Blue Grass Café. I'll text you the address."

"See you then." She ended the call. "What do you think?"

John massaged his chin. "I think what's on their forehead is a message. What's on the pouch is a declaration. And my gut says they'll intersect."

He believed whoever gave the women the gifts also murdered them.

But why?

Chapter Six

Tuesday, October 17
8:00 p.m.

Dinner had been two hours going over notes and details of the day. Asa and Fiona had found another leather purse with the same Scripture on it and Tillie's name sewn into it about three feet from where her body had been in the cave, tucked into a small crevice. The contents included mints, her car keys, pepper spray, tissues and tampons. Water had receded inside the cave, revealing it.

They'd batted around theories about the leather pouches. Were they in some kind of support group? Had they been given them as gifts or bought them all at the same time? Could someone they cleaned houses for have given them the purses? Tomorrow they'd get in touch with Amy, see what she knew of the purse, and if nothing, begin asking around.

Asa and Fiona had talked to Tillie's sister. She knew nothing of the leather purse or the Scripture. Their parents had passed years ago, and she'd tried to get Tillie to move out of the holler. Tillie's sister had left to go to the University of Kentucky at eighteen. Tillie had still been in high school. After she graduated, she went to Lexington, but after being there for three months, she was roofied at a club and assaulted by three men, according to DNA samples. She returned to the holler and started cleaning homes because it paid in cash and she needed the money. She had a few big houses in Louisville and Lexington. Worth the drive for the money. But that was the most she ever left the holler. Tillie's sister believed she'd felt protected and safe in Night Hollow.

Turned out, she hadn't been safe here either.

Tiberius had been perusing numerology books to see if he could find a solid lead on the numbers. To the killer, the numbers might have significant meaning. After they told him about the Song of Solomon Scripture, he'd searched the book hoping to solve the number riddle; as of now, it hadn't panned out. But he planned to work later into the night.

Now, he was up in his room with Owen, who hadn't found a clear pattern between where the victims were left and where they lived. It was hard to determine work locations when no one seemed to know where exactly they worked. He still needed addresses. But this one was tricky. Small holler. Tight vicinity. A geographic pattern may not emerge at all.

After dinner, they'd arrived a little after eight at the B and B. No sign of Aunt Hossie. Or Regis. The door had been unlocked, and Violet couldn't shake the unsettling feeling in her chest when she walked inside. Like the walls were alive and watching her every move.

She'd changed into sweats and a hoodie and worked for about an hour, but her room was constricting and she needed air. She padded downstairs, the wooden joists creaking against her weight, the smell of vanilla and moth balls hanging in the stuffy air. An old Tiffany lamp glowed on a mahogany buffet against the wall, and Violet caught her reflection in the mirror hanging over it.

Her father's eyes and chin stared back.

Shrugging off the ill feeling seeping into her lungs, she crept through the dimly lit living room and out onto the covered porch. The air had a bite to it, and the leaves sounded like ocean waves. She inhaled the scent of rain about to fall, earth and a hint of a rotting animal.

"Done working for the night?"

Violet's heart lurched, but she didn't jump. Turning to John's voice, she found him sitting alone in the wicker rocking chair, a cup with steam rising in his hand. "What are you doing out here?"

"I like fall nights. October is my favorite month." His voice was quiet. He hadn't changed clothes, and he sipped his drink. "There was a silver carafe of cider on the buffet in the dining room. Figured it was fair game."

"Or poisoned. This place... I sense something in this house." She wrapped her arms around her middle and rubbed her forearms.

"Like?"

"I don't know. It makes my skin crawl and my scalp prickle. Quite frankly, I feel this way about the entire hollow. It's not the people. Granted, most of them don't want us here, but I don't dislike them per se. I can't put my finger on it."

John remained quiet, sipping his cider. She sank into the thick, soft cushions on the outdoor sofa.

"You see Aunt Hossie?" she asked.

He choked on his cider and coughed. "No," he said through a sputtering laugh. "I wonder if she's even real."

"Wanna go check the fruit cellar?"

Now, he cackled. "You think she'll be facing a wall, rotted?"

"You like the movie *Psycho*?" She was surprised and impressed he knew the movie based on her vague question.

"Who doesn't? I like all of Hitchcock's films."

Now she was completely impressed. "Really? Something no one knows about me is I'm a movie buff. Old noir films, mysteries and thrillers. I don't watch rom-coms or romances. I like British crime shows. They always have unseen twists, or at least mostly unpredictable."

Leaning her head back against the sofa, she closed her eyes and listened to nature. She liked that John didn't blab too much, as if he sensed she needed silence to think. Process. This killer wouldn't be stupid enough to murder women who cleaned his house. He'd know police would be able to find a link. He'd have to at least suspect that if the bodies were discovered, the FBI would be called in. And even if he never dreamed they'd be detected, the local police still would have found the link.

Unless he was law enforcement and had them turning a blind eye.

After a few more minutes passed, John spoke. "Violet, why did you inquire about missing persons in Memphis with me? I've always wondered who you were looking for. A sister. Friend. Aunt Hossie."

Violet appreciated John's discretion when she'd gone to him. Mom had needed a colonoscopy, and Violet had taken her. In her waking from the anesthesia, she'd talked. Mostly incoherent but more than she'd ever heard as a child. She heard names. Of other girls.

You have to get out of here, Eve. Polly and Debbie too. We have to find a way out of the baby basement. No more babies.

No more babies. Meaning whoever had taken her—this

Adam—had been having babies with not only her mom, but other girls. She'd approached John about any missing persons with these names and the timeline of when they might have gone missing. Polly and Debbie had been reported missing, and then the cases closed. Parents said they'd run away and returned. Could be true. Or they could have been hiding what had happened.

Violet had tracked addresses for the two women. Debbie lived in Memphis, and Polly's last known address had been in Tucson. Debbie had died only weeks before Violet had found her, and Polly had taken her life almost two decades ago. Violet searched for their children and family members, but she'd hit a dead end. Until she got a lead back in July with the Nursery Rhyme Killer, but that family had hidden their daughter's abduction and child well. Had the means to bury it or fake a story like she went away to a home for teenage mothers and returned with a child, and Violet once again hit a brick wall.

Did she want to talk about this with John? She didn't speak of it other than to Fiona or Asa, and she did it clinically, compartmentalizing her personal feelings. Looking at herself as a survivor of a victim. She trusted John. He was one of very few people who wasn't working an angle. No underlying motives. Nothing hidden.

"My mom was abducted by a man named Adam when she was fifteen. Those women you found, I believe were also his victims. I've been trying to track him, but I have very little to go on. Mom doesn't talk about it. What I knew was from her talking in her sleep."

"I'm sorry."

Not as sorry as she was. "I'm still trying to find a lead to him."

"That why you went into law enforcement?"

"To find him. Because if I didn't go into law enforcement..." She might have ended up a criminal. "I don't know what I'd have done."

"I know where I'd be. A jailbird. I was such a delinquent growing up." He laughed. "I mean it's not funny really, but my friends used to call me Slick. Had nothing to do with the ladies but how well I could lift something off a person."

Violet hadn't pegged John for having a single criminal bone in his body. He seemed well-rounded and honest. It was in the eyes. "I'm shocked."

"Yeah, well don't judge me. I turned it around when I was nineteen. Guess all those prayers from my mama and granny that I'd come to know Jesus personally finally paid off."

No one had ever prayed for her. "I didn't grow up with a mom who was a person of faith."

"And now?"

"Meh." Her mom's words echoed in her heart. *If there was a God, and there's not, He wouldn't want you.*

"What happens if you never find this Adam?"

"Not an option." Because she had no idea. She'd hunt him until she either found him or died trying. A raw awareness jolted her eyes open, and she sat at attention, eyeing the darkness and peering beyond the woods.

"What is it?" John asked as his body went on alert, rigid and ready to move.

Surveying the tree line, she stood and inched toward the porch railing. "I feel something. Someone?"

The sound of twigs snapping drew a shiver from her. Could be anything though.

John stood and neared the porch railing, searching the surroundings. "Probably a raccoon or opossum." He turned. "You want to go inside?"

She scanned the area, thought she saw movement in the distance but couldn't be sure. "I'm going to bed." More like escaping the unseen eyes gazing upon her. Like a force salivating to approach her. Consume her.

Devour her.

Quietly, he unlatched the old Civil War painting and slipped into the secret passage. As a child, he'd played hide-and-seek in them with friends and cousins. They'd pretended to be treasure hunters or bootleggers, who were the reason behind the passages being built into the house. Slate County had been a midway point during the Prohibition era. The house had been a boarding house, a front for other things as well.

The wood was moist and smelled of dead rodents and stale air. Cobwebs clung to his clothing and hair as he batted them away and moved between the walls until he came to the staircase.

To the upstairs.

To her room.

The other agent was pretty with her short hair, but the male agent stayed in there too late, too long. He'd lost interest watching her with him. He hadn't minded watching them kiss, but he'd grown bored when it hadn't progressed past that.

The staircase spiraled to a narrow hallway between the walls. He turned sideways to maneuver his frame without brushing his shoulders against the walls. If anyone heard him, they'd only think it was mice. He didn't need his cell phone or a flashlight. He'd done this for years. Knew every inch of the hall and where it opened into a tiny room where moonshine had been stored. Her room was on the right, the one with the dolls. All the pretty little girl dolls.

Long painted lashes and red, cherry lips.

But the agent didn't like the dolls. She'd turned them all to face away from her. It wasn't the dolls she need worry about or their eyes studying the way her slender hips swayed, the way her hair flowed freely down her back after she shrugged out of her work clothes. Dainty hands and feet. A soft body.

Unlike the dolls, her lashes weren't long and she didn't paint her face. But he liked that about her. Liked seeing her naked face, nothing hidden or enhanced.

He shivered with anticipation as he approached the wall facing her bedroom. Placing his head against the raw wood, he listened. Heard a suitcase unzip and close. She was getting ready for bed. Holding his breath, his heart hammering inside his chest, he carefully peeled back the teensy eyehole cover and peeped into the room.

His breath caught at first sight of her. She was lovely out on the porch earlier with the detective. She'd sensed him. They were connected. Had to be. He felt it in his bones. Now, in the privacy of her room, he could feast his eyes on every inch. It was clear he had power to draw her to him. Or she wouldn't have looked for him in the woods.

Wanting him.

Saying yes with her eyes.

The lamplight cast the room in a soft glow, giving her skin a sun-kissed look. He watched as she readied herself for bed. He tucked his bottom lip between his teeth and bit down then swallowed hard, his breath shallow and hot.

She untucked her hair from her thin tank and tossed back the covers then crawled into the crisp white sheets. He'd been in her bed today. Earlier. Smelling her scent, caressing her pillow.

Dreaming.

Preparing.

It was only a matter of time.

Soon. He wouldn't be able to contain himself much longer.

Chapter Seven

Wednesday, October 18
9:20 a.m.

Mother lived near the head of the holler in a cabin with a protracted porch. Rockers teetered next to handmade wooden tables. Smoke plumed from the chimney on this cold Wednesday morning. Violet hadn't slept well last night. Eerie dreams had kept her tossing and turning only to awake to the sense of being watched.

An hour ago, at breakfast, where they once again saw food but no Aunt Hossie, she'd asked Fiona if she'd felt watched or weird over the fact the lady of the house hadn't made a single appearance. She'd admitted that a few times she had felt creeped on, but she chalked it up to the house being old. She couldn't explain the no-show. Not even Detective Owsley had returned after their Monday night check-in.

Which was fine with Violet. She wasn't a fan of people she didn't trust. And she was pretty sure she didn't trust Regis

Owsley. Asa had briefed them and assigned duties. Ty and Owen were staying at the SO to work on the strange numbers and the location patterns, though Violet didn't think a pattern would emerge. Selah was working from the Memphis field office to track down clubs or support groups that might link to the *dark but lovely* Scripture reference. John was with Asa this morning canvassing homes and talking to friends and the community about Atta, Darla and Tillie, and they planned to talk to Amy Miller about the purses since her phone had gone to voice mail the rest of yesterday evening. Asa said he was hoping John's slight Appalachian drawl would play to his benefit and someone could give them names of people they cleaned homes for.

Now, Violet and Fiona were visiting Imogene Boyd, aka Mother. She might be one of the last people to have seen Atta Atwater alive when Atta picked up the casserole for the new mother, Betty Jane Dwyer.

"How have you and John been working together? Good?" Fiona asked as she stepped from the vehicle and adjusted her black blazer.

"I don't do girl talk, and you know this."

"I'm not doing girl talk. I'm asking how you are working—"

"I don't do subtext." Violet locked the car door with the fob, her shoes crunching on gravel as she approached the home. That same icy sensation pricked at her skin, and she paused, scanning the woods.

"What's the matter?" Fiona asked.

"I don't know."

"Are you trying to get out of the *John* conversation?"

"No. But knock that off." She moved toward the woods. Something or someone was out there.

"Where are you going?" Fiona followed behind.

"You don't feel that? Sense it? Being spied on?" Violet asked as she proceeded to the edge of the tree line.

Fiona stopped cold. "No." But she drew her weapon anyway.

They stood and listened. The cutting noise squirrels made echoed in the treetops. A flock of birds rustled the leaves as they took flight. As if something dangerous had disturbed them. The creek water bubbled and wended downstream, and something splashed in the water.

Hairs on Violet's neck stood at attention, and leaves crunched.

Twigs snapped.

Too loud to be a small critter.

Violet's blood turned cold, and she crept toward the creek, slowly retrieving her weapon and scanning the area. She felt like a deer. Her hunter was camouflaged but keenly aware of her presence.

Near the edge of the water, something glittered. What was that? Using her core to keep balance, she finagled herself down the steep creek bank riddled with tree limbs and roots.

"What are you doing?" Fiona asked. "No one is out here. I think you're just paranoid over this place."

"You're wrong." She caught Fiona's eye. "He's out here. He's watching us," she whispered.

"Then let's go get him. We have guns."

Violet smirked. "We'll never find him. These woods belong to him." And he knew it. It's why he kept to the shadows of the forest. A place he felt in control. Powerful.

But he had no idea that deep within her lay a predator too.

The crunches and snapping grew faster. He was running away. For now.

He'd be back.

Using the large stones as steps, she carefully trekked across the creek to the shimmering item in the water.

A tiny gold jingle bell.

It was attached to a piece of twine that had been tied around an old doll's neck, as a makeshift necklace. The dark hair was wet and looked as if it hadn't been brushed in decades. It was filthy, and the fingers had been chewed on.

She lay unclothed in the creek.

"Whoever was watching us dropped it when he ran." Violet had heard the splash. She returned and held the doll upright for further inspection.

Its eyes opened. Rusted and red.

Like bloody orbs.

After bagging the doll with hopes of finding some kind of print or trace evidence, Violet led the charge up Imogene Boyd's porch. The door opened without their knocking, and a woman in her late sixties appeared. Tall and slender with a short silver bob, the woman's blue eyes were hard and the lines around her eyes and mouth were severe, but it was obvious she'd once been a striking woman.

"Help ya?" she asked.

Violet introduced herself and Fiona and showed her creds. "We'd like to talk to Imogene Boyd. Are you her?"

"I'm Wanda, her daughter. Mother's inside rolling out dough. Come on in." She opened the door wider, and they entered to the smell of lingering bacon, lemon and hints of maple syrup. The home was warm and cozy, a real wood fire burning in the corner. Hardwood floors and antique furniture fabricating the idea that they'd been passed down through the generations and might be as old as the cabin.

They followed Wanda into the kitchen. A woman about the same height and build with long gray hair in a braid down her back, flour from fingers to elbow, rolled out dough on the kitchen table. Her piercing blue eyes met Violet's, and her smile was kinder, softer than her daughter's. But she appeared equally weathered, as if life hadn't always been easy. But in these parts, Violet imagined life wasn't a cakewalk for any of them.

"Agents with the FBI, Mother."

"I'd welcome ya properly if I didn't have all this flour on me. Makin' apple pies. Y'all like apple pie?" she asked, continuing to roll dough until it was smooth and thin. Then she placed it in deep dishes and began crimping the edges.

"I like any kind of pie," Fiona said. "We're obviously here about Atta Atwater. We hear she came by the night she might have died. To pick up a casserole."

"She did. It was a chicken-and-broccoli casserole. Can I get y'all a cup of coffee or a biscuit and some bacon?"

"I'd take a cup of coffee," Fiona said. "Black is great."

Fiona always accepted drinks when offered. Not because it was polite, but because most people who offered didn't really mean it, and Fiona got a kick over putting people out. And she called Violet sadistic. But the truth was put-out people generally lied in questioning, and those who had no problem serving a beverage had no issues with interviews. Not 100 percent of the time, but often enough.

Wanda headed to the Mr. Coffee coffee pot and poured a white mug full of rich black brew and handed it to Fiona. "You sure you don't want one, hon?" she asked Violet.

"I'm sure." She noticed Wanda gawking at her. Same look she'd gotten from Sheriff Modine and Regis Owsley.

Wanda blinked and cleared her throat then busied herself with wiping down a counter.

"It's neighborly and expected by the Good Lord to take

care of those in need, and new mamas need some TLC. You have children?" she asked Fiona.

"Uh. No."

"Wanda here is my daughter. My only one. I had three boys. Lost two in childbirth. One in Vietnam. But I have lots of surrogate daughters. And sons. That's why everyone up here calls me Mother. Haven't heard my given name in probably forty years or more." She laughed through a cough.

"Did you know Atta well?" Fiona asked.

"Atta was a good girl. I can't imagine anyone layin' a finger on her," she said with strong conviction, and her gnarled fingers gripped the rolling pin tighter.

"No one she might have been involved with or who frightened her? Do you have any idea where she might have gotten a leather purse with a Scripture verse?"

Wanda rubbed her mother's shoulder. "Several leather shops in town. Could be any one." She spoke to Mother. "You need to rest, Mother. You been on your feet a spell."

"Ah, I'll rest when I'm dead." Mother waved her off. She appeared perky enough. "Atta was a precious soul. Didn't have a man in her life."

"Mother!" a little girl's voice shrieked, and footsteps stomping on the wood floor sounded before a dark-haired girl with curls approached, a black lab running after her. "Festus ate my cheese curls!"

Her hands were coated in orange paste, and the dog sat and stared at Mother with innocent eyes.

"And you'd like more cheese curls, Lula?"

"Yes, ma'am."

Mother dusted her hands on her apron and approached the little girl. "Are you sure you didn't eat the cheese curls and simply want more? Because tellin' the truth to Mother is important. The truth gets you cheese curls. Lies get you a switch from the elm tree."

Well then, every single person in this holler should receive their licks. Not a soul was telling the whole truth if even a sliver. Maybe they needed Mother to take an elm tree switch to 'em.

"I ate the cheese curls, but Festus did take my last one."

Mother kissed her forehead, and a piece of Violet's heart ached. She couldn't remember a single time her mom or grandmother had ever kissed her. She'd forgotten how painful that was until this moment, watching Mother with this child. A pretty little child too, with a heart-shaped face, long lashes.

"You can have a few more, and then that's it." Mother pointed to the cabinet. "Get her a little bowl of 'em, will you, Wanda?"

Wanda went to the cabinet and did as she was instructed while the little girl, Lula, let the dog lick away the cheese powder gummed to her fingers. Gross.

Wanda handed the bowl to Lula, who thanked her. Then the child peered up at Fiona then Violet. "I got's a little dip on my chin too." She pointed to the cleft in her chin, licked her cheese curl then stuck it right into the cleft.

Fiona laughed.

Violet wasn't about to offer to do it too. "Nice."

Lula giggled then snatched it and ate it, leaving a streak of cheese powder on her chin.

"Go on and go play, child. Us women have talkin' to do, hear?"

"Yes ma'am." She scampered off, and the lab followed.

"You the town babysitter?" Violet asked.

Mother grinned, her lower teeth crooked and a bit colored from age and years of coffee. "Lula's my great-great-granddaughter, but my door is open to anyone in need. At any time. Child or not."

What would it be like to always have an open door she could enter when she was troubled or needed help? Violet didn't even have a key to the apartment she'd lived in her whole growing-up years. Not only was it far from open, it was locked shut.

"We got word," Fiona said, "Tillie LeBeau and Darla Boone were victims one and two. Did you know them as well?" Fiona asked and set her empty coffee cup on the wooden countertop.

Mother clutched her chest and her lip quivered. "I didn't know it had been confirmed. Of course I knew them." Looking up with watery eyes, she shook her head. "Someone is gonna pay for this. I promise you that."

"We're trying to make that happen, Ms. Boyd," Fiona said.

"Oh child, call me Mother. Anything else sounds foreign."

"Is there anything you can tell us about the victims?" Fiona asked. "Anyone who gave them trouble? Did they talk about anyone creeping them out? Boyfriend issues? Anything, even if it seems inconsequential."

Mother patted her eyes with the bottom of her kitchen apron. "I can't think of anything. The girls were so sweet and good. Gave money to the Lord and were charitable. They didn't have many worries or troubles. We take care of our own up here. If there's a need, we fill it. A sore heart, we make sure to mend it."

Violet had enough of everyone's evasive answers and self-promoting justice. "Yeah, well, I doubt you're going to find a way to mend a dead body, Mother."

Wanda stepped up and scowled. "You can see yourself out."

Violet had crossed a line. Knew it. And to an old lady do-gooder.

Mother untied her apron, laid it on the butcher block and

stepped into Violet's personal space, but Violet didn't budge. She placed cool hands on either side of Violet's cheeks and searched her eyes as if searching her soul. "You've known pain, child. Bone-crushin', agonizin' pain. I'm sorry for your affliction. I understand your frustration—your job." She leaned back as if trying to make Violet's profile come into better view. She traced the side of her face with a rounded nail and touched the cleft in her chin. "You might find a killer up here in the holler, but you won't find any peace for that pain. I see it. It's in that pretty, pretty face."

Violet swallowed hard, frozen at how deep into her soul Mother had seen. Like she knew her history, from conception to now. Seen the desire to be loved while always coming up short. She had never been smart enough, good enough, kind enough, behaved enough...nothing. Even when she went into law enforcement, it wasn't enough for Reeva. For Grandmother.

Why hadn't they given her away? Let her be adopted by parents who didn't know about her conception, wouldn't hold it against her as if it were her sin to carry. She could have had a happy life. A loving family.

But it wouldn't have changed her DNA. That couldn't be altered or erased.

"If..." she cleared her throat from emotion "...if you think of anything else, call us."

She backed away, strode out the front door, Fiona behind her. Lula sat under a tree with the dog, an empty bowl of cheese curls in the grass, a couple of dolls and a little purse in her hand. Violet opened the passenger door and paused. "Hold up," she murmured to Fiona then stalked across the lawn. "Hey, Lula, can I see your pretty purse?"

"I gots monies in it."

"You do? Well, I won't take any of your monies."

Lula held it out, and Violet's heart skipped a beat as she took the brown suede purse. Turning it over in her hand, she inspected the other side. No name on this one, though.

"Where'd you get this?"

"My house."

Like the other three, it read *I am dark but lovely.*

Wednesday, October 18
2:30 p.m.

"Lay it on me straight, John," Asa said as John pulled into the parking lot of a Best Western about sixteen miles southeast of Whitesburg.

"We should have stayed here. I'm not digging that old boarding house turned B and B."

"I know but it keeps us close to the holler, and I keep thinking if they want us gone so bad, staying right in town will motivate them to help," Asa said. "Get us gone faster."

"Except it won't. They think if they clam up, we'll have nothing and leave."

"They haven't met me."

Asa Kodiak had been named the Bear by his colleagues, and it had nothing to do with his last name. Everything to do with his ferociousness if need be—whether protecting his cubs on his team or in the quest for justice. John admired him. "They aren't afraid of bears, Kodiak. Not up here."

"We'll see. Now, let's go talk to these employees and hope for a lead."

Tillie's sister had told them that Tillie had worked with Atta at a small hotel for a short time after she returned to the holler. Then they both quit. Figured they'd make more money cleaning houses, and for cash.

But someone might remember them. Have some information. Their hunt back in town had been a complete bust. No one would cough up a word about them other than they were good girls who worked hard and gave to charity and attended church on Sundays. Didn't know anyone who'd want to hurt them, but best they let the holler folk handle it.

"You know," John said as he strode to the front door, "if the holler did know who the killer is, he'd be dead. Their conversation wouldn't be to let them take care of it but to move on, things had been dealt with and there would be nothing for us to do but go on 'bout our business."

Asa grinned. "I hear the Hazard in you coming out."

Like he often heard the Louisiana bayou dialect pop out of Asa. Not really Cajun, but it was a tone of its own, especially when he was frustrated. "I'm right though. They don't have him. I don't know if they know who's doing it."

"Then it's a race to catch him first."

"That it is. If they find him...we never will. That I can promise you." They entered the lobby, and two customer service reps looked up with sunshine in their eyes.

Asa showed his creds. "I'm looking for anyone who might know Tillie LeBeau or Atta Atwater. They worked here about four years ago. Maid service." He showed them photos on his phone.

"I remember Atta," the lighter blonde said. "She was sweet. She was friends with Landra Robbins. Worked in housekeeping together."

"Landra here today?"

The young woman nodded. "I can get her for you." She picked up the phone, and about ten minutes later, a woman in her late twenties with jet black hair twisted in a bun and a housekeeping uniform stepped off the elevator with wary dark eyes.

Asa once again showed his creds and asked if they could sit and talk a moment, then they made their way to the lobby area table. "Sheila said this was about Atta. I saw the news. Didn't really know Tillie."

"We're here about that," Asa said.

"I thought for sure she'd end up dead, you know? But not by some serial killer. In the holler? How does that even happen?" Landra pursed her lips and shook her head. "I told her over and over she could get out. Do it on her own. I do. Work two jobs and have two kids because I refused to let a man put hands on me. Then she gets out and...this. Talk about being shortchanged."

"Who put hands on her, Landra?" John asked. Why did Landra expect Atta to be killed?

"Her old man."

John exchanged a glance with Asa. This was new. Nothing popped in the background check that she was married or divorced. "A name?"

"Bobby Lloyd. Atta said they were high-school sweethearts and eloped when she was seventeen. But he liked the sauce. She'd come in all bruised up. When she missed three days of work, I drove out to Night Holler. Found her place. She was seriously jacked up by him. Couldn't get out of bed. She promised she'd leave him. But then she didn't come back to work. That was last I heard. I tried to keep in touch but...you know how that goes."

Not really.

John wasn't sure her ex-husband was the Blind Eye Killer. Seemed like an impulsive, mean drunk. This killer was clever. He knew the holler, had taken the women's eyes with some measure of skill and sewn their lids closed, was then able to transport them to the cave, which he was familiar with. Violet was right—he knew he had time to indulge in their fear before beating them within an inch of their lives then strangling them. The violence fit though.

"Can you tell us about Atta? About Bobby?"

Landra rubbed the hem of her apron between her index and thumb. "Atta was sweet and smart. I always told her she needed to get out of the holler and go to college. She laughed in my face."

"Didn't think that was an option? If she had wanted out, how would Bobby have felt about that?"

Landra low whistled. "I doubt Bobby would have liked that much. She buttered his bread. He drank more than he worked."

"What about her brother? The pastor." John wanted to know why big brother hadn't intervened—or if he had.

"Atta wasn't close with him. She went to church and all but...well, they didn't see eye to eye on some things."

"Do you know if he knew about Bobby's beating on her?"

"I don't know. Probably. She couldn't hide the marks, and everyone knows everything up there. Trust me. It's not like the police didn't know," she spat. "But all his cousin did was throw him in the drunk tank, dry him out. Atta knew he'd never be charged, and she'd never get to leave." She checked her watch. "I really should be gettin' on back to work."

"Who's Bobby Lloyd's cousin?" John asked.

"I knew you'd ask that. I can't remember. I think he's a detective for Slate County."

Asa stood and John followed. Asa handed her his business card. "If you think of anything else, let me know."

She tucked it in her apron pocket. "Will do. Tell her brother I'm real sorry to hear about her."

"I will."

When they finally got the chance to talk to him.

"I'd like to find this Bobby character," John said as they exited the hotel, the fall wind cutting through his button-down shirt and sports coat. "I'd also like to find this detective."

"Won't be too difficult. There's only two of them. Regis Owsley and Alton Berry. I'm going to bank on the good Regis Owsley, who never seemed to mention he might be related to the victim."

"Yeah, I'm not liking that." John plucked a pack of spearmint gum from his coat pocket and held it out for Asa. He snagged a stick, then John unwrapped a piece before pocketing the pack. "I wonder if she was seventeen when she married, if their marriage was even legal?"

"I wondered the same thing." Asa retrieved his cell phone and hit a button. "Selah, check and see if you can find a marriage license for Atta Atwater and Bobby—no, not McGee. You've got to stop spending time with Tiberius. He's a terrible influence on you." He paused then chuckled. "It's Lloyd. Bobby Lloyd. Probably Robert. Yeah, I'll wait."

John waited quietly while Asa hung on the line. "Really? Huh. Interesting. Okay, thanks." He laughed. "Uh, no. But I'll let Fiona know you think it's a good idea." He ended the call and pocketed the phone, humor still playing around the edges of his lips. "Selah thinks Fiona and I should elope out here. In the backwoods of Kentucky."

"Leaves and mountains are pretty," John offered. "Where to?"

"The SO."

John backed out of the parking lot and headed toward Crow's Creek.

"And Fiona would no more get married while on a crime scene—and definitely not in the woods—than I'd eat glass for dinner. We uh...we never got a real full honeymoon. Long story. She's looking forward to a whole two weeks of us and the sun and sand. Murders can cease or wait, and the woods could rot for all she cares."

Murders did neither. "When?"

"I think I'm going to propose on the Fourth of July this year. Rent a boat and pay for fireworks. The good kind. It's our thing."

"You gonna use the same ring you did the first go-round?" What did one do when proposing to their ex-wife?

Asa laughed. "I do have it. She threw that bad boy literally into my kisser when I asked for the divorce. Split my lip. She's got good aim." He grinned but John glanced over and caught the regret, the remorse from past pain. John could relate on some level. "But no. I'm gonna have the stone added to a new one. 'Cause we did have a lot of good times the first go-round."

John arched an eyebrow. "You been thinking about it, huh?"

"Since we got back together this past July. We got married on a beach with friends and family the first time, and I have a feeling this time she'll want to be married in our church or a chapel somewhere by our pastor. We didn't put much stock in marriage as a covenant before God last time."

"Callie and I married in a church. Big, with stained-glass windows and a pipe organ. It was pretty."

"And your marriage?"

That wasn't as pretty.

"I'm sorry. I get investigative too easy."

John slowed at a sharp curve rounding the mountain. "Nah, no worries. It was good for a while, but no marriage is perfect."

"No. No, it's not."

"What did your analyst say about Bobby Lloyd and the marriage that was interesting?" Discussing his marriage and the failures weren't on the top of John's list today. He wished for a do-over of the night Callie left. Even if things had ended between them, at least he wouldn't carry the regret of words he'd spoken, lashing out and telling her she wasn't a good mom, didn't care about them, didn't love them. He hadn't meant those words even though he'd felt them to be true at the time.

"If I'm such a terrible mom and wife, then why do you care if I go undercover or not?" she'd thrown out with venom.

"I don't! I don't care if you go. Go, and if something bad happens while you're gone, then you'll have to live with it. And if something bad happens to you, then I guess, oh well! That's what you get!" he'd responded with equal venom. Hated himself for lashing out in anger and hurt, in disappointment.

Something bad had happened. It wasn't oh well. And she hadn't deserved it.

Seemed the people you hurt most were the ones you loved most.

"She did have a marriage license, and the marriage was legal. But she was seventeen. Bobby eighteen. Which meant a legal guardian or parent had to sign for her. Since her mom passed when she was little and they had no idea where the father was, the preacher was her guardian. He signed it. Either he didn't know Bobby was abusive or didn't care. And I don't know about you, but last I checked preachers were supposed to love their neighbor, and she was more than a neighbor. She was his sister. You protect..." Asa's voice choked up. "You protect your family," he said through a thin voice. "At least, you certainly try."

John was familiar with Asa's past, but he didn't feel words needed to be spoken at the moment and remained silent as they approached the sheriff's office. Clouds had rolled in, coloring the sky chalky gray. Heavy with rain, the wind picked up and rocked his car. He parked at the front of the SO and noticed the SCU vehicle in the same parking row.

Violet was inside.

His stomach corkscrewed, and he frowned at the physical

reaction she drew from him. He followed Asa into the sheriff's office, the smell of old coffee and cologne permeating the small station. The woman at the front desk eyed them warily. He dipped his chin and she returned it, but no one spoke. They made their way into the conference room they were using as a command center. Violet sat at the head of the table, the tip of a pen between her lips and her hair falling like a curtain around her face, touching the table. Fiona sat beside her with case files open before her, and Owen Barkley was holding a box of push pins and scowling at the map on the wall.

Tiberius Granger sat at the opposite end of the table, feet up and hands cocked behind his neck. Eyes closed.

Violet raised her head as they entered the room. "You catch him?"

Asa arched an eyebrow. "Are you kidding?"

It was hard to tell, John had to admit, but there was the most miniscule amount of mischief in Violet's blue-green eyes, which were more green than blue today with the soft green sweater under her gray blazer.

Asa threw a glance over his shoulder into the empty hallway then closed the glass door. "Atta Atwater was married at seventeen to a man named Bobby—"

"McGee," Tiberius offered as smugness pulled at the corner of his lip.

"No. Stay away from Selah by the way. She's adopting your horrible habit of bringing songs into everything."

"Janis Joplin could wail. You should thank me for introducing Selah to her."

Owen seemed to perk up at that statement and gave Tiberius a dark eye. Tiberius shrugged.

Some kind of interplay with the computer analyst it seemed. But nothing causing tension. This team had an intriguing dynamic. He'd been on task forces and within different law enforcement ranks, but this group was unique in many ways. From personalities to the way they worked with one another, spoke with each other. Like family. John hoped one of them never lost their life in the line of duty. It'd cause a chasm of grief they might not ever recover from. He shrugged the thought away and focused on Violet, who caught his eye but refrained from acknowledging him or that he was staring at her.

Asa finished briefing them on Landra's statement.

"You think Regis Owsley is the cousin?" Fiona asked and pushed away the case files.

"I do."

"I'd like a crack at him," Violet said and stood.

"Have at it," Asa said.

"John? You want in on this?" she asked.

Asa and Fiona exchanged a glance, and Tiberius scowled. "How come you never ask me to come along on interviews?"

"You're annoying, and you make me want to shoot you. Which I know you know I'm not afraid to do."

"Valid points." Tiberius thumbed toward John. "Don't annoy her, John. Chick's a crack shot."

"Don't call women chicks, Ty," Asa said.

"Yeah, he doesn't need any more paperwork to file." Fiona snickered. "He's grouchy enough."

"I'm not grouchy."

"You're a little cranky," Owen offered.

Violet huffed. "I'm outta here. You're all wasting time." She motioned for John to come with her, and he wasted *zero* time. Violet wasn't one to ride a clock or piddle.

"How do they solve cases when they horse around so much?" John asked in the hall.

"They're good at their jobs. And between us, the comic morale motivates their performance. I can only deal with it for a minute though, you know? I'm not a real kidder. We didn't joke around in my family." She shrugged. "When I joke, most of the time no one knows I've made a wisecrack."

"You're a hard read."

"Sometimes I do that on purpose." She breezed through the small bullpen, but Detective Owsley wasn't in the room.

"Why?" he asked as they searched for the detective.

"I don't know." She approached a deputy. "You seen Detective Owsley?"

"He left about thirty minutes ago. Late lunch."

"Where did he go?"

The deputy scowled. "Meat and Three Veg."

Violet blew out the front doors. "Let's take your car."

"Okaaay." The woman was a laser-focused whirlwind. He liked it. Liked her. Wanted to ferret out who she was beneath the exterior. Maybe even see who she might be on the exterior. Touch her skin. Sample her lips.

John's skin heated and flushed his neck.

"What's the matter with you?" Violet asked.

"Nothing." Nothing that he was going to confess. He needed to keep his head together.

"You're lying, but I'm going to let it pass. I just want you to know, I know you're lying." She buckled up, and John inwardly sighed. He wished she was as easy to read as he was to her.

Chapter Eight

Wednesday, October 18
3:40 p.m.

Violet led the charge, striding into the Meat and Three Veg with John in tow. Detective Regis Owsley sat at a corner booth with a cup of coffee in one hand and his phone in the other. He glanced up and registered that Violet had entered and was striding his way.

His nostrils twitched, and he laid his phone on the table. "What brings this visit?" He threw a look at John but didn't acknowledge him.

"I was searching for you, Regis. Can I call you that?" He'd like her using his first name. She'd recognized his attraction early on. At the SO, then when he lingered in her room on their first night. She'd use it to her advantage and not feel guilty in the least.

"And what can I call you?" he asked with a hint of intrigue and flirtation in his voice, but his dark eyes were cool.

"Agent." Power play. Was he secretly into being submissive to a female? It would tell her a lot about his personality, feed into his profile. She held his eye contact, watched his pupils dilate.

He liked it. Assumed it was flirtatious banter, but the wariness behind his eyes revealed he wasn't by any means stupid. He might recognize her motives and was, in his mind, using her. She'd tuck that clever, calculating mind in her pocket.

"I'm going to make a phone call," John said and excused himself. But Violet kept her focus on Regis. He'd appreciate that, and she heard in John's voice a tone that reflected his awareness of her approach and that he was giving her ample time to do what needed to be done. She'd pocket that too and ignore the way it made her feel.

A little fluttery. A little soft.

She was neither of those things. She was not vulnerable. She was not unguarded. She was not trusting.

All of those feelings brought deep pain and a wave of grief in the end. She'd learned ages ago how to carefully and meticulously craft impenetrable walls. A drawbridge hadn't been constructed or even drawn into the blueprints. Her heart wasn't a fairytale castle with the possibilities of happily-ever-after.

"Are you going to offer me a seat or sit there staring up at me?"

"I like the view." Amusement crinkled the lines around his eyes. Regis Owsley was attractive, smart and a little too on.

She ignored him, impassively. Not giving a schoolgirl titter or happy giggle. Keep him guessing. Working for it. See if he would continue or get bored. Did he like challenges? Did they bring out aggressive behavior? Their victims' killer was aggressive, but not at first. They likely trusted him. Once they were exactly where he wanted them, he'd flipped the switch. Would Regis show her that behavior?

Sitting across from him, she leaned in, tented her hands. "I heard a rumor," she said in a low, sultry tone.

He leaned in too, his hands folded and nearly touching hers. "What kind of rumor?"

"The kind involving you."

His eyes dilated again. "Sounds scandalous."

"Enough it put me on the hunt for you." And she might very well be hunting him. He could be the Blind Eye Killer. She wasn't persuaded either way.

"You like to hunt?"

"The hunt's part of the thrill," she murmured, making her voice like butter, "knowing prey is out there but not completely sure where. Nerves are heightened, pulse picks up from steady to staccato as you close in." Had he been hunting her earlier by the creek? "Like a lion with a gazelle on the Serengeti. It's a rush."

All true. That was what it felt like catching killers who believed they were invincible. Who toyed with them, miscalculating their—her—prowess. It was a powerful high. Nothing like it.

And it terrified her all the same. Because what if she wasn't a federal agent? Would that desire to hunt manifest in other ways?

She shook out of her own chilling thoughts, though she couldn't shake out of her skin, her DNA. If there were a way, she'd pay every dime to do it.

"You're a scary woman, Agent."

"You don't know the half of it." She sat back. "Enough with games. I heard you used to be related to Atta Atwater. Bobby Lloyd is your cousin."

He leaned back too, folded his arms over his chest. "Where'd you hear that?"

"Doesn't matter."

"Bobby's my daddy's sister's boy. He and Atta had a thing in high school. Wanted to get married, and I told him they were too young. Too dumb. And he already drank too much. But Wendell signed away." He frowned. Was he irritated that Atta's brother, the preacher, had given permission or something else? "We had some words over it. But he'd already done did it so…"

"Why would he do that? Was she pregnant?"

"No. He quoted Paul in First Corinthians. 'But if they cannot contain, let them marry: for it is better to marry than to burn.'" He gave them a knowing look. "They'd been burnin'."

"Arson?"

"No. Burnin' with passion. Some translations state it a little clearer than the good old KJV."

Violet would ask Ty about the Scripture. Also, Regis appeared knowledgeable of the Bible. "You felt they should continue in, what I'm assuming you mean, sin?"

"Far be it from me to throw a stone, *Agent*."

"A stone?"

"Judge." John strolled up to the table. "He's saying he can't judge what Atta and Bobby were doing because he has his own sins."

"Amen." Regis leaned back.

What were those sins? Violet would like to know.

"Bobby's drinking got worse. I threw him behind bars to dry him out a few times. And then…he left. And she quit the hotel and started cleanin' houses."

"Left Atta?"

"Atta. The holler. Ain't heard from him in about four years now."

"You don't find that odd?" John asked. "Kin keeps in touch. I know."

"He was no good for her. I didn't try to find him. Better off, she was if you ask me. The kid was a menace from the start."

He pushed his cold coffee away, and a server approached and handed him a white plastic to-go bag with foam boxes inside.

"You get the apple pie?" he asked.

"Two pieces." She winked and disappeared.

The smell of baked meats, garlic and onion, and cinnamon permeated the space between them.

"Let's say for fun our killer is hunting women who've been taken advantage of, hurt and abused. They go to the police for protection, and they end up dead. Let's say that person is you, Regis." Violet studied his facial features closely, waiting for a reaction.

He hooted and withdrew his wallet then threw a twenty on the table.

"Where were you last weekend when Atta died?" she asked.

"I'll play your game because it's the most ridiculous thing I've heard. I was sick last weekend. Stomach bug. Ask Mother. She brought me homemade chicken noodle soup and saltines. Called in all weekend. Check with the SO." Regis's jaw ticked, and he inhaled a deep staccato breath then tied a knot with the plastic bag handles.

"I'll verify this."

He leaned over John and into Violet's face. "I thought you'd be a better hunter," he whispered.

"I'm just getting started."

Wednesday, October 18
7:45 p.m.

He opened the back of the built-in chifforobe that connected her bedroom with the secret passageway, then inhaled her scent—the agent's own personal fragrance wafting inside.

She'd hung up her blazers, dress shirts and pants. Taking a moment, he let the silk of her shirt stroke his cheeks.

She wasn't frilly or fragile.

She'd come down that creek bank earlier with ease and stealth. Coming for him. He hadn't meant to drop the doll. He hadn't finished it, but she'd startled him from his trek in the woods, from his hidey-hole where he kept his treasures— the one he'd wanted to use for the doll that she had now.

He hadn't expected her to come to the woods' edge.

The agent was powerful and strong. She knew what she wanted.

She wanted him. Had felt his presence. Been drawn to him.

And he wanted to take her. He toyed with a button on her blouse and shuddered, then quietly opened the tight space and entered her bedroom. Her scent wasn't as strong in here. Her suitcase was zipped up and neatly placed by the wall under the window. Shuffling to the door, he cracked it and listened. Before entering the house, he'd made sure the feds were gone and he'd have complete access without being seen.

He was getting better at entering and going from homes without being noticed. The thrill of it flushed his skin and turned him warm like fresh apple pie. Not only was it easier to do each time, but the need to do it came faster, hotter, building like a dam of water that needed release.

Even now, he nearly salivated. Closing the door, he then hurried to her suitcase, laid it on the bed she'd made this morning and unzipped it. He let a long, soft breath escape and carefully explored each folded piece of laundry until he found what he wanted. He ran it between his fingers then stuffed it in his pocket before zipping up the suitcase and replacing it exactly where it had been.

He crossed to the chifforobe then turned back at the chair holding some of the old porcelain dolls and couldn't help himself. He wanted her to know he'd been here. Wanted her to know he had access to her and could take her whenever he chose.

He was in control. He had the power. Her gun and her badge meant nothing to him.

Meant nothing to the holler. Whatever power she thought she had, he wanted to take it.

Consume it on the altar of his will and swallow her whole.

Chapter Nine

Thursday, October 19
12:18 a.m.

Ruby took the porch steps two at a time and barged into the trailer without knocking. Nadine had called thirty minutes ago hysterical and incoherent, begging her to come. She'd barely had time to dress before she'd hopped in the car and driven up toward the head of the holler to Nadine's.

She'd called a friend to come and keep watch over Lula long enough for her to get to Nadine. All she'd understood over the phone was Nadine had been attacked. She had no idea by who.

Crying sounded from the back bedroom. The pungent odor of pot lingered, and a roach still weakly burned in the ashtray. "Nadine?" Ruby called, a sudden chill sweeping over her skin, and she zipped up her hoodie to her neck then tip-toed through the kitchen, down a short narrow hall. The door was cracked open.

Without knocking, she entered. Nadine was curled in a ball on her bed, mascara streaming down her face, hair in disarray and blood trickling from her mouth, nose and forehead. She wore an oversize sweatshirt and leggings. A man's flannel shirt was crumpled on the floor at the end of the bed.

"Nadine," she murmured and perched beside her, running her hand through Nadine's messy hair. "What happened?"

"I heard the back door open, and I thought it was Jake comin' back. We'd partied earlier."

Ruby smelled the party. "It wasn't Jake?"

"I don't know who it was." Nadine stared at the mirrored sliding closet door. "I was dozing off when it happened. Then he was here on top of me before I could do anything, and I was kinda out of it, you know?"

"You fought him?"

She scrunched into a tighter ball. "He punched me a few times, and I couldn't overpower him…but then a car pulled into the drive, and he froze, then he left." She sobbed into her hands. "Then I called you."

"He didn't have a chance to…"

"No," she squeaked. "I got up and locked the doors and looked out the window, but there wasn't a car in the drive, Rube. But I know I saw a light shine through my window, like headlights or something. He did too, because it drove him out into the night. But what if that light hadn't come right then? Then what?"

Then the story would have a more sinister outcome. Because Nadine might have been taken by the Blind Eye Killer.

And that was why Ruby believed that whoever was murdering holler girls wasn't someone who lived in the holler. Or he'd be dead already.

"I called him. On my way over."

"Why?"

"Because we need protection." She brushed hair from Nadine's face. "Your eye's swelling. I'm going to find an ice pack or something." She headed for the kitchen as the roar of a powerful engine revved and bright lights shone inside the trailer.

He was here. She'd know that engine anywhere.

The lights cut off, and then the door opened and his muscular frame entered the trailer. Black wavy hair, hanging at all one length under his chin. Inky scruff across his squared jaw added menace to his already threatening appearance. His dark eyes met hers, and his clenched jaw relaxed. "How bad?"

Ruby opened the freezer and removed an ice pack. "Beat up some, but I guess a car or something drove up and the headlights scared him away before he could do worse, though Nadine insists there was no car. Maybe it pulled away. She's still semi-high, so…"

He wore a military-green jacket over a flannel shirt and faded jeans, and his heavy hiking boots clunked against the laminate flooring as he ate up the ground and approached her. Her heart skipped a beat, and she licked her lips. He touched her cheek with more gentleness than his rough, weathered hands would seem capable of doing. "And you?" he asked gruffly. "Are you okay? Where's Lula?"

Lula. Of course he'd asked about her.

"I'm fine. Lula's tended." No point telling him with who. He'd be angry, and it wasn't worth an argument. "I just…y'all have to catch this guy. It's not safe for any of us now."

He cradled her face, and she tried not to let it affect her. Not let it seep into her bones. She'd loved him once. Truth be told, she loved him now. But he was a dangerous man. And he'd never been willing to put her before his precious business and power.

Ruby had never meant to fall in love with him. Maybe he

never loved her. Maybe everything out of his mouth had been worthless, vain words. Empty promises.

Either way, things were complicated between them.

The front door opened, and his newly favorite minion entered, bigger, longer hair tied in a sloppy bun at the back of his head and a creepy scar running through his eyebrow. His eyes met hers. He wore flannel over a Henley, jeans and work boots—no jacket as if the cold didn't affect him. "Ruby."

She hated the way he said her name. As if he were undressing her right in front of his pal, and he didn't have the decency to care.

"Greg," she said and shrugged off his presence. Something about him didn't sit right.

"I'll find this guy," Whiskey said. "And I'll end him. Nobody is going to touch my girls."

"She have a stash here?" Greg asked and spotted the roach burning. He picked it up. "Might as well partake." He inhaled deeply, held his breath then slowly exhaled.

"You would be more concerned with the product. Nadine could have been killed. And all you see is money being tossed away." Her stomach turned. Her savings under her mattress were growing. She needed a little more time. But time was running out, and the walls of the holler were closing in on her.

"Neither of you go anywhere," Whiskey said.

As Whiskey turned for the bedroom, she called, "Wait." She held out the ice pack. "She needs this. And a doctor."

He took the ice pack and left her alone with Greg. He sat on the couch toking, his feet on Nadine's coffee table, dirt falling off the treads of his boots onto the glass.

She perched on the rocking chair near the windows facing the front yard and rubbed her hands on her thighs.

"You don't need to be afraid, Ruby. We got ya."

"Really? Who had Tillie, Darla or Atta? Who had Nadine?"

"We're looking into it. We got leads."

"Leads. What, are you pretending to be a cop now? Watch too many crime shows? Maybe we need to cooperate with the federal agents in town."

Whiskey entered the room, his jaw clenched. "You're right. She needs a doc. Her ribs are broken, and she can't breathe. I don't want her at the medical emergency facility. Not with the feds here. They'll sniff that out. Ask questions, and I want this sucker for myself."

"They could catch him. Then be gone. The longer you spin them in circles, the longer they'll stay. They're not getting irritated, they're getting determined."

Whiskey cocked his head. "Where you hear this? No. Let me guess. Your *detective* friend."

"Yes. Regis."

Whiskey's nostrils flared. "You talk about the feds as pillow talk late at night? When I said keep him close, I didn't necessarily mean your bed, Ruby."

She swallowed hard. "I don't think when we talk is your business."

Whiskey stepped into her personal space. "I think everything concerning you has become my business, don't you?" His voice was quiet. But it made its mark. Reminding her that she didn't belong to herself. Never had.

Never would.

She wasn't terrified of Whiskey. He'd never lay a hand to a single hair on her head. That didn't mean he wasn't to be feared. Love and fear. How could one do both? She didn't know. But she did.

"I don't like any of those feds." Greg sneered. "Especially that detective with 'em. He's gonna be a problem. I can feel it."

Whiskey took out his phone and scrolled through it. "Well, you know how we solve problems."

"Yes, I do."

"I do too," Ruby said as her heart hammered against her ribs. "You can't touch them. The rest will descend like locusts, and then you'll never get this killer and he'll keep killing. Any one of us are fair game. Leave them alone, but give them something. Anything."

Whiskey put his phone to his ear. "Hey, it's me. We need a favor. Bring your medical kit. Nadine. Send Chris then if you can't come." He ended the call.

"Can't leave work. He's gonna call Chris. Now we wait."

In fifteen minutes, another car pulled into the drive, and Whiskey opened the door to Jimmy Russell, not Chris. He wore his EMS windbreaker and held a black medical bag. His short blond hair was windblown, and his pale blue eyes met Ruby with sympathy. "Are you hurt, Ruby?"

She shook her head. "I wasn't here. Why are you here?"

"Chris called me. He's sick. Flu. Where is she?" he asked, his tone soft.

"Back bedroom," Whiskey said while Greg looked on with glazed eyes. "And I can be sure you'll be discreet about being here."

"I won't say anything." He proceeded to Nadine.

"I don't trust him." Greg stood, arms folded over his chest.

"That's the dope talking." Ruby huffed and left them in the living room. Inside Nadine's room, Jimmy examined the wounds, then began cleaning them as he quietly asked about her pain levels and where it hurt the most.

"Do you want me to help you, Nadine?" he asked. "I can get you out of this."

Ruby froze and glanced toward the door. If Whiskey heard those words, he'd kill Jimmy. Snap his neck, bury him so deep a dog couldn't dig up his bones.

"I'm fine. I've already been through this before with Chris."

He wiped her tear-stained cheeks with a soft rag, the mascara disappearing onto the cloth. "Okay, but the offer stands." He ripped open an antiseptic wipe. "This is going to sting." He carefully applied it to the cut on her forehead. Nadine winced. "Sorry," he murmured. "Any other injuries? Any you didn't tell him about?"

"No."

"Okay. Let's look at those ribs." He helped Nadine sit up, and she winced again and cried out. "Easy, easy." He pressed and prodded against her rib cage. Her skin was already turning black and purple. "Can you take a deep breath without it hurting?"

She shook her head.

"Chest pain?"

She nodded.

"I think they're bruised pretty badly. I can't prescribe you pain meds, so take plenty of ibuprofen and shallow breaths. Restrict your activity. No running."

"Tell that to Whiskey," Nadine said through gritted teeth.

"I will. And I'm not one to condone drug use, but I smell it. If you need it for pain, smoke it. If it gets worse, you will have to see a doctor. You can go to the urgent clinic in town or have Ruby take you somewhere else."

He closed up his bag, removed his gloves, and threw them and the papers and cloths in the garbage can by the bed. "Anything else?"

"No. Thank you, Jimmy."

At the door, Jimmy leaned in to Ruby. "Make sure she rests. I'm serious."

"And I'm serious when I say you need to stop talking like that. If he finds out..." She and Jimmy had grown up making mud pies and even attended a school dance together her junior year and his senior. The last thing she wanted to hear was he'd disappeared too.

"What kind of man would I be if I didn't offer her a way out? Does she look happy to you, Ruby? Are you? Happy?"

No. But Ruby had a plan. One that wouldn't get Jimmy or Chris killed. If she could muster the courage to go through with it.

If she was willing to die.

But who would watch over Lula? Who would keep her daughter unharmed?

Thursday, October 19
7:46 a.m.

She'd packed them. Violet wasn't going crazy. But they weren't in the suitcase. Nothing appeared touched.

The doll.

Last night after dinner and a briefing with assignments for today, she retired to the room completely exhausted, but that stupid porcelain doll with black painted eyes was facing outward, like a corpse. At first she thought the lady of the house had been in here, but why only turn one doll around?

She was about to right now hunt down ole Aunt Hossie and ask who all had access to this house. The door blew open without even a knock, and Violet's irritation and anger shifted. She pulled her gray robe close against her and narrowed her eyes.

John stood with concern in his eyes. He paused at Violet's attire. "I apologize. I should have knocked. But…we have another victim. Found fifteen minutes ago. We need to move. Rain's coming in."

"Same cave?"

"No. Team's heading to the car, told Asa I'd come get you."

They had to beat the rain, try to retrieve all the evidence they could. "I'll be down in two minutes." She'd have to deal with the panty raid and creepy doll fest later. She hurried and dressed then grabbed a hair tie and twisted her still damp hair into a bun on her way downstairs.

Less than two minutes.

She and John rushed to the car. Asa, Fiona, Ty and Owen were already outside.

They all hopped into the Suburban. "What do we know?" Violet asked as she adjusted her messy bun and shivered. Nothing like a wet head in chilly, damp weather.

Asa glanced into the rearview. "Just heard from Sheriff Modine. They got a call half an hour ago. Guy out for his six a.m. hike tripped over a bloody shoe. Had been watching the news and knew about the girls in the caves. Took it upon himself and entered the cave nearby. Found her straight away."

"We know how long she's been there?" Violet asked.

"No details yet. Sheriff was on his way. I was a little surprised he called us at all."

They turned off the main road into the mouth of Night Holler and drove through the winding curves until they crossed a small bridge that led to a cordoned off muddy road. Media hadn't made it out here yet, but it wasn't quite eight o'clock. Two side-by-sides were parked on the road.

Sheriff Modine, with the bushy Tom Selleck mustache, stood by and waved at them. Asa rolled down the window.

"Can't get regular vehicles up there. We got side-by-sides. Muddy. Rain about to come in again too. Called the coroner. But no one has messed with the scene."

The ambulance was on the scene, several deputies and their cars parked in a line. One deputy stood guard at the yellow tape with a logbook in hand.

"I appreciate it," Asa said and parked. The team geared up and wore rubber boots. "I called the ERT. But we'll have to do the preliminary."

Asa drove one four-person side-by-side, and Ty drove the other. Once they arrived at the craggy opening, they got out. Violet's feet sunk into the wet earth; the smell of animal decay and rain swept through her senses.

"Ty, you and Owen cordon off the perimeter. From six feet out from the shoe all the way around, and then we'll section off the target area. Go wide." He turned to Fiona. "Outer perimeter. Look for tracks. If we had to bring in UTVs, then he had to as well. Couldn't haul a body all that way. I wouldn't think. And from where?"

The sound of another motor roaring drew their attention, and Detective Regis Owsley approached in a side-by-side. In rubber boots, jeans and a Slate County Sheriff's Department windbreaker, he approached the team. Why wasn't he here already?

"Just got word."

Violet wasn't buying that.

"In order not to contaminate the scene, the fewer of us going in the better," Asa said. "Violet, Detective Owsley, you're with me inside the cave."

"What do you want me to do?" John asked.

"Interview first responders and the man who found the body. We'll rally after we get some answers." Asa motioned for Violet to follow, and Regis brought up the rear. Probably looking at hers all the way.

"Wearin' your hair different today, Agent," Regis said.

Violet inwardly rolled her eyes. "I hope you put those stellar detective skills to use inside the cave, Regis."

Asa turned and arched an eyebrow at her use of Regis's first name, but said nothing. The cave was dark, dank and freezing. "We need more light."

"I'll get us some." Regis left them alone in the cave.

"You getting to know the detective?" Asa asked and shined a light around the opening of the cave.

"Nope. Just doing what I do."

She kept to the edges of the cave in case footprints were in the center. About six feet in, a woman in an oversize sweatshirt and a pair of leggings lay on her back, mouth wide-open. Her face had been treated like a punching bag. Violet retrieved a camera and began taking photos. "Do we have an ETA on the ERT?"

Asa snorted. "Not soon enough."

"I got floodlights," Regis said as he approached. He switched on the battery-operated lights, and the cave lit up like a Christmas tree, but there was nothing peaceful or pretty about this. The woman's eyelids had been sutured, and one was torn open, the socket empty. Regis cursed.

"You recognize her?" Violet asked.

"I do. That's Nadine Fields. Lives here in the holler. Works at Bush's corner market part-time. I get my groceries there." He shrugged. "Lived here her whole life. I don't— I just— I have no idea when this happened. She…"

"Why would you?" Violet asked. "And she…what?"

Regis's neck flushed red. "I just mean. I knew her. I'm upset, okay?"

He was hiding something.

"Violet, what do you think?"

Violet used her mini Maglite to look more closely at the vic. "Lividity is setting in, but it's not prominent yet. Less than eight hours, I'd guess. Coroner will confirm. Her shoe was left behind. It's sloppy. He was in a hurry." Why? She stared at her face. "Same numbers on her forehead as our most recent vic, and it's fresh. If he hadn't left the shoe, we might not have found her this soon. I'd like to know if she owns a leather purse with the same Scripture writing as the other vics." Amy

Miller hadn't had any knowledge of the purses. Never saw Darla, Atta or Tillie ever carry it. But Violet was unsure if Amy had been telling the truth. She trusted no one's word.

"What kind of leather purse?" Regis asked and turned away from the body.

Violet told him about the pouches that had been handmade. "Any church groups that might hand those out around here?"

Regis shook his head. "Not that I'm aware of. I'll look into it though."

Maybe he would. Maybe not.

"He's escalated," Violet said to Asa, "and with us being present—which everyone knows—why?"

Asa shook his head as Dr. Crocker entered the cave. "Move, move." His tone was gruff, and behind him Dr. D.J. Lanslow, his assistant, followed.

"We're not done photographing," Asa said and continued. He snapped photos as Violet laid down evidence cards, working to beat the rain that would come down any second and possibly infiltrate the area from above.

Was the killer's thirst too insatiable for him to wait for his usual kill time? Had he been stalking Nadine Fields? Violet knelt. "He thinks he can outsmart us. Stay ahead. But the shoe gave him away too soon. How did he miss that? He's meticulous. Careful."

"Excuse me," John called from the mouth of the cave. "You're going to want to talk to the paramedic out here. A Jimmy Russell."

"I can talk to him," Regis said.

"We'll do it, Detective." Asa left the body with the coroner, and Violet eyed Regis. Why didn't he want them talking to this Jimmy Russell guy?

"I can come with."

"No," she put her hand up to halt him, "we got it. But

thanks, Regis." She followed Asa out of the cave, and the wind whipped her windbreaker open.

John led them up the wooded hill to the edge of the muddy side road where the ambulance was parked, relaying his interview with the guy who found the body and the two EMTs. "I think Jimmy Russell might want to say more, but he wasn't going to with the other one around. Still, he might need prodded a little, but my gut says there's something he's not telling me."

A guy about six feet, blond, blue eyes and pale skin sat on the back of the ambulance along with another man, darker hair, dark eyes and a couple inches shorter than the blond. When they spotted them, the two men stood.

"Take it, Violet," Asa whispered.

"Which one of you is Jimmy Russell?"

The dark-haired man cast a thumb in Jimmy's direction, and Jimmy stepped forward, cutting the other man a side-eye as if uncomfortable having him present. John was intuitive.

John spoke up. "Mr. Leigh, why don't we head over there and go through your statement again while they talk with Mr. Russell, and then they'll come talk to you."

John led Chris away, but he glanced back at Jimmy, and Jimmy's sight dropped to the ground.

"I'm Agent Rainwater, and this is Agent Kodiak. We'd like to hear your statement if you don't mind repeating it, Mr. Russell."

He shook his head. "No, I don't mind." His voice was tenor and soft.

"You knew Nadine personally?"

"We went to school together."

"According to Detective Orlando, you treated her last night?"

"She'd been beaten up badly. Bruised ribs. Swollen eyes. Cuts to the forehead and lip."

Some of her injuries happened prior to coming to the cave then. Had it been that way with the other victims as well? She assumed they were beaten after the eyes were extracted. Swollen eyes would be hard to remove. Why was this different? Nadine might have fought, almost gotten away. The killer might not have had a choice.

Jimmy continued his story and Violet listened, watched his body language and noticed Regis and Sheriff Modine lurking, whispering. Was Jimmy committing the cardinal sin here?

If what he was saying was true, then the killer broke in, beat her up and attempted a sexual assault before the interruption of headlights—that had turned out to be nothing but some kind of light breaking through a dark room. Then he returned and finished it. She needed to chew on that one. Something didn't add up.

"Anyone else at the trailer when you arrived?"

Jimmy broke eye contact, and his sight darted to the left. "No."

Lies.

Someone was there. He was either protecting someone or afraid. Maybe both. "Why didn't she call 911?"

"I guess she didn't want to go." He shrugged.

Violet inched further into his space, and he retreated a couple of steps. "Your friend is dead. You saw the body. You know how horrific it was. You can tell us who was there with you or not. But something you need to know, we are very good at our jobs. That's why we have them. We'll find out sooner or later, but later means more women die. You want that hanging over your head?" She folded her arms then stepped aside, motioning for Asa to take charge.

Asa angled his body to conceal Jimmy Russell from Regis

and Sheriff Modine. "No one has to know about our conversation. No one will read anything in the report other than
Nadine called you and you went to help."

Because they were withholding their personal reports from
the local department. But Jimmy needed to know that he was
free from any corrupt law enforcement retaliation.

"We can't catch this guy if we can't catch a break." Asa
splayed his hands, showing their need for Jimmy to come
through.

Jimmy massaged the back of his neck. "I could... I could
die for talking to you."

"Not gonna let that happen. Who was there with you?"
Asa asked.

Licking his lips then expelling a heavy breath, Jimmy leaned
in. "A guy called Whiskey and his friend. I think his name
is Greg."

The undercover agent and Whiskey. John would want to
hear this. "What's her relationship to them?" Violet treaded
lightly to not tip him off that they already knew of Whiskey
and his presence in the holler. They didn't want to blow the
DEA agent's cover by knowing information they shouldn't.

He cleared his throat. "She... I don't really know."

He didn't want to reveal she ran drugs for the guy. "Where
can we find them?"

"You can't. Whiskey finds you, and Greg...he's nobody
really."

"Whiskey's trouble then?" Asa asked, playing the igno-
rance game.

Jimmy glanced over Asa's shoulder to where Regis stood.
"He's dangerous and that's all I can say. If I want to wake up
breathing tomorrow."

Violet scowled in Regis and Sheriff Modine's direction.
"Could he have hurt Nadine?"

"He's not above violence if he thinks it's warranted, but I don't see him murdering women and putting them in caves this way. Not his style."

But he could have beaten her up if she'd turned down his advances, then she called Jimmy, but why would Whiskey let her call? Why stick around? Could someone else have gotten to her later? Violet couldn't put her finger on what was happening.

"Have you tended the wounds of other women who have had a *relationship* with him?" Asa asked.

Jimmy checked his watch. "Occasionally."

"Any of our victims?"

Another heavy breath. "I'm already dooming myself, might as well jump off the ledge. I saw Atta Friday night. She called me saying she'd been roughed up and asked to come by for me to take a look. She needed a butterfly stitch above her left eyebrow."

"Did you administer that?"

"Yes, and I cleaned up her wounds. She left around midnight."

That jived with what Amy Miller said. She'd come into the bar around one—after Jimmy put the adhesive on her cut to close it. But it was gone when they found her body. Which meant the killer got ahold of her after one in the morning, and the adhesive likely came off in a struggle prior to the cave. The ERT hadn't found the little white strip in their search.

"She say who caused the wound?"

"No, but I suspected Whiskey."

"Why?"

"Because she refused to tell me a name. Said she didn't know." His lips twisted and his eyebrow raised in a not-buying-it gesture.

"What did Nadine say when you asked who hurt her?" Violet asked.

"She didn't know."

It could have been Whiskey too. "And did you believe Nadine?"

"I'm not sure."

Something needled her. "But you suspect it was him?"

Jimmy shoved his hands in his pockets. "Whiskey doesn't let his girls go to the hospital. To keep things quiet, he calls someone to treat them privately. Generally speaking, when they're hurt, he's at the very least indirectly connected. Sometimes, I wonder. No one asks."

"Wait, you said he calls. Who called you? Nadine or Whiskey?"

Jimmy's face reddened, and he swore under his breath. "Neither. Whiskey's usual guy was unavailable. He called a friend of mine—but he was sick that night and called me. He knows I can be trusted and wouldn't want me confiding. Yet here I am…"

"Did Atta call you after her altercation, or this other person who works for Whiskey?"

"I promise it was her."

"But a friend called you this time?"

Jimmy nodded.

"Name."

"I can't do that to him. He doesn't take payment. He only wants to help them medically and…" His face looked pained and he huffed. "I've said way more than I should. I don't want to get my friend dead."

A friend who could doctor up someone. Violet would put her money on Chris Leigh. The exchange of glances between them as John led Chris away made more sense now. "What about the one Whiskey calls—who does take his money?"

"You didn't get it from me."

"Done. It came straight from the grapevine."

Jimmy cleared his throat, his jaw working as he kicked at the ground.

Violet waited him out.

Finally, he met her gaze. "Dr. Crocker."

The coroner.

Chapter Ten

Thursday, October 19
10:45 a.m.

John should have known Whiskey would be all up in this mess. And Greg was letting it happen so he could make the arrest and get the credit for taking him down on drug charges. Women were dying left and right. Did that not matter to him? When had the lines of justice blurred? Drugs were killing human beings, and some dastardly killer was too. Both were like an open grave, never satisfied, satiated. Just a hollow throat swallowing up its victims and salivating for more.

He'd try once more to talk to Greg. To convince him to work together. Who knows, maybe they could secure one of these frightened women who ran drugs to turn on Whiskey in exchange for shelter from a killer that he clearly couldn't stop.

Unless he was doing it himself.

Or protecting someone else.

John hated the idea of using a potential victim to meet an

agenda, but it would save lives in the end, and quite frankly, he was desperate.

"What sounds good for lunch after this?" Violet asked.

John glanced up at the coroner's office in front of him. After interviewing Jimmy Russell, he and Violet were tasked with being present for the autopsy findings, then questioning Dr. Crocker. How many women had he provided medical care to under Whiskey's orders? Asa was looking into bringing another coroner in since Dr. Crocker may not be able to be trusted. If Whiskey or his men had anything to do with these murders, they might be paying Dr. Crocker to fudge his findings.

"Ask me that after the autopsy. As many corpses as I've seen, I never ever get used to it. Not the appearance or the smells."

Violet grunted. "Ashes to ashes and dust to dust. It's normal. I take the scientific approach." She walked to the glass doors. "I do hate the smells though."

John couldn't see it quite as sterile as Violet. But if that was what she needed to do in order to handle the gravity of the situation surrounding most victims they saw, then he wouldn't judge.

Before they entered, John paused. "You think Dr. Crocker is in on this? Or a witness to the drug trafficking?"

Violet left her hand on the metal knob. The wind whipped her hair around her face. "I don't know. And depending on how well Whiskey is paying him for his medical services, we may never know."

She had a point. Money talked or, in this case, kept jaws wired shut.

"So you know, I noticed your silence on the way over. Not that you're normally a well of words," he grinned, "but you have this extra furrow in your brow when something's plaguing you." He'd noticed. Studied her. Was tipping his hand.

"Uh. Huh," she softly commented but gave no indication she was upset or even a little excited to know he'd been learning about her. "Well, I do have something on my mind."

John waited, hoping she'd share. Open up. She was tightly bottled. She hesitated, and he glanced at the door, expecting her to open it, to keep her thoughts private.

"Someone stole my underwear sometime before I came back into the bed and breakfast last night."

John did a double take. Startled she shared, even more taken aback by what she confessed. "What?"

"Well, you asked," she said. She shrugged. "I should be thinking about the case, but...maybe I am," she murmured.

Confusion wrapped around his brain. He couldn't process fast enough. "Back the bus up, Violet. Someone stole your underwear? All of it? Are you sure?"

An eyebrow raised, but her eyes were clear. "Not all of it. Only a pair. They were there yesterday, and this morning they weren't...so yeah. I'm sure," she said with a measured degree of irritation. She didn't like being questioned. If she said it, then it was so. She wasn't one to mince words or be dramatic or even shoot off without considering.

"Okay. I believe you. Anything else?"

"Just the feeling of being watched. And one of the dolls in my room was facing me last night. I turned them all facing away from me the first night. They're...unnerving. Plus there's the doll we found by the creek bed. A piece isn't fitting here. Dolls. Eyes. Undergarments. I wonder if the victims had undergarments stolen prior to their deaths."

"Did you tell Asa?"

"No. I haven't said anything to anyone. No time." She dropped her hand from the door and pocketed both in her blazer, eyes squinting in the wind. "The dolls. They're female, obviously. He singled out one of them. One with dark painted hair. Is it me? Is he leaving me a message that I'm next?"

John's stomach turned. He hoped not.

"Fiona worked a case a couple years ago when she was with the Midwest Division. Caught the Paper Doll Killer. He had an agenda to string together human paper dolls. They'd decay and he'd start over...this isn't that, but...he *collected* women. What's our killer collecting? Initially, is it undergarments and then later the eyes? What's he do with their eyes? Does he have an agenda? Is he keeping them? Do the dolls represent his victims?"

Eyes—the sclera at least—could be frozen for eye graphs. They could possibly be preserved for a portion of time under the right circumstances. "I don't know."

She tucked her long hair behind her ears. "Why not leave their eyes with them? Like in their hands. They'd wake up and feel something mushy...not realizing until they panicked, ripped out the stitches, and then the awareness would zap them. Then they'd know they were holding their own eyes. That would be cruel. Sadistic. It fits what he's doing. Where are the eyes?"

He wasn't fully sure how she was connecting the doll facing her with the eyes. Other than the doll was looking, and Violet felt lurked on. "Is he obsessed with sight? Did they see something? Does he look at things he shouldn't—like the women? You think it's about the eyes—the watching. The seeing?"

"And those numbers. The numbers mean something. But they're odd. I don't think they're meant for us to understand. I mean, if anyone can figure it out, it'll be Ty. They're carved. Painfully. Like a mark. Deep enough it hits skull bone."

John lightly clutched her forearm, terror for her rising in his throat. "Violet, if someone broke into your room and took personal items, we need to tell Asa. Tell the entire team. He may be marking you."

"Maybe," she murmured again.

"Are you not worried?"

"Worried? No. Concerned...definitely." She retrieved a small round container of breath mints and took one then passed him the container. He'd rather know what they tasted like by tasting her. Completely awkward timing to be thinking it, but he suspected it had been simmering long before.

"What?" she asked as he accepted the mint.

"Nothing. Just concerned." Where was this Aunt Hossie? Did she even exist? Someone was providing breakfast for them in the mornings. If not the ailing aunt, then who? Had she seen anyone?

"I'd like to know who has free access to the home besides Regis," Violet said.

"What if it's Regis?"

"Then we act like nothing is happening. Tipping him off will only play into what he wants. If I don't show him fear or even a whiff of caring, it'll anger him. I'd like to see if I can make him angry." A thrill danced in her eyes. "If we question Aunt Hossie, she'll tip him off, so for now, we keep this between us."

"But it may not be Regis. She might have seen someone else in the house, someone else familiar that wouldn't concern her but would help us."

"I feel like we're a step ahead. For once. I'd like to stay a few steps in that direction. Give me twenty-four hours, and if we haven't caught him dead to rights, we talk to Hossie."

John reluctantly agreed.

"Let's get this autopsy and interview over with."

They entered the building, passed the pitiful security and walked down a hall to the morgue. Inside the stainless-steel, sterile room, the scent of death, decay and cleaning fluids whacked his senses and his stomach churned. He curled his nose and noticed Violet's face was stoic.

They entered, but Dr. Crocker wasn't present. Dr. Lanslow stood in his place, and when he saw Violet his face blanched and he swallowed hard.

"Where's Dr. Crocker?" she asked in her husky tone.

"He—uh—got called away."

Violet surveyed him until he squirmed.

"Do you want to know about Nadine?"

"We do." John scooted up and stared at the victim.

"She died before she could pull out all the sutures. One eyelid is intact, giving us a better idea of the skill of the sewer. It's good for the most part, but the stitches closest to the corner of her eye appear a little sloppier."

Violet leaned in, and he brought down a magnifier for her to get a better look at the sutures. "He might have been in a hurry. He didn't linger long enough to see her rip out the ones on her other eye."

"I don't know."

"I wasn't asking," she stated without looking at Dr. Lanslow. "Sexual assault?" She glanced up when he didn't respond. "I'm now asking."

"Right. No evidence of that, but she recently had intercourse. I'd say within twenty-four hours of her death."

Same pattern as with Atta Atwater, and likely Tillie Le-Beau and Darla Boone.

"I'm back." Dr. Crocker hurriedly entered the room. "I can take it from here, Doctor."

Dr. Lanslow paused then moved aside.

Violet folded her arms. "This is all so tragic. Women dying. I don't think it's going to stop, do you?" she asked Dr. Crocker.

His lips turned down. "I don't know. I hope it does. I don't want to see another woman on my table."

"No. Me neither. I'm glad you feel that way, since I have a few hard questions to ask you. A witness has come forward who will testify that you take money from Whiskey to tend to his girls. Can you set the record straight for us?"

Dr. Crocker glanced at Dr. Lanslow, who was focused on the tile flooring.

"I accept payment from everyone. I'm the holler doctor." He folded his arms over his chest. "Most of the people in our community don't have insurance and can't afford decent health care. These are my people, and I offer care and take what they can give."

Seemed like greed and underlying motives.

"Then why not allow these women to go to the emergency clinic or the hospital in Whitesburg?"

"It's not up to me to send them. I treat them or they go untreated. I'm not on the take, Agent Rainwater."

She turned to Dr. Lanslow. "I'd like to know where you were last weekend."

Dr. Lanslow frowned. "You want my alibi? I didn't kill Atta."

"Atta. First-name basis." She let out a slow breath. "It's obvious you knew her. Why lie? If you have nothing to hide, tell me where you were. Better yet, tell me why you lied."

Dr. Lanslow massaged his neck. "I have nothing to hide and I didn't lie. I was gone for the weekend. Left Friday at noon. Went hunting all weekend with my buddy Ray in the foothills of Pine Mountain. He's got a cabin."

"I need Ray's last name and number." Violet handed over a pad of paper and a pen. Dr. Lanslow scrawled the information and returned it.

"When did you get back to Night Holler?" John asked.

"Sunday around eight p.m."

Violet jotted the information, and they exited the building. John's stomach growled, and he checked the time. Eleven forty-five. "You hungry?"

"I could eat. But I'd rather you find out if Whiskey has Dr. Crocker on his payroll and if he's dirty. Do you think your undercover agent would cough up that little bit?"

John wasn't sure. They already had a witness, so there was no fear of exposing Greg's cover. "Possibly. I'll text him."

He sent a quick and cryptic text that he had a package and to meet at the bar they'd met at earlier.

"And see if you can pull anything else out of him about Nadine. If she ran drugs for Whiskey, then he'll know her personally. Know who she was involved with. Might be sleeping with. We need some serious information."

"You think her first attack and second are separate incidents? Seems odd to be coincidence." John turned the car ignition and cranked up the heat. The day was growing chillier. Rain coming in again. He was sick of cold fall rain.

"It does. But it's possible. I want to be sure. Something is off about this. Why rush and be sloppy with the stitches? There's a million possibilities, but my gut is warning me to look closer."

John's text dinged. "I can meet him at one."

"Good. That's good."

His phone rang again. He answered the FaceTime and his daughter's face filled the screen.

"Daddy!"

He'd never tire of hearing that title. "Hi, baby girl. Daddy misses you."

"I'm sick, Daddy."

"You are?" That's when he noticed her fevered cheeks. "Where's Aunt Julie?"

"Right here. Doc said it's a virus. Fever, runny nose and

cough. She'll be okay. She needed to talk to her daddy. Said Daddy will make it all better."

"Well…of course I will."

"But how, Daddy? You're not here to kiss it and make it go away."

His gut pinched. "No, I'm not, but I'll be home soon, and I can blow you a kiss and it'll help. Sound good?"

"I miss you, Daddy. I want you to come home." She sported a pouty face, and it tugged his heart taut. He'd never been away from her for this long, and it hadn't even been a full week. And she was sick. Guilt nipped at his heels.

"I know, baby. I'll be home soon. Aunt Julie is going to give you lots of love, and before you know it, I'll be there."

Big tears rolled down her bright red cheeks burning with fever. "Okay. I'll be brave."

"That's my girl. So brave." Hopefully his words encouraged her.

Julie returned. "She'll be fine. Do what you need to," she murmured.

"Love you, Stella Bella."

"Love you." The FaceTime ended and he sighed. "Well, this sucks."

"Kids are resilient. She'll be fine."

"It's not about resilience but the fact I love her and want to be there to make her feel better."

"I'm sure she'd love that."

He didn't get the impression she and her mom were close, and he'd like to know if she had any father figure in her life growing up. "You mentioned your mom but not your dad."

"I didn't know my father. Only a few stories."

As he suspected; he'd done the math. If her mom was abducted at fifteen… Violet was most likely born out of the kidnapping. He wasn't going to pry too much. It was private and probably a tender spot, but her drive to find the man made more sense. She wasn't simply looking for a kidnapper but a rapist and…her father.

"Drop me at the sheriff's office," she said. "Or I can go and wait in the car. Backup."

"I'll be okay." He appreciated her sentiment—that she cared. Mostly he cared about the fact a killer might have his sights set on her and have access to her room.

Thursday, October 19
2:30 p.m.

Violet had driven an unmarked unit to Nadine's trailer, where she was supposed to meet John. She hadn't talked to him in almost three hours, since he left to meet his undercover contact, Greg. She shouldn't be worried about him, but she was. And that needled her in the ribs. Because it wasn't the same kind of caring she felt for her team members.

She was attracted to him. But listening to him talk to his daughter when she was sick and seeing the torture on his face of not being able to be there and hold her, to make her feel better—that was even more attractive. John had a warmth in his eyes that, even on a rotten day when they were getting nowhere in this stupid investigation, radiated. He was good with people and patient.

Everything she wasn't.

He was light.

She was dark.

Dark but lovely. Lula said that leather purse without a name was at her house. She was Mother's great-great-granddaughter. Somewhere in the holler, her mother might be in danger or could possibly be of assistance—if she'd be more forthcoming than any other person up here. It was trying her patience and clawing at her bones.

She stepped out of the unmarked unit she'd parked close to the trailer in the dirt driveway. The place was surrounded by mountains and forest, and the road dead-ended.

The ERT had left, and according to the tech she talked with, there had been blood in the bedroom—on the bedsheets and lamp and on the flush handle of the toilet in the primary bath, and spatter on the headboard. The bedcovers had been tangled, but that didn't necessarily signify a struggle. The back door had shown no signs of tampering, but that might mean she'd left it unlocked. They'd printed and tagged and bagged evidence to send to the Quantico lab, including bedsheets and towels and clothing that had been lying on the floor.

The place was older but tidy. She climbed the wooden stairs to the porch and peeked in a window. A couch. A coffee table. One small recliner. She slipped on a pair of latex gloves. Turning the knob, the door opened and a waft of stale marijuana smacked her senses. The kitchen to the left was small. A table and two chairs butted up against the wall by the back door. The counters were clear. No dishes in the sink.

Violet checked the fridge. Processed meats and cheese. Milk and eggs. Condiments and a pizza box. Six pack of beer. Two gone. She glanced in the freezer. Ice cube trays and ground beef. The sound of a car drew her attention, and she spotted John. Relief expelled from her chest as if she'd been unaware of holding it inside. His expression was grim as he strode toward the trailer. She opened the door as he stretched gloves over his hands.

"Well?" she asked.

"I can confirm that Nadine Fields was a drug runner for Whiskey—a Whiskey Girl. She was reliable and never crossed him. He considered her trustworthy. Greg asked how we already knew that, but I kept our answer close to the vest. I see no reason to offer him anything more than necessary. He's not doing us any real favors. And quite frankly... I don't think I trust him."

His hair was a little mussed, and he looked tired around his soft brown eyes, but he still had light in them. Like little pops of amber shining on.

"Did Jimmy's story match his?"

"All except he said that Nadine called a girlfriend over first and she called Whiskey. Ruby Boyd."

"Relation to Imogene Boyd? She a Whiskey Girl too?"

"I don't know. He just said Ruby called Whiskey and had arrived a few minutes earlier to see Nadine's condition."

"I wonder why Jimmy didn't mention Ruby's being there."

"Maybe she was gone by the time Jimmy got there. Or maybe he didn't want to involve her."

Violet made a mental note to find out.

John stepped inside, turning up his nose at the stale but pungent pot scent. "How long you been here?"

"Not long. Did Greg think Whiskey could have beaten her up?"

"He says no. But again, I don't trust him. My wife worked for Whiskey undercover, and she ended up dead, so anything is possible."

Whiskey could be the Blind Eye Killer, but Violet wasn't sold on it. They were after a diabolical serial killer with a fetish for eyes. And pretty women. "He tell you where you might find Whiskey?"

"He's not giving him up, and I don't think anyone in town will either. He's buttering bread, supplying addicts with the goods and instilling fear in the rest. He's untouchable." John ran his finger along the cheap Formica counter. "He did say that he and Whiskey were here. He saw Nadine alive. Either Whiskey isn't the BEK and didn't hurt Nadine, or if he is, then he beat her up, got interrupted and left, came back with

Greg when called, then returned again to finish. That's a lot of trouble to go to. Not to mention he probably slept with her prior to her getting roughed up. Somebody did."

But who?

"Might be whoever was smoking that joint." He pointed to the now empty ashtray. "Maybe we'll get DNA."

They split up and combed the house. Violet was interested in finding a leather purse. All the other victims and Lula's mom had one. She hoped to find one here. That was the only connection besides the fact the first three victims cleaned houses.

Nadine did not. She worked part-time at the corner market and, apparently, the rest of the time running drugs for Whiskey.

Violet opened Nadine's closet. Nothing fancy. Sparse even. She noticed a ridge making the wall uneven, and she tugged on a panel, revealing a duffel bag shoved inside a small crevice. She unzipped the bag and found it full of loose money, a variety of bills. Was she using the canvas bag as a bank? Had she stolen or skimmed drug money? If so, Whiskey had every reason, in his mind, to kill her. He could have copycatted the previous murders, but without all the details, he'd tipped his hand.

She carried the money into the kitchen and laid it on the counter as John exited the other bedroom. She showed him what she'd found and shared her thoughts.

"You could be right. But if he knew she was taking money, why not take the duffel bag? The beatings could have been to get her to spill the tea on where it was hidden."

John had an excellent point. "Then he didn't know she was skimming, and the slight differences in the murders could be the killer was in a rush and sloppy with Nadine since we're breathing down his neck. He's panicked but can't control his urges."

John massaged the back of his neck. "Find anything other than the money?"

"No." Her sight wandered to the counter, and she spotted a purse. Brown suede with fringe around the bottom. It wasn't a pouch, but it looked similar to the others in material. She examined it. Unzipped it. Inside was tissue, old mints, loose change and few lip glosses. Looked like she'd changed purses and left the miscellaneous items inside.

A logo was stamped on the inside pocket in bright yellow. AΩ

The sign for alpha and omega. She grabbed her phone and googled *alpha* and *omega* combined with *leather goods*, and one shop popped up. AΩ Handcrafted Leathers. Crow's Creek, Kentucky.

Bingo.

"You want to shop for fine leather goods? Or at least leather goods." She held up the purse. "Alpha and Omega Handcrafted Leathers. It's local, and I'll wager that's where the other purses came from too."

"It's religious. Jesus says in the book of Revelation He's the Alpha and Omega—the beginning and the end."

"I have an address. Follow me." They left Nadine's, and in about fifteen minutes, they arrived downtown. Maybe many moons ago the downtown district of Crow's Creek was charming, but paint now peeled on wooden buildings and brick had chipped in places. Even the lopsided sidewalks appeared tired and broken.

Pots of yellow and purple mums attempted to serve as minor cosmetic surgery to give the aging town a lift. Alpha and Omega Handcrafted Leathers was sandwiched between an empty store and a donut shop that was closed, but the smell of sugar still lingered in the air as they strode to the front door.

A large wooden sign with the logo AΩ squeaked as it swayed in the breeze. A bell rang as they opened the heavy wooden door and entered to the smell of a stable minus the manure.

A rounder to their immediate left held dozens of leather belts in a myriad of colors and designs. Beside that were tables of wallets, business card holders, and purses of every size and shape. Sheaths for knives lay neatly in glass cases. The store was expertly organized, creating an aesthetic array of color across the entire landscape. Artistry at its finest. Instrumental violin and acoustic guitar played beyond the counter and hallway that led to the back of the store. Polished hardwoods looked original to the building, but what snagged Violet's undivided attention was the back wall on the right.

From floor to ceiling it was filled with leather crosses. Many of them had John 3:16 stamped into them. The only verse Violet knew by heart. It was the verse she'd heard that night as a child before walking up the aisle at the church service to ask Jesus into her heart.

For God so loved the world... The words had echoed inside her and released the pinch, giving her room for hope. Hope that for once she might be loved. Even at ten, she'd been acutely aware that she was alone in the world. But if God so loved the world then surely that must have included her. She'd take the love of an unseen God any day in comparison to the seen rejection of her mom and grandmother.

And if He loved her then maybe she wasn't the monster Reeva claimed, and He could wash away the darkness, she knew even then, that had stained her.

God help her she was dark, but He said she was lovely. She'd been told she was pretty since she was a preschooler, but to know that God thought she was lovely, knowing the ugliness that lurked in her could be washed into inner loveliness...

She swallowed hard, forcing herself to tear her gaze from the cross.

She was beyond fairytales now.

"You seeing what I'm seeing?" John muttered.

No. No, she probably wasn't. He pointed to the wall above the hallway entrance. Plaques with several carved Scripture verses and lined with leather hung in a neatly arranged cluster.

"Be right there," a reedy voice carried from the back.

"I'm not saying this guy is our killer. We are in Kentucky, and it's steeped in Christianity. Crosses and plaques sell well," John said and perused the wallets. "Hand stitching," he said from the corner of his mouth.

Violet chuckled. He sounded almost comical. Finally a door clicked, and a man glided into the hallway. His solid white T-shirt was splattered with wood stain. His jeans were worn but not raggedy, and he wore thick hiking boots. Average height. That was all that could be considered average about him though.

He was stunning.

Perfectly symmetrical features from the Greek nose to the round, sharp blue eyes fanned by long lashes. Full lips with a perfect Cupid's bow offset the clean-shaven, creamy skin. Like something out of a Dove commercial. His hair parted in the middle and hung to the tops of his shoulders in surfer waves. Nicks and calluses covered his knuckles.

But the face.

The porcelain face did not match his sinewy build.

"Can I help you?" he asked, his eyes curious.

"I don't know," she muttered, and John tossed her a quizzical expression. "Sorry." She pulled her creds. "I'm Agent

Rainwater and this is Detective Orlando. We're here investi-gating the deaths of—"

"I know." He held out his hand. "Cecil Johnson. I own this place." His accent was pleasant and carried less drawl than she'd expected.

He shook their hands. His was firm, cool.

"It's unbelievable, really. Nothing like this happens in Night Holler—or here in Crow's Creek." He sighed. "Until now. How can I help y'all with that?" His tourmaline eyes remained on Violet, studying her without gawking. A skill she was adept in as well. She'd been sizing him up without making it obvi-ous. But she was no average Joe, and it appeared Cecil John-son wasn't either.

"Can you tell us if you made these purses?" Violet showed him a picture of the ones they'd found.

"Sure. I've made them for almost all the holler girls."

"You mean girls that live in Night Holler?"

His pale eyebrows pulled together, and a knowing smirk played on his lips. "What else would I mean?"

She wasn't sure. The term could be specific or general. "Why do you put this particular Scripture on them?"

He studied the picture again, moving in closer to see. He gently touched her phone, zooming in on the small purse. "Because it's true. We're all dark inside but lovely." He caught her eye again. "You're lovely." He tossed her a staccato smile and breathed a laugh through is nose. "Very pretty."

She could say the same of him. He clearly carried an obses-sion with appearance. And she wondered… "Have you ever been told you're pretty?"

His right eye twitched. "Is that all you want from me? To identify my work?"

"The hand stitching is amazing," John added. "My aunt Alma does some cross-stitching, and this puts hers to shame."

His Kentucky drawl was a little thicker, slower, twangier as he held up a wallet with stitched edging. "I'll take this one. How much?"

"Thirty-five. Thanks." He carried the wallet to the counter and rung it up. John had diffused his irritation, but Violet had meant to evoke it—if it was simmering. Cecil Johnson did not take kindly to being told he was pretty. "I do all the stitching. It relaxes me." He glanced up at Violet. "See anything you like?"

Innuendo or a simple question? "I like that cross at the top right. With the scalloped edges."

"You a believer, Agent?" he murmured.

She went with it. "Of course. Aren't you?"

"Oh yes. My mama made sure I was purified and sanctified. Molded in His image like clay. Maybe I should have been a potter." His smile was wide and his teeth straight and white. "Would you like that cross?"

"I would."

"How well did you know Atta, Tillie, Darla and Nadine?" John asked.

He faltered and the cross fell, but he caught it before it hit the floor. "Not in the biblical sense if that's what you mean. We were friends. Went to school and grew up together."

Taking the cross to the counter, he carefully wrapped it in tan tissue paper and handed it to her. "No charge for the pretty lady."

"Unfortunately, I can't accept gifts." She dug into her pocket and pulled out her small wallet, retrieved a twenty-dollar bill and handed it to him. "But thanks for the offer."

"Thanks, but no thanks," he said with a wistful chuckle. He tucked away the bill in his pocket instead of the cash drawer. "Anything else?"

"Do you know what happened to Bobby Lloyd or Earl Levine?" John asked.

"I know they disappeared. Or left. Either way. Poof!" His fist sprang open as if he were tossing confetti. "Don't reckon we'll ever see 'em again." His eyes hinted at a delicious secret. One that was buried probably six feet in the ground times two.

"Do you know where we can find Whiskey?"

"Black Feather has a nice variety of Kentucky bourbon." Cecil ran a hand through his thick hair, and it fell right back into place.

Nice attempt at playing dumb. "The man, Whiskey."

"'Fraid I can't answer that, Agents. My apologies." Cecil Johnson was far from sorry.

"When was the last time you saw any of the victims?"

Cecil shook his head and shoved his hands into his back pockets. "I don't remember about Tillie or Darla. I saw Atta last week. She came by the shop on Wednesday to pick up a pair of boots. And I saw Nadine maybe two weeks ago at the Meat and Three Veg. She was with Amy."

Maybe they needed to interview Amy Miller again.

"Thank you for your time. And the cross."

"You're welcome. Be seein' ya."

Violet and John left the shop. The heavy gray sky released a light drizzle. Not enough for an umbrella, but enough to be annoying. "Well he was...odd."

"I feel like he should be in a painting in Paris or Greece or Italy or something." John pocketed the wallet. "I actually do like this wallet, and if he turns out to be the killer—between us—I'm keeping it anyway."

Violet laughed. "That's a little creepy. Kinda surprised it came out of you."

"Right?" He laughed with her. "You really want that cross?"

"No." It was a painful reminder that love was out of reach for her.

Her phone rang as they approached the car, little beads of rain dotting her hair and face, then sprinkling her phone as she read the caller's name.

Reeva.

"Hello."

"Violet, it's Reeva."

Well aware. "I know."

"Your grandmother fell, and she's in surgery. I—I think you should be there to tend to her."

"That's what doctors and PT are for, Reeva." She wasn't coming home to play nursemaid to a woman who hated her. She was surprised Reeva would want her to; this was more of a roundabout way of asking for Violet's help. Reeva hadn't been formally diagnosed, but Violet guessed she was agoraphobic or close to being that way. Hadn't been out of the house but a handful of times that Violet could remember. She didn't want Violet. She needed her.

"I had a feeling you wouldn't care."

Why should she? "I'm in Kentucky on a case. I'll...call you back." She ended the call.

"Who's Reeva?"

"My mom."

Chapter Eleven

Violet bristled in the passenger seat as John exited I-40 into Cordova, Tennessee. The trip had been a long seven-hour drive. They'd left around six this morning. Violet had wrestled with whether she should even come back to Memphis. Her return would be unappreciated, and she'd end up unsettled and out of sorts. The psychologist in her told her it was okay to walk away from a toxic relationship.

But here she was. In Memphis. Unsettled and out of sorts.

John had been upset over being so far away from his sick daughter, so when he'd heard her grandmother had fallen and broken a hip, he offered to drive them both back for the weekend. Violet could see to medical needs, and John could hug his daughter.

A seven-hour drive for a hug.

What might that feel like? To know someone was willing

to go that far simply to wrap you in an embrace and impart love and fatherly care. That was one favored little girl.

Asa had been fine with her leaving this morning and returning Sunday afternoon since the entire team was in the field. They would continue the investigation, building a better profile and hopefully discovering the meaning of those numbers. Ty had been at his wit's end, and that meant endless energy drinks, bad jokes to accompany them, and all-around annoyance and a few four-letter words, which Asa and Fiona now frowned upon.

John pulled into a middle-class neighborhood with nice homes and small, tidy yards.

"I live around the corner from my sister. It's easy to get Stella back and forth when needed. You sure you don't mind coming with me? I can take you to the hospital first."

He'd already offered to drop her off first, but Violet wasn't ready, and it wasn't like Grandmother was lying on the floor unattended and in pain. She was in the hospital with a medical team tending to her. "She's probably still in recovery. Nothing can be done right now anyway." She'd have John swing by the field office later and pick up her car. No need for him to be her personal Uber.

"Okay," he said softly and didn't press further.

The ride had been pleasant when not discussing her family, when it had been about jobs, cases, favorite foods, music and movies. She already knew he loved Hitchcock but was pleasantly surprised to hear of his love for chicken parm and Neil Diamond.

He pulled in behind a white Honda. "I've never brought a woman home to my sister before." His smirk slid sideways, revealing a dimple.

She failed at suppressing her own. "I imagine you were quite the heartbreaker in high school and college."

He flashed her a playboy grin and leaned in, giving her a whiff of his aftershave. "Oh, I was. I definitely was."

Violet's pulse went on the uptick, and her insides flushed. "And now?" she flirted back.

"Now?" He sobered and pierced her gaze, sending a skitter along her nerves. "I'd never break a heart, Violet. But I told you my nickname earlier. So I can't promise I won't steal one."

Slick. He'd been a little thieving delinquent.

"I've never stolen or broken a heart. And I've never been on the other side either. I'm not sure I'd know what it felt like."

Without warning, he slid a stray hair behind her ear. "Heartbreak feels like weight on your chest, robbing you of breath until you suffocate. A *stolen* heart…well, that's like a kiss that robs your breath while simultaneously breathing life into your body. You feel it everywhere," he whispered and grazed her lips with his forefinger. "Here…" He trailed that same finger down her arm and chill bumps broke out. He intertwined their fingers. "Here," he murmured. Arching his eyebrow, he lightly touched the skin below her collarbone; she swallowed, her mouth bone-dry. "Here." His last whisper.

She held his gaze, anticipating and dreading a kiss.

As if reading her mind, he said, "I want to kiss you, Violet Rainwater. But I'm not going to. Not unless I've lived up to my name."

She licked her parched lips.

He eyed them and sighed. "Not gonna be easy, if you keep distracting me like that."

"I could seduce you into it." She could be persuasive if she wanted to be. Did she want to be?

"Maybe." His voice was raspy and alluring. "But we're just gonna let it simmer, let all the spices marry."

She was about to boil over right now. Never had she wanted a man to kiss her more, but she acquiesced. "Are you playing cat and mouse because you know I like the hunt?" He'd heard her conversation with Regis at the diner.

"One thing I don't do...play games."

She laid a hand on his forearm. "If this isn't a game, then what is it?"

He leaned in, her awareness of him intensifying, and then his lips brushed her ear. "It's intention." His breath tickled her neck and zinged into her ribs causing a reactionary jolt. Pulling slightly away, he arrested her eyes. One beat. Two. "Now, come meet my daughter."

A sudden weight dropped in her gut. She'd almost forgotten he had a very young daughter without a mom. If John was going to be stealing hearts, he needed to pick hearts that were mom material.

Which she was not.

Could he not see that? Was he blind? She followed him to the front door, and he rang the bell. Pumpkins and mums were arranged in a cozy fashion, and a big wooden sign with white painted letters read *Happy Fall Y'all*.

The door opened and a petite woman sharing the same dimples, blondish brown hair and warm brown eyes as John beamed, then her sight landed on Violet. "Welcome, Agent Rainwater."

"You can call me Violet if you'd like."

"That's a pretty name. I'm Julie."

"Thank you." They entered a home Joanna Gaines would stamp with approval, and Violet smelled something delicious. Rich and decadent. Tomatoes. Garlic.

"I figured y'all would be hungry after a long drive so I cooked early. Made John's favorite. Chicken parm. He texted me earlier and told me you liked it too." Julie welcomed them inside the open floor plan. Toys littered the floor, and a cat perched on top of a bookshelf, eyeing them suspiciously.

"Swipe," John murmured and winked.

His teasing about working on swiping her heart with a delicious dish better be just that. Teasing. He might have once been nicknamed Slick, but Violet had vaulted her heart so securely not even the most famous of thieves could crack it.

Two sweaty little boys zipped inside the back door. "Mama, Jacob threw my ball over the fence again."

"He was hitting me with it!" the other child hollered in defense.

Julie folded her arms over her chest. "What have I told you two? Behave or neither of you go back outside."

They huffed and skulked through the door they'd entered, shoulders slumped.

Julie shrugged. "Kids."

"Daddy?"

The tiny voice belonged to the fragile girl who rounded the corner. Her blond ponytail had been mussed, and a few strands of curls flopped in her dark brown eyes.

"Baby!" John scooped her up, and she wrapped her little arms around his neck and peppered him with kisses. He returned them.

It was crystal clear he'd stolen her heart long ago.

Stella squished his cheeks with her little chubby hands. "I missed you."

"I missed you too," he said through fish lips, and she giggled then whispered, "I feel better."

"Good. You want to meet my friend?"

Stella suddenly realized they weren't alone, and she dipped her chin, peering up at Violet from underneath her lashes. She was a beautiful child, favoring mostly John.

"This is Miss Violet."

"Hello," Stella said shyly.

"Hello. Nice to meet you." What did one say to a preschooler upon introduction? "I'm glad you feel better."

She hid in the side of John's neck. Not a bad place to be.

"Miss Violet catches bad guys like Daddy." He met Violet's eyes. "She's very good at it."

Why did everything he now said feel as though it held hints of underlying meaning?

Stella perked up. "I'm gonna catch bad guys too when I gets big."

Violet awkwardly shifted her weight to the other foot. Bad guy thieving her panties? No problem. Making conversation with a four-year-old? Debilitating.

"You wanna see my jail? I made a jail to puts the bad guys in." She wiggled in John's arms, and he set her down. Stella grabbed Violet's hand and tugged her toward the front of the house. She glanced at John, unsure of what to do, and he winked his approval for her to go play.

But he didn't come along.

Unfair.

Inside a boy's room were pillows that had been stacked in a square and what looked like old wrapping-paper rolls propped against the front like bars. Clever. Imaginative. Plastic handcuffs and a holster on a matching belt rested on the bottom bunk bed.

"Brannon never lets me be sheriff, but when he's outside, I gets to be the sheriff." She wrapped the belt around her tiny waist, but her slender fingers fumbled. Violet squatted and helped her fasten it.

"Girls can be sheriffs too. You'll be a good one."

Stella stared intently at Violet and then offered one resolute nod. "I will be. You gots a gun?"

"I do."

"You ever shoots a bad guy?"

She had.

"Have you?" Redirection usually worked on adults, hopefully it would on a child. Stella Orlando didn't need to know about Violet's shots.

"I shot Brannon."

Violet snickered. "For telling you girls can't be sheriffs?"

She nodded again and curls bobbed.

Violet helped her adjust the belt and get the holster set on her hip. "You know, us girls have to be smart." She tapped Stella's temple. "We can't be shooting people simply because we don't like what they say. Good sheriffs have a cool head under pressure."

"I had a hot head 'cause I had fevers."

This kid was a kick, and Violet's nerves dissipated. Stella wasn't quite as scary as Violet expected. Easy. Like John. Being with him, having conversations, was like slicing into warm butter. Effortless.

"I had a fever once."

Stella found a plastic sheriff's star and clipped it on her doggie pj's. "Did your daddy make it all better?"

No. No, she'd been given medicine without any sugar to make it go down and a door shut with commands not to come out and give her illness to anyone else. She'd been about six. Maybe seven. "I got all better by my medicine."

"When Daddy was gone, I prayed and asked Jesus to make me feel better. He dids."

Probably the meds kicked in, not the prayer, but who knows, maybe she was one of the good ones God did actually love and want to be His.

"I'm glad," Violet choked out. "You want me to pretend to be the bad guy? You can throw me in jail." It wouldn't be too far-fetched. Violet had done bad things. Came from a bad man.

Stella holstered her gun and fingered a strand of Violet's hair.

"I think you're—"

Pretty.

"Good." Stella continued rubbing Violet's hair between her forefinger and thumb. "Good guys don't belong in jails." She held up a strand of Violet's hair. "I like your hairs too."

Violet heard the chuckle outside the door and spotted John leaning against the doorframe, amusement in his eyes. Violet wasn't amused; she was spinning inside.

She'd never been called good.

Only pretty. Or negative words.

"Who's ready to eat?" John asked.

"Mes is!"

John winked at Stella as she came running and slipped through his legs into the living room. John entered the bedroom, toyed with one of the paper tubes. "She's not quite got down singulars and plurals. It's cute, so I let it go."

"She's very sweet, John. Lot like her father, I think."

He dropped the tube and approached her, toyed with the end of her hair. "Thanks. I like your hairs too." He held her gaze then pointed toward the kitchen. "Let's eat. We skipped breakfast and I'm famished. I'll take you to the hospital after. You got to go sometime, Violet. I don't know your family dynamics, but the woman I know isn't afraid of anything. But this...this bothers you. I'm going to take you to the hospital... and I'm going to stay with you. And that's not up for debate."

He wanted to emotionally support her? He'd picked up on the dread she'd tried to mask as nonchalance. She wasn't sure what to make of that.

"Since it's not up for debate, fine." But she'd already settled that she liked the idea of John at the hospital with her. Near her. For her.

No one had ever been *for* her.

She met Julie's husband and her two boys now that they were seated and clean, then she sat between John and Julie.

The meal was served family style, and as they passed the food around and laughed and talked, Violet felt fully welcome.

And home.

"Sonny! Is that you?"

He bristled and ground his teeth. The storm hadn't let up in hours, and he was drenched, cold and bringing the old, ungrateful bat her dinner. Currents of resentment rolled in his gut, and he balled his hands as he hollered from the kitchen, "Yes, Mama. I brought you some dinner since you're feeling poorly."

He snatched a tray tucked between the fridge and the pantry and set her chicken soup, a sleeve of crackers and a glass of tea on it. Then he maneuvered his way through the old, drafty house, the joists creaking under his weight. He used his hip to push open the door.

Heavy burgundy curtains tamped out any sliver of light that had remained outside. Rain pitter-pattered on the roof as Mama lay in bed, her long hair loose around her shoulders and a thick, colorful quilt pulled up over her chest.

"Set that tray down and help me prop up, Sonny," she commanded.

He didn't want to come any closer. Like the big bad wolf, he feared the closer he came the better she'd smell him. And she'd know. Like she always did.

Invisible ants began to skitter across his skin, and the slow rumble started in his bones as he envisioned her catching a whiff of his sin.

He'd been taking chances. Too many. But he couldn't stop himself.

"I said come help me now, boy."

He ground his teeth and inched toward the bed. Leaning over Mama, he helped her sit up and then he snagged a pillow beside her, imagining holding it over her wretched face and watching her body writhe for oxygen. Instead, he placed it behind her back and fluffed the ones behind it. "Is that better, Mama?"

Suddenly her hand snatched him by the chin, her nails digging into flesh and her silver cross glittering against her throat like a knife. "You filthy boy!"

She knew.

Shoving his face from her, she threw back the covers and sprang to the floor in her nightgown and bare feet. "I know what you been doin' with them girls," she hissed, a sneer morphing her face from an old craggy hag into something darker, more frightening.

"Mama, I don't know what you mean," he offered calmly, but inside his bones rumbled. Ants skittered. His heart raced.

Stalking him like a lioness, she held her cross in one hand and pointed at him with the other. The crosses on the wall were like a banner above her head.

"I've been real good. Haven't done anything evil."

"Lies." She held onto the *s* and let it snake through her teeth. "You're a dirty boy."

"No."

"I know what you do in the night. I seent it with my own eyes." She inched toward him, and he retreated a step.

"I was in your room, Sonny. I know what you're guilty of. God's gonna smite you for what you done to them girls! Maybe… I can save you."

Kill her…for once shut her up.

"Stop!" Sonny shouted at the voice, but the rumble grew louder and the ants skittered faster. Temptation grew larger.

She's nothing but a hypocrite. A liar. A whore!

Kill her. Do it.

Hand shaking and heart ratcheting, he clasped the bowl of

steaming soup and slung it off the tray into her face. "Shut up! I haven't done anything!"

Mama shrieked as the hot soup singed her skin and noodles stuck to her wrinkled face. She cursed him, dooming him to fiery eternity.

Now!

A dense and looming darkness he was familiar with slicked over his skin and slithered into his joints, his muscles, to his very soul, suffocating and snuffing out logic and reason. An icy burn ravaged his chest and shaded his eyes until he could no longer see but only feel pure, unadulterated rage.

His bones rumbled. The invisible ants skittered.

What are you waiting for? She's found you out. She'll tell. Worse, she'll punish you. Force you to look at the cross. Recite the words. You have no other choice. And you want to. You've wanted to for forever. No one will know.

With a guttural cry, he lunged, knocking her haggard frame to the hardwood floor with a crack and crunch.

"Sonny! Get off me right this minute!" No longer was she in control. And she knew it. Fear dazzled her eyes with a sheen of tears.

Oh yes. Now she was finally afraid, and he was in control.

"What are you doing?" she cried.

He straddled her, pressing his thumbs into her eyes, ignoring her screeches. "You don't see anything!"

Her nails clawed his arms, but his long sleeves protected him.

He felt nothing.

A shadow knelt beside him, smelling of sulfur and fury. Invisible arms wrapped around him and filled him with dark pleasure as he watched in delight the blood trickle from the old bat's eyes.

Yesss…that's it. Shut her up. For good. Be free of her. Nasty old hag.

He listened to those wicked thoughts and let them massage his brain. Memories surfaced on a loop.

Lashed as a young boy for spying on Mama with Mr. Franks.

He reared back and punched, connecting with bone and cartilage, and felt the joy of inflicting what she had coming.

With each painful memory, he punched.

Locked in the dark. Crying to escape.

He punched.

Peeping on the girls next door during their slumber party and being punished.

He punched.

He'd prayed not to be bad. He hadn't wanted to be bad. But Mama never told him he was good. He was always bad. When he brought her flowers for Mother's Day but picked them from Miss Hazel's yard. Bad. Punished.

Her cries ebbed, but he punched and punched and punched and punched.

Until she was quiet.

Sweat slicked his body, and he dropped his arms, relaxed his rigid muscles and let his head fall backward, eyes closed. Finally, sweet silence.

Satiated and soothed, the voice in his head disappeared, but the evil presence lingered, approving, nodding.

Rain thundered on the roof and the clock ticked, ticked, ticked the seconds away.

Opening his eyes, he held his hands out before him.

Covered in blood.

"Mama?" he murmured. "Mama?" he asked louder. "I'm sorry." He lowered his head to her chest, cradling her. "I'm sorry, Mama. Look what you made me do."

The presence skittered off as it always did, leaving him

void and empty. With nothing but chaos in his brain and fear gripping his heart.

Nothing but the shame of what he'd done.

Then the knock came on the door.

"Sorry it took me so long to open the door. I was changing bedsheets for Mama."

Ruby warmed. Regis was devoted to his mom even if she was a little strange. "You're a good man, Regis. Can I come in?"

He wiped his hands on his pants and glanced behind him. He'd told her earlier to come by. "If it's a bad time—"

Regis waved off the notion. "No. Ruby, it's never a bad time when you're around." He checked his watch.

"Seems like it is." But she could use some company. Between the murders and toying with her plan, fearing someone would find her stashed money, and the Him who was lurking, she could use being near a detective. Regis had promised to look out for her, and she believed him.

"Where's Lula?" he asked.

"With Mother. She's staying for several hours."

Regis held her gaze and slowly caressed her cheek. "You look tired."

"I am but..."

"Come inside." Entering the drafty house, she noticed dishes piled in the sink. Something sticky on the linoleum floor. The lingering scent of dinner reminded her that she hadn't eaten yet. Her stomach growled, but Regis didn't seem to notice. He was preoccupied.

"I get the impression something is on your mind. What's going on, Reege?" Maybe helping him with his problems would take her mind off of her own.

"You hungry?" he asked. "I can make you a sandwich, or there might be some chicken left."

"Actually, I'm starved. A sandwich would be great, but I can do it."

"No. Take a load off. I got it." He opened the fridge and took out all the fixin's, holding them in the crook of his arm and carrying them to the counter. "Tomato?"

"No."

"Mayo?"

"Sure." She swiped a crumb from the table. "How is your mom? Mother said she wasn't doing well. She was going to swing by tomorrow and bring a pie."

"That's not necessary. Really. Besides it's supposed to storm all day, and Mother don't need to be out in it." He carried the sandwich to the table and then opened the cabinet for a glass. "Tea or lemonade?"

"Tea."

After pouring a glass and setting it by her plate, he took a chair opposite her and tented his hands on the table.

She bit into the ham and cheese on white and noticed his right hand. She swallowed and pointed to the nicked and roughed-up knuckles. "What did you do to your hand?"

He stared at it a moment and sighed. "Would you believe me if I said I punched a raw cedar wall?"

Ruby laughed and took another hefty bite. The bread was soft and sticking to the roof of her mouth. She pushed it away and finished chewing. "FBI driving you crazy? How's the investigation? Mother said they'd been by to talk about Atta."

"The dark-haired one—she kinda reminds me of you. Only cold and...feral." He wiggled his eyebrows. "I like riling her up. Except, I'm not sure it's wise. She's not like the others. She's...calculated. But I kinda like that too."

Regis had a knack for getting under a person's skin if he

wanted to, and growing up he enjoyed bullying other kids. Girls at times. But Ruby didn't judge. She had her own sins to atone for. He'd never declared feelings for her, and she didn't ask because he'd been rejected before, and she didn't want to add to the hurt. He'd had a hard row to hoe.

"I think you should cooperate, Regis. Amy said they talked to her again today. She said the woman agent was nice."

"She have short hair?"

"Yeah."

"Then that ain't the one I'm talking about."

"I'm scared, Regis. I think it's someone we know who lives in the holler or down in Crow's Creek. He's brought trinkets to Lula. He leaves them by the crick, and he knows his way in the woods. It's not a transplant." No one wanted to believe a man in the holler would dare touch one of them, but someone was proving them wrong. "He's not afraid of the fact that others have died for doing less in the past. He thinks he can evade it. Hide from it. And he has, Regis. We're helping him hide and continue killing 'cause we won't share any information with the FBI."

Regis frowned and glanced at the ceiling, his jaw working and nostrils flared. "What kind of trinkets?"

She told him about what Lula had been given. "I heard they talked to Cecil too."

"Cecil? Why?"

"They found leather pouches he made them. Made me one too. I gave it to Lula for a purse. He said—"

"When did you see Cecil?" he asked, cutting her off. He was a little possessive of her. She shouldn't have even mentioned it. Regis wouldn't hurt her, but he would punch a wall. She had no doubt he'd torn into raw cedar with bare hands.

"I stopped by the shop to pick up a gift for Betty. I got the baby a plaque for the room. It's real cute too." She tried to ease him into another subject. Everyone knew Regis and Cecil had personal issues. But she supposed that was to be expected.

"What did he say?"

"That a real pretty agent and detective came by inquiring about the purses and the stitching. He actually felt like they'd given him a compliment on the stitching being precise. I reminded him they suspected him. He didn't seem to care." She finished off her sandwich and put the plate in the sink. "You want me to do these dishes?"

"I want you to stay away from Cecil."

She sighed. Too many men in her life were dictating her choices. "I'm leaving, Regis."

The chair scooted across the floor, and she turned to face him. "I'm sorry. Cecil's trouble. Has been since we were teenagers. You know this. Stay a little longer."

"No." He didn't understand. "I mean I'm leaving Night Holler. For good." She thought saying it would bring her some courage to actually do it. She'd been thinking about it since she was thirteen years old. But staying here gave her a certain amount of protection, even if she still felt trapped and suffocated.

She didn't want this life. Never asked for it.

Once, she'd asked Whiskey to run away with her, and he'd laughed. Said they were going nowhere. Her home was here. His daughter was staying here. But she didn't want Lula raised here and going into the family business. Drugs abounded. She was lonely. She wanted better for her daughter. Money and protection weren't everything.

She'd been saving up.

"Are you being serious?" he asked and stepped into her personal space. His dark eyes held concern and something she couldn't put her finger on. "Ruby, that's like signing a death warrant."

"No one will find me…if you help me. Regis, you know the law. You know things I don't. You could help me. Help me and Lula and not get caught." Hopefully, she wasn't putting him in harm's way. She grabbed his biceps. "Will you? Help me?"

"Ruby," his eyes darkened and he grasped her hands, "you're not going anywhere."

Chapter Twelve

John glanced over at Violet in the passenger seat of the car. Something plagued her mind. Last night after dinner, he'd taken her to the hospital and, as promised, he stayed by her side. While she hadn't expressed her nerves in terms of fidgeting, her jaw had been tight until a woman entered the waiting area, and then she'd bristled.

The woman had been Reeva Rainwater, and she'd been gnawing her nails, pacing and muttering about being forced by Violet to have to be here and having no money to pay a cabdriver. From Violet's calling her by her given name to the arctic air icing the atmosphere around them, it was obvious no love was lost between them. The only things they shared were bronzed skin and dark hair. Violet had mentioned on the ride to Memphis that her great-great-grandfather had been a

Native American from the Shawnee tribe, though she'd never met anyone from her grandmother's side of the family.

Violet had handled the financial affairs, checked in on her grandmother and given Reeva money for an Uber back home all in under an hour, with the excuse that she needed to get back to the investigation. She'd planned to drive back a day early on her own, but Stella was much better, and seeing her—if only for a day—had given him the strength he needed to return to Kentucky and find Callie's killer. He'd packed a few more items, and they'd hit the road at six o'clock this morning.

It was pushing two o'clock as they exited Route 15 into Slate County. "You know if you want to talk about anything, I'm a good listener."

"I have a therapist for that." She stared out the window, her tone clipped and cold. "I'm sorry. I don't really have relationships where I share feelings. The closest I've come is Fiona, but mostly that's because she forced herself into my house and my life."

John didn't see anyone barreling into Violet's life that Violet didn't allow, but she could keep on with the tough exterior that hid a lonely and confused woman. After seeing her home life, he could understand her more. He had no idea what it would be like to grow up unloved, unwanted and reminded of it daily. But looking at Reeva Rainwater had proven that's the kind of life Violet had. To be successful now made her nothing short of a brave woman determined to overcome. Yet, he had a feeling she would never see her life this way.

"No men in your life?"

"I date, occasionally, but it never goes past a few. I don't have time. Haven't we had this conversation?"

"Have we?" He kept his eyes on the road, or he'd miss the turn off to Crow's Creek.

"What about you? Have you dated since your wife passed?"

She was A-OK talking about his relationships, but she was a vault about her own. "I dated for the first time six months ago. But I knew pretty quick it wasn't going to go anywhere. She was sweet and attractive, but she didn't...challenge me enough."

"You mean like playing truth or dare?"

He caught the tease in her tone. He was recognizing it more quickly now. "Exactly. I mean if someone won't double-dog dare me, are they even worthy of my time?"

She smirked but said nothing.

"We weren't compatible." They began the uphill wind of the mountain toward Crow's Creek B and B.

"Was she not enough like your first wife?"

"Are you doing therapy on the sneaky side with me?" He glanced over again, and she caught his eye, a little glimmer of playfulness.

"Maybe. But if you're holding back and turning women away, it might be because you're trying to find Callie again. You won't be able to do that, you know."

"I know." He wasn't looking for Callie again. Quite the opposite actually, and he harbored a fair amount of guilt over it. "I'm not comparing women to Callie. I'm not sure what I'm looking for." He and Violet had been pretty flirty over the weekend, and he would like to know her better, but she didn't make it easy. She went from hot to cold fairly fast, not to mention her job was dangerous and she didn't have the good sense to be afraid. A killer had stolen personal items, and she hadn't even batted an eye. Would she run into trouble, hoping for a fight? He had Stella and her tender heart to think about too.

Flirting might be all they had, but he'd meant it when he said he didn't play games, so he wasn't sure what to think of the signals he was sending; he was mixed up. The woman intrigued him. He admired and respected her.

They pulled into the drive, and he cut the engine. "What are you looking for?"

"I'm not looking." She unbuckled and opened the passenger door.

All right then. But her evasiveness was like dropping crumbs for a dog. He'd keep dogging her heels. Maybe she knew that. Did she play games? He grabbed his bag, and they entered the house. It smelled of maple syrup and old books.

Footsteps thudded on the stairs, and Asa made an appearance, a bag in hand. Fiona followed behind. "I was about to call you," Asa said.

Violet frowned. "Why?"

More footsteps and Owen and Ty approached.

"Why's everyone here?" Violet folded her arms over her chest, waiting.

Asa left his rolling suitcase by the door. "Got a call from a homicide detective friend in Charleston, South Carolina."

"And?"

"Hey there, Little Red Riding Hood, you sure are lookin' good…" Ty sang then bayed at the ceiling as if it were the moon. This guy was a trip.

Asa frowned and Violet pinched the bridge of her nose. "Someone with at least an average IQ talk to me."

Fiona smacked Ty. "Enough of the Sam the Sham and the Pharaohs song." She turned to Violet. "A sorority girl was found eviscerated the morning after a full moon, which, sadly, isn't weird, but they found—"

"A *wolf* tooth in her throat wound," Ty cut in. "Rumor has it the big bad wolf lurks around Charleston Harbor University. I mean, we've never hunted a Grimm's fairytale character before. That's pretty cool."

Asa frowned. "This is why you aren't coming with us. We aren't hunting an actual wolf."

"You don't know." Ty jutted out his chin like a ten-year-old.

"I'm taking Fiona and Owen," Asa said. "Putting you in charge of the investigation here, Vi."

"Great. I get stuck with Tiberius."

"Well," Ty said, "it might not be the big bad wolf, but I think I should come. In case it is."

"Okay," Asa said.

Ty's eyes lit up. "Really?"

"No," Asa stated flatly. "Figure out those numbers. Our good friend Regis is going to take us to the airport, leaving you the rental."

"I imagine he was jumping at the chance to escort you right out of the holler." Anything to get rid of some or all of them.

"He was. We'll be back in a few days unless it takes a turn."

"You seen the aunt of this house yet? Hossie?" Violet asked.

"No. But we knocked on the door to her personal living space earlier, and she didn't answer. Door was locked too. According to Regis, she went to the doctor in Whitesburg this morning." Fiona checked her phone then glanced up as the car pulled in the drive. "He's here. Let's rock and roll."

Ty put his arm around Fiona as they walked to the front door. "Don't wear red and remember not everyone in the woods is your friend."

Fiona blinked once. Twice. Unamused. Asa scowled.

"Too soon?" Ty asked and tugged Fiona's hair.

Asa didn't bother with a response and Fiona just shook her head. Guess after catching the Nursery Rhyme Killer she could handle jokes about the woods, and Ty didn't seem to mean any harm.

Ty slapped Owen on his back on the way out the door.

"Stay out of the sorority houses. They may be hot, but they're only barely legal, bruh. And more drama than you can handle."

Owen rolled his eyes then closed the door behind them.

Ty spun and clapped his hands together. "Who's hungry?"

"I'm in charge, Tiberius Granger. I will not tolerate your stupidity or your random mental iTunes playlists."

His wicked grin foreshadowed misbehavior.

Violet's jaw clenched.

"Fine." He straightened his posture and sighed. "About those numbers. Six-two-zero-one-two-three-four-five-six. I tried the sixth book of the Bible. Joshua. I tried looking at chapter twenty-one—two, zero, one. Verses two, three, four, five and six. But it doesn't make sense. It's a chapter about the Levites having towns allotted to them, but I made note of the name in the verses. Dan. We have several Daniels, Dans and Dannys in Crow's Creek and Night Hollow. I have Selah going through them. But at the moment, they don't meet the loose profile we have."

"Then it's a dead end," Violet stated.

He held up his forefinger. "I didn't say that. I also looked at Joshua chapter twenty. That's a little more interesting, but I'm not sure it meets the criteria."

"Interesting how?" John asked. "It's the cities of refuge, right?"

Ty's eyebrows raised. "Yeah. You a Bible major?"

"I'm a student of the Word."

"Ah," Ty said dramatically, "Bible *thumper*. I hear ya."

That was not what he said at all, but he didn't feel the need to correct the religious-behavioral analyst.

"So check it. Cities of refuge were places singled out so if someone accidentally murdered another person they could flee to one of these nearest cities to cry sanctuary. You know, like the Humpback of Notre Dame. Cry sanctuary!" he hollered and raised his fists.

"I'm pretty sure it's *hunchback*. And what did I say about iTunes songs?" Violet said.

"That wasn't a song. I mean, it was actually in the Disney movie, but I chanted. You said nothing about chants, Vi." He waved her off as if she were ridiculous, but John hung with him. He was going somewhere. Eventually. "My question is could these women have seen a murder or accidentally committed a murder? Could this man be a relative of someone and he's avenging them? I don't know. I mean it's not out of the strange-crimes realm, but the fact that these women all had intercourse prior to their deaths is throwing me off. And avengers don't take trophies. Where's the eyes?"

"That's what Violet said."

"Of course she did." Ty batted his hand between him and Violet. "We have this wavelength thing going."

Did they?

Violet's eyebrow raised. "We have no thing going. Stop being stupid. I told you that you couldn't be stupid."

"Did you?" He playfully winked at John, revealing he wasn't interested in Violet romantically. That was a relief. "I thought it might be the sixth book of the New Testament, which is Romans, but it doesn't have twenty chapters. So I tried chapter two. Verse one, using the zero and the one. Then verses two, three, four, five and six. We might have something worth pursuing there."

Violet blinked rapidly. "Why didn't you lead with that?"

"I needed you to know I've been working."

"Get to it already," she said, her voice low and calm and collected.

"This is about judging and condemning other people when the one doing the judging and condemning is just as bad. The hypocrites say to condemn the wicked, but they should be condemned too because they're doing the same wicked things. We're looking at someone who may have been, or felt, condemned by these women, but they were equally as wicked. And God in His justice will punish them. He could be assuming the instrumental role in punishing them. Think about it. They are dark but lovely. Sinful. Pretty faces condemning, inside rotten and wicked. Verse five says they're storing up terrible punishment for themselves by doing this. I mean, let's be honest. What he's doing to them is pretty terrible."

This could be it. The information they needed to build a solid profile.

Violet placed her finger in her cleft. "They don't see that they're hypocritical and judging and condemning...because they can't see, he literally blinds them. They're in the dark to their sin therefore he literally puts them in the dark."

"Verse six says God will judge each one according to their works."

"He's bringing the pain. The punishment of God."

"What type of man are we looking for?" John asked.

Ty rubbed the scruff on his chin. "Religious. Devout to the rules."

"Legalistic, not someone who has a genuine relationship with God." John rolled it around. "Could be anyone."

His phone rang.

Greg.

Saturday, October 21
4:35 p.m.

Violet sat across from Ty at the Meat and Three Veg for an early dinner. Greg had called and wanted to meet with John again. Alone. He'd been gone for about an hour, and even though it was only a little past four thirty, Ty wasn't waiting on him for dinner. While he could be infantile most often, he was brilliant in his field of work. Romans 2:1–6 made sense to her, even if Ty wouldn't concretely say that was what the numbers meant. He wanted more time.

But if it was spot on, what were Tillie, Darla, Atta and Nadine condemning the killer for? Or condemning others for? He might be exacting punishment, but not in direct relation to him. Which would make it more difficult to find him.

"Nadine was a Whiskey Girl, and I'm starting to think that the other women were too." She speared a cherry tomato from her house salad, and Ty peppered his country-fried heart attack and mashed potatoes.

After a heaping bite, gravy dotting the corners of his mouth, he held up his fork and chewed. "We know they all cleaned houses, except Nadine, but we know for a fact she was a Whiskey Girl. We can't find a single person who knows whose houses they cleaned. No addresses. Customer list. I don't think they cleaned houses at all."

"You think they ran drugs and that's a front to hide what they were actually doing?"

"And maybe prostitution. Not all of them have been referred to as Whiskey Girls—who we know run drugs. But holler girls, which could be a term used for a hooker. Or maybe the terms are interchangeable depending on who you talk to."

"I wondered that myself, but we have no proof," Violet said.

"They did all have intercourse before they died. Not concrete proof." Ty dabbed his mouth with his napkin. "Still something to consider. Whiskey running drugs with one set of women and pimping another set. That would make him a lot of money and even more powerful."

"Mother mentioned the women giving money to the Lord. Charitable work in the name of Christianity. Could they have done that with drug or prostitution money or both? Could that be what's set off our killer?"

"Maybe."

She sipped her water and almost swallowed a lemon seed. "I asked for no lemon."

"Well, they do what they want up here. That much is clear," Ty said. "Most everyone goes to the church in the holler. That's Atta's brother's church. He's religious."

"He has access to the women. They wouldn't struggle or expect him. Speaking of access…" Might as well come clean. "I think the killer has access to the B and B." She told him about her missing undergarment. "I don't know that I'm actually being watched. It feels like it. This entire place…it feels like something invisible is hovering and slithering, staking its claim and having its way."

Ty paused midbite. "You're freaking me out."

"You don't feel it? Sense it?" How could anyone not? It was dark and heavy like breath releasing from a vile place. "I don't mean the people—not all of them. The place. Especially the house. It's the same sensation I felt in that cabin on our first day here. The one where we found that photo of the little girl. Have you heard anything from Selah on that or figured out who the place belonged to?"

Ty shook his head. "We found who the land belongs to, but we don't know, yet, if the cabin had been rented or if he lived there. Trying to locate him." A prankish gleam formed in his eyes. "Name is Cotton Joseph Wilkes."

"Don't," Violet warned, knowing this was heading down a musical pipeline. She was not up for Ty's rendition of "Cotton-Eyed Joe."

"Well, we *don't* know where he came from or where he goes." Ty ran a roll through his thick white country gravy. "I could eat this every day."

"Ugh."

He shoved it in his mouth, his right cheek bulging as he closed his eyes and clutched his chest. "Paradise," he said through a full mouth. After he chewed and swallowed, he sipped his sweet tea. "But for real. While you were having a sleepover with John—"

"There was no sleeping over. I stayed at my town house. He stayed at his home. I never even saw his place."

"You like him. K-i-s-s-i-n-g." His shoulders moved up and down in rotation with each letter he sang out.

She tossed the lemon wedge she'd yanked from her water into his face. "I do not." But that wasn't true. She did like him. Quite a lot.

"It's cool to like someone, Violet. He's stand-up. You should go for it. He's into you."

"How would you even know?"

"I'm a federal agent."

That made her laugh.

His eyes grew big. "Look at that. She laughs. And at my expense. You're more tolerable these past few days. I think it's him. Bringing out the chill pill in you."

"Nobody says that anymore." But he might be right.

Ty pushed his plate aside and wadded up his napkin. "I'm a dude. I date a lot. I know."

"Why don't you ever get serious with anyone?" she asked and pulled a piece off her crusty French bread, dipping it in the honey butter. Bread was her one indulgence, and one didn't eat bread without butter.

"I was. Once. I was gonna get married."

Violet paused with the bread halfway to her mouth. "You lie."

"I'm not lying. I fell in love, but she...she married someone else and that was that. I'll never ever fall in love again.

Or get married." His eyes started to shine, and he blinked, sniffed. "Now, let's split a sundae, and I'll even give you the cherry on top."

He kinda already had. This explained a great deal of his infantile behavior. "Does Asa know this?"

"Nobody knows. Just you and me. Our little secret." He leaned back, arms over his chest. "Why aren't you serious or married or with a partner?"

"Because I'm a potential serial killer, and I can't be sure anyone close is ever safe." She held his gaze. She'd never voiced that fear. That she could be a killer. That she had some same tendencies.

Finally he shook his head. "I get dead serious, and you throw that ridiculousness at me? I thought we had something going here." He stood and tossed a twenty on the table. "Come on."

But he didn't know what she'd done.

One push was all it had taken.

She followed him through the cramped diner as the front door opened and Wanda Boyd entered with a woman who looked a lot like her only in her mid to late fifties. Striking, with a little too much eyeliner. Wanda waved to a server and ignored them as she made her way to the woman.

The other woman held open the door, and as she stretched her arm across the glass to give them plenty of space, Violet caught a glimpse of her wrist.

The room tilted and Violet's breath caught.

Under the sleeve of her leather coat was a puckered burn and tiny branches shooting upward on her arm.

No. This couldn't be right. She met the woman's eyes as they stood gawking at one another.

"How did you get that brand?" Violet asked, ignoring Ty looming behind her.

The woman retracted her hand from the door, and the brand disappeared under the leather sleeve. "I don't know what you mean."

"Yes, you do. I saw it. You know I saw it." She grabbed the woman's hand without thinking to see the mark more clearly.

"Hey!" she exclaimed. "Let go of me!" She tried to yank free, but Violet tightened her grip.

"Violet," Ty said sternly. "Let go."

Violet shoved the woman's sleeve above her wrist, and the branded tree came into perfect view.

Identical to Reeva's.

"You have it. You knew Adam. Tell me how you got this."

"Let me go!" The woman ripped her arm away, and Ty grabbed Violet's arm before she could reach out again. She had to know. This was a break, a lead. An opportunity.

Adrenaline raced through her veins, and her pulse pounded.

"What's going on?" Wanda demanded, approaching with a scowl.

"She has the brand. How?"

"Leave me and my daughter alone. Come on, Loretta."

But Loretta's eyes were locked on Violet. There was no hiding it.

Loretta Boyd had been one of Adam's victims.

Did Violet have a half-sibling in Night Hollow? Who?

And could it be the Blind Eye Killer?

Chapter Thirteen

Saturday, October 21
5:52 p.m.

Violet's hands trembled as she stormed from the car at the B and B. Ty had attempted to pry, but she didn't want to speak. It was all too much. She hadn't expected that, hadn't been prepared.

That was Adam's mark. His brand. Here in Night Hollow. How was that even possible? Violet hadn't been tracking a lead or pursuing that particular case, yet the very case she was working led her to this?

Violet didn't always believe in coincidences, but she had no idea what else to call it. She wanted that woman to talk. Loretta. Wanda Boyd's daughter. Mother's granddaughter.

Mother said Lula was her great-great-granddaughter. Her mother might be Violet's sister. She also had a purse like the other women. Which meant she was potentially in great danger.

Or maybe she had a brother. Could she have a brother

wreaking havoc in Kentucky? It wasn't that far-fetched that all of Adam's offspring would be corrupted moral failures. Even killers.

Violet herself had…pushed that girl.

John's car was here. He must be inside. She wanted to know what Greg had to say, but she didn't want to talk right now. Her thoughts were all over the place.

Ty blocked her at the porch. "You don't have to tell me what happened, but this isn't the first time you've freaked out on a total stranger. Need I remind you about what you did back in July? You're the lead investigator now, so you have to act like it. And I can't even believe you're forcing me to be the level-headed adult here." Ty scoffed and stomped up the porch then turned back. "I'm going to wash out the lecture taste, it's sour." He entered and slammed the door behind him.

He was right. She couldn't go grabbing people and demanding information. At least not when she was the senior investigator. Asa left her in charge because she was generally the responsible one who didn't get all up in arms and emotional about things.

Bypassing the front door, she tromped across the spongy yard, her feet sinking into the wet earth, leaves sticking to the bottom of her boots. The rain had been off and on all day and was going to start up again later this evening, bringing a cold front. She folded her arms over her chest and hunched forward, taking the crisp gales head-on.

The house was built on a hill that sloped down toward the river. As she made her slippery descent, the wind grew colder, harsher, and dots of water sprinkled her face. Leaning against a large pine, she kicked at wet needles and tried to wrap her brain around what she'd just experienced. Could she get information from Mother? Would she be willing to speak of the past and help Violet? She was all about helping people.

"Hey," John softly said as he trekked down the hill to the tree she stood under. A pinecone fell in front of her feet.

She wanted to tell him to go away. Being alone was the whole reason for coming down here. She'd handle her feelings and the circumstances alone. But instead she said, "Hey." Because below the surface, she didn't want to handle it alone. Be alone. She wanted him to be here, and that terrified her.

"Ty said you got handsy at the restaurant, and at first I thought he meant you got handsy with him. Then I realized you'd never do that." He sidled up beside her. "He told me about you snatching a lady and forcing her to tell you about a mark on her."

He didn't prod or pry. Instead, he leaned against the tree and watched the river roll as he inhaled the briny scent, the earth and the rain coming in.

"I think she knows something about my mom's abduction when she was fifteen. Their ages are close. She has the same brand on her arm. It's a tree burned into the flesh. Unmistakable. But she acted as if she had no clue what I was talking about."

No one wanted to talk. Violet didn't blame them. The trauma was unbearable, horrifying. Her own mom had spent her life in depression and bouts of anger. What had she been like prior to the abduction? What had Grandmother been like? If it hadn't been for Adam and the violence, would Reeva have grown up and married? Had a family she planned and wanted?

Violet would never know.

"I know you want to find your mom's abductor. I want to find who killed Callie. I realize I may never get him. I am at peace with that though, Violet. Are you?"

Easy answer. "No." She tucked her hair behind her ear and out of her eyes. "If you're at peace either way, why bother at all?"

He cocked his head as if she'd asked a ridiculous question. "Justice. I want justice for Callie. Someone did unspeakable things to her and left her to rot as if she were garbage and not a human being. He's continuing to do that, and he needs to be stopped. They all need justice, and I believe that we pursue it on earth, but if we don't see it, it will still come."

"In the next life? From God? Why not prevent it from happening at all?"

"Do you like making your own choices and decisions? I do. People have that freedom. All people. And not all make even decent choices. There's violence and corruption, but there's goodness too, Violet."

She supposed that made sense enough. "I haven't seen much good."

"The fact you're here on a case and are presented with a clue to the one who drives you is good. I call that providence." John slid his hand in hers. It was warm for how chilly it was outside. He squeezed. "I believe that God often directs us when we don't even realize that's what is happening. It's His divine care for you, Violet. His goodness. And wise ways."

She wished that were true. It would be comforting. "You think God brought me here on this case to give me answers to the one I want?"

John sighed. "I don't know if you'll get the answers you want or any at all. But maybe there's something more important, better than answers. Maybe there's something here you need. He knows it. You don't."

"I don't know, John. That sounds like some cheesy TV movie where it all ends happy and no one feels any aftershocks from the pain."

He brushed the stray hair back in place. "There are always aftershocks from pain. It's not cheesy." He searched her eyes. "You're not an accident, Violet. You were made on purpose."

Why would he say that? How could he say that? He had no idea that while Adam had a purpose in making her, Reeva absolutely had not. She was a blight not a blessing. There was nothing loving or special about her conception or birth. It had been in violence in the cold, dark baby basement.

"You don't know anything about me, John," she whispered through a mountainous lump residing in her throat. But the words he spoke…though untrue, made a heated trail into her heart and settled in like warm fire.

Like hope.

"I want to, Violet. I want to know everything about you. I want to unwrap it all and see what's in there." His sight trailed to her lips and her heart rate sped up. Yesterday, she'd wanted to be kissed by him, had even spurred him to do it. But he hadn't. He said he wouldn't kiss her unless he'd stolen her heart. He hadn't.

But those words. Him.

Yesterday, they'd been flirting, but now it felt like he was declaring something. It was intimate. Nothing playful or shallow.

His lips hovered over hers, waiting…

Panic seized her, and she blurted, "My father is Adam, my mom's abductor." A kiss might be the tipping point for her heart, and she wasn't ready to face it, to respond.

He blinked and paused his slow descent.

"I was conceived on purpose. I'm not sure what his purpose was. But it wasn't good. And… I have his DNA coursing through me. You don't want to know me under the surface. You can't know me. I don't even fully know myself." She pushed away from him and stalked up the hill.

"Wait! Violet, wait!" He muttered and growled then she heard his faster footsteps hurrying to catch up. He blocked her, faced her and let out a breath. "You can't drop that kind of bomb on me and then blow away like a breeze. You weren't conceived in love, but that doesn't mean you don't deserve to love and be loved."

Tears stung her eyes. She couldn't remember the last time she'd cried. It wasn't her thing, but his words, they kept coddling the tender places within her. Places she'd hardened over years of hurt and disappointment.

"You are loved, Violet."

She raised her chin. "Yeah? By who? My mom thinks I'm a monster, and she's not far off base. You don't know the things I've done. My grandmother tolerated me. Men who have been with me have only gone surface deep, nothing past pretty. So who. Loves. Me?"

"God loves you, Violet. He knew how you'd be born. Where. Knew you'd be right here. Right now. Talking to me. Arguing with me. Because you're bossy. I remember." He smirked and framed her face. "And He loves you. Die-for-you kind of love, Violet."

She couldn't. It was too much. Too hard to listen to. She wanted to reach out and stake her claim on the words. Wanted to believe that if she cried out in faith, she'd be free from the hopeless dark prison that held her captive.

She opened her mouth, and the hairs on her neck stood on end as if something slippery and sinister had nestled up beside her.

There is no God. And if there was, He wouldn't want you. Tell John what you did to Lynn Tavish. Tell him how you watched after you pushed her. Tell him. No one has saved you. No one will save you. No one can save you. You're your father's daughter. When are you gonna embrace it?

She swallowed down the aching cry and dark thoughts. Blinked back the tears and cleared her vision. "I'd rather discuss the case and what you found out from Greg. I don't want to talk about me or my soul or how Jesus loves me because the Bible tells me so. If I wanted to be preached to, I'd go to a church service. Do we understand?" It was cold. Harsh. And lies, if she would allow herself to be honest.

Disappointment filled his eyes. "I understand. I'm not sorry, but I'll abide by your wishes."

A sliver of herself wanted to take her words back and ask him to repeat the ones he'd just spoken instead—words that breathed like life and not death—but she refrained and the risen neck hairs slowly dissipated as if the sinister presence had been satisfied. She shook out of it and glanced beside her to check. See if she could see anything.

She never could. Never had.

Only her own punishing thoughts.

"Thank you." She began walking uphill again. She'd been walking uphill since she was born. "I need a few minutes, and then I'll meet you on the back porch. I want to hear what Greg said. I hope it's good and gets us somewhere."

John sat in the rocking chair on the screened-in porch, waiting on Violet to return to share the news from earlier. It was hard for him to concentrate on the case when Violet had revealed the truth about her birth and her father, though he'd suspected it.

The baggage she carried was a lifetime of heavy weight, and the rift with her maternal family had been brought into sharper focus. John's family was far from perfect, but he'd never felt unloved or unwanted. Not even during his most wayward moments.

Violet had never felt loved. Worse than never even feeling love, she believed she was unlovable. A lie developed from childhood experience and from hateful words slung in her face from a terribly hurt person. He worked in missing persons, and on the few occasions they found a survivor, the person came back empty and hollow. Without proper counseling and care, they never healed. He suspected Reeva had remained a shell of her former self.

And in the meantime, Violet had been used as a punching bag for the pain, riddled with lies, and it would take powerful truths to untangle and dissolve that and free her.

It would take…love. He closed his eyes and prayed for Violet. To feel the love of God. To see through the darkness to His light. That He wasn't outside the darkness but there in the midst and not hiding. She was blinded, and she desperately needed to see. Not what was tangible but what was real. And true. He ached for her, ached for her to see…to know. To experience.

She was a psychologist. She knew the mind, emotion. But she was deep in a web that had spun around her and cocooned her in. Reason wouldn't work. Logic was useless.

He leaned forward, resting his elbows on his knees and digging his hands into his hair. He prayed a little longer then checked his watch. She'd been upstairs for fifteen minutes. His thoughts wandered to Greg and their conversation earlier.

"I'm sorry, John. I don't want Callie's killer to get away. I owe her, so I'm going to tell you something the locals won't. Whiskey owns a bar up near the head of the holler. Back in the hills. It's called the Swallow. He coordinates out of there. If by chance you discover it and go in there, remember no one is friendly. No one is going to tell you the truth, and if I'm there, I'll be of no assistance to you. Do you understand?"

John wasn't sure if he was getting good information or an invitation to get the stuffing kicked out of him. Greg wouldn't confirm or deny that the first three victims were Whiskey Girls. He denied Whiskey being the Blind Eye Killer. But John wasn't sure Greg believed that.

"You can question him, but don't expect answers, and he might toss you out on your head. I'm not breaking cover for you. But I will tell you something else. Earl Levine and Bobby Lloyd are dead. I didn't see Whiskey kill them. Didn't have to. Bobby hurt Atta. Earl got drunk and stupid and hurt more than one of the holler girls. Quit looking for them."

John inquired about Cecil Johnson, but Greg didn't have much on him. He didn't hang out at the Swallow often. But some interesting folks did, and they would be more useful to John than Whiskey himself. With that cryptic bit of information, he'd left the bar they used as a rendezvous point.

The screen door opened and Violet entered. She'd changed into jeans and an oversize sweater that matched her eyes. Bluish-green. Her hair was brushed, and she wore a pair of Duck Head boots. "Well?"

"You wanna go out to a bar with me?"

"Are you asking me on a date?"

The tension had receded between them, and she was back to her way of teasing. "Our first date isn't going to be at a bar," he said lightly. They weren't having a first date. Things wouldn't work between them. Not because of her history or the sobering truth she'd dropped on him. John wasn't scared of baggage. He had his own nice-size trunk of mistakes, junk and shame. He couldn't forget that her job was her first love, and it was dangerous. He'd seen how Stella had quickly been fond of her. He wasn't bringing anyone into the house for Stella to get attached to, only to lose them. And there was the whole big other thing where they didn't share the same faith, and that could cause complications down the road.

But all of these factors and truths didn't change the way his heart was feeling about her. Almost kissing her had been his brain's lapse in judgment as his heart usurped the throne, and it was holding its spot for the long haul.

"Well, I'd hope you would have more class than that."

He stood and grinned as he glanced toward the house. "Should we ask Ty to join us?"

"No. He's working on the numbers and deep in it. When he finally gets in his zone, he's in. I did apologize to him and told him what he needed to know to appease him. I'll text him, fill him in on what we're doing. What are we doing exactly?"

John gave her the rundown of his conversation with Greg. "I thought maybe we'd watch from behind the scenes. See who goes in and out then make our way inside."

Violet texted Ty. Her phone dinged. She snickered. "He said be careful. Steer clear of the Wild Turkey and don't get handsy with any middle-aged women."

"You did do a number today at the diner."

"No," she held up the phone for him to see the text, "that warning was for you."

John read it and laughed. "Tell him I'll try to be a gentleman."

"Will we be able to get a vehicle up to the head of the holler?" she asked.

John opened the car for her. "He said it's a tight squeeze and with all the rain it might be muddy. I say let's take our chances."

Violet slid into the seat. "I had a feeling you'd say that."

John eased out of the driveway and turned left. "I have ponchos and flares."

"Wow. You go all out on a first date."

Saturday, October 21
8:22 p.m.

Ruby sat on a hard barstool and batted cigarette smoke from her burning eyes. She didn't hang out at the Swallow much these days, not since Lula was born, since she and Whiskey had complicated things by having her. He wasn't inattentive when he was around his daughter, he was simply absent most of the time.

Two hours ago, he'd summoned her, and when Whiskey called, you came without making him wait. And after the big blowout with Regis last night, she was worried. Regis might have told Whiskey her plans as a ploy to keep her bound to the holler. Not that Regis cared for Whiskey or felt an obligation. He didn't have any interest in him at all, but he ignored Whiskey's business without trouble. Because he'd been told to. Period. And if he didn't want to disappear, he followed the rules.

Mostly Regis hated that Whiskey and Ruby had been something once. And that they had a child together. When she'd told Regis she was leaving, he explained clearly why that would never happen.

Their conversation had heated until she finally stormed from Regis's house. She never should have told him. But she needed someone, and Regis had some authority. Except he wouldn't use it to rescue her and Lula, to help them make a better life.

The music was louder than the laughter. Cadie Rae was playing darts with Jerry Billings and tossing back shots. Bella Dawn was in a secluded booth with a frisky Greg. Bella Dawn wasn't a huge fan of Greg personally, but no one would know that. Not that he was unattractive or unappealing—he wasn't. He was actually easy on the eyes, and he always smelled good underneath the hint of booze. But since the day she'd met him, there was something off about him. He'd been handsy with Tillie and Darla at one time, until Atta.

Then he never strayed. But Atta was now dead, and it appeared Bella Dawn was his new toy. Ruby sighed and fiddled with the toothpick lying on the counter, her stomach in knots.

She had no idea what Whiskey wanted, and he was nowhere to be found. He had no problem making her wait.

"Hey," a soft tenor voice said. Cecil Johnson slid onto a stool next to her. He wore a brown sweater and jeans and hiking boots. His hair had been pulled back in a low ponytail; a few curly strands that wouldn't fit fell around his face. "What are you doing here? You're too good for this place."

"I could ask the same of you, CeCe." CeCe. A nickname he didn't particularly like, but it was a habit from childhood. "Sorry."

"It's okay. Old habits die hard." He ordered a Miller Lite in the bottle. "You never said what you're doing here."

"Neither did you." She sipped her vodka tonic, hoping it would settle her nerves. "Whiskey called. I'm waiting on him to emerge and grace me with his presence."

His laugh was light and shimmery. "I don't understand why you still bother with him." He shrugged. "At least you got your girl from it. Saw her with Mother the other day in town."

She did have Lula. Her one ray of hope. "Because when Whiskey calls, you come. And you know that." And part of her still wanted him to want her. She was a mess. "Why are you here?"

"Just…felt like a drink."

Donnie Ray set his beer in front of him and winked. Cecil bristled.

"Ignore him. He's a jerk." She finished off her drink, letting the warmth flow down her throat and pool in her gut, relaxing her. She looked to the right where the stairs led to rooms above. Heavy boots bounded down one step at a time until Whiskey's frame came into view. He spotted her then motioned for her to follow him behind the doors into the back of the bar, where patrons were only allowed if invited.

To do business. And to his private quarters.

"Gotta go."

"See you, Rube." She looked back and sighed. Then she approached Whiskey, and he opened the doors and led her through to the back room. She'd been here a million times before. They passed an open area where a few men sat hunched over poker tables, a different smoke hovering in the air. Nothing stunk worse than skunk. He led her to another narrow staircase that led to his private living quarters.

Inside his studio apartment, he opened the fridge. "I got that wine you like. You want a glass?"

"Sure." He was buying her wine. What was the occasion? He opened the merlot then poured it in the stemless wine glass that had been sitting in a drying rack. Someone had used it before her. It wasn't Whiskey.

A woman.

The rejection mixed with envy. He poured a bourbon neat and sat beside her at the table. She sipped her wine. "It's good. Thanks."

After a drink, he scooted closer. "Ruby, you know I trust you more than anyone in this holler."

Doubtful.

"Okay."

"I wouldn't ask you what I'm about to if it wasn't dire straits." He sighed and she smelled mint and whiskey on his breath. His dark hair hung in his eyes, and she had the urge to brush it back, but she kept her hands balled on her lap. "You know Nadine was my best girl…"

Ruby's breath was stolen, and her lungs turned to concrete. He would not. Could not ask what he was about to.

"Baby," he lightly caressed her cheek, "I got a big, big score, and I don't trust anyone else to do this. I know you stopped doing side jobs for me because of Lula, and I fully approved and still do. She needs her mama, and work was dangerous.

But this is the mother lode, babe. Please. I'm asking you to do this."

Asking, or was it phrased for courtesy's sake? "Whiskey, don't ask me this," she squeaked, her voice suddenly hidden. Her hands trembled.

His eyes hardened. "It has to be your choice."

Of course it did. She had a measure of protection some in the holler didn't have.

"I would never endanger Lula."

No, just Ruby. "I can't, Whiskey. I can't risk it."

His jaw hardened, and he balled his hand at his side so tightly his knuckle popped. He wouldn't force her. Couldn't.

"I was hoping you'd do it because you love me, but… I see you don't. Guess Regis won that one."

Ruby stood. "This has nothing to do with Regis Owsley. It has everything to do with I hate drugs. I have a daughter."

"And I know you don't want her around all this." His eyes narrowed. "Let me offer you something no one else can or is willing to. You run this one time for me. Deliver the product, bring back the money. You can keep twenty percent, and I'll get you out of this holler."

She snapped her attention toward him. Met his dark eyes. "And Lula?"

"Free to go. I know it's what you want. You think I don't know about the money under the mattress, Ruby? You'll never make enough to leave when you want. I know people. You can change your whole identity if you choose. Go anywhere. Make a life. I'll make sure you have enough to get settled and for Lula. Maybe she'll be something better than we ever were. Are." He shrugged, and she saw the truth in that. He did want better for their daughter, but he wasn't above using her as leverage.

If she did this one run. She could get out as soon as it was over. Go anywhere. "Can I trust you?"

"Have I ever lied to you, Ruby?"

No. "Then tell me one more truth. Did you ever love me?"

He inhaled and framed her face, slowly kissed her lips. Warm with the taste of spicy bourbon. "As much as one man can love a woman like you," he murmured against her lips and tears stung her eyes, but they didn't burn as intensely as those four words flamed over her heart.

...a woman like you...

"I'll take your deal. I want enough to get in a good place with a decent car and money in the bank. I want Lula in a good school, and I want far out of here."

"Done." He grinned and kissed her hard on the mouth and then drew her closer. "Since you're here...let's seal that deal."

A tear threatened to surface, but she forced her cries to remain silent and in the dark.

Chapter Fourteen

Saturday, October 21
9:52 p.m.

Violet and John crouched, hidden in the bosky area on the east side of the Swallow, a two-story building that reminded her of an old country mill. The top floor had an outer deck, and a few people had congregated up there to drink, talk and make out. She'd seen worse.

Classic country music filtered into the night air along with the scents of marijuana, cigarette and wood smoke. Trucks and UTVs were scattered in the open area in no real order.

John had parked half a mile down behind some brush, and they'd hoofed it the rest of the way. She'd made a good call on the shoes. The ground was soggy and downright muddy in some areas. The trees rustled, and rain splattered on her face. She studied the patrons cycling in and out. Some looked to be there for a friendly time, but there were more sinister-looking faces and what might be some underhanded exchanges going on in the parking lot. But that wasn't why they were here.

The only familiar faces they'd seen enter in the almost hour they'd been scoping out the place were Cecil Johnson and Amy Miller—Darla Boone's roommate. She'd been zero help aiding them in discovering who Darla cleaned for, which was why Violet was almost certain the victims were Whiskey Girls, running drugs and possibly prostituting themselves under his authority. People benefited from it, or they were too afraid to talk for fear they'd disappear like Earl Levine and Bobby Lloyd.

"I really do not like this guy Whiskey. Let's go inside. Shake the branches of the tree with our presence and see what falls out. Nonchalant."

"Easy for you to say. You're always nonchalant." He playfully nudged her shoulder.

They strode through the parking lot, turning heads, then entered the establishment, noticing but ignoring the wide eyes, scowls and whispers as they slowly moved through the fog of smoke and couples slow dancing to "Anymore" by Travis Tritt.

"That takes me back," John muttered as they scanned the crowded bar.

"To what? The womb?"

"Eew. I meant listening to it in my teenage years because old country was cool. Now you've ruined it for me." His voice was pleasant, but his eyes were wary as they scanned the bar, the patrons, hoping to spot Whiskey. A man like him, John had a feeling they'd know him when they saw him. A few men in the corner had halted their game of pool to glare. Others scattered or looked away.

John led them to the bar with a nicked wooden top and non-fancy barstools. Violet sat next to Cecil Johnson. "Hello again," she said. He didn't seem to fit in either, but he appeared relaxed.

He pulled on his beer then set it down with a quiet click. "Hello again, Agent. Doesn't seem like your kind of atmosphere. Official business?"

"I'm always on official business, Mr. Johnson."

He turned his attention to John. "How you liking that wallet?"

"Very nice, thanks." John leaned against the bar then paused as his sight landed in the corner booth.

"I never asked what you plan to do with your cross."

Violet kept her gaze on John and the booth, then he turned. "I'll be back." He headed for the hall near the bathrooms.

Cecil repeated his earlier statement.

She shrugged. "I don't know. What would you do with it?"

"I'd probably hang it somewhere I could see it often. Let it remind me of my sins so as not to repeat them. A sin repeated isn't a mistake, you know." He tapped his spindly finger on the bar. "Another, Donnie."

"Another what, CeCe?"

Cecil eyed the bartender. "You know, Agent, some men play dumb. Some...they just are. Consequences of inbreeding."

Donnie came across the bar, but Cecil was fast—lightning fast—and pulled back. "Tsk-tsk. You don't want to do that, Donnie." Their eyes met, and Donnie backed down.

Was he afraid of Cecil? Cecil didn't appear tough, not compared to the bartender's brawn, but his eyes...those intense blue eyes were cold. Piercing.

Cecil shifted on his stool. "Would you like to dance, Agent?"

She met his gaze. "No, thank you."

"I see."

"Nobody wants you here, pig!" a deep voice boomed. Violet swiveled as the old-school jukebox quieted, clicked, and Three Dog Night's "Shambala" filled the smoky atmosphere.

She noticed the drunk in the far corner huffing and puffing. It appeared John had it under control, but she kept an eye on him in case it escalated.

That was when a ruckus broke out on the opposite side of the bar.

Two brawny fellows in saggy jeans and ball caps low over their eyes pushed one another as the electric guitar riffed, introducing the song.

Curses ensued and the shorter man cracked a pool stick and came for the other guy in a drunken vengeance. Their friends worked to break it up to no avail, and tables toppled and chairs tipped over.

"You going to do anything about that?" Cecil casually asked as he sipped his beer.

"Nope." Violet could care less if the locals kicked the junk out of each other. She hoped it'd get rowdier, then it might produce Whiskey.

Beer bottles crashed to the floor, shattering glass. A crowd grew. Sides were taken.

John glanced at a man in a corner booth, but the guy downed his bourbon and kissed the girl beside him. John threw his hands up and entered the fray to bring order. As if a badge would bring peace to this war. And why did he look to the man for any help? Must be the undercover DEA agent—Greg.

John hollered, "Police!"

It fell on deaf ears.

And Violet looked on. Waiting.

"Your buddy's gonna get his head bashed in, you know. That's Bear Wheeler and his cracked-out crew. Ain't nothin' good comin' of this."

The commotion spilled into the bar area and the dance floor, knocking couples to the floor and inciting men to take up for their women. The only thing missing was the cartoon swirls of smoke around them.

A pool ball flew over their heads and crashed into the mirror behind the bar.

Violet ducked and turned to check on Cecil, but like that earlier lightning move, he'd already vanished. She crouched under the bar, searching for John in time to see a barrel-chested guy coldcock him.

Now, she was going to do something about it.

Growling under her breath, she pulled her weapon and left the credentials where they belonged. The floor was littered with glass, peanuts and napkins, slick with alcohol, blood and broken furniture. Violet was ready to shut this mess down.

John was on the floor rolling around with the jackwagon who'd sucker-punched him. She began her march to end it all when a sound caught her attention.

Crying from behind the bar.

Not a woman's cries.

A child's.

She weaved and bobbed through the chaos and clutter to find a little boy about three, maybe four, in race car pajamas crying for his mommy and holding a little cowboy rag doll. *Who brings a kid to a bar?*

Another bottle struck the wall behind the bar.

The floor was a sheath of shattered glass. The boy had on footy pajamas—no shoes. "Stay there. I'm coming to you." Then she planned to stalk down the parent or guardian and kick the dumb out of them for bringing him here then abandoning him. "It's okay. It's okay," she kept offering as she maneuvered around the shards. She scooped up the baby. "Where's your mama?"

"I don't know. I fink hers upstairs." He hiccupped and clung to Violet's neck like a vise.

"Okay, let's get you out of here. Then we'll find your mama." And kill her.

John would have to handle the guy on his own. He was a big boy. Right now, this child needed help. She found the closest exit, but it was packed with people trampling one another to get away. Weren't there bouncers in the bar?

The room behind the bar. She had no clue what was back there, but it was her only clear shot. She kicked the door open and entered a large illegal gambling room. Full of tables with men and women drinking, playing... She covered the child's eyes. Some things going on were highly inappropriate. A guy stood.

Violet pulled her gun and aimed it at his face. "Sit down." She'd pull the trigger, and her tone conveyed it. The man sat.

"What's going on out there?" a woman asked through slurs.

"Nobody moves until I'm out the door with this child." Violet strode to a door on the east wall at the back of the building and opened it with the hand she had around the little boy, keeping her eyes on the room full of inebriated patrons. Once she was outside, she kicked it shut and took off around the front. The fight had made its way into the parking lot.

She had no vehicle. No one trustworthy to take the child. She rushed toward the tree line and into the brush then placed the child behind a large tree trunk. Was John okay? Worry thumped in her chest. "What's your name?"

"Mason."

"Mason. I'm Violet. I'm a police officer, and I'm gonna make sure you're okay." But who was going to look after John? And where was Whiskey? "You hang on to the little cowboy..." She noticed the scarf covering its face. Like an outlaw. It was sheer material. Like racy underwear. She touched it and noticed it had been cut. Her stomach roiled as thoughts snapped through her mind until her attention was snagged by a woman racing from the back of the bar along the edge of the property, a purse in hand. A shotgun blast fired, and she squealed and ducked.

"Over here!" Violet hollered. "I'm a federal agent. Come to me!" Otherwise the woman might get her head blown off.

The woman crouched and darted toward her, long dark hair blowing in the breeze. At least the rain had let up.

Thunder rumbled.

Lovely.

The woman approached, her face shadowed but her form was tall, lean. Violet smelled the sweet scent of perfume, cigarette smoke and alcohol as she crouched beside her.

"Miss Ruby!" the little boy cried and reached for the woman.

"Mason? What's going on out here?" Her voice was sweet and soprano. Violet snagged her cell phone. "I found him inside behind the bar. Do you know him?"

"Yeah. His mom is Bella Dawn. A friend of mine. I'm Ruby."

Violet shined the light to see the woman. Her heart jumped into her throat, and she swallowed hard. Long dark hair. Blue-green eyes. Squared jaw...the subtle hint of a cleft in her chin. Not as pronounced as hers. High cheekbones.

"Ruby Boyd?" Violet asked through a dry mouth.

"Yeah."

Violet lost her breath.

It was undeniable.

She was staring down her half-sister.

John took another punch to the ribs and tossed out his police procedural knowledge. All the announcements he might declare as the law would fall on deaf ears. Between the music, the brawl and the screams, no one would hear and no one cared.

He swung around with a right hook and laid the guy out on the ground.

Three rounds fired inside the building, sending the frenzy into a state of shock. The fighting died down, and cries from women could be heard under what tables were left upright.

Violet. Where was she? Had she been hurt? He'd been tied up in the thick of it and unable to find her.

A guy picked up a chair, and another shot whizzed beside him, leaving a hole in the wall next to his head. John whipped in the direction of the gunfire.

Violet stood in the open area, gun aimed and icy fury in her eyes. "Next one to move gets a bullet to the brain. Am I clear?"

She searched the bar, her sight landed on John and she sighed.

"Enough." A sharp voice cut through the noise. Greg stood with a shotgun. "Party's over." He cursed the place out and called out Bear Wheeler and Joey Jacobs to make their way upstairs. They'd started the brawl.

"Miss Law Lady, you can put your weapon away. Now. We got this under control."

Violet appeared bored. "I think I'll pass, thank you."

Why hadn't he done this earlier when John was getting the stuffin' beaten out of him? The only reason Greg even intervened was Violet coming in guns blazing, literally, which she could get in a lot of trouble for. He stood on shaky feet; his ribs and head ached. His nose and lip were bloody, and his hand hurt from the punch he'd thrown. He hobbled through the debris to Violet.

"Everybody out," Greg said.

People began exiting. Trucks rumbled. Headlights flashed through the windows. "There's a kid out there. I left him with someone he knows. My gut says he's in good hands, but I want to make sure we get them somewhere secure."

"Who would bring a child into this place?"

"Someone named Bella Dawn. When I find her, I'm gonna snatch her bald-headed."

And she said she didn't have any maternal instinct. The place emptied faster than a church full of sinners and John locked eyes on Greg. "You'd have come to the rescue earlier, might not be such a mess here."

"I was busy." He sniffed and John kicked through the trash and stalked outside. He needed to cool off. Striding toward the creek, he let the cold fill his bones, put the fire out. Greg was busy? No, more like he was enjoying the show. John could have been killed. Maybe that was what Greg wanted. Maybe the tip tonight was a setup.

"Hey." Violet met up with him. "Ruby's looking for Bella Dawn. She wouldn't leave without Mason. You and I both know Whiskey's up in that bar. I say we go back in and find him. Process of elimination." She shined the cell phone light on him. "Man, you're looking rough."

"But it's manly and attractive, right?"

"Whatever you say." She chuckled. "I would have come sooner but...the kid. And I'm not leaving until we get him somewhere secure. I'm not sure that means going back to his mom."

He winced. "I'm with you. I need some aspirin. Big time."

She touched his cheek, and he flinched. "Sorry," she said.

"Don't be. Under different circumstances, I'd welcome the touch." He groaned. "You can get in a lot of trouble for shooting in an open bar with civilians, Violet."

"Yeah, because these guys are gonna be willing to cough up a secret bar that runs illegal gambling, drugs and, I'm quite sure, hookers. They do things their own way up here.

I couldn't beat 'em with the badge. I joined 'em. It's not like we were in Atlanta at a mall."

Guess she had a point. A flash of lightning bolted across the sky and cast light on something near the water's edge. "Hey, shine your light over there." John moved toward the pink material. Violet followed. Lying under a bush was a torn piece of a garment. "Doesn't that look like the partial shirt Atta Atwater was wearing in the cave?"

"Yeah," Violet said as she squatted and examined it further. "I can't tell, but is that dark spot rain or dried blood? There's a broken beer bottle over here too. We need to bag this." They took photos. No crime-scene kit on them to document it better. They did what they could.

"I'm going to go get a plastic bag if they have one and be back. You stay here." John raced inside. The place was empty, wrecked. Voices from behind the bar drew him, and he entered the room.

Greg stood next to a guy with chin-length dark hair. Next to him, a woman stood with a small child—must be the one Violet saved. He froze as he set his sights on her face.

The resemblance was uncanny. Shocking even.

"What are you doing in here?" Greg boomed. His eyes narrowed, and he took a menacing step toward him. Was he serious or in character?

John raised his hands. "Hey, man. I need a plastic bag. Clean if you got one." He glanced again at the woman holding the child.

"Get him the bag, Greg," the woman said. "He's here to help."

Greg cursed.

"Are you Whiskey?" John asked.

"Who's asking?"

John retrieved his badge. "Detective John Orlando. I'm here investigating the murders—"

"I know what you're here doing. I have nothing to say or to do with those girls getting killed." He glanced at Greg. "Get him a bag. Get him gone."

"Actually, I'm not going anywhere until we talk. Here or at the sheriff's office. Either way. You pick." John steeled himself for another fight. Instead, Whiskey slid a chair toward him with his foot, turned it around and straddled it.

Greg left and returned with a plastic bag. Fury in his eyes. John handed the bag to the woman. "Can you take this to the federal agent who gave you the child? She's down by the creek. Then tell her to come back in here."

"What about Mason?" She gripped the child closer to her.

"Take him with you. Do you know where his mom is?" John asked. Poor kid. He was likely traumatized. But if Violet trusted her gut with this woman taking care of the child, he would too.

She shook her head then looked to Greg. "Do you know where she might be?"

The boy's mom must have been the woman with Greg earlier. "She took off long before I intervened. Not my problem, Ruby."

Ruby. The same Ruby who had called Whiskey the night Nadine died? Ruby opened her mouth, but Whiskey spoke. "Take the agent what she needs. Get the child out of here. Go home. We'll talk tomorrow."

John had questions for her, but she had a small, frightened child. Now was not the time.

She nodded and obeyed.

"What do you want to know, Detective?" Whiskey asked.

"Where were you last Friday night?" He'd start with Atta's disappearance and work his way back to the earlier victims.

Violet entered with a huge lump in her coat pocket. She

stood in the doorway madder than a wet hen, but she wasn't flaming. It was in the icy eyes and calm and cool composure. She slowly let her sight land on Whiskey.

His eyes widened. "You look—"

"I know."

She and Ruby could pass for sisters.

"We've been chomping at the bit to talk to you."

"He was telling us where he was last weekend."

"Well?"

"I was here like I am most weekends. I can give you a dozen witnesses or more." He tucked his hair behind his ears. His cocky grin begged to be punched off. Whiskey could trump up any number of liars. This was pointless.

"We found a piece of Atta's shirt outside the bar. Putting yourself here really doesn't put you in a good place. And we have a witness who says you and Atta had a row last Friday night. What about?" Violet asked and stepped inside the room, owning it and embellishing what they actually knew.

"I had no beef with Atta. She was cool. Never gave me any trouble."

Probably too afraid. Like his other drug runners. But they couldn't ask about that. They weren't supposed to know it.

"She left here beat up. And since you're the man in charge, wouldn't you know it? And why didn't you do something about the brawl down here tonight?"

"I just call that Saturday night, sweetie. And I was upstairs occupied. Didn't hear anything outside my own room." He glanced up. "Ask me where I was when Tillie and Darla got killed. Here. I have more alibis. And Nadine? I tried to help Nadine. When I left her, she was beat up but alive and doctored. Ask Ruby. She was there."

Violet slightly winced. "I plan to."

"There's blood on Atta's shirt," John said.

"Great. I hope it helps you find the sick mother that's doing this. It won't be mine." Whiskey pointed to Greg. "Bring me a brewski and get the guys cleaning up this place."

"On it." He eyed John as a warning to keep his mouth shut then left the room.

"What about the boy's mom?" Violet asked. "Do you know where she might be? His dad?"

"His dad could be anybody in this holler," Whiskey said through a tired laugh. "'Cept me. I'm not sweet on Bella Dawn. But you're pretty." He winked.

John bristled. Whiskey was doing nothing but reiterating what Violet already thought about herself—superficial.

Violet cocked her head. "I take out the trash. I don't sleep with it. You have a nice night." She stalked out of the room, and John followed.

Out in the hall, he sighed. "Now what?"

"Now, I talk to Ruby Boyd. In detail. I should have stuck around and not gone to Memphis. I could have already interviewed her," she mumbled and buttoned up her coat. "I had her take Mason to Mother. She can watch over him until they find his mom or someone responsible can take guardianship. PS, he had a little cloth cowboy doll and the scarf or bandana around its neck was made out of sheer panties. I'm almost certain of it."

"Were they yours?"

She arched an eyebrow. "Hardly. But it's weird. The bandana thingy. My underwear gone. The purses. Even that homemade necklace around that plastic doll at the creek. Something is way bizarre."

Right up her alley. And tomorrow, they'd go to church and talk to Atta's brother, Wendell Atwater. Maybe he'd know more about Whiskey and his relationship with his sister. As far as the undergarments, he wasn't sure, but he had a bad feeling about all of it.

Chapter Fifteen

Sunday, October 22
11:35 a.m.

Violet hadn't been thrilled about going to a church service. She hadn't attended since she was ten years old. She, John and Tiberius sneaked in as the singing commenced and attempted to slide into the back wooden pew unnoticed.

Not so much.

Violet gazed out the window at the side-yard cemetery protected by a four-foot wrought-iron fence with a large cross monument in the center.

The rain had cleared, and sharp blue poked through the mildly cloudy skies. The sun had stretched out to warm the air, but the breeze remained chilly and somewhat damp.

John sat beside her and Ty on the end. His pinched lips indicated he was as irritated as Violet with their situation. John, however, nestled in comfortably, as if he belonged amongst

God's children. If Violet had that many kids, she'd probably pull a flood and wipe them all out too.

Wendell Atwater, preacher man, stood at the lectern and talked about mercy. God's mercy and God's children extending it to others. According to Wendell, mercy was when someone received something they didn't deserve, and all could come and receive what they didn't deserve—salvation.

She scratched at the itch inside her chest, cleared her throat and scanned the sanctuary. Families were tidy and paying attention. She recognized a few from last night. Kids colored and whispered and were thumped on ears to hush up and listen.

The crumpling of candy or cough drop papers rattled, a purse zipper *zzzz*'d and sporadic coughs barged in on the preacher's words. Wendell himself was tall and lithe with pale blond hair parted neatly. Clean-shaven face and blue or maybe green eyes. Hard to tell from where she was sitting.

He wore a pale gray suit with a clip-on tie and no wedding band on his left hand. He ended in prayer and an invitation to come to the altar and find mercy from God. Violet ignored the "every eye closed and head bowed" part and surveyed that no one was coming to the event at the altar. Maybe no one wanted mercy or felt they needed it.

Or maybe they were too ashamed to publicly declare they did. Like Violet.

The lady who looked older than God Himself began playing the piano, and everyone stood instinctively and sang. The child Violet had sent with Ruby was standing on the pew sandwiched between Mother and Wanda. Mother stroked his hair. He was dressed in a blue T-shirt and denim overalls. Knowing Mother, she kept a clothes pantry on her back porch. She'd have *SALT-OF-THE-EARTH* engraved on her headstone, no doubt. One that was already picked out in this very cemetery. But Loretta Boyd and Ruby were absent.

"Everyone is welcome to stay for the monthly potluck. Brother Charles brought his cornhole, so you fellas remember the sermon. Show some mercy."

Everyone laughed and began filtering out.

Violet and John swam upstream, heading for Wendell Atwater.

Mother blocked the aisle. She wore her hair long and wavy past her shoulders, a soft navy blue dress with a pink shawl around her shoulders and shoes like a Shoney's waitress. Her lips were painted a soft shade of pink.

"Ruby told me what happened last night at the Swallow." But it sounded like *Swallah*. "Thank you for seein' the child to safety. He's well-tended now."

The little boy looked up at Violet. "I know you."

Violet rustled his dark cap of hair. "I know you too." She returned her gaze to Mother. "Any news on..." She let her sight trail to Mason.

"Not yet but I'm sure everything'll be fine. She's probably sleepin' it off. Like Ruby and Loretta." Wanda took Mason's hand. "Let's go get some fried chicken and cake." The little boy nodded. He didn't have the cowboy doll this morning.

"Is this behavior normal for Bella Dawn?" Violet asked Mother.

"Leaving Mason in a bar to fend for himself? No. But sometimes she takes him there. He's usually seent to. We try to look out for and take care of one another. Not judge. Show some mercy."

Guess Violet's judgment on taking a child to a bar was showing.

"Y'all stay and enjoy a good lunch. We know how to fry some chicken and maybe even a rabbit or two. Sit around the people with no underlyin' reason. They might be more willin' to open up to you."

Violet planned on staying. "I will. I wanted to talk to you about something."

"I'm sure you do," she said as if she already knew what it would be about. She patted Violet's arm and slipped down the aisle. John was in line to talk to Wendell. Ty had split during the invitation and hadn't returned. She met John at the stage as the last woman left.

They introduced themselves. John shook his hand. "I know you're busy, but we need a few minutes."

"Of course," Wendell said as he retrieved a bottle of water from the lectern and motioned for them to have a seat on the front pew. After a swig, he popped a breath mint. "I don't know anything that would help you though. Atta and I weren't as close as I would have liked us to be. I loved her. Tried my best with her."

"What do you mean by that?" Violet asked.

Wendell sat on the altar steps, his elbows resting on his knees and his hands folded under his chin in a prayerlike manner, the tips of his fingers touching his nose. "Our daddy was a drunk and used us as punching bags until he died. Atta was only seventeen. We were free, 'cept Atta went and fell in love with a boy like Daddy. I was home from seminary, and she asked for permission. I knew if I didn't allow it, she'd end up living in sin with him. They were already...well... I gave consent and went back to seminary. Then he left. Best thing for her, I guess, but she...she and I never saw eye to eye on much of anything." He ran his hands through his perfectly straight hair, mussing it.

"When was the last time you spoke to or saw Atta?"

He inhaled and slowly released it. "I don't know. Wednesday maybe Thursday last week. We didn't do family dinners or lunches. Occasionally, I checked in on her to see how she was doing. Make sure she had enough money. I saw her in town one of those days. At the corner market. She acted usual. Small talk. I told her about the monthly potluck. Told her she should come." He closed his eyes. Then he opened them and shook his head.

"Where were you last Friday night to Sunday morning?"

"Here."

"Anyone see you?"

"No. It was just me."

Not the greatest alibi.

"Anyone you can think of who might want to hurt her? Whiskey?" Violet asked.

"Whiskey hurt Atta? Not in a million years."

"Why?"

"I've said more than I should. I get a certain amount of leash being a clergyman, but I know when I'm overstepping. I'll say this though. I've seen some of his men overstep with the holler girls when they were drunk and—" He cleared his throat as he glanced toward the back.

Regis Owsley stood at the entrance into the sanctuary.

"Excuse me. I have a flock to attend to." He slipped past them and stopped next to Regis. They spoke in low hushed tones then Wendell disappeared. Regis, who had been in the fifth row on the left side during the service, waved then followed Wendell out.

"What do you think that's about? You think Regis is trying to protect Whiskey?" John murmured.

"It's possible." Something else had been sticking in her craw though. And she had to tread lightly. "How long was your wife undercover in these parts when she was murdered?"

"A few months. Why?"

"She would have hung out at the Swallow. I did see a few from last night here."

"Yeah. But if I want to keep Greg hidden, then I can't bring her up. And nobody's mentioned it."

"Well, she was found a county over and in a coal mine. But what if we did bring her up? We could say we found another victim with similarities and interrogate Whiskey and Greg—keep him hidden still. I want to see their faces in regards to Callie. What name did she go by?"

"Allie Walker. Her maiden name. Keeping it close made it easier. But she had an undercover legend."

"What is it?"

John paused. "Why do you want to bring Callie into this now?"

Violet wasn't sure how to answer without revealing her line of thinking. "Because if we didn't know about her, then bringing her up earlier would have given them a red flag. But tomorrow, we'll have been investigating a full week. We've had time to run database searches, and she would have popped. Just...trust me, okay?"

John frowned. "Yeah. Okay."

"Later tonight, maybe tomorrow, let's go back to the Swallow and ask questions." Music drifted in, and she motioned John outside. "For now, let's mingle and you can go play cornhole. Bond with the men."

John snorted. "Pretty good sermon though, huh?"

"Sure." Talking about mercy. Not on today's list of topics. She headed straight for the women and, more specifically, Mother.

Mother glanced up and handed Violet a plate. "I had a feeling you'd make your way over."

Violet declined the plate. "I'm not hungry."

"And it's not polite to turn away food when being offered. Never been taught that?" Mother handed her a plate full of fried chicken, potato salad, some kind of macaroni concoction and a yeast roll that hit Violet's senses and changed her mind about being hungry. Fried food wasn't her jam, but she acquiesced to Mother's wishes.

"Can we go somewhere and talk?" Violet said and accepted a foam cup of sweet tea, or what would more appropriately be called sugar in a cup with some ice and a little tea.

"Of course." Mother led the way through the commotion of games, chatter and kids running amuck in the isolated cemetery on the hill, flanked by trees and wild growing bushes. Mother opened the iron gate, and they entered the sacred ground where family and friends had been buried years before. Violet would guess fewer than a hundred headstones dotted the hilly ground.

Mother sat on a stone bench and patted a seat for Violet. She sat beside her and pulled the fried skin off the chicken and picked off a piece of the breast.

"You're leaving the best part."

"I hear that from time to time." She split the yeast roll and sandwiched the hunk of chicken inside, making a chicken slider of sorts. "Have you talked to your granddaughter in the past couple days?"

"I have. But Wanda, not Loretta, told me about the scuffle at the diner."

"I saw Ruby last night. I know why you and Wanda looked at me like you did when I came to your house. Why I remind Detective Owsley of someone and why Sheriff Modine seemed taken by me. It's pretty obvious."

"Yes, it is."

"Loretta wouldn't talk to me, but I'm hoping you will. What happened to her? How much do you know?" She almost prayed to God that this woman would help her. Could help her. But she was afraid she'd be talking to no one. Or worse,

He wouldn't care to listen. To hear her at all. And Grandmother would be right. He wanted nothing to do with her.

Mother's ample chest rose and fell as she expelled a long, shaky breath. "It's not my story to share, child. But I can tell you that Loretta was a stubborn child. She didn't want to fall into line or do as she was told. Thought she knew better, was wiser than us adults who've lived life. Seen things. Typical teenage things, I suppose."

Violet was well acquainted with rebellion.

"She ran off at thirteen. Scared us out of our minds, and I prayed the Good Lord would bring her to her senses and back home. She was gone for about four years. When she returned, we discovered she was pregnant with Ruby."

"Did she say anything about the man? My own mom called him Adam. Did she speak of Adam?"

Mother shook her head. "No. Loretta said very little. She'd been traumatized, held captive and impregnated. She admitted running away had been a grave mistake, as I told her it would be every time she threatened it. She saw it my way then. Sometimes one has to experience it the hard way to truly grasp reality. We decided to let the past stay there, and we never spoke of it again."

Mother was in her mideighties and from a different era when talking about feelings and therapy would seem unnecessary.

"But we raised Ruby and loved her as our own. Taught her in the ways of *our* family, and the holler accepted her as its own. She only knows the basics of her birth. But she doesn't ask questions. There's no point. It's over." She laid a hand on Violet's forearm. "It's over for you too. Put it to rest, Agent. I know you have a law and order mindset. But justice has been served in God's way."

Violet wasn't sure about that.

"I don't know. He might still be out there, abducting and getting women pregnant. And for what? Why? And what of Ruby? Does she take after her mama...or...?"

"We gave her our values. Our way of thinkin'. Our teachin'. She's one of us. A strong woman. And I suspect you're a strong woman too."

Maybe the sociopath gene skipped Ruby. "How old is she?"

"Thirty-four this spring."

Making Violet barely a year older than her. "Where did Loretta run away to?"

"Memphis."

The common location. Meaning Adam had lived in the Memphis area at the very least. "Where in Memphis?"

"I don't know. She wasn't in the city long before he took her. I don't know from where. I'm sorry. But again, you can't let this gnaw at your bones. Leave Loretta alone, honey. She's made peace, and you pokin' around is only gonna hurt her and bring up things she's tried to let go."

That may be true, but if Loretta knew where she'd been taken from, Violet could get Owen to cross-reference that location with where Reeva had been abducted. He might be able to find a geolocation pattern, and she might be able to pinpoint where Adam had lived or still lived.

No point raining on Mother's parade. "I understand. Thank you for the food."

"How's your mama?" Mother asked.

"I don't suppose she's ever been what she was before. We... she kept me, but she never wanted me." Not like Mother and this community had received Ruby, embracing her and loving her regardless of how she'd been conceived. "She thinks I'm my father's daughter."

Wasn't she?

Mother took Violet's plate and wrapped her arms around

her in a hug she felt clear to her bones. Had any woman ever hugged her?

"Now, you listen to me. No woman belongs in a man's hands without it being her own choice. I'm sorry about your mama. But that's no excuse not to love you. To raise you right and teach you to be a woman who holds her own dignity and strength. That man was not your father. He has no power over you. You stop talkin' like he does. He sired you only. God has made you strong and capable. You aren't weak, child."

Violet's eyes burned. Why hadn't Reeva seen her this way? Why couldn't Violet have been Loretta's daughter? She might have had a different life, one with family who loved her.

"We might start out havin' to survive, Agent. But we can turn survivin' into thrivin'. I've had to do it on more than one occasion, and I've taught my own daughter and any daughters of the heart the same thing." She reared back and cupped Violet's face. "Ya hear me?"

"Yes, ma'am."

Mother patted her cheeks. "Now, go get some banana puddin' 'fore it's gone."

Violet headed for the food tables. She tossed her plate in a tall metal trash can and bypassed the desserts then wandered back toward the church. John and Tiberius were playing horseshoes with some of the men, including Dr. Crocker. Dr. D.J. Lanslow bowed his fiddle with the rest of the band. Seemed to her he'd been up here more than just a time or two like he'd said when they first met. She tucked that nugget away.

Inside the church, she crept toward the altar. She didn't have the same unsettled feeling here as she did at the B and B or anywhere in the holler, but she was unsettled all the same. She fished her cell phone from her pocket and found Reeva's name and pressed it.

The phone rang six times until she finally answered.

Violet put it on speaker and laid her head on an altar stair. "Hello, Reeva. How's Grandmother?"

An irritated breath filtered through the line. "She's gone to the rehab facility, but she's tough. Are you in Kentucky?"

"I am. I need to ask you a question. I met someone here who I think you might know." Would she open up? Talk?

"I have no kin in Kentucky, Violet."

"What about Loretta?" She held her breath and hoped.

One beat. Two.

"I don't know a Loretta."

Violet inwardly sighed. "She has the same mark as you. She's from Night Hollow. That ring a bell?"

"No. We didn't exactly share addresses and numbers. It wasn't summer camp." Her words were clipped and bitter.

"No. I know that. But she has the mark, and she was taken by the same man in Memphis. The man you call Adam. My father."

"Violet, you don't need to be anywhere within miles of him. He's evil. And you keep wanting him, gravitating to him. Maybe that's why he wanted to fill and populate the earth with his precious offspring."

"Is that what he said? What he was trying to accomplish?"

"I don't know or care. I don't want to talk about him." Her tone was resolute. Violet would get nothing more.

"Okay. Reeva, why didn't you give me up for adoption?" She'd never asked that before. Too afraid of the answer, but now she needed to know. It mattered. "If you couldn't love me, someone else might have been able to." Mother, Wanda and Loretta had loved Ruby.

A slow, shallow breath released. "Because it was my job to keep an eye on you. Because no one else would have known what you are. Who you are. Because they wouldn't have known your father. A liar. The devil himself. I kept you in check. I made sure you didn't do more damage than you could have. That's why. You are your father's daughter. I saw it when he held you for the first time."

Violet squeezed her eyes shut. "I see." Her stomach quivered, and she balled her hand to control the trembling. She'd hoped that there might be a hint of love, even a sliver. But she'd been kept to be monitored and held back from unleashing evil.

"Is that all?"

"Yeah. Yeah, that's all." She ended the call. She wasn't going back. To keep hoping.

Hope had been lost. Tossed right into the abyss.

"Hey."

She snapped her head up, and Tiberius leaned against the back wall. "How long have you been there?" Heat flushed her cheeks.

"I'd say a few seconds, but I'd be lying." He approached the altar, perusing the pews and the cross hanging on the back wall, then dropped lazily beside her. "I was raised in a cult. It was jacked up beyond belief. God said this and God said that, and I don't think God was anywhere near that place or those people. Then my mom left only to join another one, in my opinion. My dad's still in. With my brothers."

"You don't have to feel obligated to share a family secret because you eavesdropped like the jerk you are."

"Oh, I know," he said as he casually leaned back, his elbows on the altar stair. "It's just we all come from messed up people, and we've all been raised in messed up places. You should still have a birthday party."

She never celebrated hers. No one ever had. It was more a day of mourning. This past July when the team celebrated Ty's, Violet didn't want to go. But she had. Because people should be celebrated. And it had been fun, though she'd never admit it.

"None of what she's saying is true about you, Violet. You should know this being a head doctor and all. It's no different than how the religious people behave. You believe what you're told over and over. They're told there is a God and He is good. They must do x, y and z to get to heaven. They believe it, and they pass it down. But it's not real. That woman who birthed you—'cause she sure ain't no mama—she's lying to you. Out of her own pain and suffering. She's projecting. The fact I'm diagnosing this is sick."

She did know this. Clinically. The facts behind the motive didn't make the heartache less achy. "You really believe there's no God?"

"Do you believe there *is*?"

"I did. Once. It felt real."

"So do virtual-reality games. Or the interactive rides at Disney." He rubbed his palms on his knees. "I don't know, Violet. I mean maybe there is. Something has changed with Asa and Fiona, and it's stuck. I definitely like them better. At least on most days. But then religions brainwash you. I was brainwashed for a long time."

"Can we talk about something else?"

"Yeah, this is making me sweat." He laughed. "Lab results came back on the sutures. They're made of catgut, which I'll tell you is not what you think. Well, it is. It's intestines. Just not of cats. Sheep and goats. But still. What the—"

"Isn't catgut used as strings for violins?"

"Who thinks, 'Hey I need some new strings for my fiddle. How about this here sheep intestine.' What is wrong with people?" He shook his head, dazed. "Anyhoo, most catgut sutures have been replaced with synthetic material."

"But it's still used for instruments."

"Yeah."

"Did we ever confirm Dr. Lanslow's alibi? He went camping at a friend's cabin. Ray Smith. Did Ray confirm it, and even if he did…can we ask around to see if he's telling the truth?"

"Yeah. I'll get on that. Have Selah make some calls. Get some information on Ray. Who are his friends, where does he work…the usual."

Violet stood. "Can we keep this between us?"

"I mean the team is gonna wanna know Ray's alibi." He grinned knowingly. "Yeah. Can you keep mine in the vault too? Only Asa knows, but that's because he's the SAC and has our files."

"Exactly. Fiona knows too—about me. I told her back in July. She's been trying to help me find leads on this Adam."

"Sounds to me he believed it was a mission by God as a new Adam. In Genesis, Adam was told to be fruitful and multiply and fill the earth. Now, life spans are shorter. It would take more than one Eve to get the job done. No offense."

"None taken."

"He never made contact with you?"

"Not that I know."

Ty frowned. "Let me do some digging from the religious angle. I'll be discreet."

Violet appreciated it immensely. "Thank you."

"Be nicer to me though."

"I'll consider it." She heard footsteps.

Regis entered the sanctuary. "Bella Dawn is still missing. Her car and purse are still at the Swallow. No one's heard from her. I don't think she's sleepin' off a bender or shackin' up anywhere. I think we got us another Blind Eye victim."

Violet pinched the bridge of her nose and caught the glimmer around Regis's neck. "I didn't take you as a jewelry owner, Regis."

He lifted it from his shirt. "Oh this? A cross my mama gave me. Does that have anything to do with Bella Dawn missing?"

Maybe.

And maybe he knew it too.

"I'll be at the SO." He left the church.

"I really don't want to find another dead girl." This was crazy.

"Me neither. But I think we're gonna."

Chapter Sixteen

Sunday, October 22
6:55 p.m.

John slowly circled Bella Dawn McDaniels's beat up Ford Taurus that sat at the far end of the Swallow. Violet and Ty had found him playing horseshoes and delivered the news. Right now, they were assuming she'd been taken.

Local law enforcement had been dispatched to search several of the nearby caves. They'd been combing for hours. Ty, Violet and John had gone to Bella Dawn's house to talk to her mom. They'd wondered why Mother still had the child and not the grandparent, but when they'd arrived, she'd been stoned out of her gourd. She was zero help.

Friends and neighbors hadn't seen her come home. The people at the Swallow might have been the last to see her alive, including John, Violet and Greg. Bella Dawn had been coiled around him in the back booth most of the night, until the fight went down. Interviewing last night's patrons was going to take a while. John's stomach rumbled, reminding him hours had passed since they had lunch at the church social.

The ERT had processed the car, and he and Violet then went through it, but they hadn't found anything special or telling, only a car seat, empty wrappers and sippy cups.

Violet had made sure that little boy was now in good hands. John hadn't missed the genuine care and concern in her eyes. The woman had up a shield, but it wasn't as impenetrable as she let on.

"I'm not sure she ever made it to her car," Violet said and tore off her latex gloves, shoving them in her blazer pockets. She studied the outside of the bar then looked back at the Ford. "I think the killer was here last night. He hadn't planned on taking a victim, but, in the chaos, it was a prime opportunity. She knew her killer. She went with him. Why leave Mason?" A frown narrowed her eyes and caused a faint line to pucker across her brow.

"She might have asked to go get him, and he lied or shoved her in his vehicle by force. No one would have paid attention due to the chaos." An altercation would have blended in, making Violet's theory of the killer seeing an opportunity and taking it make perfect sense.

"Perhaps. Let's go inside. See if we can get more information."

"It'll be as easy as getting blood from a turnip," John stated and motioned with an outstretched arm for her to take the lead.

"What exactly does that mean?" she asked as she approached the bar.

"I have no idea. But my mamaw used to say it so..." John opened the door for her, and they entered the Swallow. Tables and chairs had been righted, and the broken chairs, glass shards and junk had been swept up and removed. The mirror behind the bar was still missing shards and the place smelled of booze and bleach.

A woman in her twenties wiped down the bar. "We're not open yet, hon."

"Well, hon," Violet said with a stringent tone, "we need information not a drink. You here last night?"

"I was. Talk about a nightmare." She tossed the bar rag over her shoulder and shot another glance in John's direction.

"I'd like to talk about Bella Dawn. You see her here?"

The girl darted her sight behind her then fiddled with the edge of the rag hanging from her shoulder. "She was. Got here a little after five. She brought the boys dinner."

"What boys?"

"Whiskey and his crew. They ate back there." She pointed to the back room. "She went upstairs with Mason until about seven. Put him to bed and came back down. Hung out."

John rubbed the back of his neck. "Why would she bring her son into a bar? And what's your name?"

"Mellie. Whiskey lets her bring Mason sometimes. If she can't find a sitter and has to…"

"To what?"

Mellie bit her bottom lip. "Look, if you need Whiskey, he's in the back with Greg and Terrance. I just tend bar," she lowered her voice, "and I need this job."

They didn't need the rest of her sentence to put together what was going on. Bella Dawn had come in to work for Whiskey. Put her kid to bed. Was sweet with Greg until it was time to meet up with a buyer, then went on her run. Maybe the Blind Eye Killer hadn't taken her. Maybe whoever she made an exchange with had. And if she was Greg's informant, then it made it more likely.

Whiskey came through the door, wearing a gray hoodie and jeans and black motorcycle boots. His hair was pulled back in a short ponytail. A strand of bangs had fallen from it and hung over his eyes. He paused and looked from Mellie to John to Violet and back to Mellie. "Take five, Mel."

She scurried behind the door.

"What brings you back?"

John let the irritation roll off his back. "Two things. One, Bella Dawn is missing. If you haven't heard."

"I heard."

Greg pushed through the doors. Jean jacket over flannel. Worn jeans. A faded red baseball cap on his head. He stood next to Whiskey, arms folded over his chest. Menace in his eyes and a clenched jaw.

"We saw you with Bella Dawn last night," Violet said. She eased onto a barstool as if she had nowhere to be and was in no hurry. She leaned her right elbow on the bar. "You two seemed friendly."

Greg laughed. "Friendly don't mean we're friends, Agent."

"You haven't heard from her since last night?" she asked, eyeing him coolly.

He shook his head.

John couldn't discern if Greg was playing his part or if he was legit being a jerk.

Violet paused a few beats. "The other reason we've come is because we've run the killer's signature through our database to see if we could find other victims that fit or are similar. We got a hit. Victim died about four years ago. Right over the county line. Name's Allie Walker. Got a photo here."

She did? John was not prepared for this. Greg shot him a glare, and he tried to convey he too was at a loss. Violet held out her phone for Whiskey, and he squinted. It was there.

Whiskey recognized his wife.

Violet then showed it to Greg. "You know her?"

"Why would I?"

She looked back at Whiskey. "You do. Don't you?"

Greg raked a hand through his hair. "What we know is you're looking in all the wrong places." Whiskey put his arm on Greg's, but Greg gave him a look and Whiskey gave a slight nod. "Things aren't always what they seem around here, Agent. Go take a peek in room five. Upstairs, last door on the right. You want answers to Atta and maybe the others..." He pointed upward. "As far as that chick. We ain't ever seen her."

John's insides flushed hot, and he balled a fist. This was Greg's open chance to give him something. Anything.

But maybe he was.

Maybe it was upstairs behind the last door on the right.

The hallway was narrow, and the hardwood nicked and scratched. On either side of the hall were three rooms with closed doors, but the sounds of music, laughter and prostitution filtered into the hallway.

"Brothel?" John whispered.

"That's my guess." It had briefly crossed her and Ty's minds that Whiskey did more than make meth and run drugs.

No sound came from the room where they stood. Violet hoped this wasn't a trap. After Callie was brought up, Greg had been angry, and Whiskey had appeared confused and irritated. He was quick to let Greg give them this nugget.

She hoped it didn't backfire.

She carefully turned the knob and quietly opened the door. The scent of cheap liquor and dirty socks whacked her senses. Blinds were closed and the dim room revealed a dresser with an older model TV, a small round table with two wooden chairs by the window and two nightstands flanking a queen-size bed with a sagging mattress.

Tangled in dingy white sheets and out cold lay Wendell Atwater.

He was in black-socked feet, the suit pants from earlier today and a white undershirt. Half a bottle of Chivas was propped against his chest.

"Well, this wasn't what I was expecting." A slow hiss escaped John's lips as he inched toward the bed. Wendell's chest rose and fell. At least he was breathing. John leaned over him and gave him a light pop on the cheek with the back of his hand. "Wake up, preacher."

"I wonder if he'll want us to show him that mercy he preached about when we get him awake." Surely receiving mercy wasn't license to get sloshed. Was this a habit or something he'd given in to since Atta's death? Whiskey and Greg's implication was that today wasn't a first time.

John grunted and smacked him a little harder. "Wendell," he said sharply, "wake up. Up."

Wendell groaned and stirred. One bloodshot eye opened then closed, and he groaned again, then his eyes sprang open. "Detective?" he slightly slurred, still smashed.

"Yeah. And Agent Rainwater. We'd like to ask you a few questions."

"I'm going to find a cool washcloth and maybe a cup of coffee." Violet walked into the hall, the scent of perfume and booze lingering. She tromped down the wooden stairs and into the back room, where Greg, Whiskey and two other men were gathered at a table with beers in hand and a pizza in the middle of the table.

"You hungry, honey?" Greg asked.

Violet detested this man. He was playing no game.

Out him. Say the words, and they'll do the rest. You know you want to.

She did. They hovered on the edge of her tongue. *He's undercover.* That was all she had to say. "How long has Wendell Atwater been passing out in room five?"

Whiskey picked a piece of pepperoni off his slice and popped it into his mouth. "A decade. But just in that room. He's been drinkin' since he was twelve. Takin' after the old man. In more ways than one."

Violence? Was Whiskey implying Wendell Atwater was the Blind Eye Killer? No. If he had definitive proof, he'd have killed him himself for choosing girls that worked for him. But maybe he needed the proof and was using Violet and John to get it in order to enforce his own brand of justice. Holler justice. And that was why he'd told them about room number five. "I need coffee to sober him up."

"That doesn't really work."

"Well, I need it anyway." She drilled her gaze into Greg's. John might keep his secrets, but Violet had a side John couldn't begin to dream of. "Give me a reason," she whispered. "One reason."

"A reason for what?" Whiskey asked.

Greg dropped his pizza and stood. "Mellie has some made. Faster we help her, the faster we get her out of here," he said with a few choice names for Violet. She ignored them. Didn't deny them.

Once behind the bar and alone, Greg cornered her, blocking her against the wall. "If you so much as breathe a word—"

"You'll what?" she hissed back and straightened her spine. "If you don't start cooperating with us, I will make sure he knows who you are and who Callie was, and then I'll let him kill you and sleep sound all night long. Because he will kill you, and I have a hunch he'll make it slow and torturous. Do you understand *me*?"

Greg studied her, searched her eyes and found the truth, then chuckled. "You should do undercover work." He dropped his arm and poured what looked like hours-old coffee into a foam cup. "I think Whiskey made Callie. She was kinda like you. Crazy. She followed him and saw an exchange. One that could be tied to a pretty powerful politician. She called and told me what she'd seen and that she had photos. We were supposed to meet up, but she didn't show. I knew he had her killed. I'm not just trying to bring him down for drugs. I want him for Callie. I need him for Callie." His tone softened.

"And Bella Dawn?"

He kneaded the nape of his neck. "It's hard to know who you are when you've been told for so long who you're supposed to be. Sometimes I think I am Whiskey's guy. That I belong here. I get... Doesn't matter. I don't know where Bella Dawn went. But I know who she was with when she ducked out."

"Who?"

"Regis Owsley."

Violet hadn't seen him. But that didn't mean he hadn't been there.

"I don't know who the Blind Eye Killer is. Nobody does and that's the problem. Because we never don't know who is up to no good around here. He's a ghost."

"Do you think it's Whiskey?"

"Maybe. The M.O. is similar to the way Callie died. I can't always account for his whereabouts. No one suspects him. He wouldn't have any reason to murder those women, which puts him under the radar. But I don't want John to know any of this. He'll...he'll mess things up. He's a straight shooter, and he is by the book. But I got a good feeling, you and I...we're alike. Keep John off me. I will avenge Callie."

Violet blew a heavy breath. Greg didn't want John to bring down Whiskey because he wanted to. For the same woman. This was going to get messy.

"Could Wendell be the killer?"

"I don't know. I really don't, Agent. Maybe. He's violent when he's drunk." He glanced back. "I've got to go, but I'll give you a peace offering. Keep a close watch on Ruby Boyd and Amy Miller."

"Why?"

"Because they're the only two holler girls left. They're marked." He headed for the door.

He didn't say Whiskey Girls. And there were far more than two women left in this holler. "Why? What does that mean? Is the killer targeting Whiskey's prostitutes?"

Greg glanced at the door. "I'm not the bad guy. I play one, and sometimes slip over the edge. But I don't want any more women to die." He disappeared behind the door.

She related on some level with Greg. She'd been told her whole life who she was and who she was to become. For a moment, she'd embraced it.

One push.

She shook out of the memory and brought the coffee up-stairs, foregoing the washrag. Inside, Wendell was sitting on the edge of the bed, his head in his hand. Violet handed him his coffee.

"Why are we up here, Wendell? Whiskey seems to think it might be you who beat up Atta. Did you kill her too?"

"No. No!" He sipped the coffee, and after he swallowed a sob erupted, spittle flying from his lips, leaving them wet and puckered.

"But you did see Atta last Friday night, didn't you? Because you were both here. You've had a guest room here for over a decade, Wendell. We know." Violet wanted someone to tell the truth for once.

"Yes. I've tried to be the person I know I'm meant to be. The man God wants me to be." Another sob escaped, his shoulders bobbing as he cried. "I beg Him to take this demon away from me. And for a while, I can resist. Until I can't. Then I look in the mirror, and I see my father. Not my heavenly father. My dirtbag of an earthly dad. The man I don't want to be. I'm exhausted and ashamed."

Violet wasn't here to offer counsel or consolation. "I understand that, Wendell. Wanting to be someone else. The better person crying to be let out. But what I need to know, besides your sins, is am I going to find your DNA on her swatch of clothing and on a beer bottle we found by the creek outside the bar?"

"I don't know. Maybe." He wiped his mouth. "I came into the bar. I was gonna have one beer. But it turned into more. She came in. We got in an argument."

"What about?"

"The fact the holler preacher was once again drunk at a bar ran by a criminal." He drank the coffee, sniffed. "But who was she to condemn me! I boiled over and followed her outside, where we had it out and… God help me, I hit her. I slapped her right in the mouth. I'm not sure how the beer bottle broke. I think I hit it against the tree to scare her. Maybe even hit her with it. I can't remember." He held up his right hand. "Cut my hand." His bloodshot eyes drilled into hers. "When she took off, I grabbed her, the bottom of her shirt ripped clean off. But I did not kill her. I came back inside when she stormed away. And the next thing I knew, I woke up in this room. That's the last I saw her."

He'd lied about his alibi to hide the fact he was a drunk. A mean one. "We're going to have to retrace and recheck your alibis for Tillie, Darla and Nadine. Were you here last night?"

A slow nod. "I was upstairs. Drunk."

"Did you see Bella Dawn?"

"Briefly, when she brought Mason upstairs. I didn't kill these women. I didn't kill my sister."

But he'd been angry that his sister had condemned him, and he knew about her own sins. It fit with Scripture in Romans, and Wendell Atwater had proven himself to be a liar with a violent temper if drunk. "I guess we'll find out, won't we?"

Outside in the hall, she asked, "Do you believe him?"

"I don't know. He fits the loose profile we have. He's definitely a solid person of interest."

Violet had several persons of interest on her radar, but she needed time to process everything before snapping to conclusions and speaking too soon. "Your boy Greg said Regis was here last night. Saw him escort Bella Dawn out the front door. Now, maybe he's telling the truth. Maybe he's casting light on Regis for other reasons."

"To get us off his back."

"Perhaps." But not for that reason. Too much information and too many personal issues weighed like a bag of bricks on her skull. She wanted to be done with this day, this investigation—her past. Wendell's words about being his father had struck her deeply. "I need some air."

She clomped down the wooden stairs, spotted the bottle of Jack on the bar and swiped it—not like they'd care, and who would they call anyway—then she strode out the front door toward the creek, the wind picking up leaves and swirling them in the air, swaying trees and sounding more like beach waves than wind in the branches.

Greg's and Wendell's words in her brain were doing what the leaves were doing around her now. Blowing round and round. Unsure where to fall and settle.

It's hard to know who you are when you've been told for so long who you're supposed to be.

Who was Violet?

I've tried to be the person I know I'm meant to be. Wendell's words kicked her gut, and she twisted off the top of the bottle as a dark thought ran through her mind.

You know who you are. You can't keep pretending you're not your father's daughter. And you'll do it...you'll push someone else. Pull a trigger. It's going to happen. You're safe for no one.

The swollen creek ran over sedentary stones down the bed with a whoosh. A squirrel zipped across a log that had fallen over the creek.

She grabbed a yellow leaf and traced her finger across the edges of the diamond-shaped pattern.

Footsteps approached, and without looking, she knew it was John.

Chapter Seventeen

Sunday, October 22
7:53 p.m.

"You think that's smart?" John asked and pointed to the bottle she'd lifted from the bar.

She held it up. "Call me Slick." But she still hadn't taken a drink. "I don't want to think at all, John. That's the point." She set the bottle down by the tree roots. "I don't even drink. Losing my inhibition means I might do something volatile. It was impulsive." She closed her eyes and leaned her head back on the trunk of the tree. "Do you believe that people can change? Look at the preacher. He doesn't want to be a mean drunk, but he can't help himself. He tries to be a good person, but he can only fight so long and hard before he succumbs to his true nature."

What was she fighting?

"Because if a man who claims to be a preacher of God can't

do it, seems the rest of us are without hope of being anything more than what we are. Depraved and cruel. Inhumane."

Violet was searching for age-old answers that couldn't be found in any of her textbooks.

"I think our base nature is dark," he said. "We hate and murder. Lie and steal. Cheat and covet. We betray and look out for ourselves and do what feels good to us—and those things aren't always good things. There will always be a streak of darkness in us all."

"But?"

"But we can know light and have light live in us. Shine through us. Battle that darkness we struggle with but not alone." He hated seeing her in inner agony. "Wendell Atwater has a streak of darkness. He battles alcohol, and he may always battle it, but that doesn't mean he's not a man of faith or that he won't eventually win the war—if that's what's going on here."

"It makes him a hypocrite."

"No. A hypocrite would judge others for it and then do it in secret with no shame. What I witnessed was a man severely ashamed of his sins. Kicking himself for giving in to that temptation. And trying to hide it—not to keep indulging but from the shame, the guilt and the fear."

She shifted, leaning her shoulder against the trunk. "You don't think he's the killer then?"

He suspected about every man in this holler. "I don't know. Some killers do feel remorse for their kills. In a twisted way. It's possible he did it and feels that heavy shame but believes in his mission. If so, he'll do it again."

"I killed a girl once," she whispered.

Had she drunk some of that whiskey before he made it out here?

"You did what?"

"Well, almost. I killed her in my heart before I attempted

to in reality, so I may as well have. Lynn Tavish. I hated her. I was fifteen. And I was pretty. Never hit an awkward stage. She hated *that*." Her words weren't arrogant or prideful. Simply facts. "She was vicious to me. Blocked my path on the school bus, humiliating me. I never fought her, or even spoke. Just went back up to the front of the bus. She harassed me in the halls. Spread vile rumors about me. None true. And every day, I wanted to kill her. I spent study hall daydreaming of ways I'd do it and not get caught. Then one day...I executed the plan."

John's stomach turned, and he wasn't sure how to respond. His mind reeled. What was he supposed to say to this kind of confession?

"I left a note in her locker from a boy I knew she had a crush on. Said to meet him out by the lake near her house. At the gazebo at midnight. She came. I saw her walk onto the gazebo from where I stood on the dock. She saw me, but I was far enough out and dressed in dark clothing. She didn't know I wasn't him. And when she got to me, before she could even realize I wasn't Terry Travis, I listened to the voice in my head that said to push her."

John's blood turned cold.

"All the harassment and humiliation. All the pain and hate and rage within me... I pushed Lynn Tavish off the dock of the lake. Knowing full well—having planned it intentionally this way—that she couldn't swim."

The wind blew down his shirt, and he shivered. The swollen clouds moved and shifted, leaving the air damp and dark and cold.

Her voice was quiet and hollow. "She flailed and fought, and I thought it would be louder. But it's quiet actually. Her body stilled, and she slipped under the black water. One second...two... And then I slipped out of my shoes, and I jumped in. I wasn't sure if I was going to drown myself too or hold her under. But I just... I brought her to the surface, laid her on the dock and rolled her on her side, smacked her back. She coughed up water and gasped for air. Then she looked up at me, and the horror in her eyes was startling. She was terrified of me, and I'm convinced that's what kept her from ever telling anyone what I did." She broke off a piece of tree bark and rubbed it between her fingers. "I was terrified of me."

"But you didn't kill her," John said.

"Not technically. But I hurt her. I knew then Reeva was right. I was my father's daughter. What kind of person could do that? None. But a monster could. I think she was right to keep me and not give me to a loving family. To monitor my evil tendencies."

John pawed his face, his adrenaline racing and his brain buzzing. "But you didn't kill her, Violet. You jumped in, and you saved her because you knew it was wrong. Or...did you think you'd get caught?"

Violet's laugh was icy and soft. "I knew I'd never get caught. I'd created a rock-solid alibi and slipped into her locker to retrieve the note I wrote. No way to trace it to me. That's cunning. Like my father."

"You were fifteen and abused—if not physically, at least verbally. Your rage and pain weren't really about Lynn Tavish, but Reeva Rainwater. You needed help, Violet. You needed counseling."

"Monsters can't be fixed." She pushed off the tree.

John framed her chilly cheeks. "Violet, you are not a monster. You're a woman who needs some things in her life untangled and brought to light. You didn't kill Lynn Tavish."

"But I wanted to! I plotted and almost executed it. Don't you understand?"

"But you didn't," he said with force, holding her face firm

in his hands, leaving her nowhere to gaze but at him. "You didn't. You saved her. You. Saved. Her. You saved Mason last night at the bar. You save lives every day and stop monsters. Why do you do that?"

"Because I love the hunt. The thrill of tracking them and seeing them behind bars."

"Why?"

She frowned. "What do you mean why?"

"Why is it a thrill?"

She closed her eyes. "Because I can stop them."

"Why do you want to stop them?"

She kept her eyes squeezed shut, her lips clamped tight.

"Why?"

"Because they're monsters. And they deserve to be locked away forever for the destruction they've wreaked on victims and their families. Because maybe one of these days...it'll be my dad. And he'll pay for making my life a living hell. For robbing Reeva of her innocence and what should have been a wonderful time in her life. For forcing her to give birth to a child she never wanted and shouldn't have had." Her voice grew louder, her words faster, tears flowed freely. "One of these days, I'll be able to put him in a prison and hold *him* captive. And...and maybe my mom will finally love me." A cracked sob escaped, and she collapsed against him as the aching sobs destroyed his heart and clenched his gut.

This woman had been alone and afraid her entire life. Never wanted. Never loved. Never told she was anything but pretty. No one had ever championed her, had a tea party with her, told her she could be anything, and yet she'd become a successful, intuitive, intelligent psychologist and federal agent. She was brave. She was resilient. But Violet saw none of these things.

Her body convulsed against him as her hopelessness, fear

and pain flowed in tears. When was the last time she'd cried? Had she ever? John embraced her with strength and tenderness. If she was willing to be vulnerable and trust him with her secret, her shame, her deepest hurts, he would not treat it lightly, would not let it be in vain.

His hand smoothed her hair, like he did when Stella had nightmares and needed to feel safe and protected and cared for. He said nothing, allowing her to pour everything out. To collapse against him in her desperation. To feel. This place had brought it out. Seeing another victim and survivor, her half-sibling, had brought all the muck of her life to the surface.

He thanked God that He'd given John the privilege of being the secure place for her to fall and land. Silently he prayed for Violet and for all those lies to be untwisted and truth to prevail. For the light to open her blinded eyes to see that God was real. He existed. She needed Him. And He loved her.

Slowly her sobs turned to steady tears and then to sniffs and shallow breaths. He slid tear-matted hair from her cheeks and looked into her watery eyes.

"Do you hate me?" she whispered.

"No," he murmured. God help him he might love her. Using his thumbs, he wiped away tears dotting her cheeks. "I think you're brave and strong, Violet. Thank you for confiding in me."

"I feel stupid."

He stared dead into her eyes. "You shouldn't. You're not." He carefully, chastely placed a kiss on her forehead, held on and lingered, feeling the warmth of her skin. His blood raced at the connection.

Violet raised her head, her nose grazing his and her lips meeting his. Soft. Full. Too tempting to not taste, to explore and get lost in. Her arms slipped around his waist, and she pressed in, but he pulled back a hairsbreadth and whispered,

"I can't kiss you like this, Violet. Not when your emotions are raw and you're confused. And I said I wouldn't kiss you before I stole your heart. And before you say another word— you don't know if I have or not. Not like this."

"No one's ever turned me away." Confusion clouded her eyes.

His gaze deepened. "Don't misunderstand. I'm not at all turning you away. I'm...postponing."

Thunder rumbled and rain began to fall in a steady stream, dotting her face and eyelashes. "A rain check then."

With more restraint and willpower than he'd ever used, he let his hands drop from her cheeks. "Count on it."

They raced to the car. He opened her door, and she jumped in then he followed suit. The rain slammed against the roof and concealed their view.

Violet's phone rang. "It's Tiberius." She answered and put him on speaker.

"We got all kinds of stuff to tell you," she said.

"Yeah, well me first. I cracked the numbers. Romans sounded good, but I've been thinking about the phrase *holler girls*. We both thought they might be more than drug runners, so I ran down the prostitution angle."

"Cleaning houses probably *is* a front for prostitution." Violet told Tiberius about the rooms upstairs at the Swallow. "And Bella Dawn was all over Greg last night. Then there's the fact no one will talk. Greg did say that Ruby Boyd and Amy Miller were holler girls—and targets. I didn't get much more than that out of him though."

"That only helps me confirm my new theory. And it changes everything about who we're looking for."

"Where are you?"

"I'm back at the B and B."

"We'll meet you there."

★ ★ ★

Violet went inside the B and B and straight to her room and private bath, where she washed her face and brushed her hair. Had she really confessed her most horrible acts to a man who epitomized everything that was good and noble and kind? Everything virtuous and honorable. The man wouldn't even kiss her in a vulnerable state for fear of taking advantage of her! Was he for real?

In his arms, warmth had encompassed her, chasing away the cold that dogged her heels. A brightness radiated and kicked down darkness's door, and she'd felt it clear to her bones.

But then she'd felt stupid.

You're not.

And she'd believed him.

No lies. No games. Only honesty and truth in his spoken words. In his eyes—like amber sunshine arresting and capturing her but not against her will. She'd wanted to be drawn in, drawn close. Held near. Held dear.

Had John Orlando stolen her heart? She wasn't sure. But he'd at least circled her ribs and cased the joint, leaving a mark.

Staring in the mirror, she studied her face. She'd revealed the ugliest part of her life, and John hadn't run. What might that mean? And was God real?

"Are You real?" she whispered. "Did You see me when I was a little girl walking down that aisle? Were You there at all? Are You here now?"

She blinked then dried her damp face and headed back downstairs to the covered porch where Ty, John and Agent Kip Pulaski from the Louisville field office sat sipping coffee. Once again, it had been left out on the sideboard in the dining room by the mysteriously absentee aunt.

"Well, hello again, Agent Rainwater," Pulaski said. "How goes the investigation? I hear the holler's lips have been locked up tight. Not surprising. Thought I'd pop over and offer you some services."

"Why, because Asa isn't in charge, and you don't think a woman can run the show?"

"Chip on your shoulder and fiery. Nice." He didn't appear offended. "Agent Granger's been fillin' me in."

Ty looked up, his hair a disaster and his normal scruff now a short beard. He tossed her an apologetic glance. "I thought we could use all the help possible."

Violet wasn't sure. She also had trust issues. She sat on the wicker sofa beside John. Pulaski sat across the glass coffee table in a wicker rocker, and Ty sat between them on the outdoor sofa. The coffee smelled rich and nutty. But she wanted information right now. Coffee could wait.

"I told them about Wendell already," John said.

"And the numbers?" Violet asked.

"I got to thinking about prostitutes—"

"Which I don't tend to agree with," Pulaski stated. "I know we got drug running going on, and the rumor is Whiskey uses women to do it. DEA has a close eye on him, but I don't know that he's running holler hookers."

"We're not saying he is," Violet said. "But we are running down the possibilities. We have nothing else concrete to track. Ty, what were you about to say?"

"The numbers are interesting," Ty said. "Not necessarily meant for us as a calling card. But an exclamation point in blood so to speak. Proverbs six. Verses twenty, twenty-one, twenty-two, twenty-three, twenty-four, twenty-five and twenty-six. He's dropped the 'twenty' in front of all the numbers except for the first verse. He marks the two and the zero, then uses singular digits—probably for space constraints, but he doesn't want the numbers anywhere else. The forehead—the mind—it matters."

6-2 0-1-2-3-4-5-6.

"What's the verses say?"

Tiberius picked up a black King James Version Bible. "I'll read it for full effect. 'My son, keep thy father's commandment, and forsake not the law of thy mother: Bind them continually upon thine heart, and tie them about thy neck. When thou goest, it shall lead thee; when thou sleepest, it shall keep thee; and when thou awakest, it shall talk with thee. For the commandment is a lamp; and the law is light; and reproofs of instruction are the way of life: To keep thee from the evil woman, from the flattery of the tongue of a strange woman. Lust not after her beauty in thine heart; neither let her take thee with her eyelids. For by means of a whorish woman a man is brought to a piece of bread: and the adultress will hunt for the precious life.'"

Violet let the words percolate. "Can I see it for myself?"

Ty handed over the Bible, and she read it again and again.

"I went onto BibleGateway, which is a Bible website, and entered *prostitute* in some more modern translations. A few stuck out, and I looked them up in an older version, the King James Version. It doesn't use the word *prostitute* but *whore*, but it means the same. When I saw verse twenty-five...that was that."

"The eyelids."

"The eyelids," he confirmed. "All people are driven by belief in something. False or true. If a person is religious, then their religious beliefs will directly influence their behavior. What they do or don't do. What is right and what is wrong. This man is warned not to lust. To keep himself from an adulterous woman or prostitute or any woman who might be seductive in speech or form. The batting of the eyes is the expression here concerning eyelids. If he were to succumb to the seduction, he'd be sinning against God, and it could cost him his life."

Violet tracked with Ty. "But he can't help himself. Then

he feels rage and hatred for his actions and for the prostitute. That's why they had intercourse, but it wasn't rape. He paid for services. Then he went into a rage. Brutally beat them. Took their eyes and sutured their eyelids to prevent them from ever batting their eyelashes or luring him."

"Or anyone else," John said. "He might be trying to protect other men from falling into the same trap, which is exactly how he'd view their actions—a trap."

Violet nodded. "A preacher wouldn't want any of his congregants to fall into this snare. But would he pay for his own sister's services? Would she be participant to that?" If it was Wendell Atwater, how did his sister fit in?

"Maybe he caught her in the act with someone in his congregation, and while her death fits the same pattern, the one thing missing is he wasn't the one to sleep with her." John then looked to Kip, who hadn't chimed in at all. He sat quietly and held up his hands revealing he had nothing to add.

"There's some other verses," Ty said, "that talk about darkness. Deuteronomy mentions those groping in darkness blind but unable to find their way out, oppressed and no one coming to save them. It's about spiritual blindness. I think he may be using the blinding and the caves to bring this Scripture to life. They grope hoping for someone to save them, then instead of rescuing them, he beats them. Strangles them. Proverbs says he's to tie the words of wisdom to his neck to continually be a lamp to guide him. I think that's why he chooses strangulation for the manner of death."

Agent Pulaski low whistled. "You're building a big profile on a Scripture that might not be right."

Possibly, but Violet's gut screamed they had it on the nose. "We need someone to concretely confirm these girls are prostitutes."

John huffed. "Who? People are complicit or have actively

participated. But the Scripture used on the leather purses makes more sense now."

I am dark but lovely.

"Cecil Johnson. Let's talk to him. Now." They were running out of time. Bella Dawn was missing. Most likely already dead. Atta was taken on a late Friday night and found on Sunday. Nadine was rushed. Time wasn't on their side. "Ty, you and Agent Pulaski—since you're here to help—go take a crack at Wendell. Go down the angle we've discovered she's a prostitute. If he's not the killer, that may be why they were in a fight. She was at Whiskey's bar. He came in. Saw her with someone or working the floor. They got into it. He hit her. But take a good look at all those rooms and get him to allow you to search his place and church without a warrant if you can."

Ty and Agent Pulaski stood. "However I can help," Pulaski said. "What are you going to do?"

"John and I are going to see Cecil Johnson. He's on my radar." Right along with Regis Owsley, Dr. D.J. Lanslow and Dr. Crocker. "Ty, anything new on the hunt to confirm Lanslow's alibi?"

"Selah is digging. I'm going there personally tomorrow morning before I track down Jimmy Russell to find out why he didn't mention Ruby Boyd being at Nadine's place that night, and if I have time, stop in at the Black Feather and see if the story we've been given about Atta Atwater coming in after a fight can be corroborated. Hey, maybe I'll get a break and Mr. Anonymous Caller will be there and fess up."

Doubtful. "Sounds good." They dispersed, and she and John got inside his car. On their way to Alpha and Omega Handcrafted Leathers, she ruminated on a long list of suspects. Every person in the holler as far as she was concerned.

They pulled up to the curb and saw the light on inside the leather shop. Good. Cecil was here even at this late hour. Violet hurried to the front door. Locked. She knocked. Waited. Knocked again.

Finally, Cecil stepped into view wearing a white sweater and dark jeans. The light cast him in an ethereal glow. "Is it me or is he ridiculously beautiful?"

"Not that I like to discuss men's looks, but…yeah. He's what we'd have called a pretty boy back in the day."

Cecil opened the door. "Agents. Nice to see you made it out of the Swallow alive." He swept his hand for them to enter. "What can I do for y'all tonight?"

"We need a favor."

Cecil's eyebrows raised as if he'd expected this visit. "If you're wondering if I gave Bella Dawn a purse, I did."

"Are the women you gave leather purses to, these holler girls, prostitutes?" Violet asked. "I got the feeling you were withholding last we talked about that. Is that why you call them dark but lovely?"

Cecil looked up at the wall of plaques filled with Scripture and the crosses. "They are dark in their sinful ways. But they are lovely. Aren't they?" His blue eyes pierced hers. "Yes, Agent. They sell themselves to men."

"Do you buy what they're selling, Cecil? Are the purses gifts for their services?"

Cecil frowned. "Do you need anything else?"

"Do you have Bella Dawn?"

He stared at her and sighed. "No. Last I saw Bella Dawn was when she left the bar with my brother."

"I thought she left the bar with Regis Owsley."

"She did."

Chapter Eighteen

Sunday, October 22
11:54 p.m.

The moon was a thumbnail slicing through heavy clouds peppering the night sky. The rain had finally slacked, but the air was cold and wet. Plumes of breath rose from his lips as he trekked through the hills southeast of the old place. He hated it and loved it.

He slipped by the yellow crime-scene tape rattling in the wind. Past the cave and onto the worn footpath from childhood. How many times had he pretended to be hiding in the forest from gnarly hags?

Or his own mom.

But she had no power over him anymore. No forcing him to be someone he wasn't. He entered the clearing to the old cabin where he'd been born and spent the early years of his life before they'd moved into the other house.

But he liked it here best. In the silence. Isolated. No one telling him what to do or who to be.

No one telling him no.

He was careful on the rotted porch. He hadn't been back here since the agent and detective had snooped through his private things, invaded his space. When she'd looked through the woods into his eyes.

The wind howled and whistled its way inside. His latest doll he'd been making with the agent's pretty red undergarment was almost finished. Lula liked the first doll so much she'd probably like this one too. Wood shavings from his last project littered the floor underneath the chair.

He approached his old bedroom door and cracked it open. On the twin bed with the dirty mattress, Bella Dawn lay.

He'd bound her hands and ankles before leaving this morning. Her torn dress hung off her shoulder. If she hadn't put up such a fight, he wouldn't have had to tear the pretty blue thing. The curves of her collarbone were exposed. Feminine. Delicate. Like a porcelain doll.

He laid a plastic to-go bag on the rickety table and glanced at his old pencil box, then he sat on the side edge of the bed.

She drew up her legs, but not far enough out of his reach. Finally, she was in his grasp. He traced her bare legs with his index finger. Soft and lovely.

Bella Dawn flinched and whimpered.

"You don't have to be afraid of me, Bella Dawn. You know me."

Her hair was a disaster. Matted and stuck to her face from tears; mascara had run and caked in smoky trails. "I brought you something to eat."

Slowly, he eased the duct tape from her lips, but she hissed anyway. "Sorry. But I can't have you yelping out here." No one would suspect he'd bring her this close to where they'd discovered Tillie, Darla and Atta. Someone would have to be stupid to do that. Or smarter than them. Here in this cabin is where he first dreamed of touching a girl. Wanting a girl.

It should be here that he could. In privacy. Without any interruptions.

He finished peeling back the tape, and she shrieked through a hoarse croak.

He uncapped a bottle of water and held it up. "You thirsty?"

She halted her screams and stared at the water as if it were life. He had control. He decided if she got to have a drink or if she would not. She nodded and he eased the bottle to her cracked, dry lips and let her partake her fill. She gulped half the bottle; rivulets of water dribbled down her chin.

"Please let me go. I won't tell. I'll say I needed to get away. Please."

"They're looking for you, you know. I even led a search party myself." No one would suspect him.

Except Agent Rainwater. She was another matter altogether. He was going to have her. Patience. No rushing.

"Please, my son…"

"He's with Mother. Snug as a bug in a rug." He caressed her cheek. She flinched and he frowned.

"I don't know why you're doing this. You know I'd be willing to do whatever you ask voluntarily. Even…even here and like this. I don't understand!"

"Has it ever crossed your mind I don't want to have to pay someone? That a willing and free yes would mean more." He picked up the paper sack and pulled out a club sandwich. "Hungry?"

"No."

That word again. "Fine," he clipped. He inched closer, framed her face and kissed her. "So pretty." Then his hands wrapped around her neck. "So…fragile."

And he squeezed.

Monday, October 23
11:02 a.m.

John crouched in the tall grass behind two towering pines, his binoculars searching the old trailer and property up near the covered bridge. After last night, they'd decided to do a briefing over breakfast at the little coffee shop in Crow's Creek. John, Ty and Violet had ordered a light breakfast and strong coffee. Agent Pulaski had stuck around but forfeited breakfast this morning. Violet planned to talk to Regis today about his brother, Cecil. He knew full well they'd noted Cecil as a person of interest, and yet he'd kept his yap shut tight. Why? Violet wanted to spearhead that questioning.

Ty and Agent Pulaski's crack at Wendell didn't pay off. They couldn't find him. John was fairly certain they'd find Bella Dawn, but it would be too late. This killer showed no mercy, and he didn't prolong things. By now he knew his time was short. He wouldn't hang on to her.

But it was possible their killer was law enforcement. Which was why John had crept up to the Swallow soon after their breakfast meeting to watch for Greg and Whiskey, follow them and hope to find the meth lab. See Greg in his element. Violet had asked him questions the other night that raised hairs on John's head. Questions that John hadn't entertained until he realized Violet's motives. Greg had been undercover a very long time. He had tasted power and the freedom to do whatever he wanted. Whiskey ran this holler and maybe even the county. With Greg rising in power, he had access to darkness he might find enticing. Maybe he didn't want to bring Whiskey down at all. He was prolonging the bust because he liked the criminal life. He had money available that he wouldn't as an agent. Women.

What if Callie realized this and he killed her? He could be the Blind Eye Killer. John had no idea about his religious beliefs. He was seen with Bella Dawn. The murders didn't happen prior to Greg's arrival. He was bent on keeping John out of the loop with the reasoning that he needed more time. But what if he was stalling out because he was enjoying this life?

Enjoying getting away with murder. Whiskey wouldn't suspect his right hand. The DEA wouldn't. He was the inside man. The good guy.

But what if he wasn't?

That was what Violet had been thinking, and she didn't trust John with the information. He understood. He was emotionally invested in ways no one else on the team was. He needed to see Greg in his element. Determine for himself if he was undercover or if he'd become the legend written about him. Had he been influenced by the dark side? It was seductive. Even Callie had trouble coming out from her personas from time to time depending on how deep, how far and how long she'd been under. But she'd craved it. Thrived in it. Lived for it.

Far more than she'd lived for a normal life with him—with Stella.

John watched as a car pulled up. Ruby Boyd and Amy Miller exited the vehicle.

Greg stomped out of the rickety trailer, speaking to Ruby. She ignored him and met Whiskey at the door. He touched her face and kissed her. She didn't look happy at all.

Amy stayed down by the stairs with Greg. The front door closed, and all that was left was Greg and Amy. He ran his hand through her hair, tilted her head back, his eyes devouring her. John clenched his teeth as he whispered in her ear. Amy wasn't fighting, but she didn't appear to be as enthralled as Greg. Greg glanced up at the covered windows, then he led Amy inside. John beat his fist on his palm. If he had to guess, these women were being trafficked. Neither Ruby Boyd nor

Amy Miller seemed to be there out of free will. A beat-down, forlorn expression cast down their countenance. Greg had succumbed to the darkness. No one was around to pretend in front of. If he could see Amy Miller wasn't thrilled about his hands on her body, then he didn't care.

And John wasn't having it.

He kept low and moved through the tree line toward the house. What was he going to do? Out here, he wasn't in control. The law meant nothing. They could end him, bury his body and he'd never be found. No one out here confessed, confided or even considered aiding the law, or they did it anonymously.

He had no backup.

But those women were inside and helpless. Hopeless. John couldn't idly sit by. He was out about twenty feet from the trailer, gun in hand, when the front door opened and Ruby and Whiskey left. Ruby had a big black duffel bag on her shoulder. She tossed it in the back seat and they drove away.

But Greg and Amy, and at least one other man, remained inside.

He covered his mouth and nose as the scent of rotten eggs and cat urine permeated his senses. They were cooking it up in there. He crept closer to the trailer. The windows had been covered with black garbage bags, keeping prying eyes out.

No telling what they might be doing to Amy, especially if they were high. Now or never. He sprinted for the trailer when a huge boom sounded and a whoosh of fire exploded through the back window at the end of the trailer, engulfing it in flames.

John grabbed his phone and growled at the bad reception but got a weak signal and called 911 then circled to the front door and ran up the porch steps. The fire would spread quickly. John had to get in and try to help any survivors of the blast. He slung open the front door, and a scrawny guy with a scruffy beard, panic in his eyes and fire extinguisher hollered, "Who are you?"

"Where's Amy? Where's Greg?" Fumes nearly knocked him back, and then Greg appeared inside the kitchen.

"What is going on?" he boomed then coughed, soot on his face.

"Where's Amy?" John hollered, the flames licking the walls and devouring every inch. The heat grew stronger, and sweat trickled down his temples.

"Who is this?" Scrawny Guy said.

"We got to go! Now!" Greg said. "It's gonna blow! Richard, leave it. We gotta get out of here!"

"I can save it. I can!" Richard, aka Scrawny Guy, tried in vain to salvage the mess. Greg rushed to him and they fought, Richard cuffing his chin and knocking him backward.

"Greg!" John hollered. "Where is Amy?" He wasn't leaving without her.

Greg got to his feet, and Richard had run down the hall to the back bedroom.

"She's dead! She died in the explosion. Move, John!" He bolted out the door, and John followed as a boom deafened his ears, the trailer shook and the impact sent him flying off the porch and onto the ground with a thud that stole his breath and rattled every bone in his body. His vision was spotty, and his hearing was muffled like being underwater.

Richard hadn't made it out.

Hands wrapped around his shirt collar and yanked him from the ground.

Cursing and hollering spewed. John blinked and regained his senses and his breath. Greg had him clutched by fistfuls of his shirt, his face sooty and eyes furious.

John shoved him backward. "Get your hands off me!"

"Why are you here? How did you even get here?" Greg screamed, spittle flying from his lips. "What did I tell you!" The entire trailer was on fire, and smoked billowed and smothered them. John coughed and the faint sounds of sirens wailed in the distance.

"I came to find out if you were the killer." He shoved him back. "I saw you with Amy Miller. She didn't seem too into your groping." Greg came for him again, but John blocked him. "Keep your hands off me."

Greg coughed and sputtered. "You think I'm killing women? You think I was forcing myself on Amy Miller?"

"I saw you groping her." Saw the manhandling. Leading her inside.

"I'm being watched twenty-four seven. You could have blown my cover. Would have if Richard had made it out alive."

"A man died. All you're worried about is your cover?"

Greg's nostrils flared. "Whiskey already suspects someone on the inside of leaking the Swallow to you and that agent with a mouth. I haven't worked this hard to have you come in and screw it up."

"I don't believe you!" John's fury exploded like the trailer. Greg drove out of the county to meet with John. No one was watching him drink at that bar or withhold information. He was lying. What else had he been lying about?

"Did you kill my wife?"

Greg's eyes widened then his fist connected with John's face before he could duck. John swung back, defending himself, and clipped Greg on the chin. Greg hunched like a linebacker and rammed him until he hit the ground again.

Greg reared back, but John caught his fist before the punch landed.

First responders drove up, but John ignored them.

Vehicle doors opened and closed.

"You think I killed Callie! I *loved* Callie. I understood her."

"She loved me!"

"Well, that's not what she told me when she was in *my* bed."

What? Time stilled and shock spread, not allowing his brain to process. Callie and he had issues, but she wouldn't have done this to him. They'd loved one another. Fury unleashed and he shoved Greg off of him, straddling him and drawing back his fist. "That's not true."

"It is." He put his hands up in surrender. "I loved her and she loved me, John. I want nothing more than to bring Whiskey down and find out who killed her. *I* want to be the one to do it. I owe her." He sighed. "I'm not a serial killer. As soon as Whiskey left, I ignored Amy. I tried to get her out. I knew it was gonna blow. I'm sorry Richard stayed inside. But there was nothing else I could do. He was high and irrational."

John couldn't do it. Couldn't punch Greg. He dropped his fist and slid to the ground beside him. He glanced up and Violet stood nearby. Then Detective Owsley drove up and ambled out of his marked unit. "Didn't expect you to be here, Detective Orlando," Owsley said.

"I, uh…thought I might find Whiskey if I followed this guy. Find some concrete evidence if he's our killer. But Whiskey isn't here, and by the time I arrived, the place had already blown up. I went for survivors, and it blew again. There are none except myself and him."

Regis eyed them both as if weighing his words as truth. Greg said nothing.

Violet slowly approached John. "Are you all right?"

She'd heard it all. How humiliating.

Callie had been having an affair, and as much as he wanted to deny Greg's words, he knew they were true. Callie had betrayed him. He'd feared she might leave him for the job, but never for another man.

John stood and lightly touched her cheek. "Mostly."

"I had the scanner on. Heard there was an explosion and had a sick feeling you might have done something stupid and be here." She looked into his eyes, bit her lower lip and whispered, "I was scared for me too." That might be the most forthright Violet had ever been about how she felt concerning him. It soothed a sliver of his sore heart.

"Who was inside, Heart?" Greg's cover last name.

"Richard Green, Terrance Filmore and Amy Miller. I'd just arrived, like he said. Had no clue what was going on."

Regis rolled his eyes and walked toward the back of the inferno.

John locked eyes with Violet again. "Thank you. For coming to my rescue."

"Day late and a dollar short." She gave him a close-lipped smile. "I'm sorry."

About Callie.

"Yeah. Me too." But right now wasn't the time to sulk or cry over it. Bella Dawn was still missing.

"Local police can handle this. It isn't directly linked to the Blind Eye Killer." Violet paused. "Is it?"

John shook his head. "I don't think so. Not anymore." If Greg was keeping John from investigating in order to avenge Callie, then keeping tight-lipped made sense. "I'm not going to say for certain. Nothing is certain."

"That's the truth."

"My car is about two miles back off the road behind some trees."

"Of course it is. I want to talk to Regis since he's here."

John followed Violet behind the blazing trailer toward the tree line where Regis Owsley stood watching the place burn.

Violet cast her attention on Regis. "Guess what I found out?"

Regis shoved his hands in his cheap black dress pants' pockets and cocked his head. "What's that?"

"Your brother is Cecil Johnson."

Regis's eyebrows scrunched. "You say that like I'm supposed to be surprised. I know he's my brother. Half-brother. Same mama different daddies. But I figure you can gather that from our last names."

Smug and annoying.

"Why didn't you tell us this? He's a suspect, and you should have divulged that information. You have a conflict of interest."

"I don't have a conflict of interest though. Cecil isn't the Blind Eye Killer, Agent. Not to mention you have no evidence proving he had any involvement at all."

"We have the leather pouches," John said.

"Okay. So. He made a few pouches for friends he grew up with. Go ahead and put me on your list too then. I made some wood crafts for two out of four." He laughed and Violet knew he was right. They had nothing but circumstantial evidence.

Violet moved slowly and ate up the distance between them. "Who says you're not on my list? Maybe higher than your brother." She sniffed and locked eyes with him. "I'm on the hunt."

"Your scent's off."

"Why didn't you tell us that you left the Swallow with Bella Dawn Saturday night? You never mentioned you were even there."

Regis's eyes widened. Now that news surprised him. "Who told you that?"

"Your brother for one," she said flatly.

He inhaled sharply. "I went by to check on a friend. Couldn't find her. The commotion was breaking out, and Bella Dawn was on the run. She'd been popped on the cheek with broken glass, but she was fine. I helped her outside to the parking lot. Asked about my friend."

"What friend?"

His nostrils flared. "Ruby Boyd."

"And then what?"

"Then I left Bella Dawn by her car and went looking for Ruby again. I couldn't find her and gave up. The brawl was contained, and I went home. Period."

Violet stared him down. "You're no longer privy to any information on this case. Not until we officially clear your brother—and you."

"Have fun with that." Regis's cocky words grated Violet's nerves, but she ignored them and climbed back up the hill.

"I hate that guy." She growled beneath her breath.

"He goads you because he has zero respect for you, but he also wants to sleep with you." John wasn't a fool. The lust clouding Regis Owsley's eyes was unmistakable.

"Fat chance." She climbed in the driver's side, and John eased into the passenger seat. His head ached and his back felt like he'd been almost blown up. "If he's not the killer, he's at least complicit or hiding something. Could be hiding the fact he knows what's going on and has been turning a blind eye—or engaging it."

"Drugs and prostitution?"

"Why not? There are no rules up here." She looked at John. "And that's why I'm not playing by any."

Chapter Nineteen

Monday, October 23
2:45 p.m.

Violet had left John back at the B and B. He needed to rest.
Ty should be back from Whitesburg and hopefully had information from Ray Smith regarding Dr. D.J. Lanslow's alibi. If
Ray didn't corroborate Dr. Lanslow's alibi, then the doctor
moved up on the person of interest list. He was hiding something and Violet's gut wouldn't let up. But now she wanted
answers to something else.

Mother's suggestion to let things go might be good advice,
but Violet couldn't let it go. She was closer than she'd ever
been. Reeva might not admit to knowing Loretta Boyd, and
Loretta might not want to talk about the past, but maybe she
could get something from Ruby Boyd. Mother said Ruby
didn't know anything, but that might not be true. Ruby might
know more than Mother realized.

She knocked on Ruby's door and waited a beat. Two. A car

was in the dirt drive. Someone was surely here. Violet walked around the back. The creek rushed and whooshed. The yard was kempt, and a few toys were organized in a row at the back of the house. She climbed the small deck stairs and rapped on the back door.

Ruby Boyd peeked out of the sheer curtain hanging over the window of the back door and dread filled her blue-green eyes. Violet expected as much.

She slowly opened the door.

"Can I help you?" she asked softly. She was dressed in faded jeans and a thick brown sweater. Her hair was pulled up in the same messy bun Violet wore on the weekends when she cleaned house.

"Can I come in?"

"Um…okay." She swung open the door, and Violet smelled cinnamon.

Inside, the kitchen was tidy with navy Formica countertops in a U-shape. The living room was full of toys, and Lula sat on the floor near the coffee table with a cookie in hand and a puzzle on the table. She glanced up but didn't speak.

"I baked cookies. Would you like one?"

"No thanks. I don't do much sugar."

"Coffee?"

"Coffee sounds good."

Ruby motioned for Violet to have a seat at the kitchen table. She eased into a wooden chair with white backing and caught Lula's eye.

Lula dramatically waved. "I know you."

"Yes, we met at Mother's. You were eating cheese curls."

"I like cheese curls. I'm doin' a puzzle. You like puzzles?"

"I love puzzles. I get to do them every day at my job."

"Lula," Ruby said. "Mind your business while we talk, okay?"

"Yes, ma'am." She occupied herself with the puzzle on the coffee table.

Ruby opened the fridge. "How do you take it?"

"Like this."

"Me too." She closed the fridge door and sat across from Violet, stealing glances to see their similarities—ones hidden by the shadows the other night.

Violet cupped her mug with both hands. "I don't really mince words, so... I'm your sister."

"I know," she said softly. "Mama told me you were here. That you'd probably come by to find me. It's strange." She sipped her cup.

"It is. What did your mom tell you?" Violet sipped the cheap coffee and waited patiently.

"Mama, I gotta pee."

"Okay, hon. Go." Ruby sighed. "Do you have kids?"

"No."

"I don't see a ring."

"Reason for that." Ruby was stalling. Violet would give her a few more questions before redirecting.

"Ever been married?"

"No."

"Me neither. I thought maybe Lula's father might..." She sighed and glanced at the counter. Nothing but a large black duffel bag. But it connected with her statement, which was about Lula's father, and the duffel bag that John said earlier she was carrying from the trailer with Whiskey. Whiskey must be Lula's father.

She sipped her coffee again. "All I knew growing up was Mama made a bad choice when she ran away. Running away never solves problems. It only proves you're better off in the holler." But the look in her eyes revealed she might not believe that.

"Why did she want to run away?"

Ruby scraped her thumbnail back and forth on the table. "Guess she wanted out of this life. This place. Thought she'd be better on her own even at that age. But she was in Memphis for less than a month when she met a man. He was kind to her and asked her if she wanted to go for pizza—she'd been living on the streets looking for reputable work. She said yes and he took her. He did things to her. Marked her. Grandma Wanda says that she was gone almost four years with no word. No idea why she chose Memphis other than she adored Elvis."

"Mother said your mom didn't know she was pregnant when she returned home."

"She didn't." Ruby sipped her coffee. "Mama started feeling sick. Dr. Crocker came. She was a few weeks pregnant."

Why had Adam let her go without a baby? Did he think she couldn't produce and wasn't worth his time? "Did she say how she got free?"

"No. Grandma Wanda said one day the phone rang, and Mama was on the other end. Asked her to come pick her up at a bus station in Memphis. She did."

"No one ever called the police?"

She shook her head. "Grandma Wanda said it was over and they were going to just forget it since she was home and well, and she knew Mother and Grandma Wanda had been right all along. The world is much scarier than here in the holler." She glanced at Violet. "Is that what happened to your mama?"

"Basically. But I was born in captivity, and then he let her go." She leaned forward, uninterested in the past for a moment. "What scares you in the holler? Because I'll tell you something. This place doesn't feel good to me. I'm ready to get home."

She peeped at the duffel bag again. "Where's home for you?"

"Memphis."

"I've never been anywhere." She shrugged.

Lula came bouncing into the room, her panties sticking up from her pink cotton pants. "I washed my hands."

"Good girl. If you'll let me and the nice lady talk, you can have another snickerdoodle."

"I will." She snatched a snickerdoodle. "Can I go play by the crick?"

"No. Stay inside today, okay?" Ruby rubbed her thumb and forefinger together and glanced out the window. What was she concerned about?

"Okay."

"Lula tells me you have a leather purse. Cecil Johnson gave you that?"

"Yeah," she said, surprise in her voice. "Cecil's a good guy. Just a lot of...issues. Like everyone else, I guess."

"He give you any other gifts?"

"I got gifts from Him," Lula said and bit into her cookie.

"From Cecil?"

"From Him."

Ruby's cheeks reddened. "She's not talking about Cecil. She's talking about something else."

"Show her the doll, Mama. And my other stuff."

A doll. Violet's stomach turned. "Gifts from who?" Violet frowned. "Someone you know?"

Lula ran from the room and hurried back with an arm full of things. "My gifts from Him."

Ruby sighed, worry furrowed along her brow. "You have enough on your plate with solving what's happened to Tillie, Darla, Atta and Nadine. This is—"

"Underwear." Violet plucked the doll from Lula's arm. "Do you know who made this or who these belong to?"

"They're my mom's silkies."

"Lula, what did I say about another cookie and being good? Go watch your cartoons." Ruby snagged a bag of candy and a silver compact from Lula's arms. When Lula was in the living room watching TV, Ruby rubbed her temple. "Those are my undergarments, and that compact was Atta's. I gave it to her for her birthday last year. The candy—she kept a bag in her car. Total Skittles addict. Someone has been leaving these gifts for Lula down by the crick. She's never seen him. Only his back. She calls him *Him*. It's nothing to worry about, just weird."

Violet would beg to differ. "Someone came into your home and stole these. Then he fashioned a dress from them and made a doll to give your preschool-aged daughter. And you won't let her go play outside. Nothing to worry about? Really?"

Ruby collapsed in the kitchen chair. "I have a friend in the sheriff's office, and he's been looking into it. Says it's nothing to worry about. He put new locks on my doors. And anyway, no one is going to hurt me." She stared at the floor either in shame or because she couldn't look Violet in the eye while lying to herself.

"Why?"

"Because..."

Because she felt she had a measure of protection because she had a child with Whiskey, a relationship, unlike the other women. That wasn't enough.

"Just because Whiskey is Lula's father and whatever that makes him to you, doesn't mean you're untouchable, Ruby. Women he 'protects' are dying. I think the killer stole underwear from Bella Dawn. I found it as a scarf on Mason's doll. Now she's missing. Did any of the other girls mention they'd had undergarments stolen?" None had children, but that didn't mean he wasn't stealing their underwear. He'd stolen Violet's. It had to be the same man.

"I don't recall it. No. But then I never said anything about mine so…" Ruby rubbed her lips together. "And as far as Whiskey and Lula, who told you that?"

"I'm good at the dot-to-dot game. Are you a couple?"

Ruby's laugh was icy. "No. But he looks out for us." She eyed the bag again.

"What's in that bag? You don't want me to know, but you're giving it away because you keep drawing attention to it."

Ruby stood and walked to the counter, let her fingers graze the canvas material. "You have no idea how great you have it. You get to go wherever you want. Make your own choices. Nothing to fear. Hide from. You save people's lives. You do good." She turned then. "I wish I had your life."

Irony. Violet had been wishing for Ruby's life. But now that she had a closer look, was maternal love enough? "If you have people looking out for you, then what are you afraid of? Who are you hiding from?" Violet carried her cup to the sink and set it beside a few other dishes. "You wouldn't want my life, Ruby. I'm here because of dead people. I show up when death isn't prevented." She laid her hand on the bag, noticed their nails had the same shape. "I could help you though. Whiskey only looks out for Whiskey. You know that, right?"

Ruby's eyes filled with tears. "I'm leaving," she whispered. "I'm leaving Night Holler. I'm taking Lula, and we're getting our own life. A better life."

Why was she telling her this? Because there was no one else to tell. Because she needed support and help. "Do you need me to help you get out from under him?"

She shook her head. "He's going to help me. But you're right. He's only helping me because I'm going to help him. But we'll be set. We'll have money, and I can go somewhere nice. Where Lula can grow up and be someone better than who she'd be here. Better than me. Anything besides me."

"You could come to Memphis. I can help you." The words

tumbled out, and she instantly regretted them. How could she help Ruby and her daughter? She wasn't that kind of person. She didn't get personally involved.

But she was her sister.

And Ruby wasn't a serial killer. Wicked. Vile. She was under the thumb of a man who imprisoned her with fear and bargained with her life. "What's in this bag?"

"I can't tell you. And I know by law you can't look. It's not tied to your case. But it's going to buy me freedom."

Violet doubted that, but she was impressed with her cleverness. "If what I think is in that bag and you get caught… you'll lose your freedom and your daughter. Does your mom or Mother know about your plans?"

"No." She grabbed Violet's hands, pleading in her eyes. "And you have to promise not to tell them."

It would endanger them, and she was trying to protect them. That was why she was talking to Violet. She was an outsider who wouldn't tattletale. "Okay. But if you change your mind and you decide you don't want to take this risk," she handed her a business card, "you can call me. I—" What was going on with her? "I'll help you. I can help you get set up in Memphis."

Ruby half smiled. "I believe you. Maybe, maybe I will."

"In the meantime, you can't trust anyone, Ruby. Not even Regis Owsley. I know you're friends. No one. Keep your doors locked. This guy has a religious background and is serious about it. He's killing women who clean houses." She pointed to the duffel bag. "What do you do for a living, Ruby? Are you a Whiskey Girl?" Her heart sped up, and her blood turned to ice.

Ruby looked away. "Not exactly."

"Are you a holler girl? Do you really clean houses?"

She ran her bottom lip between her teeth. "I'm between jobs," she murmured. "Now. But I, for real, cleaned houses."

Violet noticed Ruby hadn't actually denied prostituting or drug running though. Maybe she had done both. She wanted out. She might have also legit cleaned some house to save up money to leave. Violet recognized shame reddening Ruby's cheeks. But she had helped Violet piece together the difference between both girls. If someone wanted a Whiskey Girl, they wanted drugs. If they were after sex, they asked for a holler girl.

But both came from Whiskey.

Monday, October 23
4:52 p.m.

Exhaustion added invisible weight to Violet's limbs as she opened the door to the B and B. After another hour with Ruby, she'd concluded maybe she had the better life. No one forced her to make her choices or do things she didn't want.

Whiskey.

He was at the crux of this whole holler. Calling shots. Running drugs and prostitution and no one would stand up to him for fear of disappearing like Bobby Lloyd and Earl Levine. You touched one of his girls—his possessions—and you vanished. The rules, however, didn't apply to him. He could beat up on the girls and call in a doctor on the take to fix them up. Those who weren't afraid and could do something about it stood by.

Regis Owsley. Was he paying for Ruby's services? He called her a friend. Ruby hadn't come out and admitted to prostitution, but it was pretty obvious. Anyone else cleaning houses was a prostitute—if Cecil Johnson was telling the truth. Why would he lie about that? And she had a purse. Violet had asked about clients of the victims, but Ruby kept her mouth shut—fear had her bound too.

Except she was leaving. Probably doing a major drug run, which could put her in greater danger, but Violet hadn't been able to talk her out of it, and technically she had no idea what was in that duffel bag. Could have been gym clothes. No judge would give her a warrant to search it properly. She hadn't been playing by the rules, but deep down she didn't want to see her sister go to prison for drugs. Not when she wanted out and felt trapped. It had to be a big payoff to risk it all.

"Lord," she whispered, "maybe You're not real. But if You are, I get You don't want me. Ruby…she's not me. She's a desperate woman who needs help. Please help her. Amen or something."

As she entered the bedroom, she noticed the dolls hadn't been turned faces out. Since the disappearance of her underwear, she'd been strategically packing her suitcase and keeping it tucked in the chifforobe for harder access.

Earlier, Asa had called from Charleston for a briefing and she'd refrained from sharing what she'd experienced personally about Adam, Ruby and the underwear. She did fill him in on the investigation and that the meth lab had blown but John was relatively unscathed.

He'd found out his wife had been unfaithful and with Greg. Violet had expected John to pummel him to a pulp, but he'd dropped his fist as if it wasn't worth it. The man had taken his wife and taunted him with it.

Violet would have reacted differently. Pushed him off a dock.

They were entirely different. And according to John, the difference was God.

She didn't have the energy to think about that. Right now she wanted to know why the killer was giving dolls to little children. The only other holler girl who had a child was Bella

Dawn. Later, Violet would check in on little Mason and see if he'd been given any other trinkets or toys too.

She opened the chifforobe, grabbed her suitcase and noticed a draft of cool air on her hand. That was odd. She peeped around the sides and noticed the piece of furniture was flush against the wall. She pulled on it to scoot it forward, but it was anchored. Who anchored old clothes closets to the wall?

Tiny sharp chills scraped against her spine as she hauled her suitcase out and then felt around the back of the sturdy piece of furniture until she found a small moon-shaped groove on the upper right side. She slid her finger into the groove and pushed; the back of the chifforobe gave way.

"What fresh—" An icy draft chilled her skin as she inhaled the scents of damp earth, must and rot. She grabbed her gun, mini Maglite and cell phone from the dresser, turned on the light, then climbed through the chifforobe to a narrow hallway that ran inside the home. Wooden walls and flooring were covered in dirt, bugs and cobwebs.

Whoever had stolen her underwear and messed with the dolls had gotten into the room through the chifforobe. Someone who had knowledge of the passageways. Regis for one. Cecil was his brother; he'd have knowledge. Anyone in the holler might know about it.

A narrow hallway branched out to the left and opened up to a small room, which was backed up to Fiona's room. She entered. The room was sparse. A few jars on shelves. Two chairs. Cobwebs, dust, wood shavings and rodent pellets. Holes in a few walls from termite damage.

Exiting the room, she shined her light down the dim hall, following it and batting away cobwebs. The place could have been used as part of the Underground Railroad or for boot-legging. Maybe both. Up ahead was a set of stairs that descended to the first floor, possibly to a basement. Violet hadn't explored the house. She decided to start now. She descended the old wooden stairs, keeping light on each one in case they were rotted, until she came to a large rectangular door with a latch. She undid the latch and pushed on the door. It opened up into the formal living room, the covered porch beyond it. Stepping out, she turned and closed the door to see a large Civil War painting.

"What are you doing down here and why have you been rolling in spider webs?" John approached her and picked the sticky webbing from her hair, his nose scrunched. He'd showered and smelled clean and alluring. His hair was still damp, and his chin was bruised.

"I found a secret passageway."

"Are we in the *Clue* movie now, Miss Scarlet?" John grinned then sobered when he realized she wasn't messing around.

She pointed to the painting. "It's a door. One of probably many in this creepy home. It leads upstairs into my chifforobe."

"What?"

"Let me show you."

"I just showered." He picked another cobweb from her shirt and brushed the dirt from her shoulder.

"Well unless the water is out, you can take another." She opened the painting. "You'd make a terrible Indiana Jones." She stepped inside and heard him huff as he stepped in behind her. John had to walk sideways down the passage, his shoulders too broad.

"At least we didn't find Aunt Hossie in here."

"There's plenty more hiding spots," Violet muttered and began shining the light on the walls, running her hands along them until she found a slight bump in the wood. She carefully pulled, and a small round opening appeared.

Just enough space for an eyeball.

She could see inside her room. See her bed. The dolls. Her stomach tightened into a ball as she replayed the past week in her mind. Getting dressed. Going to bed. A ball of anger rose, filling her cheeks with heat. "He's been watching me."

John nudged her aside and peered through the hole. "When I get my hands on him... Do you think there are holes in all the rooms?"

"Probably." She felt along the walls and found two more. Her phone rang, and she flinched. "It's Ty." She answered and put him on speaker. "What's up?"

"What're you doing?"

"Peeping in holes." She peered through another one. "Where are you?"

"I don't even want to know what that means." He chuckled. "Right now, Agent Pulaski and I are back with the search party for Bella Dawn. Three things. First, the barmaid confirmed that Atta Atwater had come in around one a.m. the night she went missing and she did have a butterfly stitch. She had a couple of drinks, talked to Amy Miller and then left alone, which must be true since her car was in her driveway. Doesn't mean someone didn't follow her from the bar."

So Jimmy Russell and Amy Miller had both been telling the truth. "Next."

"Jimmy Russell said he didn't bring up Ruby because she's a friend and he wanted to leave her out of it for personal reasons. I pressed. The reason. Whiskey doesn't want Ruby anywhere near this investigation and what Whiskey wants Whiskey gets."

"I really hate this guy." Whiskey didn't want Ruby anywhere near them, not when he planned to use her for a big drug run. "And lastly?"

"D.J. Lanslow's alibi has burned to ash. Turns out he wasn't at the cabin at all. But Ray was and he had company from

Friday through Sunday night about nine. Woman in town named Carlotta Joyner."

Where was the good doctor who played fiddle with catgut and had zero alibi for the weekend when Atta died? He had ties to all the victims. "I knew he was holding back when we first arrived. Any news on Bella Dawn?"

Ty sighed. "No. The search party is tired, and the rain's coming in again. They've postponed until first light tomorrow. We're not going to find her alive. I think everyone knows that."

If they found her at all. "What about mines?" She swung a glance at John and mouthed *sorry*. She hated to bring up bad memories of his wife. "No one is connecting Callie Orlando's murder to these women except us, and we've kept that private. Maybe he's gone back to a mine because he knows locals are searching caves. See if you can get a local team to revisit where she was found and neighboring mines. It's worth a shot."

"Agreed. What are you going to do?"

"Go find out why D.J. Lanslow lied about his alibi." She paused. "Hey, did you get a call from Quantico about the bloody shirt we found and the beer bottle? We should have heard something. Asa called Rebecca personally and asked if she'd do me a favor and put it at the top of the list, especially since Bella Dawn is missing."

"No. But FedEx picked it up at the SO and took it. I'll call. Check on it. They should at least be able to tell us if it's Atta's blood or not and if they could pull a print."

"Call me when you hear something. I still haven't ruled out Wendell Atwater." She ended the call. "We can go do our jobs or wait here for Perverted Peeping Tom to show back up. My guess is it's Regis Owsley, but I can't ignore Cecil Johnson. He meets the Blind Eye Killer criteria too."

"Well, you can't sleep here any longer. You're being spied

on. And stalked. It's been over twenty-four hours. We need to talk to Aunt Hossie."

"This is all the more reason to stay and not to talk to her. He doesn't know I know his little hiding spot. Tonight, we'll catch him. You in the walls and me as bait."

John grunted. "I don't like that."

"'Cause the cobwebs?"

"No." He brushed off the idea with a toss of his hand. "Because it's dangerous."

"For you. You're the one who's gonna be back there with him." She gave him the eye. "It's a sting, and we're trained to do them. If he doesn't show up, we talk to Hossie and we stay in Pikeville. But I have a feeling he's going to show."

"Fine."

Now to hunt down D.J. Lanslow and find out why he was lying.

Chapter Twenty

Monday, October 23
6:26 p.m.

John listened to his GPS tell him which turns to take as they headed for D.J. Lanslow's home. Violet hadn't said much more about the passageways or the peeper. She had a point. If they ambushed him in the tunnels and it was the Blind Eye Killer, they could close out this case and he could, hopefully, find out if he'd killed Callie too.

While he'd rested earlier, he hadn't actually done much resting. He'd prayed and did a fair amount of tear shedding and called Stella to hear her sweet voice. Callie had cheated on him. For how long? Prior to going undercover? Was that why Greg had asked her to join the team—they'd worked together before. He'd concluded those answers didn't matter.

What mattered was finding who killed her. And moving on.

"I saw my half-sister today. While you were in your room."

John had a feeling she'd attempt to see Ruby. "And how did that go?"

Violet dug inside her pocket and pulled out a roll of Mentos. She offered him one, and he held out his hand. "Beneficial but not in the way I wanted personally. But she's a holler girl. And she might run drugs for Whiskey, though she never said either directly. All this time I've been wishing for her life, thinking how it must have been to grow up being loved by her mom and grandmother. Only she gets roped into prostitution by Whiskey and pressured to do a run for him. One I'm guessing Nadine was supposed to do before she was murdered."

"Do you think her family knows?"

"No. I think she's trying to protect them. The less they know the safer they are. But they might. No one can stand up to him. And those who could, won't." Violet shook her head. "I want to help her, John. I sense she's lost."

Pot meet kettle, but he refrained from voicing it aloud. "What about you?" They hadn't talked about the breakdown at the Swallow where she'd emptied herself out in tears.

In one hundred feet, turn right onto Juniper Lane. John turned on his blinker.

Violet let out a long breath. "I prayed. For Ruby's protection. That's the closest I've gotten to God in a long time. I don't know."

"You know what I think?" He slowed as the GPS instructed him to take the next left onto Golden Lane. "I think God brought you here for more than a case. I think He's showing you, Violet, that He is real. He hears your cries and knows your heart. That's what I call providence."

"God had to use a serial killer to get me here? How 'bout a way that didn't include a bunch of brutally murdered girls? How about save them and get me here another way? Seems kinda cruel." Violet popped another Mentos.

"I don't think He orchestrated these murders, Violet. But I do think He uses things meant for evil to bring about His redemptive purposes."

"Maybe. I don't know. This place. It feels different than any place I've been."

Maybe it was because she was now on the cusp of change, of turning her life completely around. He couldn't be sure. But something was stirring inside her, or she'd have never uttered a prayer, and the fact that it wasn't even for her but for her sister revealed selflessness. One who wanted to save lives, not take them. Violet was willing to risk her own life to help someone she barely knew, but she was blood—kin—and she would fight. That was no serial killer.

That heart at the root was a warrior. A rescuer.

"When this is all over, I'll help you get her the aid she needs."

She half smiled as the GPS let them know they'd arrived at their destination on the left. "Thank you."

Dr. Lanslow's home was a modest ranch style in a small middle-class neighborhood with mature trees and tidy lawns. They exited the car and approached the house. The shades were pulled, but a hint of light flickering from a TV revealed he was here at around six thirty in the evening. "If this goes well, let's get food after, and also if it doesn't."

"You mean if it turns out he's not the killer, and we don't have a shoot-out or have to book him?" Violet asked and retrieved her FBI credentials then rang the doorbell.

"Something like that. But either way, I'm hungry."

"Don't worry. It won't come to that. I only need one bullet to end it," she said as the door opened and he studied her cool, stoic face. He believed that wholeheartedly.

Dr. D.J. Lanslow opened the door wearing sweats, a wrinkled T-shirt and a forlorn expression. He had bedhead and a five-o'clock shadow. Didn't appear he'd been to work today. "Doctor Lanslow, we need to talk to you. Can we come in?" John asked.

"Sure," he mumbled and opened the glass door. They stepped into a clean home, no clutter in sight. His violin case was propped against the entryway wall. He led them into the small living area. A fire blazed over gas logs, and the TV was on the news station. "Have a seat."

They chose the brown leather couch, and he slumped in his recliner. Four empty beer cans were crumpled on the table next to him. Violet motioned with her chin for John to take the lead.

"We wanted to go back over everyone's alibis. You were with Ray Smith, camping at Pine Mountain when Atta Atwater went missing, yes?" John asked.

He raked a hand over his face, and John noticed his bloodshot eyes. "Yeah."

"Right. See we know that's not true. Well, half of it is. Ray was in his cabin all weekend but with a woman named Carlotta, and they say you were never there. Let's try this again, shall we? Where were you the weekend Atta Atwater went missing?"

Violet caught his eye then looked away, and he followed her gaze to the Ten Commandments hanging on the wall with a leather cross next to it. Looked like one from Alpha and Omega.

"Are you religious, Doctor?"

D.J. used his hands to dry wash his face. "I attended seminary with Wendell. We grew up together, but I never actually went into the ministry. Dropped after first semester. I wanted to serve in other ways. I went to medical school, but I didn't give up my faith or anything. Why?"

"What's your violin strings made out of?" Violet asked. There went giving John the lead.

"Catgut," he muttered. "Why?"

She looked at John again, and he leaned forward. "Alibi?"

D.J. sniffed. "No point living anyway. Might as well jump." His tone was low. Depressed. He was grieving. That's what was happening here. John recognized the pain in his eyes and the hopelessness. "I wasn't camping with Ray, but I asked him to be my alibi long before you came into the picture. I needed it for Dr. Crocker, to take off work without being questioned. I was in Lexington for the weekend. Apartment hunting. I leased a place. I have the proof, and you can call the apartment manager. I have receipts of places I ate. Gas receipts."

John frowned. "Did you not want Dr. Crocker to know you were moving? Why would you hide that alibi?"

"Because I was getting the place for me and Amy."

John frowned again. "Amy Miller?"

D.J. nodded.

Amy Miller, who had been killed earlier today in the meth lab explosion. Amy Miller, who Greg had messed with. "Dr. Lanslow, I don't mean to offend or add pain to your grief. I do understand what it's like to lose someone you love. But...it's come to our knowledge—or at least what we're gathering—that Amy Miller might have been a holler prostitute. She 'cleaned houses' like Atta Atwater, like all our victims except Nadine."

D.J.'s eyes filled. "I know," he whispered. "But we fell in love, and she wanted out. We were going to run away. Once I had everything in order. Get married. She didn't want to do what she was doing, but...her mom died when she was ten, leaving her alone with her stepfather, and he...he abused her. She left him at sixteen and became a holler girl. It was money, food, protection. She was naive and lost—she thought it was hope. Thought it was going to be freeing since she was in charge, but she was never in charge, and by the time she realized it, she was in too deep."

"How does Whiskey keep these girls in line? Threats? Do they all run his drugs or just Nadine? Would you be willing to testify? We could put him away for drug and sex trafficking."

D.J. wiped bleary eyes, and his brow knit together. "Whiskey doesn't have anything to do with the holler girls. He runs drugs. Everyone knows that. He does provide protection for them. And Nadine did sometimes prostitute to buy weed. Whiskey Girls didn't get drugs for free."

"What kind of protection?" John asked.

"He's the muscle if men get rowdy or hurt them. Almost every man around knows if they hurt the girls or do something they don't want done—they're dead."

Like Earl Levine and Bobby Lloyd.

"That's why Amy did it. She needed money, but more so she wanted protection from being hurt again. She realized that was totally screwed up, but she was in and once you're in… you're never getting out. Not alive."

All these victims appeared to have had abusive pasts by men. Girls like Atta, whose father and husband beat her up. Or Tillie, who had been sexually assaulted in college. D.J. was right, at the time it would appear to be a better deal for the girls. It would feel as though they had control when, really, they had none. They had exchanged one abuse for another.

Reality hit John with a one-two punch. "Is that why you needed a fake alibi for Dr. Crocker? He doesn't just tend to the girls for Whiskey, does he? He's far more than the holler doctor. He runs the show. Whiskey is his front. His muscle."

D.J. frowned. "Whiskey is no one's front. People are afraid of him, sure. He has some power, and he's been running drugs and other criminal activities only because he's *allowed*. But neither he nor Dr. Crocker run this holler, Detective Orlando."

Violet and John shared a confused glance. "Then who does?"

D.J.'s laugh was humorless. "Mother. Mother runs this holler and has for decades."

"Have you come to check on Mason, hon?" Mother asked as she rocked on her porch, an afghan over her lap and a steaming cup of what smelled like apple cider in her hands. "He's asleep."

Violet's skin broke out in chills. She'd trusted Mother with the child's welfare and placed him in the arms of a madame! She'd felt maternal love from her and wished she was part of her life. But had she been born into this family, she'd have been forced into the family business. According to D.J., holler girls had been run by a Boyd Mother since Mother herself was a girl. All daughters were required to prostitute, and any other girl who needed protection or covering came to Mother. Mother had said she had many surrogate daughters.

No wonder Ruby didn't want Violet to tell her mom or Mother. No wonder Loretta ran away so young. She wanted out. Violet's stomach had been in knots since they left Lanslow's home.

Violet glanced at John, who stood behind her. "No, I'm here to make sure he gets as far away from you as one can possibly get. I'm here to make sure you can't traffic another single child, girl or woman."

Mother's sharp blue eyes narrowed. "Excuse me, missy?"

"Don't call me missy." Seething words sat on the edge of her tongue, but she held them in regrettably. "You turned out your own daughter and granddaughter, who ran away to escape the same fate. And your great-granddaughter."

Mother stood, the blanket falling to the porch floor. She was dressed in a long skirt, and her feet were tucked into thick boots. When she slammed her mug onto the table, the cider splashed out. "And look where that got Loretta. Stolen. Some man had his way with her for almost four years, controlling her, forcing her."

"How is that any different from what *you're* doing? Forcing. Controlling. Letting men have their way," John said.

"No." She pointed her bony finger at him and then Violet and descended another stair, her long gray hair blowing behind her. "I empowered them to take control of their life. They choose who and when and how much. And they give the Good Lord back His due. They help the poor and the needy and learn how to be kind and decent. Like I had to learn."

Violet had no words. Mother's reasoning was stunning, twisted. Disgusting.

"When poverty came, my drunk of a daddy left us. And my mama did what had to be done to put food on the table. One afternoon, one of the men had an interest in me. Instead of letting him take me, Mama gave him a price and a limit to what he could or couldn't do. They didn't get to run the show. We did and we still do. Men are violent, so we allow them to indulge their violent tendencies—by protecting the girls. A man hurts them or doesn't comply, and they get hurt."

They get dead was what she meant.

"And when we get our clutches on this killer…he won't see another day either."

Did she even care that she was basically revealing murderous intent to a federal agent? Imogene Boyd thought she was invincible. Because she had been since she was a girl. A child. And in a sick way, she believed she had God on her side because she used some of that money to do good things in His name. Violet knew little about God, but there was no way He was condoning this wicked nonsense.

"You're nothing but a con woman, brainwashing these girls who have already been abused to believe you actually have their best interest at heart." So much so they'd all kept their mouths shut to protect her, right along with the men—out of fear of being murdered or fear they'd lose their good thing.

"You wouldn't understand."

"No, you don't understand, but you will. We'll see how much you like being forced into doing something you don't really want to do. See how you like living in fear. You're going to prison for trafficking, for impeding an investigation and anything else I can possibly find to make sure you suffer for your own sins. To free these women. Lula will never know this lifestyle. Ruby and I will make sure of it."

"And so will I," John added.

Mother's lips tightened. "No one in this holler will testify. You have nothing but hearsay. You think I'm stupid."

Violet held out her phone to show she'd recorded it. Might not get admitted in court, but it was worth a shot to get someone to testify. "You think I am?"

Mother saw the recording, and it turned the tables in Violet's favor. Fear flooded her face. "I can give you something you want. In return, you delete that and you walk out of here. I'll deal with who's been murdering my girls."

"I'm not interested in Whiskey's drugs or who he's murdered for himself or at your request or command. If he's the Blind Eye Killer, you'd have already dealt with him. You got nothing I want."

Her eyes told a sinister tale. "I'm not talking about Whiskey. I have Adam," she cooed. "You want your father more than anything. I can give him to you."

Violet's heart thudded in her chest, and blood whooshed in her ears as the world tilted. "You're lying."

"I'm not. I didn't tell you everything then. I will now." She came down from the porch. "Adam fancied Loretta. More than the other girls who were trapped with her. He never wanted to part with her, so he tried to steal her away again. But holler girls don't leave, so *he* stayed."

Violet's knees turned to water. Adam was here. Under her nose. Had she encountered him? Did he know she was his daughter? "Where is he?"

"She's lying, Violet," John whispered. "It's a last-ditch effort."

She wagged her forefinger. "I'm not. And I want a promise you'll pack it up and leave. Let us handle this ourselves. Our own way. Like we always have. Like I always have."

The thought was tempting. Too tempting. She could find her father. Get answers. Know the truth about herself. Was she safe to be around or would she end up like him in some form or every way?

The front door opened, and Loretta Boyd stepped out and down the stairs. Her aging lines were deepened by worry, her eyes wide and frantic. Was she still in the business? She hadn't wanted this life for Ruby, and she'd run away, only to have a horrific thing happen to her, solidifying Mother's logic that she was better protected here. Did she also know Adam was still in the hollow? Were they...an item in some sick way?

"Loretta, go back inside. This doesn't concern you."

"Yes, it does," she said softly, and that was when Violet noticed the pistol in her shaking hand.

Violet drew her Sig, aimed it at Loretta, hoping this thing would not go south; she didn't want to hurt Loretta. John pulled his weapon too.

"Ruby's missing. I went over to see about her, and Lula was

in the house. Alone. I dropped her at Betty Jane's. She said Ruby went outside to talk to someone, and she never came back inside. He's got her."

"Loretta, put the gun down and tell me who has Ruby," Violet pleaded. "I can help her."

Loretta faced her grandmother, ignoring Violet's instructions. "Everyone is dead because of you. Because you've terrified us into thinking we can't leave. We can't marry. Oh, but we can have children just like you did. Especially if they're girls. But we can't do anything else. I didn't want to be a holler girl, and I didn't want Ruby to be one either, and Lula will not know this life." She raised her gun, hand trembling.

"Wanda will decide that when she takes the helm," Mother said. "Put that weapon away. This minute!"

"Loretta," John said softly, "put down the gun."

"Loretta, put the gun down," Violet added when she ignored John. "I'm not going to ask you again, and I don't want to shoot you." But she would. "Mother isn't going to hurt anyone else. Neither is Wanda."

"Oh, I know. Wanda's dead. I went over there after I dropped off Lula at Betty Jane's. But she wouldn't listen. Said Mother was right. And I knew it was never going to be over."

Mother gasped.

Violet's stomach sank.

"You saw firsthand what happens to those who leave me and my protection." Mother took a step toward her granddaughter. "We do what we do to survive, to keep control and order. Put that gun down. We'll deal with what's happened to Wanda," she said through a stern voice.

Maybe that was why her own mother had turned her out. It would have been during the Depression in an already poor part of the country. But now. Now things were different.

Loretta shook her head. "You're done."

Violet dove on top of Loretta, but the gun fired. She could only hope it missed Mother.

It didn't.

A pool of blood bloomed near her upper right shoulder.

John bolted for Mother, applying pressure.

Loretta dropped the gun and stared at Violet. "They're okay now. Find Ruby." She collapsed on the ground.

Violet retrieved Loretta's gun and pocketed it, then called 911. Loretta didn't move; she lay motionless.

Mother's breath was haggard.

Violet knelt beside her. "Tell me who Adam is. Where is he? For once in your life, do the right thing. Tell me." Mother's blood covered Violet's hands. An ambulance siren whirred.

"Loretta, where is Adam?"

Loretta's eyes were hollow, vacant. She murmured, "…close…"

"I did the right…thing…" Mother said. She closed her eyes, but she had a pulse.

Violet had more time.

Chapter Twenty-One

Monday, October 23
8:35 p.m.

John's mind reeled as locals and deputies littered Imogene Boyd's yard. News traveled fast.

Sheriff Modine approached him and waved to Violet, who now stood by the porch. Local deputies had taken Loretta Boyd into custody for killing her mom and attempting to murder Mother. He prayed a judge and jury would go easy on her. She'd been through nothing but pain her entire life at the hands of her mother and grandmother. Mason had been taken to the same neighbor's house as Lula. Poor kids had been jostled around and confused. He had no idea if social services would be called in or not. Things worked differently up here.

"Quite a situation we got here," Sheriff Modine said.

"If you call two missing women, a shot old lady, another one dead and four other dead women a 'situation.' Then yeah,

I guess so." Lives had been destroyed. "Did you know about Mother? The prostitutes?"

The sheriff sniffed. "What I know doesn't matter. I'm one man. But I believe the Good Lord is doing what's necessary to cleanse this place."

John narrowed his eyes. "You a religious man?"

"I'm a God-fearing man. I don't believe no whores belong in the holler. But sometimes the law...well, it ain't enough. Not when lawlessness abounds. I figure she's gettin' what's comin' to her. Feel pretty bad for Loretta. Seems a waste she's goin' away."

The sheriff knew and had done nothing. Either out of powerlessness, fear or laziness. Or he was lying and was all up in the mess. "Guess I'll get to the paperwork. Hate the paperwork." Sheriff Modine ambled away, and John walked over to Violet. "Have we done a background on the sheriff?"

"I don't think so. Why? You think it's him? He's older than we initially projected. He's probably, what, late fifties or early sixties." Her phone rang and she answered. "Hey, Ty." She frowned. "Okay. What?" She put the phone on speaker. "Say that again for John."

"I said, Mother—Imogene Boyd—didn't make it. I just arrived at the emergency clinic. Talked to EMT Chris Leigh. She died on the way here."

Violet blew a heavy breath. "She knew where my father is. Here. In this holler."

"What?"

"Yeah. But that can wait."

"Good. 'Cause I heard back from the lab. The material that matched Atta's shirt and the bloody beer bottle never made it to Quantico. They checked. Double-checked. Triple-checked. I called FedEx next."

"And?" Violet demanded.

"And the FedEx delivery guy remembers getting the package with my signature, but on his way to the hub, he was stopped by a sheriff's deputy. Only he says he was in plain clothes. Stopped him for a routine traffic violation—which he denies—then said he smelled pot. Which he says was impossible, but one did what one was told by the law up here. He forced him out of the truck and did a search. Let him go."

"He get a name?"

"No, and the car wasn't marked. But he got a photo. He was pretty ticked, and he snapped it to a million people on Snapchat. I have it. It's Regis Owsley."

"Send it to me."

"Already did," Ty added then hung up.

The sheriff doubled back. "Oh, hey, Agent. When you get a minute, I'll want a more formal statement. You come on by my office. We'll have us a proper chat."

"Yeah. Whatever." Violet massaged the back of her neck.

Modine laid a hand on her shoulder. "Don't be too upset. You can't win 'em all."

"I'm not throwing in the towel yet."

"No." He grinned. "I suspect you won't. I like your tenacity, kiddo." He spun on his heel and left her and John to themselves.

"As if he cares about anything formal," she groused.

"I have zero respect for that man," John mumbled then refocused. "We need to talk to Regis."

"Now's our chance." She stalked toward Regis's car, John picking up the pace to keep in step with her.

Regis exited with a scowl on his face. Violet blocked him from moving past his open car door. She showed him her cell phone with his picture by the FedEx truck.

Regis studied the photo, his nostrils flaring and resignation in his dark eyes.

"Afraid your blood would be on Atta's shirt, on the broken beer bottle? After her fight with Wendell, did you try to play the hero but it backfired? You got into an altercation and then you abducted her? Is that what you did with Bella Dawn too? Seize an opportunity? Did you kill them both?"

"What nonsense is this?" Regis shoved her arm out of his face. "I didn't kill anyone."

"Then why did you stop the FedEx truck and lift the package, and don't give me any cockamamie excuses, Detective. This is what I call the end of the hunt, and you in cuffs is my victory. Maybe I'll take a photo and send it across social media."

Except John was pretty sure Violet had no social media accounts. Had they caught the Blind Eye Killer? Was it Regis Owsley?

Regis threw up his hands. "Wait. Okay. I'll admit to lifting the evidence. But not for me. I was protecting someone."

"Who?"

"My brother. Cecil's the Blind Eye Killer."

Violet wasn't sure if Regis was telling the truth or lying, but she did get the sense the brothers were playing a dangerous game with one another. Cecil had coughed up Regis's name concerning Bella Dawn and being at the bar—which had surprised Regis. Now Regis was casting light on Cecil.

"What makes you think Cecil is the Blind Eye Killer?"

Regis huffed. "Why not? You already have him on the suspect list, and you know even less about him. The truth is Cecil has been peeping in on girls since he was fifteen, and over the years it's escalated. I've kept an eye on him, kept him in check. Cecil has some problems—"

"Well, welcome to humanity, Regis. We all have problems. You've been covering for him."

Regis closed his eyes. "You don't understand. My mother doesn't have all her faculties. Never has. And she'd wanted a girl. When Cecil was born, she said he was too pretty to be a boy, and she named him Cecilia. Didn't know who his daddy was, so there was no father to contest it. Most folks had no idea he wasn't a girl—even me. I was only three when he was born."

"What does this have to do with being a peeper or a killer?" John asked, losing his patience.

"Mama raised him as a girl. He wore dresses, played with dolls. Mama made him dozens of rag dolls. He loved them. He played with the girls, but he also liked to get rowdy with the boys—Mama wouldn't let him. He had no idea he was a boy. She never let us change clothes together or be in the same bathroom. But then puberty hit, and things changed. He started liking girls. Mama jumped all over him for that and whipped him good. He was not to be lookin' at girls. One Sunday, he walked in on our cousin and realized her girl parts didn't match his girl parts. 'Course, he knew he wasn't like other girls. He wasn't filling out like them. But Mama would hear nothing of it. Then his voice changed. Kids realized he wasn't a girl. He had an Adam's apple. Mama still forced him into dresses, braided his hair and sent him to school as CeCe."

Violet's stomach turned. What was the deal with all these crazy, abusive moms, from Mother to Reeva to Regis's?

"By the time he hit fifteen, he was twice the size of Mama, and together we told her he was no longer going to wear dresses. Boys messed with him in ways you can't imagine. Girls wouldn't go out with him because he'd been a girl, at their sleepovers when they were younger, and it was too strange. Too weird. He didn't know who he was or who he was supposed to be."

Identity confusion. Violet wasn't unsympathetic to his

plight. But it didn't give him a free pass to become a serial killer. "And then what?"

"I should have done something. I didn't. I saw him suffer, and I let him suffer. He didn't fit anywhere. When he started peeping, I kept him at bay. Or at least I tried. But I owe him for not doing something sooner to help him."

"You are supposed to be upholding the law."

"I didn't think he was the killer until after Atta." Regis shifted uncomfortably.

"Why after Atta?"

"I went by his place the Saturday morning after Atta went missing. He was asleep on the couch. Blood on his shirt and Atta's locket she wore with a picture of her mother inside on his chest. It scared me. Cecil said Atta gave it to him, but I knew that was a lie. Then when we found Atta and the purse, I knew it was from him. He'd given them to all the girls he had tried to date over the years, the ones that had rejected him."

Violet connected the dots. Cecil had a twisted and tragic upbringing. "The dolls in my room at the bed and breakfast—"

"Cecil's old dolls. He's still obsessed with them. Makes dolls for the kids in the holler sometimes."

The rag doll Him had made for Lula Boyd. Cecil was the Him. Atta's compact and candy. They'd grown up with CeCe—the name the bartender had called him that had set him off. Not Cecil. It was too strange, off-putting even. In his mind, they lured him in with their eyes but forced him to pay for services, which in his warped way would be the sin. He couldn't say no. He hated that they said it, unless he had cash.

Maybe he saw himself in those women.

Dark but lovely.

He identified with them but hated that he did. Murdering them was murdering himself.

"He has Bella Dawn—or had if she's already dead," John said. "And he's got Ruby Boyd. Where would he take them?"

"I know." Violet swallowed hard and put the pieces together. "John, that photo we found of the little girl in the cabin. That's Cecil. The cabin means something to him. To the growing-up years."

"We moved when Cecil was about twelve," Regis said. "Right before he had trouble at school when puberty hit. And the man Mama lived with…he wasn't always kind to Cecil. Or any of us."

Cecil would see the cabin as a safe haven before bad things happened. "I saw wood shavings in the passages in the house—"

"How did you find those?" Regis asked.

Violet ignored him. "I wasn't focused on them. But the shavings in the cabin. It connects. The cave where the bodies were found is close by."

"We didn't see any blood there, though."

"No. But maybe we wouldn't. He knows how to use needles skillfully, and if he put them under then removed their eyes, it wouldn't be a huge amount of blood. Towels, a sheet—burns easy enough. He beat them up prior to taking their eyes, but he focused on their faces, breasts and genital regions." He beat them in areas he was supposed to have but didn't. Hatred. He was beautiful but missing key parts of the female anatomy, which caused him so much bullying by his peers. "He keeps trinkets in that old box—the photo for one. He's keeping their eyes somewhere. Somehow." Violet called Ty and sent him for a warrant to search Cecil Johnson's home. They had probable cause. Especially since Regis saw the bloody shirt and Atta's locket in the house.

"Let's go to the cabin. We might find Ruby. Maybe even

Bella Dawn." Though the timing of the other bodies said it was unlikely Bella Dawn would be found alive.

"And what about him?" John pointed to Regis. Would any deputy actually arrest him? Could anyone be trusted?

"I can talk to him. If you find him. I can reason with him. Get him to tell you where they are." Regis's plea fell on deaf ears.

"If you could do that, then why haven't you already?"

Violet called Agent Kip Pulaski, who was still at the search for Bella Dawn. He and Regis were friendly, but he was the only one she trusted to book him. After he arrived, she and John headed for Cecil Johnson's childhood home.

As they parked on the edge of the road, black, ominous clouds rolled in. The wind gusted, blowing Violet's FBI windbreaker open. She buttoned it and hunched as a few drops of icy rain dotted her face. She drew her weapon as they approached the cave where they'd found the victims, Violet's boots sinking in the mud.

"What's our game plan?" John asked as they hit the muddy path that led to the cabin. Violet stayed to the edge of the woods, using the branches for as much covering as possible. The rain began a steady fall. She gripped her gun and squinted. "Cabin's not big. Cecil works during the day. Why don't you call the shop and see if he answers?"

John searched for the number then called, but it dropped. "No cell service."

Violet ground her teeth. "Let's proceed with caution then. Secure the perimeter before we go in. You take the east side, and I'll take the west. We'll meet at the back door and go from there."

Violet darted from the tree line, but John caught her arm and drew her to him, then quickly kissed her cheek. "Be careful. Watch your back."

She touched the warmth radiating on her chilly skin. "You too." Dashing along the edge of the woods, keeping behind trees for shelter, she glanced up at the hanging bridges connecting to one another in a maze. Would he be up there lying in wait on the bridge or in one of the two tree houses?

With her back up against the outside of the cabin, she edged along the side, peeping in broken windows. The two bedrooms on her side too filthy to see through. She had no way to tell if Bella Dawn or Ruby were stashed inside. She eased to the back door.

John wasn't there.

She waited. Surveyed the area then texted him.

Text wouldn't go through.

She opened the back door and stepped inside the dark ramshackle cabin. Wood, earth and decay reached her nostrils. The damp air slithered over her skin, and her breath plumed before her.

She stepped forward, listened then took another step. No sound but wind whistling through broken windowpanes and the skittering of trash blowing and skimming the old wooden flooring. Chills broke out along her skin, and she ran her bottom lip through her teeth as she proceeded to the small hallway that connected the two bedrooms.

The door to the left was ajar and she approached, finding it empty, but the one to the right—the one where they'd found the photo of Cecil—was closed. Where was John? Violet had a sick feeling ooze in her belly and shoot a burning sensation into her throat. She eased down the wall, glanced back at the other room, then reached out and laid a hand on the doorknob, the metal cool against her fingers.

Violet opened the door and shined her light, then gasped.

Chapter Twenty-Two

Monday, October 23
9:13 p.m.

"I'm a federal agent, and I'm here to help you." Violet rushed to the twin bed, shocked that Bella Dawn was alive, but she'd been through the wringer to say the least. A half-eaten sandwich lay in a to-go box on the night table. She removed the duct tape as gently as possible, but Bella Dawn winced. "Sorry. I know it hurts."

Bella Dawn didn't speak. Violet grabbed the old box she and John had riffled through. She removed the pocket knife and slit the ropes tying Bella Dawn's wrists to the iron posts of the headboard.

"You're safe now. Get dressed as fast as you can." They were going to lose all kinds of evidence by not bagging her clothing, but right now getting the woman out of this pit was more important.

Bella Dawn sat stunned. Violet shined the light in her eyes.

She was in shock. Her skin was like ice to the touch. The blanket Cecil tossed across her body had slipped off—probably due to her trying to break free, which meant she'd been lying bare in the cold, shivering for hours in this weather. Could she get her to move? And where was John?

"Bella Dawn," she said with more grit and force. She patted her cheek. "How long has Cecil been gone? Talk to me."

Violet laid the knife on the table, grabbed Bella Dawn's flimsy dress and yanked it over her head, maneuvering her arms inside like a child's, then pushed it down over her torso and down her hips. Not much material to keep her warm. Shoes. Did she have shoes?

Bella Dawn's pale blue lips chattered.

Violet pulled her phone in a feeble attempt to call in backup, hoping for once there would be at least one bar.

No service.

She gritted her teeth and grabbed her mini Maglite.

"No," Bella Dawn whimpered. "No."

"No, what? You're okay. You're safe."

A scuffle of shoes on hardwood.

Violet snapped to attention as a hand brought something crashing down, cracking her skull and sending her skittering to the floor.

"She might be. For now. But you aren't," a reedy voice said. Cecil.

Pain radiated through her body, and spots formed before her eyes.

She thrust her leg up and out, kicking him in the A-frame. "Run, Bella Dawn. Go!" Violet rose to her feet, nausea rushing over her. Where was her gun?

Violet took advantage of his crumpled state and drop-kicked him in the face; the sound of bone crunched against her boot, and she knew his nose was annihilated.

Bella Dawn's adrenaline must have kicked in. She bolted from the room.

Cecil howled and cursed, and she kicked him again until he was facedown on the floor. She had no cuffs. She spied her gun on the bed and went for it, but Cecil grabbed her waistband, ripping her away from the bed, from her gun. She fell backward, hitting her head again and crying out in pain. His body was strong, compact. Sinewy.

He was tougher than he looked. But she'd already witnessed how fast he could be at the bar.

"You saw me that day you were here. In the woods. Looked right at me. Smiled."

His hands wrapped around her throat as he straddled her body. She hadn't seen anything. Most certainly had not smiled. But she'd felt something. Had it been him? She reached up to stab his eyes, but he withdrew his head out of her reach. "You look like her, you know? Like Ruby."

"Where is Ruby?" she croaked as he cut off most of her air. Her throat ached and chest burned.

She bit his hand and he howled, releasing his grip. She hissed and punched him in the sternum. He lost his breath, and she shoved him off. Reaching for the gun would take too long.

Jumping up, she shot past him into the littered living room, tripping over a glass bottle and hauling it to the back door. Outside the temperature had dropped, the rain falling in heavy sheets. No stars. No moon.

Instantly her hair was drenched, matting to her head. Water ran down her windbreaker and sent a chill over her body, and her head hammered. She bolted straight for the forest. Where was Bella Dawn? She darted behind a huge tree and forced her pulse to slow. It beat in her ears like a deafening whoosh, and she needed to listen. The rain hid footfalls. Good and bad for her.

Everything was black. Only shadows and shapes. No thunder. No lightning to give her a second to see.

She was blind, but she had sight. This was only a small sliver of what his victims had experienced. Before he came out of the darkness, not as light and salvation, but an instrument of torture and death. She was being hunted.

A bloodcurdling scream pierced through the rain from above. The tree house. The hanging bridges with rope railings.

Bella Dawn must have scrambled up to hide, and now Cecil had her.

"Come out, pretty agent. Come up and play house with me." His laugh singsonged in her direction.

He was using Bella Dawn as a bargaining chip. "Lord," she whispered, "I'm asking for Bella Dawn's safety now. She's been through enough."

Cecil had the upper hand. She needed to get it back. She went with her gut and what she knew about him and his psyche, hoping it would work in her favor. "Which one of us will play mommy, CeCe? I know how much you enjoy dollies." Hit him where it hurt, fuel his rage to the point he wouldn't care about Bella Dawn. He'd come for her, and she'd be ready.

Violet knew killer instincts.

He called her a few choices names. "I mean it." His voice shook, proving she'd struck a nerve. "I'll throw her from the bridge. Come up right now."

"Why? So you can throw her off when I get up there? I'm not an idiot. Send her down. I'll come and play." But he wasn't going to like her version of house.

"He's dead. That detective you're constantly with. I killed him. He's lying in blood on the side of the house."

John. Was he lying about John or was it true? Was he dead in the rain? Her heart hiccupped, but she had to incapacitate

Cecil, rescue Bella Dawn and come out alive before she could chase down John.

"So, if you're hoping to be saved, Violet—no one is going to save you. No one saved me. You know what it's like to cry every day because you're forced into a role you never wanted to play? To be convinced you're someone you're not? I believed I was Cecilia! Yes, I liked dolls. I like to make dolls. See the kids enjoy them."

"With their moms' panties on them?"

He was quiet. "I wanted them to know I could enter their homes. Take what I wanted. Take them. But I didn't. I was gentlemanly. And yet... I was still rejected."

"Until you did. You took Bella Dawn."

"Do you know what I went through? Pretty girls didn't want me. I was a freak. A girl. Too feminine. I tried to be chivalrous. Kind. Not like those men who pay to go thirty minutes and walk out. They use them. Even my own brother! But he gets more respect than me."

"You were told you were too pretty to be a boy. Know what I was told, Cecil?"

She made her way to the ladder closest to the tree house near the cabin. But Cecil's voice was farther away, coming from the other smaller tree house. She skulked through the forest, weaving between trees, climbing over brush, using the rain to block noise.

"What?" Cecil called.

"That I'm my father's daughter."

"Big deal."

"My father is a wicked, wicked man, Cecil. He caught young girls and imprisoned them. I'm gonna catch you. I haven't decided yet what I'm going to do with you, though. Put you away or put you in the ground."

She made her way through the shadows, watching the

bridge outline and working to find the end of it. Fine. She'd come up. It was her only shot to save Bella Dawn and make Cecil believe he was in control and getting his way.

Finally, she found a small ladder attached to a towering tree that led to a small open platform.

Bella Dawn cried out again.

"Regis won't protect you, Cecil. How do you think we got to the cabin? He knows you're the killer. He told us you'd be here." Fudging the truth never hurt an agent. "And he really won't protect you now. He's going away. I've already caught him. He's in jail right now. This town won't hide you. They'd rather see you go. You're a joke to them, Cecil. You know it. I heard the bartender teasing you, saw him winking. You have no respect and nowhere to hide."

She wasn't one to bully or goad, but he'd tortured, maimed and killed four women, and she needed his fury focused on her right now, not Bella Dawn.

"You're lying about Regis." His voice sounded unsure.

"I'm not. I have no reason to lie, Cecil. Regis told us about your bloody shirt and Atta's locket. How would I know that?" She climbed methodically and carefully up the tree until she made it to the top. The bridge swayed in the gales.

She stepped out onto it. "Let her go." Another shaky step. A few pieces were broken, and one was missing. She stepped over them and kept her arms on the thick wet ropes.

Twenty feet away, Cecil stood with Bella Dawn's neck in the crook of his arm. "Push her behind you and let her go. Then it's me and you." Time to crack him. "But to be very clear, my answer is *no*."

That did it. He shoved Bella Dawn behind him and stalked toward Violet. "Run, Bella Dawn!" She'd unleashed a rage with her blatant rejection.

She turned to run, and her boot cracked a wooden rung

on the bridge, her foot slipped through and she pitched forward. The bridge tottered, and Cecil was now in a dead run.

She scrambled to find her footing, but he was on top of her and the bridge was teetering. Her arm slipped through the rope rails, and she lost her balance, shrieking. Using her free leg, she swept Cecil's leg, toppling him over, blocking the path to the platform a few feet away. She had no other alternative than to dart the opposite way toward the sturdier tree house, closest to the cabin. Missing boards slowed her pace, and the rope handles weren't secure.

She was up maybe thirty feet. Rain dripped into her eyes, and her throat and lungs burned from the cold. But she had to make it to the tree house. Leaves and branches brushed her shoulders, but she kept moving. Not looking back. Unsure how far behind Cecil was. The wind rustled the trees; the rain was deafening.

Adrenaline raced through her bones at the thought of his slender fingers grasping ahold of her, pinning her down. If he caught her, he would do to her what he'd done to all the others.

What he'd been planning to do to Bella Dawn when he was done using and abusing her. What he would do to Ruby?

Ruby!

She had to live to find Ruby. She had to live to find John. Was he dead?

Must keep a level head. Get Cecil on the ground, where she had a better advantage. The tree house was about ten feet away.

Cecil slung a curse and a sick promise, but she didn't let it slow her pace. She reached the tree house, slid across the floor and onto the rickety rungs that had been individually nailed to the tree.

Making her descent, she glanced up. Cecil stood with malevolence in his eyes. She continued descending. Her foot slid off the wet rung, and she shrieked and grasped onto the rung above her, her nail bending back with a sharp pain.

He'd catch her now.

But he was gone when she looked above.

Her heart leapt in her throat.

Did he know a way down she didn't? Was he waiting below to get the jump on her? Heart pounding and hands trembling, she paused. Did she go back up? She was less than halfway down.

Before she made her choice, a raucous cry broke through her confusion, and before she glanced upward, she felt something hard and rough and wet. With great force, it rammed her face. She lost her grip. Writhing and grasping at anything to anchor her back to the tree, she continued to fall backward, meeting nothing but air.

As she free-fell, Cecil stood with a large plank of wood from the tree house, sinister eyes drilling into hers.

Screaming registered in her ears.

It was her own.

Then she saw and heard nothing.

Monday, October 23
10:03 p.m.

John groaned and touched the back of his head; it was wet and sticky. Blood and rainwater.

Rainwater.

Violet!

How long had he been lying here? As he'd come around the corner, he'd been blindsided, bashed in the head. Once. Twice. Cecil must have thought he'd killed him. He felt dead. He struggled to his hands and knees. A severe bout of nausea hit him, and his mouth watered. His skin broke out in a sweat, but the rain slicked over it in cool streams.

Propping himself up against the wall of the cabin, he inhaled deeply when a hand grasped him from behind. He reared back to attack and heard a woman's voice.

"Help!"

Not Violet.

Bella Dawn.

"He's gonna kill her. He pushed her out of the tree house."

John's heart lurched into his throat. Bella Dawn's condition was severe, and the best way to protect her was to get her out of here. Then he could find Violet. "Can you get to the road?"

She nodded.

"I have no signal. Here are my keys and phone. Take the car, and when you get a signal, call the police and the ambulance then drive to the emergency clinic. Ask for Agent Tiberius Granger. He might still be there. Can you do that? Repeat it back to me."

She repeated his instructions nearly verbatim.

"Good." She had her faculties. He put his hands on her shoulders. "Be brave. You can do this. Go! Hurry!" She bolted from the cabin toward the path, and he ran the opposite direction toward the tree house, praying he would make it in time.

Ahead, a shadowed figure straddled Violet. "Police!" he called, and the figure hauled it into the woods. He gave chase, his shoes sinking in mud with each step. He paused and knelt by Violet, feeling for a pulse.

Thank God! She had one. "Help's coming. Hold on," he breathed and followed who he assumed to be Cecil into the woods. Unable to see and not having knowledge of the terrain, John feared Cecil had the upper hand. The rain canceled out noise, and he knew the chase was useless. Retreating, he returned to Violet.

"Violet, can you hear me?" He softly patted her cheek, then began checking for injuries. She had a small cut on the side of her head, facial abrasions and nicks along her hands, probably from falling. He wasn't sure if anything had been broken or not. Her eyes fluttered open.

"John," she breathed. "It's Cecil. Get Cecil."

"I know. I will."

She reached up and held his hand, no strength in hers. What if she had internal bleeding? What if she was dying this very moment? "Violet, hang on." He needed her to hang on. He didn't care about her job being dangerous anymore. He cared about her. He wanted her in his life. Wanted her to live to become the special woman he knew her to be, but she didn't know. He wanted her to know. "I need you in this world. Do you hear me? You hang on. For you. For me. Please."

Her eyes closed. "Ruby? Bella Dawn?"

"Bella Dawn is safe." He hoped. "I haven't found Ruby. But we will." Again, he hoped.

"I'm tired," she murmured.

"Stay awake. Look at me." He squeezed her hand. "I haven't even asked you on a date. We'd order some kind of healthy food, 'cause you're crazy, and watch Hitchcock movies. Pick them apart."

A wan laugh slipped through her lips. "We're living a... Hitchcock movie...how 'bout...Disney?"

"Wow, you do have a concussion." Violet Rainwater was no more Disney than the sun was cold. He kissed her hand. "Whatever you want."

"Get...get Mason away from Mother...find Adam..."

"You can find Adam." She was confused, disoriented. Mason was with a neighbor, and Mother was dead.

A noise breached the rain. Relief flooded John, and he laid his forehead to Violet's. "Bella Dawn got a signal. Hear that?" Sirens wailed. "Hang on for me."

"If I was...a good person, John...I'd fall in love with you." She closed her eyes again and released a long, shaky breath.

If only she knew no one was at the heart a good person.

Ambulance lights flashed and the blue lights of the sheriff's department. The sound of UTVs hummed and appeared with first responders. Jimmy Russell and Chris Leigh ran for them carrying their gear bags, a cardiac monitor and a backboard with straps. Two deputies arrived as well.

"I just cleaned these boots," Chris muttered.

Jimmy placed his bag down and gave Violet a once-over. "Hey, Agent Rainwater, you remember me? Jimmy Russell?"

She grimaced.

"What's going on? How you feelin'?" He assessed her, his gaze roaming her extremities and his fingers resting on her wrist, taking her pulse.

"I feel like…I was shoved…from about fifteen to twenty feet…by Cecil freaking Johnson."

Probably more like twenty-five. John told them what happened and how Violet ended up on the ground. "He's in the wind though."

"You're a brave woman," Jimmy said. "You could have died."

Chris laid the board out flat. "You're safe now, Agent Rainwater. They'll find Cecil."

"But… Ruby. No Ruby."

"Shh…it's okay now," Chris said. "On a scale of one to ten, ten being the worst pain imaginable, rate your pain for me."

"Seven. Maybe eight. Could be nine."

Chris chuckled as Jimmy placed her in a cervical collar. "You lose consciousness?"

"I don't know."

"She did." John touched her foot. "She was unconscious when I approached."

Violet groaned.

"We'll get you feelin' better once we get you in the ambulance." He really looked at John now. "You got a head wound, pal. You need to be transported?"

"No."

"I had a feeling you'd say that." He dug in his bag. "Let me check you anyway. Okay?"

Fine. He allowed Jimmy to examine his head.

"She wasn't in there...she's...she's not...wasn't in there." Violet raised her hand as if trying to reach out for John.

"I'm here. Rest, Violet," John said.

Jimmy frowned. "You should really let us transport you. I don't think you need stitches, but it's a serious bump. Were you knocked unconscious?"

Yes. "I'm fine. Really."

"Head wounds shouldn't be taken lightly, Detective."

"He didn't have them together...why... John... Ruby..." Violet was slurring her words and murmuring. "My head hurts."

"I hear ya." Chris knelt by Violet. "Hush now, Agent Rainwater. We're gonna take care of you."

"But—"

"Rest. Okay?" He strapped her to the board. "We need to hurry, Jimmy."

Jimmy left John, slipped off Violet's shoes and socks, felt her pulse in her foot and then cut her jeans up the front to the crotch, cut her sweater to her sternum and her sleeves to her armpits to check for other signs of injury.

Once they had Violet secured to the Gator, Jimmy headed down to the ambulance and Chris cleaned and butterflied John's injury.

"I'll be okay." He didn't have time to go to the hospital when Cecil was still out there and Ruby was missing. He walked with Chris through the path and out to the road leading to the cave. Once they got there, Jimmy counted to three, and they lifted Violet into the ambulance. She cried out, and Jimmy rested his hand on her hand.

"Time to get feeling better." He administered pain meds through an IV. "Any minute now."

"I'll be at the hospital soon. You take good care of her."

Chris saluted. "We will."

They closed the doors and hopped into the ambulance. John turned to the deputies. "I need a radio stat." He jumped in the front of one of the vehicles and hit the radio. The team had been keeping it on to hear calls, and it was the only way he knew to get to Ty since he'd given Bella Dawn his phone, not that he could get a cell signal up here anyway.

Ty heard him. "Talk to me. I was back at the SO when I got a call from the emergency clinic that Bella Dawn was in there ranting about Cecil Johnson and needing me because he hurt Violet. I'm back at the clinic now. Bella Dawn is with the doctors. Is Violet okay? What happened?" He continued to pepper him with questions.

"She's on her way there now. We need an APB on Cecil Johnson." He gave him the CliffsNotes version of what transpired.

"You go get that piece of dirt."

"I will. I promise you I will."

After ending the call, he radioed Sheriff Modine, got an APB out on Cecil Johnson as they headed straight for the SO to talk to Regis. If anyone knew where Cecil might have gone or taken Ruby, it was him, and if he talked, he might get leniency on the tampering with evidence charges.

Cecil could run, but he couldn't hide. And if Ruby was still alive, he was on his way to her right now to finish her off before fleeing town.

He might be crazy enough to try and get rid of Bella Dawn and Violet.

She'd need extra protection at the emergency clinic.

Chapter Twenty-Three

Monday, October 23
11:11 p.m.

Violet floated. Up. Up. Up.

No pain. No dread. Her thoughts were like evaporating clouds being stretched apart, disjointed.

Her brain was fuzzy and unhindered.

Lynn Tavish stood on the dock.

Violet lurked in the darkness, aware she was going to push her in and drown out everything mean and nasty Lynn had done and said. But in this new unencumbered memory, she hadn't actually seen Lynn Tavish even though it was indeed Lynn on that dock.

Instead, Violet had pictured Reeva Rainwater walking on the dock toward her, her face snarled and her words penetrating Violet's skin and bones like hot metal. Words that had been branded on her heart like Adam's brand on Reeva's skin. A shadowy presence swirled, turning her thoughts cold.

You'll grow up to be just like him...given time.

You hate her. You want to kill her. That makes you a killer. The only time you're happy is when you're fantasizing of her death. How you'll kill her and get away with it.

You're cunning and clever. No one will ever know. You won't even be suspected.

She hates you. She never wanted you to be born. You're not worth giving life.

Reeva's words rattled around her hollow chest.

I wish you were dead. You're a monster.

You're your father's daughter.

Unloved. Unwanted. Unworthy.

She shoved Lynn Tavish into the waters to drown out the words, the pain—the unbearable pain.

And now she remembered her own words at shoving Lynn into the water.

"So long, Reeva."

The cold wrapped its bony arm around her shoulders. *That felt good, didn't it? You should jump in too. Breathe in the water and end it.*

You should have never been born in the first place. If he hadn't taken Reeva...you'd have never been born.

She shouldn't be here. Never should have been here.

No purpose.

No hope.

That was how it went down. Except...that wasn't what she remembered now; there was more to the chilling memory that was now freed and coming to light.

Warmth had chased away those frigid thoughts and filled her with new thoughts, glowing and full of hope.

Jump in...and save her. You are not your father's daughter.

And she'd known somehow, deep within her, that if she saved Lynn, she too would be saved. Violet had—jumped in. She'd rescued Lynn Tavish. She hadn't truly wanted to murder the girl; she'd projected the pain and the hate for her mother onto her. She wanted to drown out Reeva. But until now those thoughts had been submerged. Now, they bobbed to the surface.

"I don't want to kill you, Reeva," she whispered now as a tear trickled down her cheek. "I want you to love me," she murmured.

"What's that, Agent?" Chris asked.

God, was that You? Was that Your voice? Your warmth? Your promise? Would You… Could You…love me?

She opened her mouth to cry out, but the meds had thickened her tongue like cotton growing inside her mouth. Instead, she cried out of the darkness of her soul for salvation.

Suddenly, Chris cursed and the ambulance veered.

"Someone's in the road. Hold on!" Jimmy now swore and swerved again, then the ambulance smacked into something, the impact jostling her.

"Chris… Jimmy…what's happening?"

"Violet, hold tight." Jimmy cursed. "Chris…can you hear me? Chris. Chris!"

"What's happening?"

"It's okay, Agent. Chris hit his head, but he's okay. Just… let me see how bad the damage is to the ambulance. We hit a tree. I'll be right back."

A door opened. She thought she heard another door open. Had the other one closed? Her head was still fuzzy, and she was floating. She closed her eyes, let herself lift upward.

A scuffle jarred them open.

Jimmy screamed. Something heavy banged into the side of the ambulance, then another thud.

In the haze, Violet ripped out the needle in her arm. She may not have all her faculties, but she recognized a struggle when she heard it. She shook off the fuzz, but her mind was like water bubbling down a brook. "Chris…" She scooted to the front of the ambulance. Both doors were open. Chris was in his seat.

His throat had been cut.

Her heart rate spiked. "Jimmy!" she hollered, but it sounded faint and far away.

She fumbled to open the rear doors and managed to get them free. Jimmy stumbled around the corner, blood covering his face. "Agent…we gotta…we gotta get out of here. Now!"

Jimmy's head and hands were covered in blood. "Jimmy, can we drive?"

"We hit the trees too hard. We gotta run for it. Can you? Can you run? We don't have much time," he said through heaving breaths as he shoved her into her shoes and helped her out of the ambulance. "I don't know how long he'll be down or out."

Cecil.

He'd found them.

Could she run? She couldn't focus. Think straight or clearly. "I can do it."

Jimmy put his arm around her, supporting her as they hobbled off the road into the woods. Violet tripped over a tree root and lost her balance, falling. "I don't know if I can run."

Jimmy winced. "You're bleeding."

She looked down at her knee. She'd cut it. But they had to go. Had to move.

"I'm okay," she said, feeling nauseous. She stood with his help, and they moved as best they could with the drugs in her system keeping her off-kilter. "What did…what did you give me?"

"Morphine. Low dose. It should wear off quickly."

The woods slanted uphill. "Where are we going?"

"Away. Somewhere we can hide."

At least it wasn't raining.

Jimmy pushed her behind a tree and covered his lips with his index fingers. "I heard something." He peeked out from the trunk of the tree and surveyed the darkness. Violet rested her head on the tree, grogginess attempting to render her useless.

She should care. She should be of use.

But she couldn't.

"Cecil knows these woods better than I do. He and Regis practically lived out here." He listened a moment longer. "Okay, let's go again. Easy. We're gonna make it."

That was what everyone said before they died.

As they skulked through the woods, Violet's morphine began wearing off and the pain returned, but her faculties were clearing up too. "Where are we going?"

"I think there's a chapel on the other side of the hill. Used to be a little settlement down there of miners. But when they all moved, the chapel was abandoned." His breathing was labored, and she paused.

"How bad are you hurt?"

"Not terrible. Let's keep going. We can hide there."

"Can we call for help?" She winced as she tripped over a log. "Does Cecil know about the chapel?"

"I don't know. It's possible he stumbled on it as a kid. It's how I found it. Used it as a hideout." He ushered her along again. "Not any cell service out here. It's remote if you can't tell."

At the crest of the hill, she spotted a tiny wooden chapel with an old rugged cross on top.

I'll save you.

The fleeting thought from the past returned. She hadn't imagined it; it was real.

But God hadn't saved or rescued her. She was still drowning in the dark.

Stumbling, they approached the old chapel. Jimmy opened the door, and she darted inside.

"How long do we wait here?"

"Till light. When we can see better, I'll head up the hill and back out to the road until I get cell service. Call in the sheriff. Maybe they'll catch him by morning light."

"How far are we from the road?"

"Far."

Violet looked around the chapel. Only about five pews left. Two on one side, three on the other. A cross hung on the back wall by a set of descending stairs. "What's down there?"

"Basement." He peeped out a window. The clouds hung heavy, concealing moonlight.

"Probably need to get away from the windows, Jimmy." Violet tightened his coat around her and gawked at her filthy legs. "You think there's a bathroom down there?"

"Outhouse."

Eeew. Everything hurt, and she rubbed her lower back and temple at the same time.

"Pain meds wearing off?"

She nodded. "But I'll deal." She rubbed her right wrist, which he'd bandaged in the ambulance. Sprained. Her sides were tender and sore.

"Bruised ribs I imagine. You're breathing okay. Probably not broken or floating."

"How did Cecil ambush you?"

"He stepped out in the road, and I swerved. Hit the tree. He opened the passenger door, sliced Chris's throat while I was coming around the van. I got the jump on him, but he's fast."

"I can attest to that."

"We struggled, and I rammed his head into the side of the ambulance. When he went down, that's when I got you out."

Things were coming back now. "Why didn't you radio for help?"

"Because it was jump out of the ambulance or risk him opening my door and doing to me what he did to Chris." He shook his head. "Chris's married. Two kids. What am I gonna tell his wife?"

Violet listened as Jimmy talked about Chris and his wife and kids. Barbecues and all that, but something stuck in her craw. But now she was thinking about Ruby. Why hadn't she been in the cabin? In the other room? If Cecil had her, why not take her to the same place he took the other holler girls—like Bella Dawn?

Because Cecil didn't have Ruby.

"The Blind Eye Killer is still out there."

"I know," Jimmy said. "That's why we're in here."

"No…it's not Cecil. Cecil's a predator. His voyeurism escalated, and he took Bella Dawn from the bar and cast suspicion on his own brother. But how did he intersect with Atta? He had her locket, her things." She glanced up. "Didn't you say she came to you and you fixed her up?"

"I did."

"Did she mention an altercation with Cecil or seeing him before she left the Swallow?"

She rubbed her head, willing the cotton to clear.

"No. Just there'd been a fight. She didn't want to talk about it. Maybe it was Cecil. Nadine didn't know it was him. I believed her. But he knows better than to touch a holler girl. He must have a death wish or something. Although, Mother is dead and Wanda too. Loretta is going away, and Ruby isn't going to take over."

They couldn't even find Ruby.

But she wasn't at the cabin. Why?

Chapter Twenty-Four

Tuesday, October 24
12:24 a.m.

John's eyes were dry and itchy, and the coffee he'd been drinking while studying Google Earth and marking likely places on a map to give Owen Barkley a head start when he arrived with the rest of the SCU team had gone cold. Ty had called them earlier when Violet hadn't arrived at the emergency clinic and the ambulance with a dead Chris Leigh had been found.

Did Cecil have Jimmy and Violet? Had he murdered Jimmy and taken Violet? She would be doped up and vulnerable.

He couldn't lose her. He'd almost lost her hours ago.

Regis told them about the basement at the leather shop, but Ty had called to say it was clean, no sign of Ruby or anything that would point to Cecil being the Blind Eye Killer. The search for Cecil was still on. Between roadblocks and locals out helping, they'd surely find him.

John told Ty about the secret passages in the house and the

wood shavings, the peeper holes that Violet had found. That went over like a lead balloon, but he called out the ERT to comb the passages as well as Cecil's basement just in case and was going to find Aunt Hossie. She would know about the passages, but she might not know Cecil used them or made peepholes. But she needed to be talked to because she might have insight into where Cecil would go.

But what if Cecil didn't have Ruby? Ruby had a duffel bag on her counter. Lula said Ruby had gone outside to talk to someone and never come back. But did she have the bag with her? Was it still on the counter? Violet said Ruby was going to run drugs for Whiskey. A bad exchange might have happened, and she wasn't connected to the killer at all. He went outside, shivered at the cold. It had begun drizzling again. He swallowed and grabbed his phone. He sent a text to Ty to check on that duffel bag. It could be a game changer.

Next, he needed to make a call he absolutely did not want to make. But he needed Greg to help Ruby.

He called the number. On the sixth ring, Greg answered. "Hey."

"Hey. Look, I'm not calling about Callie. I know about the run Whiskey enlisted Ruby for. Is it possible that she's not been snatched by a killer but the exchange went south?"

"No. Whiskey isn't faking the search for her. She was supposed to make the drop at eight o'clock tonight. An hour away. Be back by ten p.m. tops. But at eight thirty, the buyer called pretty hacked that he'd been stood up. Whiskey thought Ruby might have double-crossed him and skipped town. But Lula was at a neighbor's house. She wouldn't leave her. He went to her place. The duffel was on the counter. Everything accounted for."

That put her abduction between when Violet visited her

around three o'clock and eight o'clock, when she was supposed to meet for the swap. "Has he had any leads?"

"No. He's looked in places the law wouldn't or doesn't even know about." He was quiet, then: "And...and I'm sorry about what happened. That's not why I requested Callie for the job. She was always good at what she did. It progressed."

John didn't need to hear how it happened. Didn't want to. "If you hear anything, call me. Violet's missing too and Jimmy Russell."

"Do-gooder Jimmy." Greg laughed. "As if Whiskey didn't know he and Chris Leigh were trying to help women get out from under running drugs and attempting to rescue holler girls. 'Course Chris didn't know Jimmy was paying for their services half the time." He swore. "Talk about a hypocrite."

"Call if you hear anything. Please."

"I will. I promise."

John ended the call and collapsed in a chair in the bullpen. He paid for their services and tried to get them out.

Sitting straight up, he caught the eye of Tiberius, who entered with a laptop in hand. "What?"

"What is the profile again on this killer? A guy who believes prostitutes lure him into sin, then he gets angry at them for it and beats them, removes their eyes 'cause of the verse about them enticing men through their eyelids—batting the eyes."

"Was that a question?" He crinkled his nose. "I'm confused."

"Jimmy Russell tries to help the holler girls, but they don't accept his offers and he pays for their services. He knows medical stuff. He has access to sutures and morphine. Is he religious?"

Ty's eyes widened. "I don't know." He typed furiously on his phone, then the swoosh of a text being sent went out. "John, if it's Jimmy Russell...he's probably with Vi."

That was what terrified him most. But she didn't know it might be Jimmy. Why would he want her? She wasn't his target. Prostitutes were. She might be safe with him against Cecil, if it was Cecil who had wrecked the ambulance and killed Chris. "I can't wait on a background search from your analyst." He stalked to the jail. Regis was lying on his back, eyes closed. "Jimmy Russell. What do you know about him?"

Regis opened his eyes and sat up. "Jimmy? He's a good dude."

"Is he religious?"

"I suppose he still is. His mama definitely is…although she was kind of a slut according to the rumor mill. Why?" He swung his legs over the cot and leaned his elbows on his knees.

"Like a prostitute?"

"No. Like affairs with married men who sometimes took care of her financially." He grinned. "Well, I guess that's the definition of prostitute, huh?"

"Sounds like."

Regis batted the idea away with his hand. "It was rumors. Jimmy was golden. Always at church, quoting Scripture and gospel-do-gooding, even went to semin…ary…" He sat up straight as if information hit him.

"He went to seminary?"

"Yeah. Him, Wendell and D.J. But D.J. quit and went to med school, and Jimmy came home and went to paramedic school. Funny, huh?"

Nothing about this was funny.

"You don't think it's Jimmy?" Regis said. "I thought it was Cecil. Cecil had Bella Dawn."

Cecil had Bella Dawn, but she'd lived longer than Blind Eye victims. "It's possible Bella Dawn was his first abduction and assault. He saw the opportunity. He was at the bar that night too." They weren't dealing with just one killer but one

up-and-coming serial rapist and potential killer, and one serial killer—the Blind Eye Killer.

John beelined it back to the bullpen. "We have two different men doing two different things. Not in conjunction
with each other. Cecil probably has no idea who the Blind
Eye Killer is, and the BEK probably had no clue what Cecil
has been up to until now." Violet had only been transferred
from the clutches of one sicko to another.

"Jimmy was expelled from seminary for sexual immorality.
Soliciting and fornicating with a prostitute. It's on his record,
but they didn't press charges." Ty rubbed his chin and cheeks.
"He fits like a glove. He's attracted to them. Pays for services
and regrets it, but he can't help himself for going back. He
offers to get them out of the business and the life—it'll save
him and others from succumbing to their wiles and sinning.
But they won't get out. Because they don't think they can.
They're too afraid. And he pays again. This time, he's en-
raged. If they'd let him help them, he wouldn't have sinned,
failed again. It's their fault. In a fury, he beats them, and then
he makes sure they can't see. They can't allure anyone else.
If they won't be saved, he'll pronounce judgment." Ty shook
his head. "What will he do to Violet?"

"Nothing. As long as she doesn't put the pieces together."

Or had she already? Her concerns about Ruby not being at
the cabin might have been her connecting the dots.

And Jimmy Russell might have picked up on that.

Tuesday, October 24
12:47 a.m.

"How do you know Ruby won't take over?" As far as Violet knew, Ruby hadn't told anyone of her plan to leave the
holler and quit the family business.

"What?" Jimmy asked. "I just don't see it."

"Why? No one else thinks otherwise."

He released a long sigh. "I tried, Agent Rainwater. I tried to spare you. But you're smart. Everyone said so. I'd hoped Cecil would take the fall for all this since he'd been caught with Bella Dawn and tried to kill you. Idiot. He deserves to be in jail. Then you started connecting the dots. Realizing Ruby wasn't with Cecil, and she should be. Wondering why I didn't call in our accident by radio. You aren't giving me a choice now."

Violet stood achingly still, listening but also calculating an escape. She didn't need his big introduction. Jimmy Russell was the Blind Eye Killer. In her stoned-out stupor, she'd put together the fact that Cecil didn't meet the Blind Eye Killer pattern or signature. She should have realized it sooner—but then she was fighting for her life and Bella Dawn's. Jimmy staged the whole thing. Cecil was never in front of the ambulance. It was a ploy to pin it all on him. Clever too.

"I liked Chris, but he was collateral damage. Not to mention he brought all y'all here to begin with by making that stupid anonymous call to the State Police. I jabbed him with morphine then swerved."

Jimmy cut Chris's throat and used his blood to make it appear as if Jimmy was injured. He'd blame Cecil for Violet's and Ruby's murders.

Violet's stomach revolted. "Do you have Ruby?"

"With the cold temps I'm thinking I can mess with the time of death a few hours."

Violet's blood froze. "What do you mean? Is she dead?" She scanned the chapel. There was one other door near the east wall, but she'd have to get past Jimmy to get to it. Could she make it to the door they entered on the west side in time? Not in her condition; her mind was moving faster than her other muscles.

"I—I can't help myself, Agent. I have to have them. I know it's wrong. I know it's a sin. I pay every time and have for many years. But it's not my fault."

"No? They force the money out of your wallet? They chain you to a bed and make you do it? They come to you? No."

His eyes narrowed, and he stepped toward her, fists at his side. "You don't understand the need. It lives inside me. It's hungry. Insatiable. It's a darkness that overtakes me. It's who I am."

Violet knew a thing or two about that. The darkness that lived inside. But John was right. She had choices. She could have chosen to let Lynn die. She chose right. She'd wanted to do right when she'd felt the warmth chase away the cold shadow and thoughts. "You're wrong. You make the choice you want to make. But you blame others. You blame the women not the darkness in you. You probably blame your mama too."

Violet had blamed hers.

"My mama's dead. I killed her with my own two hands. That hag had it coming."

Lynn had it coming too. And Reeva and even Mother.

"Maybe so, but we don't get to murder everyone who hurts or offends us. That's lawlessness."

She spotted an old hymnal. It was the best she had. She inched toward the pew to draw it out of the wooden slot. "What about the woman about four years ago? She was found in a mine. Eyes sutured."

"She was in a bar outside of town. I thought she was a hooker. I propositioned her, and she turned me down. But I wanted her. I did. Things got ugly, and I found out she was DEA. She would have turned me in. I had no choice. She shouldn't have been dressed like that! Dancing like that!"

"Yeah. It was all her fault. Have some restraint!" Violet

had the hymnal in her hand. All she had to do was nail him in the face, giving her a fighting chance to run for the door.

God, help me.

She meant the prayer. Maybe Grandmother had been wrong, and John, Asa and Fiona were right. Maybe there was a God who loved her in all the broken mess she was in. Maybe He would save her. And save Ruby. "Where is Ruby?"

"She's here of course."

That changed everything. She glanced at the stairs. Noticed an old wooden chair by the wall. "Take me to her." She slid the hymnal back inside the holder and eyed the chair. All she had to do was incapacitate him long enough to get to Ruby. "Is she alive?"

"She is. With the search parties, I haven't been able to take my time. I offered her a way out that night at Nadine's and one other chance later. Neither took it."

"You broke into Nadine's? That was you?"

He shook his head, and she eyed the chair again and made a step toward the stairs, but he was in front of her, blocking her, paying too close attention. "I suspect Cecil now. But I had no idea then. Chris did call me. I fixed her up. She wasn't a holler girl, but I know she prostituted at times. Later I came back to check on her, try one more time. She would tempt other men. She tempted me. Wanted to thank me for free for helping her."

Violet believed him. Cecil was interrupted. He'd almost made his fantasy reality; the need would be strong. When he spied the opportunity, he took Bella Dawn from the Swallow parking lot, casting suspicion on Regis.

"I want to see Ruby."

He pulled a gun then. "Happy to oblige. Cecil is still going down for all these murders. Down the stairs slowly."

She crept toward the back wall where the stairs were located, Jimmy right behind her. If she grabbed the chair, he'd shoot her, and she'd never have a chance. If she could get him closer to her, she could disarm him. At the top of the stairs, she paused. "If you let me put you in prison, you won't be tempted." It was a lame attempt, but she needed him closer.

He took another step and one more, until she felt the gun pointed into her shoulder blade. "I don't think so."

But as she turned, she felt a prick.

Not a bullet.

A needle.

It'd backfired.

Chapter Twenty-Five

Tuesday, October 24
4:51 a.m.

Violet rolled onto her side, fuzzy in her head again. Jimmy had dosed her with another shot of morphine. Now she was in the basement in the pitch-black dark, and the smell...the smell was undeniable. Rot.

Death.

Was Ruby down here, but dead? Someone was dead down here. She breathed through her mouth. Her hands were tied behind her back, and her ankles were bound. Her eyes wouldn't adjust to the blinding darkness. The concrete floor might as well be a sheet of ice.

The smell, it was days old at least. Couldn't be Ruby. Had someone else gone missing but not been reported?

I killed her with my own two hands.

Jimmy Russell's mother. She must be the rotting stench.

"Is someone there?" a shaky voice whispered.

"Ruby?" Ruby was alive!

"Yes. Violet? Is that you?"

"Yes. Are you okay?"

"No," she cried. "I don't want to die, Violet. I can't die and leave Lula here. You don't understand."

"Yes, I do." Ruby didn't know that Mother had been shot by Loretta, that Wanda had died by her hands too. "Lula is safe."

"No, she's not. Not if she stays in the holler."

Might as well tell her now. "Ruby, your mom shot and killed Wanda and then Mother earlier today." Or was it yesterday? Time had eluded her. "When she realized you'd been kidnapped. Mother died on the way to the hospital."

A thought struck her. Everyone in the holler knew not to harm a holler girl. Jimmy Russell knew this too.

I'll deal with who's been murdering my girls. Mother had a whiff of suspicion or knew that Jimmy was the killer and was waiting on the SCU to leave to deal with him. Jimmy was in the ambulance with her. Instead of helping her live, he may have taken the opportunity to help her die instead. Loretta had missed her aim when Violet tackled her, hitting her shoulder region.

"Mother is dead? Grandma Wanda? Wanda was to take Mother's place when she died."

Loretta had chosen to end the cycle. Granted, she'd done it the holler way instead of legally. The only way she'd known how—through violence and rage. She'd done a terrible thing for a good reason—her freedom.

Violet had pushed Lynn—pushing, in reality, her mom—for freedom.

Neither act would bring it.

Violet had chosen to save Lynn with the hope that in return Violet would be saved. In a way, it had saved her. The trajectory of her life would have been drastically different had she let her die, whether or not she got away with it.

Save her and I'll save you.

She'd been saved from drowning every day in the guilt she'd have if she had let Lynn succumb to the water.

"Well, it's over now."

They had to get out of this black pit. She had no idea where Jimmy was or what he was doing. She worked on the scratchy twine he'd used to bind her. But the knots were small and tight. Pins and needles ran through her fingers, her sprained wrist in fiery pain and ankles too.

Using her core, she brought herself into a sitting position and scooted until her back reached concrete. Placing her shoulder blades against it and digging her feet into the floor, she pressed against the wall and slowly scooted upward until she was in a standing position. She couldn't walk or shuffle. She hopped. Hopped again.

"What are you doing?" Ruby asked.

"I'm going to get us out of here, whatever it takes." Ruby deserved a new life. A fresh slate. Some hope.

Violet did too.

She hopped into something hard. She winced and backed into it, feeling along cold but smooth edges. Like metal. Long. As she continued touching, feeling, her gut clenched.

It was an operating table.

This was where he put them under and removed their eyes then stitched them up. It was what he would do to Ruby. Maybe to Violet. Her heart rate sped up, and she swallowed hard.

"Violet, what is it?"

"Nothing. Just furniture." No point adding to her terror. "How did Jimmy get you? Lula said someone came over. You went out to talk and never came back."

"After you left, he came by the house to check on me. Jimmy's always been a good friend. He was going to be a preacher, you know?"

"You're running fast and loose with *good* and *friend*, Ruby." Violet felt a tray next to the table. Metal clinked and rattled. Instruments. Another wave of nausea hit her.

"But he was."

"He never paid for services?"

Silence gripped the room.

"He asked if I wanted help getting out. I told him no because I didn't want to put him in danger. The less anyone knew about my plans to run, the better. That's why I said yes to him when he asked to pay for some time. I was trying to protect him."

Violet's heart sank. Ruby's twisted beliefs on the definition of protection needed to be redefined, but she was scared, desperate and trying to survive.

"Lula was inside, so...so I got into his car."

Violet didn't need any more details. "After, he went into a rage and blamed you for making him pay for services, didn't he?"

"Yes," she cried.

"And he hit you."

She sniffed and quiet sobs came from her corner. Violet had never been a hugger, but she badly wanted to hug Ruby now.

"How did he get you here?" Violet asked.

"He jabbed me with a needle, and I was floating. When it wore off, I realized I was in the dark. Unsure where. I still don't know where I am."

"You're in a chapel in the hills." The metal tray was too high for Violet to snag an instrument, preferably a scalpel. If she knocked the tray over, he'd hear it. If he was even inside the chapel. Where was he? "How are you bound?"

"Wrists behind my back. Ankles tied."

Atta and Nadine didn't have marks around their wrists and ankles. He was able to subdue them, keep them under, until he got them to the cave. But with the chaos around Cecil and the police searching for Bella Dawn, he'd had to postpone his ritual with Ruby.

She rose on her tiptoes, her backside meeting the edge of the table. If she could roll onto the table and flip onto her side, she might be able to reach a tool and cut herself free.

But time was short. She might turn the whole tray over, might need to, and that meant risking the noise and Jimmy coming downstairs. She had no choice but to chance it. Wedging her backside up against the side of the table, she rocked back onto it. Once she was on securely, she rolled to her right side and scooched backward toward the tray of instruments. Finally, she could touch it, but she couldn't grip anything.

She growled under her breath. There had to be a way.

"I prayed for a way out, Violet. Whiskey's offer was tempting, and I was willin' to take it 'cause I didn't care about the price. I knew one would come with it. I'd never truly be free of Whiskey, but I'd rather have dealt with him than Mother." She sniffed again. "I didn't know I had a sister who was coming to rescue me with no strings attached. God brought you here for this reason. I know it. Maybe you can help Bella Dawn if it's not too late. I don't know where she is, but that smell…"

Violet paused her attempt to gain a scalpel. Ruby thought God was using Violet as a rescuer? "That's not Bella Dawn. She's been found and alive. Cecil took her. He's Lula's Him. He's also still on the run."

Violet had found Bella Dawn.

Because she'd found the cabin.

Because she'd found the wood shavings in it and then found the passage and the wood shavings.

Because she'd felt eyes on her. Felt a draft in the chifforobe. Used the chifforobe for her baggage since her underwear was missing. All these little things that she never connected now fit dot by dot by dot.

She was here because of her choice of career and that was to find Adam.

And Adam was here. There was much more going on she had no way of knowing about. "Ruby, don't put all your faith in me yet."

"Violet, my faith isn't in you. It's in God. To use you."

A prostitute teaching her about faith in God. Violet was no judge of trafficked women surviving. The irony—Mother had required their church attendance and efforts to help others, yet they couldn't help themselves.

"Ruby, why do you have faith in God when you've been trapped into this life? Wouldn't you think God would have rescued you already? Sooner?"

"Faith isn't based on timing but trust. Wendell once talked about these Christians in prison for their faith. They were beat daily and starved. They prayed God would free them, but more so, they prayed God would keep them faithful to the end. They died. But they never stopped hoping. Neither have I."

"And if we die here?"

"I die in faith."

Violet couldn't say the same. But she wanted to.

God, I have to knock this thing over and get something to cut us away. To unbind us so we can break free and get out of this horrible place. Help me. Help us. Help me to see.

"Ruby, I want you to cry really loud. Okay? He won't care if you cry. If he's even up there. It'll help muffle the sound."

"That won't be hard."

"Now!"

Ruby began to wail.

Violet slapped the tray to fall toward her. Instruments clattered to the ground and onto the table. The tray rattled as it hit the floor, echoing. She grabbed onto something slight, felt a pinch and burn. The scalpel! It had cut her, but she didn't care. She gripped it and worked at cutting the twine.

It snapped and fell away, and she made haste cutting through the binding on her ankles. "Keep it up. I'm…halfway there. Got it."

She hopped off the table, thankful Jimmy had put her shoes on her feet, and shoved her hands out in front of her using them to guide her from running into anything else. She followed Ruby's cries to the corner of the room.

Hollering and cursing reached her ears then the deliberate stomping on the stairs. Violet's hand shook. She couldn't see!

Then a tiny ray of light popped on the stairs. Jimmy was using his cell phone flashlight to descend, and that one tiny beam opened her eyes to see the edge of the stairs and the wall butting up against them. She maneuvered around the operating table, trying not to scatter fallen instruments across the floor.

She tripped over something and fell. To break the fall, she put out her hand and it landed onto something cold and mushy.

And fleshy.

Vomit hit the back of her throat as she realized she'd probably landed on Jimmy Russell's dead mother. Jumping to her feet, she raced to the brick wall and backed up against it, heart pounding…waiting on Jimmy, the scalpel gripped in her clammy hand.

Jimmy entered her view, facing Ruby, and shined his light on her. She was bound and huddled in the corner with a bloody lip, hair matted to her cheeks, but she continued to cry.

"Shut up!"

All she needed was for him to take one more step.

He took two. She jumped forward, slashing the back of his neck with the scalpel.

Grabbing his neck and turning, Jimmy howled in pain, and the light shined directly into her face, blinding her. She lurched forward and drove the scalpel into his eye then yanked it back out.

Jimmy dropped to the ground, releasing his phone, and she snatched it up, using it to see the contents on the floor.

A syringe!

She raced toward it and snatched it as Jimmy dove onto her back, pushing her flat against the cold concrete.

His fist met the back of her already aching head, his weight crushing her bruised body. Cursing and wailing, he punched her again. Spots danced in her eyes, but she grabbed the metal tray and brought it up and over her head, knocking him in the face and off balance. He toppled to the side, and she jammed the syringe into his neck, pushing until nothing was left inside.

He grabbed his neck then slumped onto the floor, still and unmoving. "I think it's morphine, but I don't know, which means I don't know how much time we have."

The bloody scalpel lay nearby.

Slice his carotid. He deserves it. End him.

Violet snatched the scalpel, gripping it tightly.

Do it.

Something Fiona said to her in a conversation this past August when Violet was frustrated over not finding any leads, when she'd felt suffocated by it, bubbled to the surface of her mind.

When you know you need hope, when you know you need to be saved, you say it. Then you reach out for light in darkness. That's what I did. It's really the answer for anyone. But I couldn't reach out until I recognized that I needed to reach...and then... I found God had already stretched out His arm to meet mine. He grabbed ahold, and He didn't let go. I've been walking in light ever since.

She did need hope. She needed rescuing and saving in many ways. She needed the same light Fiona and Asa walked in.

"Lord, I need You. Not to help me get out of this or to even stop me from doing what I want to do to this monster. I need You for me. Just me," she whispered.

A warmth enveloped her heart, like a burst of sunlight to a winter night.

End him.

No. She got to choose. Taking the twine he'd bound her with, she used it against him and tied his hands behind his back and his ankles together. No longer was their captor a threat to either of them. She'd disabled him.

"Come on. We're out of here."

Out of the basement.

Out of darkness.

She cut Ruby free then they leaned on one another and climbed the stairs into the chapel and out the front door as dawn broke over the horizon.

Into beautiful light.

Chapter Twenty-Six

Tuesday, October 24
5:21 a.m.

The cold had frozen Violet's bare skin that had been exposed from Jimmy cutting her clothing earlier, but inside warmth radiated in her bones. Ruby leaned against her as they trekked arm in arm on the road to civilization.

A new life for them both. One of freedom and faith.

"How's Memphis sounding to you?" Violet asked through chattering teeth.

"Pretty good, sis. Pretty good."

Headlights bounced around the curve, and blue lights flashed. The Suburban came into view, and three deputy cruisers followed. Violet uttered words she never had before. "Thank You, God." And she meant it.

They waved from the side of the road, and the vehicle screeched to a halt, Ty in the driver's seat. The back doors opened, and Asa, Fiona and Owen clambered out, but John blew out of the passenger door and raced to her, grabbing her and knocking her off balance. "I was terrified." He framed her face and studied her features. "I was afraid I wouldn't make it to you in time."

Ruby pointed skyward. "God beat you to it."

John glanced up. "You're right. He did."

Violet leaned her forehead against his. "He definitely did," she whispered.

Asa bolted for the woods, several deputies on his tail. "Dead or alive?" he hollered.

"Alive. Mostly," Violet stated.

Asa paused and snapped his head in her direction then raised a forefinger as if indicating they'd discuss it later then ran into the forest. His voice carrying on the wind, he called, "Good job, Vi!" Their Kodiak bear would disarm evil then come console a cub. That's how he was.

Ty swaggered toward her, clearly seeing they were in one piece, a cocky grin on his face, Owen right beside him, cheesing. "You been clubbin'?" Ty asked and pointed to her jeans slit to the crotch and her sweater revealing her midriff and bare arms. "Looks like you been clubbin' and can't hold your liquor."

Owen mimicked bass from a speaker as Ty laughed, then Owen hugged her. "I had my mama and my grandmama prayin' for you. Asa actually had the nerve to tell the pilot to fly faster. And I think it scared the pilot enough that he did."

Violet shook her head at their idiocy, but she loved that they loved her. Funny, until right now she hadn't realized that while her mom and grandmother didn't love her, she did have the love of family. Guess she'd been focusing on what she didn't have instead, and it had blinded her to what she did. "You two are annoying." She wasn't ready to toss around the *L* word so freely.

"We love you too," Owen said.

Fiona looked at Ruby. "How are you?"

"I'm okay. Now." Ruby blew a heavy breath. "I'm definitely getting out of here." She glanced at Violet. "Probably coming to Memphis."

"Memphis, huh?" Fiona dug into her pocket and pulled out a pink business card with gold edging. She placed it in Ruby's hands. "You'll want this."

"What's Ruth's Refuge?" Ruby asked.

"It's a place where women survivors of domestic violence and trafficking can get help, housing and a new start," Fiona said.

Ty leaned over, his mouth dropped open and his eyes widened, then he narrowed his eyes and snatched the card from Ruby. "Where did you get this?" he asked Fiona.

"The director came and spoke to our women's ministry at church about the program. She was really great."

"This woman? Bexley Hemmingway?"

"Yes." She snatched it back and handed it to Ruby again. "Why?"

"Dark, almost black hair. Blue eyes. About five five?"

Fiona cocked her head. "Yes. Again, why?"

"Because she's supposed to be dead." He glanced at the card once more then stomped a few feet into the woods.

Fiona sighed and drew her piece. "We'll talk later. I hate the woods and killers in the woods."

Violet smirked. "I know you do."

She turned, but Violet stopped her.

"I reached out, and you were right. His hand was already there."

Fiona's eyes sheened with moisture. "I have to help arrest a killer, and it's not nearly as bad to the bone when one is crying." She kissed Violet's cheek. "But I'm glad." Then she motioned for Owen to join her.

Violet caressed John's cheek. "Give me one second." She called Tiberius's name. He continued to lean against a tree, his eyes swirling with turmoil.

"You okay?"

"Not really."

"You want to talk about her? It?"

"Not really. But you need to have that program vetted thoroughly before you send Ruby and her kid into it."

Fair enough. "Okay, I will. Let's talk about something else." She looked up into his eyes. "God is real," she breathed. "He was always there, but I didn't see until I was blind. And then I saw. I could see. He's real, Tiberius. He's real."

Ty studied her a moment then kissed her forehead. "You have a concussion. But whatever got you through that, I won't deny. Okay?"

He'd have to hit his darkest moment to see the light too. He'd have to recognize he too needed to reach, and she would pray that he would. He nodded once and ventured farther off into the woods.

John met her at the edge of the tree line. "Did you want to kill Jimmy Russell?"

Oh yeah. And she could easily have done it and been justified. "There was this fleeting thought, but I chose not to drown him, so to speak."

John's grin sent her belly whirling. "I think we have a lot to talk about. For now, let's get you warm."

"Cecil?"

John shook his head. "He was found dead at his leather shop. Two to the head and one to the chest."

"Whiskey? That's execution style."

"Greg said they entered the leather shop, and Cecil was

clearing out money from a safe to flee town. He denied having Ruby, and before Greg could blink, Whiskey popped him. He got what he wanted. To arrest Whiskey for murder."

"But not Callie's. Whiskey didn't kill Callie, John. Jimmy did."

"I figured." John put his arm around her. "I got what I wanted. Justice. Jimmy Russell is going away for a long time."

She shivered, and John steered her toward the Suburban.

"You believe Greg?" she asked and climbed into the passenger seat, the hot air warming her. "You think that's how it went down?"

John rubbed his hands together. "I don't know. Maybe Greg let Whiskey kill Cecil to get him on a murder charge since he couldn't get him long enough for the drug charges he could pin on him. Or maybe it did go down that way. We'll never know, I suppose."

Ruby joined Violet in the vehicle, sitting behind her.

An ambulance arrived, which she refused to enter, but they brought out Jimmy Russell and loaded him inside.

Tuesday, October 24
9:48 a.m.

Violet grabbed the fresh towels laid out for her in the bathroom. Without Cecil being around, she wasn't concerned about peeping toms. She showered away the grime and stench of death then changed and took over-the-counter pain meds. No more loopiness.

The rest of the team had returned to the SO to finish up the paperwork on the investigation. The local deputies had identified the dead body as Jimmy Russell's mother. Jimmy Russell had been treated at the hospital in Whitesburg and would be charged later today. The Blind Eye Killer was done tormenting and murdering.

Ruby had been admitted and given fluids, and then she was going to pack up Lula and follow them back to Memphis in a couple of hours. She planned to visit Ruth's Refuge but stay with Violet until she could get on her feet with no one expecting anything in return. Violet had a spare room, and it was time to tear down the murder board and all the dead ends she'd been tracking to find Adam. Lula could have her own space.

Sheriff Modine had called and asked her to meet him at the church where they'd attended Sunday service. Said he had a few things he wanted to share with her. She wasn't going anywhere alone.

Adam was still close by, and she'd yet to discover who he was.

She met John in the foyer. He was leaning against the wall waiting on her, sipping a cup of cider. In the other hand, a fresh foam cup for her.

"Where'd you get that?"

John pointed to the dining room. Violet followed his finger in time to see the back of a figure slip around the corner.

"Aunt Hossie?" Violet whispered. "Did I just see Aunt Hossie? Finally? Now?"

Nodding, John handed her the cup of cider. "She legit had gout. Ty said her niece on her late husband's side helped out with all the food. Regis wasn't lying."

"I'd resigned to the fact she didn't exist." She snickered. "Or was dead."

"Unseen doesn't equal nonexistent or dead. I guess you know that by now." He winked and opened the front door.

Violet paused on the threshold and turned back. "Thanks, Aunt Hossie. We appreciate all you did to provide for us during our stay."

She didn't hear a reply. But she didn't need one. She fol-

lowed John to the car and buckled up. He pulled onto the dirt
road that would lead to the holler church.

"Hey," Violet said. "How did you know where to find us?"

John sighed. "We found out Jimmy Russell had been kicked
out of seminary, so we visited the Swallow—found Wendell.
He told us that they used to play in that chapel as kids. It's
where Jimmy felt his calling."

"Not the Lord's calling," Violet said. "Did they find the
victims' eyes?"

John's lip curled. "Yeah. In a small cooler behind the old
pulpit." He switched on his turn signal. "We got the shirt and
beer bottle from Regis's house. Since we know Jimmy killed
Atta, all we can come up with is that Cecil was at the bar and
saw her and Wendell get into it. The necklace must have fallen
off in the altercation, and he took it. Like a trophy. Some of the
blood must have transferred to his shirt. Maybe he picked up
the swatch of material Wendell accidentally ripped away and
got blood on him that way, or he may have even encountered
her, touched her, talked to her. Then she went to Jimmy's. We
don't know for sure, but that's our best guess."

They wound up the long road leading to the church, and
Violet's gut knotted. John parked behind Sheriff Modine's
cruiser. "You want me to go with you?" John asked.

"No. Just...be here for me?"

He held her hand. "I'm here for you, Violet. As long as
you'll let me be."

"I feel like there's subtext there. But that can wait a minute."

His smirk undid her. "I'm patient."

She got out of the car into the cold. But she was wearing her heavy leather coat, jeans, and boots and wool socks.
Sheriff Modine opened the back door of his cruiser. Inside
sat Loretta Boyd. Violet didn't hide the shock and looked up
at Sheriff Modine.

"Loretta's no real threat. Known her all my life." He leaned in and helped her out. She wore cuffs though. The pain in his eyes and gentleness in aiding her told Violet all she needed to know about these two. Modine loved her. But he couldn't get her out of this one. Why hadn't he gotten her out before now?

Loretta let a shaky breath release. "Hello, Violet. Let's take a walk."

Violet looked at Modine for permission.

"I'll be here. Y'all go on."

Loretta led Violet to the private cemetery, opened the wrought-iron gate and they entered.

"Thank you for rescuing Ruby. Funny… I was trapped in what we called the baby basement—at least at first, and Ruby was trapped in a basement too." She looked at Violet, touched her chin dimple. "You were his first daughter, you know."

"All I know is I was a monster until he held me," she whispered. But she was done with letting Reeva's words hold power over her, killing her. She craved more powerful words. Stronger words. Life-giving words to put to death the lies.

"He called me Eve," she said. "I was one of the first girls he took to help him fulfill the command God had given Adam. Be fruitful and multiply. He believed he was the reincarnated Adam. Dozens more came and went. Most conceived quickly, and then once the babies were healthy at three months, he let them go. I'd come from a pretty bad situation, as you know. When he told me he loved me, I believed him. When he told me that I was his true Eve, I believed him. He gave me privileges he didn't give the other girls. I was their midwife, if you will. I'd seen babies be birthed before, here in the holler. I'd make him dinner, and we'd eat in the kitchen. I shared stories of the holler. What I had been made to do. Only havin' to do it with one man was way better than many."

How utterly tragic.

This explained why Reeva didn't know a Loretta Boyd. She would have known her as Eve.

"How is your mom?"

"Broken." She shared her childhood with Loretta. Her mom's words to her. Why she kept her. "She said I'm exactly like him. Cunning and clever and diabolical. I suppose that's true. I can be."

"Is that all she ever said?"

"'Fraid so."

"Can I tell you one more story about Reeva? The Reeva I knew was a smart aleck and defiant. She was always tryin' to escape and hatch new and better plans to do it. Each time, they almost worked. She endured pain the rest didn't. She fought back, tried to convince the rest of us there was hope. Tried to help me see that what was happenin' to me was wrong. But she had no idea that in my mind, it wasn't that bad. I wasn't on the streets. I was eatin' and not beggin' for food. I was… with only one man."

"I'm sorry," Violet murmured then tried to imagine Reeva full of spirit to fight back. The woman she knew wasn't much of a fighter unless she was punching at Violet through her words.

"When you were born, it was like you were wailin' to be set free. And your mom couldn't console you because she was afraid for once. Babies do better in capable arms. When Adam held you, there was no fear in him, no weakness, and you quieted. I was there for that."

"You helped birth me?"

"I did. Your mother loved you. At first, she didn't respond well, but then I saw that maternal love and her anxiety at not being able to help you, fear for what Adam would do—or not do, like lettin' her leave with you."

"But I quieted in his arms and not hers, and she didn't see

a baby that belonged to her, but one who belonged to him, therefore I must be like him."

Loretta sighed. "I think so. Adam named you, and she clearly let the name stand."

To remind her that Violet was her father's daughter, not content anywhere else but with him.

"When I gave birth, I chose Ruby. Violet was a royal name to me. Red was too. Strong. It was the only way I knew to bond two sisters. The only girls Adam ever conceived."

How could she know that? "If he let girls go after the babies were healthy, how did you get to leave when you didn't even know you were pregnant? Did he think you wouldn't and release you?"

Loretta's lip quivered, and a tear slipped down her cheek. "No. Your mom…she came back for me. After he let her go, it was a couple of weeks, I suppose. Adam had gone to work— Reeva knew the routine. Clever girl. She'd been able to see underneath the blindfold. That's what he did when he took us—blindfolded us so we didn't know where we were. Then when we produced and the baby was healthy, he blindfolded us again and took us back to the place we left with him."

But Reeva had seen. Calculated the route and returned. That was brave and bold. Clever and cunning even, but why hadn't she called the police?

What happened to that courageous girl?

She'd remained broken and unhealed.

"You know what she said?"

Violet shook her head.

"She said, 'Eve, you can't see what's going on, but I can, and I'm gonna see for you. You ain't got to go home, but you got to get out of the baby basement.' At that time, I was the only girl left—for the moment. She didn't bring me to her home but to a pay phone near the bus station. I called my mom. She came and got me. When I got back, Mother told me, 'That's what happens when you leave the holler. You don't get to live your own life, make your own choices.' God saw fit to bring me back, and I would submit, but then I found out I was pregnant and that delayed it—for a while."

Violet shivered under her coat. Her mind whirred and buzzed. "Mother said Adam is here."

"He is. He and I…we had a relationship—"

"No, you had Stockholm syndrome."

"Maybe. Probably. He came for me days later. I'd told him everything about my life, where I was from, but it never crossed my mind he'd show up."

She was his Eve, and he didn't think she'd produced. Little did he know.

"He underestimated who Mother was and the people she controlled." Loretta walked to the back corner of the cemetery to a boulder. She pointed to it. "He came, but he never left. He's been buried here for decades, Violet. Never to hurt another soul." She turned and looked at Violet. "He never got the chance."

Guess now it didn't matter why Reeva hadn't told the police. It wasn't even worth asking.

But now she had no answers to the questions she had always wanted. No way to look Adam in the eye to see if it was true. Was she her father's daughter?

"Reeva didn't have to come back for me, didn't have to save me. But she did. You didn't have to save Ruby either. You could have left her down there. I think you're your mother's daughter more than your father's." She cocked her head. "Or maybe you don't have to be either. Maybe you can just be who you want to be."

Loretta was right.

"Thank you."

Loretta quietly made her way back to Sheriff Modine, but Violet remained at the grave. She had other siblings out there. She could find them. Instead of looking for Adam, maybe she should have been looking for other brothers.

"I'm not you. I may have your DNA in me, but I don't have to be you. I will not be you." And she wouldn't be bitter like her mom either. She heard footsteps. Knew it was John. She stood. "Wanna meet my father?" she asked and pointed to the boulder.

"Not particularly."

She shoved her hands in her coat pockets, looking at this man before her. Quiet when he needed to be. Challenging and consoling. Kind and patient. He'd brought her into his family without fear, and she'd been accepted.

John was right. She believed God had brought her here for more than a case. He'd brought her here to set her free, and she was—free. She had much to learn, but she was free.

"Did you get all the answers you wanted?" John closed the distance between them.

"No. But I got what I needed."

She grasped the lapels of his coat, gazed into his eyes. "Do you want to kiss me, John?"

His eyes held the answer, and his lopsided grin corkscrewed her belly.

"I do."

"Then I double-dog dare you." She challenged him with the words.

His arms slid around her waist as he drew her against him. "A double-dog dare. Can't pass that up," he teased as his lips met hers, explored gently, cautiously and tempered with restraint, but she felt the heat beneath the simmer.

They'd let it marinate a while longer.

John eased back from the kiss, pecked her lips once more. "Does this mean I've stolen your heart?" John lightly teased.

"Hardly. You're not that slick." She framed his face. "It means I'm entrusting it to you."

His thumb caressed her cheekbone. "I like this way better. I'll be good to it. I promise."

As they walked to the car, she leaned against him. "You better. 'Cause you know I only need one bullet."

"Hmm…" John chuckled under his breath and opened her car door for her. She slid inside and noticed something was off. She patted her holster, then snapped her attention to John, who stood beaming like a kid on Christmas morning.

"Bullets are useless without a gun, darlin'." He held up her weapon.

"Oh, you are slick."

He leaned into the car, handed her back the piece and kissed the tender spot behind her earlobe. "You have no idea," he flirted through a whisper.

No, but she was ready to find out. Ready to leave the past behind and pursue something new, something greater, stronger and brighter.

Something like hope and truth.

And love.

★ ★ ★ ★ ★

Acknowledgments

Rachel Kent, my agent, thank you for your friendship and for believing in these stories even though they get a little creepier than you like! You are a rock star!

Shana Asaro, my editor, thank you for believing in this thriller and adding the most valuable input to make it even better. Working with you is pure joy. You speak my love language when you tell me to make it darker and creepier. Ha!

Susan L. Tuttle, my friend and author, thank you for brainstorming with me, for Voxing back and forth for months and, really, years and for being the first person who lays eyes on the story and keeps me from screwing it up. You get me.

Jodie Bailey, my friend and awesome suspense author, thank you for pulling me out of a hole and making me laugh and inviting me to a writers' retreat where we made creepy things creepier and funny things funnier.

Special thanks goes to:

Shane Simmons of *Hillbilly Talk with Shane Simmons* for your expertise on hollers. I appreciate you answering my questions, and your YouTube videos were gold. Y'all subscribe to his channel! It's educational and entertaining!

My friend and author of the *Paynes Creek Thrillers*, Heather Sunseri, for helping me with Kentucky living and recommending several documentaries to watch for life in the hills.

Author Beth Pugh for looking at some geographical locations and enlisting her husband to make sure I wasn't too off the mark. If I was, it's all on me.

"Mr. Anonymous," who is a federal agent and my friend. I appreciate you answering all of my endless questions. I might have stretched a few things; that's on me!

To the following professionals for helping me with some medical information: Hannah Ott (who I had in daycare, so that makes me feel ancient), Bree Eichler and Tressie Downes. Anything I stretched for the sake of fiction is also on me.

TP, you love and support me daily and give me all the money to do all the things. Please don't make me sleep in the guest room if I get any weirder or creepier.

Lastly and most importantly, Jesus my Lord and Savior, who rescues us from dark places and gives sight to the blind. Thank You for rescuing me.